Glass and Feathers

Glass and Feathers

Lissa Sloan

Darkling House

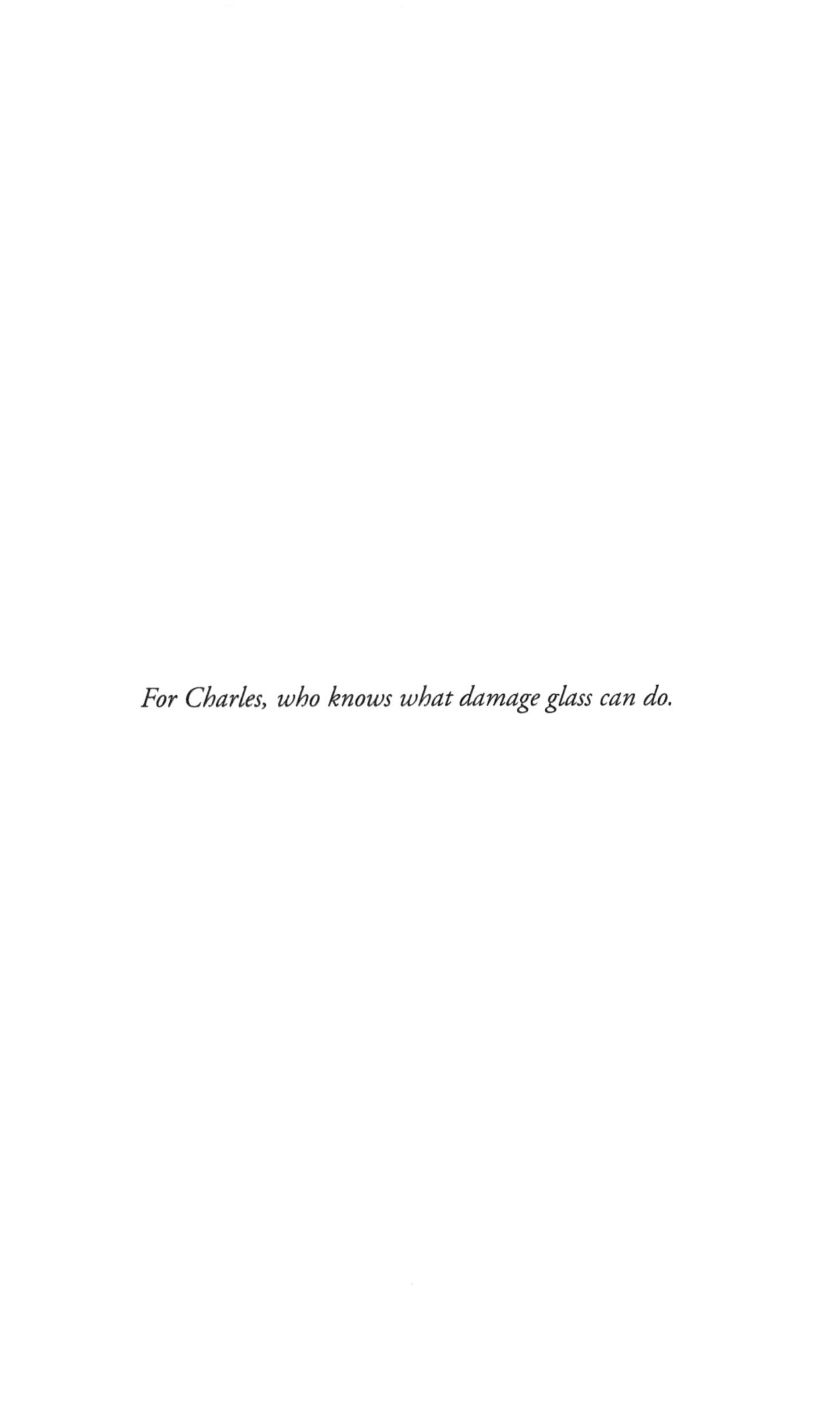

For Charles, who knows what damage glass can do.

PART ONE:

THE PALACE

ONE

The glass was smooth against my skin, cool as a fish. The slippers curved around my feet, holding me in a firm grip. I shifted my toes, but there was little room to move them.

Stillness, my dear. Even though the queen wasn't in the room, I could hear her voice at my ear. *Elegance. Grace.* As if by naming these qualities, she could make them soak into me.

My fingers wouldn't be still either. I clenched my hands into tight balls and watched the queen's ladies gathering around the new gown. During all these months at the palace, they had ordered me so many gowns, I couldn't imagine how more would fit in my wardrobe. Still, they insisted I have another gown. Another fitting.

The lady who always wore opals leaned out from the group. "Oh, your highness, it's perfection." With her black curls streaming down her neck and her body posed in an elegant line, she looked like she was made of oil and canvas, not flesh and bone.

I didn't know what to say, but it would be rude to say nothing. So I opened my mouth, hoping I sounded like a girl who knew all about perfection. "I'm sure it—" but the lady I thought of as Opal had already turned away. This was how it always was. They never really saw me. But being seen was something I couldn't risk. I stopped talking and stayed on my stool, waiting until I was wanted.

I tried easing my heels out of the shoes, but the glass resisted. The ladies still had their backs to me, so I leaned down and pushed the slippers off my heels with a finger. I drew out my toes, and I was free.

But a moment later the maid was kneeling in front of me, one of my shoes in her hand, waiting for me to present my foot. I looked at her stupidly. "They will need to know if the hemline is right, your highness," she breathed, her eyes on the slipper she held. She was keeping me from making another mistake. She was trying to be kind.

So I complied. I slipped my toes first into one shoe, then the other. I smiled and nodded, indicating she could go. She faded away, back into a corner. Under the cover of my petticoats, I pressed my heels down, forcing them back into the shoes. The glass scraped my foot.

"Your highness?"

I jumped as if I'd been caught stealing. Or pretending.

The seamstress was ready at last, so I stood and let her tie and pin and fasten me into the new gown. As she arranged the drape of the skirts in the back, I watched myself in the looking glass, wondering if this would be the gown to give me whatever I was missing. That thing that would make me like Opal and the others. But when I glanced at their faces, I could see it would not. I knew them well enough by now.

"Such a lovely color," said the lady who always wore pearls, one hand straying to her hair to be sure each red curl was in place. They all were.

The lady who always wore rubies nodded her admiration for the pale yellow damask. "Yes." She opened her wide blue eyes even wider. "And the cut is exquisite."

"It falls so gracefully," mused Opal. Pearl and Ruby, who followed Opal's lead in everything, murmured their agreement. "But perhaps…"

Behind me, the seamstress's hands stiffened at my waist. "It is everything her highness asked for." She spoke as if I were not in the room. As if the yellow damask had been my idea. She came around me to join them.

"Of course," Opal assured her.

Ruby nodded. "The gown is perfect."

It was perfect. It must have been. The fabric and color were the latest in fashion; every embroidered flower and ribbon and bit of lace were exactly where they should be, just like every other gown I had. The wearer was the problem. The *something* that wasn't right was me.

"It *is* everything her highness asked for." Pearl laid a consoling hand on the seamstress's arm. "She only needs, you know, that little something more."

The seamstress caught on and smiled in relief, her pride restored. "Perhaps some jewels in the hair," she suggested.

Ruby cocked her head and set her mouth in a lovely frown. "Or some lace at the neck."

This seamstress was not the only one I'd seen in my dressing room. She was one in a long line of artisans: milliners, lacemakers, jewelers, who came to outfit the new princess. Of course, they had needed to come; I'd come to the palace in a coarse wool gown, my apron stained with ashes. I'd had nothing better. Only the slippers on my feet were worthy of a prince's bride. Now my dressing room was filled with gowns and cloaks, stomachers and petticoats, hats and gloves and jewels.

And I had to do more than look the part. I had to speak and move and think like a princess. Nearly every day someone came to remake me, to contort me into something new. Perhaps the ladies would stop calling them in when they were finally successful.

If. If they were.

But they had never sent a shoemaker.

"What about some new shoes?" I offered.

They would have to be new. Nothing from my old life was fine enough. Certainly not the wooden clogs I had worn in the stables or the garden. Or the old, faded shoes I had worn inside, the ones with a low heel, the undyed leather soft and yielding against my skin. Of course I could not wear those.

But anything new—silk or satin or dyed calf skin, trimmed with braid or gold or bright jeweled buckles—would be more forgiving than glass.

But at the mention of shoes, the ladies looked at me as if a piece of furniture had spoken. My cheeks went hot. "Perhaps with…with some embroidered flowers at the toe," I fumbled. "Wouldn't that be," I groped for the sort of word Opal would use, "sweet?"

The word caught on my tongue. I sounded ridiculous. It was no wonder I never spoke that way. The ladies still said nothing. I looked down at the toe of Pearl's shoe, peeking prettily out from under her skirts. "Or a bow. Or a buckle."

At last Opal spoke. "Oh, no, your highness." Her black eyes fixed mine. "You have the finest shoes in all the land. We were all completely," she thought a moment, "captivated by you. The whole kingdom has heard all about your slippers and your lovely, dainty feet. Everyone you meet will want to see them. Without them…" she sighed and raised one shoulder in an apologetic shrug. She left the rest of her thought unsaid, but her meaning was clear. Without the slippers, I had nothing to recommend me.

She was more right than she knew.

She laid a slender hand on my shoulder. "A princess cannot disappoint, you know."

I was the first to look away. I was perfectly capable of disappointing, and we all knew it. But it was true. Whenever I met someone new, they inevitably glanced down at my skirts, hoping the fabric would shift enough to expose the famous slippers. "I know," I said to the flowers on the carpet. "I just thought a change…" My voice died away.

"Of course she wants a change." I thought for a moment Pearl had become my ally. "You must have a new glass pair made. Simply tell us who made those, and we'll have him in to make you some different ones."

Ruby was smiling now, baring straight, white teeth with a bit of a point. "We'd be delighted to meet him, wouldn't we?"

"But the slippers—"

"Yes, of course, your highness." Opal looked sympathetic. "We know."

After my wedding, I had told them all how I had gotten the gowns and the glass slippers. Everyone had heard about the hazel tree at my mother's grave. The tree that granted my wishes. I didn't tell them what else the tree had given me, though. I didn't tell them about the last wish.

"It's a charming tale." But *tale*, when Opal said it, did not mean tale at all. It meant *lie*. It meant that, even though I'd been proclaimed a beauty at the royal balls, and even armed with those rich dresses and exquisite shoes, I was nothing special. I couldn't possibly have won the heart of a prince. Not without something more.

She waved an elegant hand, as if it didn't matter, as if she didn't blame me for pretending to deserve a prince. "So, the slippers were a gift. Never mind. You can call the maker in and pay him properly this time." She raised her perfectly curved eyebrows as she came to take my hands. "It's only fair, isn't it?"

The others were closing in around me. Pearl, still in the guise of a friend, drew in beside me and murmured, "We wouldn't tell anyone."

"Even if he made a pair for each of us as well." Ruby's voice was silky in my ear. "It would be our secret. No one would know they aren't as magical as you say."

My stays were tightening around my ribs. I pushed my lungs out against them and drew in some air. "I've told you before." I tried to keep my voice steady, like Madame always instructed in my elocution lessons. "I don't know who made them."

Opal squeezed my hands in a way that might have been affectionate, then dropped them. She returned to her position beside the seamstress. Ruby and Pearl followed. "Then there is nothing to be done." She spoke as if she didn't care one way or the other.

But that wasn't true. They all wanted a pair of their own. *No one in the kingdom can work glass like that,* I heard Ruby say one day when I came into a drawing room where they sat talking. Opal made a graceful gesture and murmured something I didn't hear. She noticed me then and pretended to be pleased to see me.

She cared. They all did. But it didn't matter, I realized suddenly. A new pair of shoes, even glass, wouldn't have the same magic as the ones now on my feet. I couldn't replace them. Ever.

The ladies had gone back to suggesting ways to make me more acceptable. "What about a blue taffeta?" Pearl was saying.

"Mmm," Ruby purred, "you'd look enchanting in blue, don't you agree, your highness?"

I caught myself worrying my wedding ring, moving it around and around my finger with my thumb. I grasped my hands together in front of the yellow damask to stop myself fidgeting. "I already have a blue taffeta."

"No." Opal looked thoughtful. "Not taffeta. Brocade. Brocade has a gravity to it." Gravity was another quality that would have to be stitched and pleated and embroidered into me.

I spoke a little louder. "I have enough gowns for the moment." The ladies all turned toward me. "I think."

There was silence. "I do so appreciate all your help and advice, and I don't know what I'd—" What should I say? That blue brocade wouldn't make me into something I wasn't?

I wouldn't say that, I thought with a flash of anger. Opal wouldn't admit to a weakness that way. None of them would. But they could smell mine the way a pack of dogs smells illness in another creature. They knew I was not one of them.

"I only mean that surely I have plenty of dresses for now, and I think I should concentrate on—" I meant to sound confident, but I was only loud. Madame would shake her head at me.

I was relieved when Opal broke in. Now I wouldn't have to decide what I should concentrate on. "Why, of course, your highness." The tone of her voice was like a bell, lovely to listen to. She exchanged a glance with Ruby, who made the slightest nod. "We won't trouble you any longer." Her manner, which had grown so intimate and friendly lately, was cool and formal, as if we had just met. "We know you'll want your own ladies to attend you; surely they'll be joining you here soon."

I opened my mouth, but no sound came out. Ruby laid a gentle hand on my arm. "We really have been neglecting her majesty." Her eyes were wide and her expression grave. "She is patience itself, of course. But we only wanted to see you settled here, and now it seems you have everything you need." She said it as if she wanted only the best for me. As if she liked me.

At last I got a word out. "But." That was all I could manage, though, and the ladies ignored it. Giving me a formal curtsy, Opal, Ruby, and Pearl swept out. The seamstress gathered her things and hurried after them, as if what I had was catching.

My feet shifted in the glass slippers as the maid unfastened my pins and ties. I studied myself in the mirror and tried to see what others saw. But the girl in the glass only confused me. She was the same one my mother had called lovely. The one my husband called beautiful. And the one my stepmother called ugly. The one who needed *that little something more.*

Who should I believe?

My reflection would not answer my question, but still, she was trying to tell me something. Something I didn't want to hear. The ladies didn't know it yet, but I did, and I had to admit it. To myself at least. The whisper in my head had been growing more insistent for some time now. Telling me I had found yet another way to fail.

I had pushed it down and pushed it back, telling myself I was worrying over nothing. I was imagining things. But now, feeling the sharpness of the slippers against my skin, I couldn't deny it any longer. Whether my feet were growing bigger or my shoes were growing smaller hardly mattered.

The glass slippers no longer fit.

Two

Once, in the beginning, the shoes had fit. I was sure of that. There had been no tightness, only a shiver of anticipation as I slid them on my feet. When I appeared at the palace, I was the talk of the ball. Heads turned, people whispered, women exclaimed and pointed me out to their friends. *Beautiful,* they said. *Enchanting. A Picture.* Men followed me with their eyes, murmuring to one another, *Lord, if I were a younger man…* they said. *I say, wouldn't you like to…Yes, I would.*

Without the soil of the garden on my hands or the soot of the hearth on my face, even my own family didn't recognize me when I appeared at the ball. So I couldn't have been myself. I was only playing the part of another girl. A girl who belonged here.

Alone now, I crouched on my dressing room sofa and held the slipper up, turning it around to see it from every angle. It didn't look any smaller. I looked down at my feet. They didn't look any bigger. But there were red marks on my toes and heels, from where the shoes pressed into them. And all around the top of each foot was a pale pink line where the opening of the shoe gripped my skin.

Perhaps these pale pink lines were the cost I had to pay. After all, every wish comes at a price.

What would people think if they knew? In their eyes, I would be as bad as my sisters: the girls who had cut their feet to fit the slipper. I had cheated every bit as much as they had, and everyone would know.

They'd all look at each other with knowing smiles: Opal, Ruby, Pearl, the queen, the king. They would say they'd known it all along. *Oh, I could tell the first time I saw her,* one of them would say with a sadness that barely hid her delight. *That something was wrong about her. You know.*

What the *something* was, she wouldn't say, but the others would nod, still too polite to imply I hadn't come by my good fortune honestly. Yes, they knew. They all knew. *And can you imagine if there had been children?* Now they would all stop nodding and shake their heads instead, imagining the shame of it. *I said it from the first. She was so unsuitable for him really, my dear.*

And the others in the palace, from the stables to the gardens to the kitchens, would think exactly the same. I was marked, as if with a bit of garden dirt under my nails that would never wash off. *If only you could have seen her,* my maid would say to the grooms, footmen, cooks, and scullery maids assembled in the kitchen to hear the story. *No idea how to behave, or dress, or wear her hair. I'm almost sorry for her. But she asked for it, didn't she? She got her wish.* They would laugh. I would have provided them some entertainment.

I would be gone by this time, of course. Where to, I didn't know. Wherever they sent failed princesses. Wherever they sent girls who deceived their way to a crown.

There was no one I could tell. I ran my finger around the pink line on my foot. I never wore stockings under the slippers. It was the one bit of nonconformity everyone indulged me. Stockings would spoil the effect of the clear glass surrounding my foot. If I had worn them, I could have tried thinner stockings now, or gone without. Just to give me a little room. But there was no more room.

There was a noise from the bedroom, and I started, tucking my feet under my skirts. My husband stood in the doorway. I let out a shallow breath. He was the reason I was here, the one reason.

He stayed there, his eyes on me like I was the only person in the room. I was, but he always looked at me like that, no matter how many people were around. He had looked at me like that from the night we met. *Your eyes,* he'd said during our first dance, *they're green as leaves with the sun shining through them. You'll get tired of me staring, but I don't think I can stop.* He hadn't stopped, but I had never tired of it. It was intoxicating, and I still wasn't used to it. After all, I didn't even know if that look was real.

He glanced around, realizing the room was empty, and then he smiled the smile I fell in love with. The one that was only for me. It started at his eyes, slow, almost cautious at first. But it was infectious. By the time it reached his lips and the dimple in his left cheek appeared, I was warm all through. "Where is everyone?"

"They le—" We had been married for months now, but sometimes I still had trouble stringing a sentence together around him. I always had to guard my tongue. Who knew what I might say?

I tried again. "They're with the queen."

He sat down beside me, putting an arm around my waist. "Will they be—" He stopped and leaned down, picking a pearl bracelet up from the floor. I'd put it on that morning and must not have noticed when it fell off. He laid it around my wrist, but the clasp would not fasten. "Hmm." He frowned, but I could tell he was pleased. He winked at me as he stood and walked to my dressing table.

He came back with a hair pin and a nail file, and in a moment, the clasp was open. "Here we are," he murmured, his nimble fingers shifting the workings inside.

I watched him, head bent, absorbed in his work, until he straightened and wrapped the pearls around my wrist again. "There," he said, clicking the clasp into place.

"How are you so clever with your hands?"

"Not terribly royal." He gave me a wry smile and put an arm around me. "Mother would be…"

"Disappointed," we said together.

I leaned my head against his shoulder. If only I could be so careless about the queen's opinion.

"So, when will your ladies be back?"

"They aren't my—" I didn't want to trouble him with something like this. "I don't know." How could I explain? He would only get that puzzled expression he sometimes had these days, as if he wondered why I failed to make the right impression. My wish only affected him, so perhaps he couldn't see what others saw.

When I didn't say more, his fingers squeezed my waist, a little prompt. I changed the subject. "What are you doing here?" During the day he was always busy with princely things: appearances, court matters, affairs of state. None of them required me.

He withdrew his arm and rubbed his eyes, a lock of soft brown hair falling onto his forehead. "I've got to take the marquess on a tour of the park."

The marquess was here. So he and his wife would stay for dinner. The last time they had been here, the marchioness had gone on about what a good appetite I had. But then she'd turned to my husband, batting him playfully with her fan and saying, *She's far too thin, your highness. You'll need to fatten her up.* Why, I had wondered. Did they slaughter princesses like livestock?

I sighed. "At least you'll have a nice ride."

He let out an annoyed breath. "I'd rather stay here with you."

"Then do," I begged him. "I'll tell you a story."

He smiled, but shook his head. "Tell me one tonight."

I went on anyway. "Let's see…" My fingers played idly across my knees and onto his as I tried to think of a suitable one. "Unwanted visitors…"

He gave a soft laugh in spite of himself, and I went on.

"Once, there was a little girl with golden hair. She was walking in the woods one day when she came upon a house. When she knocked, no one answered, but she—"

"I'm sorry, darling. I can't concentrate now." He took hold

of my hands. "Tell me tonight."

"What's wrong?"

He shrugged. "Unwanted visitors." He gave me a pained smile. "They give me a headache."

I jumped up. "Let me get you some mint tea." I had never been to the palace kitchen gardens, but surely there would be mint growing somewhere. He caught my hand before I'd gotten far. "It's good for headaches," I laughed as he pulled me back to the sofa.

"There's no need for that." He stretched out, laying his head in my lap. "I only have a moment. I just came up here to change." He reached for my hands and laid them over his eyes, sighing. "Mmm, your fingers are cool."

For a moment I let myself imagine a garden: the soil warm under my bare feet, the mint leaves rough and pungent on my fingers. I could almost feel the steam from the kettle as I took it off the fire and poured the boiling water into the teapot. We would sit across a scrubbed wooden table, just the two of us, telling each other stories and drinking tea.

Where this was, I couldn't tell. Nowhere I had ever been or was likely to be. Telling stories wasn't dignified. And I was not to do things for myself anymore. Things like dressing myself or pinning up my hair. Things like fetching water and making tea.

So why did I long to do it so much? The queen and her ladies would disapprove.

It all tumbled out, then, before I even realized I was talking. "They say they have been neglecting the queen, that I'll want my own ladies now."

He moved my hands and looked up at me, his eyes that unfathomable color I could never quite name. "You don't mind, do you? You never wanted an entourage." His lips curved a little mischievously, trying to get me to smile. "At least not that particular one."

I tried to smile back, but failed. "You don't…" It was heresy to say it. "You don't like them?"

"You beautiful thing." He squeezed my hands. "If I had liked them, even one of them, we never would have had a ball in the first place. Mother was determined to show me no girl could surpass her choices. Her plan failed spectacularly. Because of you."

"She'll never forgive me." I sighed.

He reached up, twining one of my curls around his finger. "Then I'll just love you all the more."

His words warmed me for a moment. Until I remembered about the ladies. "But who would I get instead? Not my sisters."

I knew what everyone thought. I caught the whispers, snatches of conversation people thought I couldn't hear. They were mostly about my stepsisters and their lack of breeding, pretending to fit the glass slipper. Even better was the story of my wedding and the punishment they received there. *Blinded!* I heard a lady say once, savoring the word as if she had never tasted anything so delicious. *Yes, by a flock of birds. All those cruel little beaks! Can you imagine?*

My husband was frowning a little. This was his usual expression when my family was mentioned. At first, I thought it was out of loyalty, because of how they had treated me. But now I wondered. What if he blamed me? For belonging to a family like that. Was it only his good manners that kept him from frowning at me the same way? And what if he knew all I hadn't told him? My skin went hot and cold all at once.

He sat up, taking my hand. "Don't worry." He bent his head to try to catch my eye, "we'll find someone. I could ask—"

"No, darling, don't bother. I'm sure I can think of someone."

That was a lie. There was no one I could ask, but I couldn't bear the thought of someone else, or a group of someones, chosen by the queen, or even my husband, floating into this room. Perhaps they'd be wearing jade and jet and sapphires instead of opals and pearls and rubies. But they would be the same, pretending to be my friends. Pretending they liked me.

"As you wish." He kissed me, his lips warm on mine. "I've

got to change. They'll be waiting on me."

I kept hold of his hand. "But your headache…Shouldn't you stay?"

"It's better now." He pressed a kiss into my palm before he stood up. "Your touch works wonders."

I stayed where I was on the sofa, wishing it were as easy as everyone made it sound, replacing something. Finding a new group of ladies, or a new pair of slippers. As if I could simply order them. As if I could walk into a shop, saying, *Yes, I'd like two ladies in waiting. No, three is too many. I don't want them too fashionable. Just someone I could talk to. Someone who wouldn't think there was something wrong with me.* The lady in the shop would look uncomfortable. *No, we don't have anyone like that, I'm afraid.*

A huff of air came out my nose, not quite a laugh. Even in my imagination, it wouldn't work. And as for Pearl's suggestion, *You must have a new glass pair made*, it was just as ridiculous. As if all I had to do was go back to the churchyard, back to the hazel tree at my mother's grave, and order a new pair.

Or wish for one.

I must have stopped breathing for a moment, imagining doing just that. Then I sat up straight, air rushing back into my lungs. What if I could? Wishing had worked before. I set the slippers on the floor, forced my feet into them, and ran to the stables.

THREE

The stables had a familiar scent, of straw and animals and manure. The queen and her ladies would have wrinkled their noses in distaste, but I was not like them. The rough wood of the stalls, the muffled sounds of the animals, even the smell of the place soothed me. In the stables my stays did not squeeze so tightly around my ribs. In the stables I could breathe.

I picked my way along the rows of stalls, past fine carriage horses and long-legged hunters and massive draft horses, each bred and trained for a particular task. Except for one in the last row, a shaggy mare with a patched brown and white coat and a friendly tilt to her ears. Perhaps her owner was a craftsman or a traveler, someone just passing through. She did not belong here.

At home, I would have come to the stables with an apple or a carrot in my apron pocket. Here, I had nothing. But there was a sack of oats nearby. I took a handful and held it out to her, my hand flat under her nose.

Behind me, one of the grooms coughed. "The carriage is nearly ready, your highness." When I turned, he blushed and turned his face away. He looked as if he had come upon me naked, not stroking a horse's nose as she tasted the lace at my elbow.

"Perhaps you would like to wait outside." The groom held out an arm in the direction he wanted me to go.

I did not want to wait outside; someone might wonder what I was up to. But a princess should not wait in the stables with the animals. I leaned my forehead against the mare's neck and tangled my fingers in her mane, inhaling her warmth. Then I followed the groom outside.

I stood in the courtyard, twisting the ring around my finger, then sliding it back and forth over my knuckle. The queen always looked at me sternly when she caught me doing this. She had given up her dead mother's wedding ring for me to use as mine. Another thing to resent. I wasn't ungrateful; it was an elegant, costly thing, the gems set in the shape of a rose. But it was heavy on my finger. I still wasn't used to the feel of it.

When the footman opened the carriage door I hurried inside, hoping no one had seen me. It would get around, of course, this little excursion of mine. But was it so very odd, to take a drive?

Once we left the palace behind, I watched out the side window, willing the carriage to go faster. I hadn't been this way since my marriage. I hadn't looked back then; I hadn't wanted to. But now I had decided to return, I couldn't wait to be back in the churchyard. I couldn't wait to see the tree.

All those years ago, just after my mother died, I planted a hazel tree at her grave. I couldn't say why. I only knew I couldn't bear to leave my mother alone under that hard, unmoving headstone. *Dutiful daughter,* it said without feeling. *Beloved wife,* the carved letters declared. *Devoted mother.* I couldn't bear to bury a seed and wonder when, or if, it would push out of the earth and return to life. I had buried enough.

So after the burial, after everyone left, I stayed behind. I planted a twig, right into the ground as I'd seen the gardeners do with willows. Surely I could do the same. It was slight and bendy, with a single flower at the tip, its tiny pink fingers just peeking out of the bud. It would grow, I told myself as I patted the dirt flat around the twig. It had to.

But I didn't quite believe myself. My hands still in the dirt, I begged the little twig to take root, my grief pouring, streaming from my fingers and into the earth like water. The ground warmed, and my skin tingled. I grew dizzy, but I stayed where I was. At last I curled into a ball beside the twig, the lightheadedness too strong for me to stand. I think I even slept for a time.

When I sat up, though, I was sure the little branch was taller, the flower more open. There were even a few tiny branches sprouting from the sides. I was shaky and weak, but it would grow now. I was sure it would.

It must have just been my wishing that it was already growing, to make me think that it was. That was what I thought. But afterward, it grew so quickly that a pair of turtle doves even settled into its branches to nest. It was taller than a grown man by the time winter came that year. If anyone else had come to the grave, they would have seen it too.

But I was the only one. My father was too grieved at first. And later, I never knew why he did anything. So it was only me at the grave tending the tree, the tree that granted my wishes and changed my life.

The carriage hit a bump, and I looked around, not knowing where I was. We were near the church now, but I realized I didn't know how to tell the driver to stop. When I traveled with my husband, he never seemed to speak to anyone. Everything was arranged in some silent language of gestures I didn't understand. I knocked on the glass separating me and the driver, but nothing happened. I knocked again, harder this time. He turned on the box and looked over his shoulder, taking in my ungloved hand, now open against the glass. His eyebrows furrowed. I pointed to the church. "Can we stop here?" I spoke loudly. I didn't know how thick the glass was, or if he could hear me through it.

We came to a stop, and the footman opened the door, just a crack. "Are you quite well, your highness?"

"I'd just like to go inside for a moment." He didn't move to open the door any wider. I tried to look like someone who deserved to have her requests granted. "There's no harm in saying an extra prayer, is there?"

It wasn't a lie. A wish is a prayer of sorts.

The footman looked puzzled. I had access to the royal chapel at the palace. Why would I stoop to enter a common church? At last, he inclined his head, opened the door, and handed me down. His long strides soon overtook me, so he opened the church door and stepped in first. Perhaps he thought he would announce me. I stifled the laugh that came into my throat at the thought. But he simply held the door open, waiting for me to go through into the empty sanctuary.

I couldn't have him following me into the churchyard, though. I stopped beside him, trying to imagine what Opal would say, what the queen would say. Something commanding like, *You may leave me,* or, *Wait at the carriage.* But my stepmother had taught me too well. I wasn't used to speaking up for myself. My mouth wouldn't form those words, even if they were expected.

"I'd like some time alone," I managed at last. "Would you mind waiting for me at the carriage?" He stared at me, his mouth slightly open. My words confused him, like my knocking had confused the driver. Maybe I shouldn't have spoken at all, just made a dismissive gesture with my hand, something curt and sharp. But after a moment he bowed and left, closing the door behind him.

I pulled off the slippers and crept to the back door. Shoes in hand, I slipped into the churchyard.

The grass under my bare feet was soft, the soil warm. I wanted to run, to fall face down, arms spread wide on the earth. But something held me back. Once, I had visited this tree every day. It had been my only friend. But I hadn't been here since my marriage, not since the prince slid the lost slipper onto my foot. Now I was a stranger.

As I walked across the churchyard, a feeling of warmth crept up my chest and into my throat, stinging my eyes. I wiped my cheek with the back of one fist. I knelt in front of the gravestone, laying the glass slippers in front of me like an offering.

I knew that wasn't the way it worked. You cannot offer something you don't want, expecting something better in return. But I did it anyway.

My mother's gravestone looked abandoned and unkempt. It would; no one else came here. I dug my fingers into the grooves of the carved letters, trying to scrape out the bits of dirt and leaves that had blown in and settled there. I worked my way around the stone, pulling weeds and tossing them to the side. But on one side of the stone I stopped myself, my fingers on a small seedling under my hand. It was just a few inches high, sprouting diamond-shaped leaves with jagged edges.

A weed is only a flower growing where you don't want it, my mother had said to our gardener once. She was cajoling him into leaving a creeping vine, a weed, in our garden, because she liked the flowers and the shape of its leaves. She had never cared about what should or shouldn't be in a garden, only what pleased her.

I spread my hand out on the ground beside the seedling. What sort of plant would it be, I wondered. If I pulled it, I would never know. I left it there, along with a sprig of ivy on the other side. I would let them grow. She would have liked them.

I glanced toward the church door. I was running out of time. With my hands still touching the earth below the little seedlings, I closed my eyes. Before, I had whispered to the tree. I had told it the stories I could tell no one else: how my father wouldn't look at me, how my throat clenched at the sound of my stepmother's voice. *Ugly. Lazy. Worthless.* How I wished to go to a ball and pretend to be someone else, just for one night. And then a second night. And a third. And on that third night, I asked for something more. Something I never should have wished for.

That all felt so long ago. The tree was like a person I no longer knew. I had never even said thank you. I had never said goodbye.

I should say those things now, I told myself. And so many more. But the only word that came out, over and over again, was *Please.* In that *please* was everything I needed: I needed a new pair of glass slippers. I needed them to always fit. And I needed them to have the same magic as before.

I don't know how long I knelt there like that, but when I came to myself I was lightheaded. My fingers tingled; the earth was warm under my palms. Something was tickling my forehead where my skin touched the gravestone. I opened my eyes and looked up, wiping my cheeks with the back of my hand.

The little seedling had snaked its way up the side of the stone, pushing out leaves and thorns and white roses as it went. The ivy had done the same on the other side, meeting the rose at the top, where the two plants twined together.

Over the years since that first time, when I made a hazel tree grow from a twig, I had learned to control this unexplainable thing I could do. Sickly plants would grow strong, fruit would ripen, and buds would open at my touch if I willed them to. But sometimes, like now, it still happened when I didn't intend it to. And I never got used to it. I reached out a finger and touched one of the roses, a half-smile on my face.

I rose and slipped around the gravestone to the tree, looking for any sign that it had granted my wish. My heart hammered in my chest the way it had done before, when the shoes first appeared. I could almost feel that sweet sense of anticipation.

Before, when all I wanted was to go to a ball, it was autumn. I didn't think about the way the leaves fell with each wish the tree granted. Not then. When its first gift appeared, the glass slippers and a leaf-green gown, a flurry of golden leaves fell to the ground. With the second gown of red and gold, still more leaves rained down. And the tree was half bare by the time the last gown, silver as icicles, lay draped across the branches.

Then, with the tree still half clothed in leaves, I made the last wish. I did not wish to be in love with the prince; I knew I was already. I didn't wish for us to be in love. I didn't question my own feelings, only his. I hoped he was in love; I thought he was. But that wasn't enough. I had to be sure. So I clutched the silver gown to my chest and wished. To secure my happiness, and mine alone.

I was a fool.

I wish the prince would fall in love with me. As those words dropped from my lips, all the remaining leaves swirled off and around me in a rush, settling over the glass slippers on my feet. The glass heated against my skin, so hot it nearly burned; a gust of wind swept the leaves clean away, and I knew my wish was granted.

I clutched the silver gown to my chest and hurried home to put it on. The tree that granted my wishes stood at my mother's grave, forgotten. It was completely bare.

It wasn't bare anymore, though. Autumn and winter and spring had come and gone since that last wish. Summer was nearly gone too. There were new leaves now, the color of that first gown. But they were not all green. I saw that as I circled the tree again and again, searching for a glint of glass and brushing my fingers through the leaves. Half the leaves were dry and brown; they came away, crumbling and dead in my fingers. The turtle doves' nest lay on the ground at a bereft angle.

That was all. There was nothing in the branches for me.

I sank to my knees, my hand closing around one too-tight shoe. Those crumbling brown leaves told me all I needed to know. The tree's magic was spent on my foolish wishes. It had nothing more to give.

My hand tightened around the shoe, and I raised my arm. The feeling rising up from my stomach and into my throat was not clear and liquid like grief or tears; it was black and muddy. But unlike tears, it would not leave me; it clogged in my throat and stuck there. I froze in place, one arm wrapped around myself and the other hanging in the air, poised to hurl the slipper against the gravestone. In the silence and stillness before I let go, I could hear the sound of the shatter and see the way the shards would catch the light as they flew into the air.

But that wasn't how it went. The slipper hit the stone with a sick cracking sound; then it slid onto the grass unharmed. The black, muddy feeling tried to escape me in one ugly sob, but it remained inside. My arm dropped, and my fingers lost their strength, as if my bones had disappeared. I hadn't been brave enough to do it properly.

And I had stayed too long. I must get up and return to the church, to the carriage. I must go home. The palace wasn't my home, but whatever it was, I had to go back. My legs refused to gather underneath me, though. If only I could curl up there and let the earth come up around me. If only the magic that came from my hands would work in reverse, drawing me underground. But it didn't work that way.

It was the thought of what people would say that made me move at last. *Yes, she snuck off from the castle in the middle of the day. She was just lying there in the dirt of a common churchyard. The servant had to carry her back to the carriage.*

Oh, my dear, someone else would say, *it's the prince I feel sorry for. We did so want him to be happy with her. But what can you expect?* Unsaid would be the words, *from a girl like that.*

Planting my feet and hands, I pushed myself off the ground. Then I leaned down and picked up my shoes, wishing the slipper had broken into pieces against the gravestone. It would be out of my hands, then. No more pretending.

But the next moment I regretted the foolish thought. I couldn't destroy the wish within the slippers, no matter how tight they were.

Unable to look at the tree, I fixed my eyes on its roots. "Thank you." The words felt hollow in my mouth, but at least I had said them.

Once back inside the church I sat, grateful for the solid wood of the pew underneath me. A final hope stirred, and I held up one slipper. What if the tree had not replaced the shoes, but changed them, stretched them? It was only the littlest bit of room that I needed. Maybe just looking at them I wouldn't see the difference.

But I did see something. Along one side was a crack, thin as a hair and forked like a streak of lightning. Hitting the gravestone had damaged it after all. Even in the cool of the church, my skin went hot all over. Was this how my story would end? My perfect love, my new life, my reinvented self all sabotaged, broken by my own hands?

There was no way to know until I put them on. I set the slippers on the stone floor beneath the pew, ready for my feet. I positioned my toes above them and closed my eyes, desperate to remember what it felt like to have my feet slide in effortlessly. Just like they used to.

Behind me, the church door opened, and I jumped, guilty. It was the footman. "Your highness?"

I pushed my feet downward. It was not smooth or effortless. The glass fought against me. I pressed my lips together and forced my heels down. The slippers did not want me anymore, but despite the crack, they did not break.

It felt like there was a hand around my throat, squeezing, but at last I managed to speak. "I am coming."

FOUR

Back inside my dressing room, I pulled the slippers off. The impulse to hurl them against something solid had returned, but I didn't give in. One crack was bad enough.

I sat on the sofa and examined my feet. The grooves where the edges of the shoes bit into my flesh were deeper. What had been a faint pink line this morning was darker now, angry. On my left foot, a bit of skin along the groove had come loose. I pulled at it. But it was like a hangnail; pulling one bit of skin only left a bigger piece hanging. Now it was worse.

My trip to the churchyard had made me late, and the maid would be in any minute to help me dress for dinner. I fumbled around on my dressing table for something to use on the bit of skin. The table was stocked with every tool a princess would need to make her beautiful. There were boar bristle hair brushes, sable brushes for rouge, powder puffs, dainty silver hair pins with rounded ends. Not a single thing was sharp.

I couldn't go down to dinner like this. Someone might see the flap of skin, or the little spot of blood. They would wonder what was wrong with me. So I continued searching, knocking over bottles and opening drawers.

Finally, my hand closed around something with an edge: a nail file, the same one my husband had used to fix my bracelet. Its end was pointed to go under nails and remove the tiniest trace of dirt. It wasn't designed for cutting skin, but it would have to do. I sank onto the floor, my weapon in hand. It was only a little sharp, so I had to saw at the skin, but in a minute it came free, a trickle of blood sliding toward the carpet. I tied a handkerchief tightly around my foot and stood. It was time to undress.

My fingers fumbled at my bodice, unfastening it as quickly as I could. I had just managed to get down to my underclothes when the maid arrived. I sat on the stool at the mirror, hiding my bandaged foot under my petticoats.

The maid didn't see me, though. She just stood in the doorway, the yellow damask gown over one arm. She surveyed the dressing table with its drawers open and their contents spilling out. The line of her mouth hardened.

I tried to slow my breathing. "I'm afraid I've made a bit of a mess," I murmured, making up a lie to tell her. "I couldn't find my earrings with the pearls."

She looked sad. "You're wearing them, your highness." No, not sad. Disappointed. Of course I had picked the ones I was actually wearing.

My hand strayed to my ear to feel the supposedly elusive earring. I turned to the mirror. "How foolish." I couldn't look at her anymore.

Draping the yellow damask over the back of the sofa, she bent down to pick up the dress I had just taken off. "If you would wait for me to undress you, your highness, your gown would be less likely to be damaged." Her tone was flat as she inspected the bodice. I had torn something.

"Of course." I made my mouth into a smile. "I'm always forgetting things like that." Now she was holding up the underskirts, stained with grass and dirt from the churchyard. "I was outside," I blurted. Obviously.

The maid said nothing but folded the offending clothes, hiding the damage, and set them aside. Later, she would take them away and do the best she could to repair the damage I had done: sponging the delicate fabric, bleaching the linen, mending the rips, replacing any missing trim or buttons. The way she made my worn dresses look like new seemed like a kind of magic. But I knew better. I had done all those things for my stepmother and stepsisters too many times to count. And I'd been every bit as capable at it, if not more so. It wasn't magic at all; it was hard work.

The stained gown forgotten for the moment, we began the evening's ritual. First, the maid tied and pinned and fastened me into the yellow damask. When I had to stand, I stood on one foot, concealing the bandaged one beneath my petticoats. She didn't seem to notice.

Then she brought out the curl papers and heated the iron. People used to remark on my soft, honey-colored curls and the way they caught the light, but here, my hair did not please. It had to be smoothed in some places, set into regimented ringlets in others. With the curl papers in place, the maid covered the yellow damask and began to work on my face, powdering away my freckles, giving my cheeks a bloom they did not have.

At last the curls were arranged and the jewelry fastened. The pearl earrings did not suit the gown in the least. But I had said I wanted them, so I would have to wear them. The maid leaned down behind me, studying my reflection. *It will have to do,* her expression said. *I've done my best.* Aloud, she only said, "Will there be anything else, your highness?" Her words were the same every night.

So were mine. "No, thank you."

She would leave now. Just another moment. But just as she reached the door, she stooped to pick up one of the glass slippers.

"Never mind." My voice was awkward, filling up my ears. But she was too well trained. She looked around until she saw the other, poking out from under a couch. If I crossed the room first, she would see my bandaged foot. So I stayed, frozen to my stool, as she picked up the other slipper and knelt beside me, holding it out for me to put on.

We looked at each other for a moment. Then I reached out and snatched the shoes. I did it like a thief, like someone who doesn't deserve what she takes.

"I'll do it," I said. "You may go." She didn't move. She stared at me, face frozen. "Don't worry." I hoped my tone was teasing. "It's only a pair of slippers. I think I can manage." She left, closing the door behind her with a disapproving snap.

I untied the handkerchief, and the breath I was holding came out in a rush. The bleeding had stopped. I stuffed the bloodstained handkerchief into my bodice and squeezed into the slippers. The clock in the castle's highest tower struck eight; it was time to go down.

As the tolling died away, the clock on my mantle began to chime, a feeble echo of the bell in the tower. I should have been used to it by now, but I was always surprised to hear it, chiming just a little late.

FIVE

That was the beginning. I had started, and now there was no stopping.

It was only when I got back to my dressing room after dinner that I noticed it. My left foot, the one missing the piece of skin, didn't hurt as much. As soon as the maid was gone, I sat on the sofa, knees drawn up, and examined my feet. The left foot had a small red cut where I had used the nail file, but the other red marks looked lighter, less angry than the ones on the right.

Could it be that simple? Had taking off that tiny bit of skin made all the difference? I studied the right foot, searching for a place to start. But there wasn't one. While the skin was swollen, it was unbroken.

But I still had my weapon. The palace maids were almost invisible. I never saw them at it, but while I was away, they always repaired any damage I had done, restoring pins and brushes and powder puffs to their rightful places. Tonight was no different: the nail file waited in its drawer.

I bent my knee and brought my foot up on the stool beside me. I gripped the nail file, uncertain of where to start. The outer side was more red, but there were no broken pieces to make an easy beginning. I pinched a bit of skin between my fingers and sawed at it with the edge of the file, but I got nowhere. It had been dull before. It seemed even duller now.

I tossed the nail file onto the dresser. What I needed was a knife. Surely the castle was full of them. There were all sorts of weapons hung decoratively in the great hall. They were too big and clumsy for my purpose, though. The kitchen, stables, and gardens would have better knives. But I would not be allowed any of those.

I was allowed a meat knife, though. The kind that sat at my place every night at dinner.

My heartbeat quickened. It would work, I told myself; I would do it tomorrow night. A meat knife was just what I needed. I could smuggle one back to my room easily enough. Then I could shave off a bit of skin here and there; in time it would heal, and everything would be like before. My shoes would fit, and no one would ever know.

"Darling?" I jumped at the sound of my husband's voice from the bedroom. "Why are you taking so long? Come to bed."

I let out a shaky breath. For one more night, my feet would have to please as they were.

I dropped my wedding ring into the jeweled dish on my dressing table, as I did every night. It had always been a little loose on my finger, and I was afraid it would slip off while I slept. Then the queen would never forgive me for losing it. In its little dish, it was safe.

I stood at the door to my bedroom, our bedroom, with my hand on the latch, my forehead touching the door. I longed to ask him what was wrong with me. How had I gone from the mysterious princess who was the talk of the ball to the girl who was so awkward she had to be instructed on how to walk and speak and hold a knife? Why didn't I fit?

Perhaps I should have asked him, but between all his princely duties, those audiences, appearances, and meetings that didn't call for a princess, we had little time together. In fact, the only time we seemed to have alone was at night in our bedroom. And I was so happy, there in the dark with him, that I forgot everything but the way he made me feel. Afterward, in the safety of his arms, I could whisper stories of stepmothers and ogres and wolves, of brave milkmaids and clever tailors. But if I ever tried to ask him then, my voice failed me. I couldn't get the words out.

"Darling?" he called again.

Frozen outside the door, I forced my lungs to breathe in and out. In and out. But every breath brought me less air. What would he think if he could see the marks the glass made on my skin? If he knew my body, just like everything else about me, perversely refused to fit? If he knew his love for me was nothing but a wish?

I shook my head and dug my fingernails into my palm. My husband was the one person I didn't need to fear. His love was guaranteed by the magic I'd wished into the slippers. I had never had them off longer than the space of a night, and the magic always held at least that long. So why was my stomach so cold? The room behind that door was our own little cottage in the wood, away from the people of the palace. Away from the things they said and the way they looked at me. He was happy with me there, I was sure of it. We were in love. We were happy.

I turned the latch.

I couldn't say how it happened, but somehow we were on the bed before I could blow out the candles.

For a moment I let myself drown in the feeling of being wanted, of being exactly what he wanted. But I wasn't, and I couldn't let him see that. "Let me just get the candles, darling," I whispered between kisses.

"Don't," he whispered into my neck. "You're too perfect in the candlelight." He opened my dressing gown with one finger. "I want to see you." His eyes in the candlelight were a deep shade I had no name for. They followed his fingertips down my body, from my shoulder to my hip, to my thigh, my ankle.

I pulled my feet underneath me. "It's just that I've got a bit of a headache tonight," I said quickly. "The light hurts my eyes."

I held my breath as he sat up, his brow furrowed in concern. The last thing I wanted to do was hurt him. In his arms, I was everything I wasn't on my own: loved and confident and brave. And I'd never refused him anything before. I'd never so much as hesitated.

But he didn't seem upset; his voice was gentle. "Darling, you should have told me." He rose and blew out the candles. The flames turned to smoke and disappeared.

"It's not that I don't want to," I said when he returned to bed. "I'm feeling better already."

"Are you sure?"

"Of course, it was just the light."

"Well then," he whispered, "come here." But I could hear it in his voice. The disappointment. Even from him. It left me wondering how strong my wish had been. What blows could it weather? And what would it take to dissolve it into nothingness?

Six

He was gone the next morning when I woke up. Most days, he was up and dressed well before I was. But often, he would kiss me before he left. Not *always*, only most of the time. He was just in a hurry today, I told myself.

He was busy most of every day, while I was never wanted before dinner. Until then, I had nothing to do but prepare. My one duty was to charm the guests with my witty conversation, my graceful dancing, my beauty. Night after night I failed to do so. People would only stare at me, half smiles on their faces. As if I was an exotic bird: pretty to look at, but singing in some savage language they didn't understand.

So every morning I began again, with advisors, clothes, jewelry, lessons. There was always something more to try, a new skill I must acquire or perfect. But this day, when I asked the maid who was coming, she wouldn't look at me. "No one, your highness," she said, and busied herself with collecting my breakfast dishes.

I had shown too much independence the day before. The queen's ladies were not coming. They sent no one else to work on me either; no one was coming to instruct me in dancing, walking, or smiling. Once the door closed behind the maid, the day was my own.

But I wasn't used to my own time. Here at the palace, I could not sweep a hearth or bake a loaf of bread or weed a garden bed. And what else was I good for?

I wandered from room to room, looking for a way to pass the hours. I prowled around the shelves in the library, running my fingers over the gold titles embossed on the spines.

For a while I sat at the piano in the music room. But my fingers kept slipping off the keys with a sick sensation that made my heart drop into my stomach. When I first arrived at the palace, the queen had sent the music master to hear me. *Your voice is perfectly suited to choral singing, your highness, and your playing…* He'd kindly patted my hand. *Well, one can't excel at everything, my dear.*

Of course I could not play like Ruby or Pearl. Since my father's marriage, I had only been allowed to dust my mother's piano and rub it with beeswax, never play it. The servants here used lemon oil, and the smell made my head ache.

By midday, I was in the rose garden with my workbasket. This was my favorite spot in the castle grounds. I found an old stone bench in a sheltered corner where the wind wouldn't disturb my needlework. Pulling the slippers off, I tucked my feet underneath me and brought out my embroidery. On the cloth were two figures, a man and a woman, standing side by side. I had nearly finished their clothing, but the heads remained undone. I never liked doing faces; they never turned out the way I imagined them. I would work on the flowered border instead.

Yet, I never finished these needlework projects. I wasn't making anything necessary, so I couldn't bring myself to care enough about how they looked. I would much rather be doing something useful.

Only my husband knew what I could do with my hands in the earth. I tried to tell my father once, shortly after my mother died. But he only waved me away. *Yes, yes, my dear. Very nice.* He wouldn't look at me. Flowers made him think of my mother, I suppose, and he couldn't bear to, then. When my stepmother saw I could do something her daughters couldn't, she hissed that I was unnatural and forbade me doing any more of my *trickery* ever again.

But she could not stop me. She had taken everything else from me; she would not take my gift. I used it in secret and took a savage pleasure in growing the biggest pumpkins, tastiest carrots, and most beautiful greens anyone had ever seen. *Hard work,* she would say, when she felt like being kind. *Isn't that better, dear?* I would smile and agree that it was.

It was because of her that I kept my attentions to the palace gardens secret as well. To dirty my hands here would be unthinkable, as well as unnatural. So, as I did at my father's house, I made sure no one saw me. I never stayed long, but if I found myself alone, I would slip off my gloves and lay my hands on the earth, sometimes only for the space of a breath or two. There was always something I could do.

But the palace residents often took a stroll this time of day, and someone might see me. A princess couldn't be useful, but she couldn't be idle, either. I sighed and looked back at the flowered border of my needlework. Today I must be satisfied with stitching roses, not growing them.

I studied the roses closest to my bench before choosing a color of thread. They had an overblown, end of summer look to them. They were nothing like the flawless ones that appeared on my breakfast tray every morning. There was always a single rose in a vase, tucked in among the pots of jam and marmalade I never ate. Unlike the ones on my tray, the roses in the garden had a warm and comforting scent. My daily roses were tightly closed and perfect, but they had no smell whatsoever.

I heard footsteps behind me. It was one of the gardeners walking toward the door to the orchard. He tipped his hat to me stiffly.

"Do you have a pair of scissors?" I asked.

He stopped and looked at me curiously. "Can I do anything, your highness?"

"I'd just like one of these roses, that's all."

He scratched his ear, his mouth half open as if he didn't understand me.

"I'll do it myself if you'll lend me some scissors." I thought fleetingly that I had another use for something sharp, but tonight's meat knife would be better than a pair of scissors. Meat knives are designed for cutting flesh; scissors are not.

He patted his pockets. "I don't have any on me at the moment, your highness, but don't you worry now. I'll have a lovely bouquet sent up for you. These ones here are past their prime. Though for some reason, they've lasted far longer than usual this year."

Then he leaned toward me and lowered his voice. "I've only got a whisper of the gift. But you're just like my old granddad, you are. The way you make things come alive." He winked and grinned at my shocked expression. "I won't tell no one."

Then he spoke louder, as if he expected to be overheard. "We've far prettier ones. I'll send you some of those." Off he went, toward the orchard, or perhaps the hothouse, where the prettier roses grew.

I stood, speechless. He knew about me. I must not have been as secretive as I'd thought. But the gardener didn't seem aghast. On the contrary, it seemed I wasn't alone.

I leaned back over to the rose with the beautiful scent. My sewing scissors would be too small to cut through the thick stem. But the blossom was nearly off anyway; a little tug brought it into my hand. I tucked it into my bodice where no one would see it. But I could feel it against my skin and smell its scent. Just a little.

From the palace behind me, I heard women's voices. It was the queen and her ladies, and they were coming closer. Stuffing the rose farther into my bodice, I hurried back to the bench and sat, shoving my feet back into my shoes. I pulled my needlework into my lap and arranged my skirts, the perfect picture of a girl who had not been stealing roses.

But when they entered the garden, no one noticed me. The queen sighed elegantly, her head turned toward Opal. "I'm afraid it is a hopeless business, pet." Opal, Ruby, and Pearl followed behind her, nodding their sympathy for whatever the hopeless business was. I was sure I knew.

Do you mean me, your majesty? I imagined asking her. *Am I the hopeless business?* I couldn't, of course. I didn't need eavesdropping added to my list of sins. *So ill-bred,* the queen would say later, when they were back in her chambers, *listening to other people's conversations.*

The ladies blocked the only exit. I couldn't simply steal away. So I stood, setting my workbasket down on the bench with a bit of a bang.

But they took no notice, and the queen continued speaking. "I've been telling—"

"Good morning, your majesty." As one, they turned my way. My cheeks grew hot as I realized I had interrupted her. But there was no help for it. At least she wouldn't continue talking about the *hopeless business.*

The queen smiled. Her expression was not warm, like her son's. It was the smile an adult would give a child she would rather not be saddled with. At least she wasn't angry that I had interrupted her. She opened her arms, not widely, not as if to embrace me or even the idea of me. Her elbows stayed near her sides. Her gesture was half-hearted, but like everything she did, graceful.

"Good afternoon, my dear." It was afternoon, not morning, as I had said. "Won't you join us?"

"Thank you, your majesty." I moved to follow the queen's ladies, but they parted, Ruby inclining her head in an indication I should walk next to the queen. They fell in behind me, and I was trapped.

As she surveyed the garden, the queen made a tsking noise. "This area is so old fashioned."

The ladies all nodded gravely. "Oh, yes, your majesty," said Pearl. The other two agreed.

But I was silent. I loved this garden. It was where I first met the prince.

It was the night of the first ball. I had just arrived, and already I could tell the palace was no place for me. Once I reached the other side of the ballroom, I disappeared into the garden and walked up and down the torchlit path, trying to decide whether to go back in or scale the wall and escape.

Along one wall was a line of rose bushes. It was autumn; their blooms were gone, but the leaves were green still. Except for one bush I feared would not come alive again in the spring. I crouched down beside it, running my fingers over the brown and crumbling leaves.

Oh dear, came a voice from behind me. I hadn't heard him coming up the gravel walk. *The queen will be disappointed this wasn't cut out before tonight,* the stranger said ruefully.

I knew nothing of the queen and what she liked. *Perhaps she prefers a sick plant to a missing one,* I suggested. *Perhaps she prefers the symmetry?*

Hmm…well, she detests imperfection of any kind. The young man sat down beside me, with no apparent regard for his fine clothes. *So, neither would be acceptable, I suppose.* He glanced over at me, his eyebrows drawing together in a worried expression. *Do you not like the ball?*

*I…*I didn't have the words to answer. My stepmother's cruelty, the leaf green gown, the exquisite glass slippers, the stares and whispers of the dancers, and now a bit of concern from a stranger had all been too much. *I've never seen anything like it,* I finished lamely.

I was not used to speaking to young men, especially kind, handsome ones. My stepmother would call me *stupid* for not making good conversation. I cast about for something else to say. *Do you know the queen well?*

As well as anyone, I suppose. She's my devoted mother. He sighed. *Look at the great lengths she's gone to so she can find me a wife.*

Oh. I was even less accustomed to speaking to princes. But, prince or no prince, I didn't want this kind young man to leave. What could I say that would interest him? I preferred the surety of stories to conversation. I knew the words, everything was familiar, and it would all make sense in the end. *Would you like to hear a story, your highness?*

He raised his eyebrows. *What about?*

I took a breath, surprised at my daring. *A choosy queen.*

That night, hiding from the ball with the prince, I'd had no idea how choosy his mother truly was. But I learned quickly enough. So today, I wasn't a bit surprised as the queen frowned at the rose garden around her. She didn't ask my opinion of it, and I was glad. I had spent more of my energy here than in any other garden. When I came here, it had been planned out, with each plant in its place, but under my hands the borders faded. Creeping vines stole in and blossomed among the rose bushes. Ivy and woodbine trailed up the walls. It was perfect.

We passed out of the rose garden as the queen remarked that one day she would have it all torn out and redone. "Not now, of course. In the spring, perhaps." As we walked into the next garden, she turned to me. "Now, my dear, I understand we still need some ladies for you."

I could feel Opal, Ruby, and Pearl at my back, their eyes on me, but I didn't turn around. "I, uh…" I faltered when I caught the queen's sharp expression.

Words, my dear, Madame would have said, had we been in one of her elocution lessons. She hated words that were not words. So did the queen. But knowing that made it all the more difficult not to let any escape.

"I mean, yes, I suppose so."

The queen smiled, complacent. "There are plenty of suitable girls about. I'm sure we could find some who would do for you. Let me think." She gazed upward, speaking more to herself than me. "Perhaps my nieces." She brightened briefly. "But then they are from the North." This idea didn't please her.

This was just what I didn't want. "Thank you, your majesty,"

I blurted. "But I wouldn't want to trouble you. I'll find someone, um—" I bit back the sound that was not a word before she could glare at me again. "Someone suitable."

She looked down at me, her expression cold now. "Why certainly, my dear. We will say no more about it, then."

I forced my lips into a smile.

The queen undoubtedly kept a list of my crimes in her head. Every awkward bit of conversation, every *um* and *er,* every graceless step, and every twist of my wedding ring were all marked on her list. Now she would add my refusal of her help, underlined so she wouldn't forget it.

The next garden was regimented, orderly, the way she liked things. Still, the queen wasn't satisfied. She sighed again. "There's no color here." It was true, most of the flowers here had bloomed in the spring and were faded now. Or they had died, and the gardeners had clipped them down, erasing any evidence of decay or ugliness. I looked around, searching for a spot of color, something that would please her.

At last I saw a glimpse of pale purple poking out of the earth, a meadow saffron. Their petals made a burst of color in the autumn when most plants died, even though the leaves didn't appear until spring. They were a kind of miracle.

The gardener's wink had made me too bold. I shouldn't have done it. But my hands were quicker than my thoughts. Before I knew it, I had whipped off my gloves and knelt on the garden path, my hands spread beside the tips of purple petals, calling, "Look, your majesty." In a few days they would be up and open anyway. But it would please her, this little thing I could do. For once she would smile at me. The tingling feeling leapt out of my fingers.

Determined, the purple petals pushed against the soil, moving up and up as my lightheadedness grew. They emerged from the earth, supported by pale stems, opening to reveal tiny orange threads at their centers. I sat back a little, my head still floating too much to take my hands away from the ground. "I've never seen them this color before." I couldn't stop myself from smiling as I turned to the queen. "But there are white ones and pink ones too. They're called—"

The words died on my tongue when I saw the way they stared.

My husband had stared too, the first time he saw what I could do. It was that first night in the rose garden, and I was telling the story I had promised, the one about the choosy queen. As he listened, the prince absorbed himself in arranging a group of stones from the path.

Before the princess went to bed that night, I was saying, *the choosy queen ordered that a single rose petal be placed in between the lowest two mattresses. She thought to test the girl by*—I stopped, staring at the stones on the path. He had made them into the shape of a bird. *That's incredible,* I breathed.

Mother wouldn't approve, he murmured, a half-smile on his face, and set down another stone, finishing the bird's little tail.

Something prickly brushed the skin of my wrist, but I ignored it. *What sort of bird is it?*

You choose. He looked up, his slow smile spreading as our eyes met. *What do you think?*

I leaned closer to the bird of stones, remembering that afternoon when birds had come to my aid. *If you have picked the lentils from the ashes in two hours' time, you may go to the ball,* my stepmother had said. Overwhelmed, I'd wished for help. The turtle doves from the hazel tree had flown in the window, and with them were pigeons, wrens, and finches. Thrushes and mockingbirds and blackbirds. The sparrow had been the last to leave, dropping the last lentil into my palm and flying away.

A sparrow, I said, looking up.

But he wasn't looking at me anymore. His eyes were on his upper arm. A branch from the dying rosebush had crept up his back and was peeking over his shoulder. The dead, brown leaves had fallen off, replaced by new, green ones and pale pink buds. We looked behind us to find the entire bush was green again, and blooming.

It was one of those times when it happened all by itself; I wasn't intending to make it grow. I must have looked a little proud of myself, for he stared at me, his eyes wide. *Are you doing that?*

In answer, the bud on his shoulder opened before his eyes. I watched him, a little hopeful, a little afraid.

He smiled, amazed. *You are a wonder,* he breathed. Then he stood, holding out his hand to help me up. *Will you come and dance with me?*

That first night in the moonlight, and many times since, the prince had called me *a wonder.* But now in the sunlight, the queen and her ladies did not think so. They stood frozen on the garden path, their eyes equally round in an expression I could not quite name.

When the queen found her voice at last, it was icy. "Stand up, my dear." Her mouth hardly moved as she spoke. I wobbled to my feet, heat rushing to my face. She closed the gap between us, and I looked down, hoping she wouldn't see the stolen rose crushed inside my bodice. Her tall form cast a shadow on my hands as I brushed the soil off. "We have plenty of gardeners to do the work here."

She said *gardeners* as if it were something shameful, not an honest job requiring skill and knowledge. She reached out a finger and put it under my chin, forcing me to look at her. "My son has told me of your *fondness* for flowers." Her voice grew even colder when she mentioned him, the son I had stolen from her. "No doubt he indulges you, but this," her gaze dropped to my dirty hands, "will not do." Her glove was rough against my skin, as if it would cut me. "You are a lady, are you not?"

At last I managed a weak whisper. "Yes, your majesty."

With that, she turned and walked down the path, telling the others the milliner would be waiting for them. Opal, Ruby, and Pearl followed in her wake in a graceful swirl of silk. They did not look back.

When they were gone, I made my way back to the rose garden, not seeing anything around me, just following the path. I picked up my workbasket and went back to my room, my limbs feeling like stone.

Back in my dressing room there was a huge vase of roses the gardener had sent. They were perfect and beautiful, and all the same color pink.

They had no smell.

SEVEN

Why is the truth so hard, and deception so easy?

There's no need to be nervous, I told myself as we walked into the great hall that night. *It's only a little extra pretending.* But I could never escape the feeling I didn't deserve to be in this sparkling room. And if I had any doubts, my pale reflection in the countless mirrors would remind me. They were everywhere, ornately framed and arched at the tops, magnifying the light from scores of candles. They made the room seem even bigger, even brighter than it already was. But the mirrors never did the same for me. I was just myself, a ghost of the girl I should be.

My husband pressed my fingers before letting them go. I willed myself to hold on to his reassurance as he pulled out my chair. Glancing behind me, I watched as the girl in the mirror covered her meat knife with a quick flick of her napkin. None of the elegant diners at the table seemed to have noticed as I turned to face them.

The queen's ladies moved, smiled, and spoke to the court gentlemen with practiced ease, as if playing an instrument. After all, that was what other people were to them. Instruments to play on. Entertainment. They paid no attention to me, but I knew it was far better to be ignored, especially tonight. I sat, pulling the napkin and knife onto my lap. The knife would be safe there until I could find the right moment to slip it into my garter. No one would know.

Then it was time for the usual: the small talk with people I hardly knew. My husband chatted easily with the duchess, as he did with everyone. While he listened to the news of her estate and her family, his hands were busy with his napkin. He was knotting it and shaping it. Into what, I couldn't tell. An animal, perhaps.

If he was unconventional, no one minded. He charmed everyone without even meaning to, just by being himself. I did not. The palace guests listened eagerly for the stupid things I would say. So, I had learned to guard my tongue. Or try to at least. But tonight, my mind was on the knife in my lap, and I spoke without thinking.

I was proud of myself for asking after the duchess's son. I remembered she had one, after all, and that he was away from home. Doing what, I couldn't remember. Then I heard Pearl's shocked inhale, followed by a sickening silence. The duchess sat back in her chair, her mouth slightly open, as if she wanted to respond to my question, but didn't know how. The table around us had grown unnaturally still.

Then I remembered. The duchess's son was a soldier. Had been a soldier. He had gone to the wars, and he had died, shortly after she had last been to the castle. I had written the condolence letter myself. It was one of my few duties. I had been given a script, so I wouldn't say anything wrong. All I had to do was copy it.

I did my best to repair the damage. "How thoughtless of me." My hands flapped as if they could erase my foolish words. "I was just remembering your last visit, and how very proud you were of the captain…and for just a moment I for…" I faltered. My hands landed on the table, useless.

My husband intervened. "I'm sorry you never got to meet him, darling." His warm hand covered mine. He turned to the duchess. "I miss Red."

Red. The captain's childhood name perhaps. I hadn't known that.

"All these wars," he muttered under his breath, shooting a dark look at the back of the king's head. As a future leader, my husband had been trained to fight when he was a boy. But he had no stomach for killing. And, as he was heir to the throne, his parents wouldn't have allowed him to go to the wars his father insisted on waging anyway.

He breathed in as if he wanted to say more, but stopped himself, looking down. Then one corner of his mouth turned up as he untied the knots of his napkin and began something new. "Did he ever tell you why we stayed in the woods that night when we were boys?"

The duchess shook her head, bemused but relieved at the slight change of subject. "He said you two wanted to have an adventure, and that was all I could ever get out of him." Her eyes searched his face. "And he swore it had all been his idea, and you insisted it was yours."

My husband folded his napkin into a triangle, a rueful smile on his face. "To tell you the truth, madam, neither of us intended spending the night at all, but we didn't have a choice in the end. Red was always collecting animals, you see." He turned to include me, finishing a knot at one point of the triangle. "He was forever rescuing wounded birds, orphaned foxes, any creature he thought needed help." He reached over and squeezed my hand again.

The duchess was nodding and smiling, her eyes bright. "And his highness would fashion little homes for them." She faced me, looking less hurt now. "He was always so clever with his hands."

His highness waved that part of the memory away, as if it no longer described him, as if his clever hands never made anything of value anymore. Then he continued, folding one corner of the napkin over the rest; perhaps it was a wing. "Well, that day, we found a bear cub who had lost its mother. Red insisted it would die without our help and that we had to take it home. He had it in his arms when the mother appeared." The duchess gasped, and my husband grinned, twisting another corner of the triangle into a curved neck. "So we spent the night up a tree. I suppose it was an adventure, but we knew better than to tell anyone what kind."

She dabbed at her eyes with a lace handkerchief, while he made a few knots at the end of the neck, forming a head and beak. "If I knew about that, I'd have blistered his backside." She ended with a gentle sound between a laugh and a sigh.

My husband looked up with a warm smile. "Why do you think I had to promise not to tell? But I don't think Red would mind you knowing now."

He looked back down at his creature. It was a swan. There was something so lifelike about it, I expected it to flap its cloth wings and fly away. But before it could, the prince untied the knots and returned it to his lap. It was a napkin once more.

He had repaired the damage I had done, and I could breathe again. He was always coming to my rescue this way. I loved him for it, but how could he not resent me for needing it so often? Perhaps the magic of the slippers blinded him to the girl beneath the wish. Did the girl he loved even exist?

The talk turned to happier things, and I said no more. I was silent through the soup, and as the servants changed the wine glasses and cleared away the first course. But as the line of silver platters approached, filled with roast venison and beef, pheasants and ducks and geese, meat pies and herb salads and oysters, it was time to act.

It was so easy. I dropped my spoon, then I bent to retrieve it. While under the table I quickly pulled up my skirts and tied the meat knife into the garter I'd worn for just that purpose. I sat back up, spoon in hand, letting my skirts fall back into place, and it was done.

Then it was time to go. Unlike my husband, I didn't have important duties. I couldn't arrange for a servant to call me away on an urgent matter of business. But it was always possible for a lady to fall ill. Between the rich food, the dancing, the stuffy room filled with people, and of course, the tightly laced stays, if a lady had to sit down, or even retire for the night, no one gave it a second thought. How many ladies were not really ill but escaping, I had no idea. But plenty of ladies did it, and it always worked.

I had never fainted, and I had never pretended to. But I had watched ladies here do it often enough. I had seen all their tricks. I ran one hand over my face, then held on to the table as if to steady myself. Still clutching the table, I put my other hand to my chest. Taking deep breaths, I sat for a moment wondering if I would need to collapse onto my husband's shoulder. But he noticed at last.

"What's wrong?" he asked in my ear.

I shook my head, my hand still on my chest. "I'm fine."

"You aren't." His eyes were dark with concern. "Here, have some wine."

I took the glass he offered me and drank a little. "That's better." I put the wine down and sat back in my chair. "I just felt a bit lightheaded for a moment. I'm much better now."

His hand found mine in my lap. "Are you sure?" I tensed, hoping he hadn't felt the knife.

He deserved better. He deserved someone who would stay through dinner, someone who was honest. I couldn't even fit in my own shoes. But I would fix that when I used the knife tied into my garter. I had to go on.

"Yes, darling." I moved his hand back to his lap and patted it. "I'm perfectly…" I trailed off, letting my hand go back to my face, then my chest. I dropped my hand suddenly then, falling toward him. As I knew he would, he caught my arm, holding me upright.

"Well…" I spoke softly. "Perhaps I'm not completely well after all. I think I had better go and lie down." His expression changed then. Was it worry? Or was it a flash of annoyance I saw on his face? "I'm so sorry to be a bother," I whispered. That was true, even if nothing else was.

"Don't be silly." There was a crease between his eyebrows. "Shall I go with you?"

"No, no." I turned my face from the other diners, who sat ready to gobble up this little bit of gossip to discuss as soon as I'd gone. *Did you see how pale she was?* they'd say. *Do you think she's…Oh no, my dear, she only wants attention. So ill bred.*

"You should stay," I told him. "I'll just lie down for a bit, then maybe I'll come back down later." I pushed back my chair.

He stood and offered me his hand, then gestured for a servant. "Don't bother coming back down." He ducked his head, forcing me to look at him. "Go and rest."

I went. The servant gave me his arm and we walked slowly, me with my other hand resting gently on my skirt so I could feel the knife underneath. It stayed in place, and the ghostly girl in the mirror vanished as I went through the door.

EIGHT

*T*he pain was a relief.

Back in my dressing room, I had wrapped my fingers around the knife and tried to stop my hand from shaking. Perhaps I had performed too well in the dining room, for now I did feel a little sick.

I closed my eyes and imagined fitting the shoes again, like the first time I put them on. My hand grew steady then, and the knife felt solid and sure.

It hurt, but with a satisfaction that no pleased look or kind word could give. With the knife on my skin, I was strong. I shaved some flesh from each side, and a little off my heel. Then I wrapped a handkerchief around my foot and tied it tightly to stop the bleeding. The left foot was really no better than the right, so I took the knife to it as well.

When both feet were bandaged, I stared down into my wash bowl. Curled in the bottom were the pieces of me that didn't fit. Good riddance, I thought, and took them to the windowsill. I unlatched the window, pushed it open, and flung out the contents with an odd feeling of triumph. A feeling so thick and dark I could get drunk on it. I leaned out the window, taking deep gulps of the cool night air until at last my breathing slowed.

I turned from the window, leaning my back against the wall. Now my feet would heal, the shoes would fit, and there was nothing I couldn't do. I could begin again.

I poured some wash water into the bowl and cleaned the knife. Now, all I had to do was hide it. I looked around the room, thinking, then I went to the drawer I never used. Almost as soon as I arrived at the palace, I was given an entire wardrobe worthy of a princess. But there was one item of clothing I never wore, even in my rooms: stockings. I'd been given a drawer full of them nonetheless, and tonight it was just what I needed. After rolling the knife up in an old pair of woolen stockings, one of the few reminders of the girl I was before, I stowed it in the back of the drawer. I never opened this drawer, and my maid didn't either. No one would ever know.

I dumped the water out the window, and it was finished. My feet hurt, but then they always did these days. I would just have to keep them covered while they healed.

I pulled a thick pair of stockings over the handkerchief bandages and undressed alone. Nagging at me was a fear that the maid would sense what I'd been doing. She would see the new freedom on my face and find me out. Perversely, I wanted someone to know, but I couldn't risk it. I fumbled into a nightgown and got under the covers, suddenly too tired to even draw the bed curtains.

But I was too uneasy to sleep. I lay awake, wondering if my husband would come to see how I was. If he did, I would have to keep pretending I was ill. Still, I wished he would come.

Some time later I heard the door from his dressing room creak open. He crossed quietly toward my dressing room, then, seeing no light there, he stopped. I tried to make my breathing slow and even, as if I really were asleep. He stood over me for a moment, and I felt the warmth of his hand on my forehead, brushing away a stray bit of hair. Then he was gone.

Hot tears stung my eyes. From relief or disappointment, I couldn't tell. I knew it was still early. He had to return to the guests, and that was for the best. Even so, there was something comforting about his presence, the weight of his arm over me, the rhythm of his breathing as he slept. It was no use trying to sleep without him.

It was after the clock struck midnight when he returned. I heard him in his dressing room taking off his clothes. Finally his room grew dark, and he closed the curtains and came to bed. He whispered my name then, as he slid underneath the blanket, and leaned over as if to kiss me on the cheek. As before, I pretended to be asleep. Then he sighed and rolled away from me. He hadn't kissed me after all.

He hadn't even touched me.

I lay awake until nearly dawn, unable to banish a new thought that repeated, over and over in my head.

What if my wish was wearing off?

NINE

*B*right sunlight shone through an opening in the heavy window curtains when I woke. I was thick and slow from lack of sleep, and the exhilaration of the night before was gone. Now I was wrung out, as if I had cried for a very long time. The space beside me was empty.

As I sat up and leaned over to reach the bell pull, my husband came in from his dressing room. He pulled one of the curtains aside, letting in a stream of sunlight, and sat beside me on the bed. He was fully dressed; he had probably been up for hours. "How do you feel?" His eyes were intent on my face.

"Better." I squinted against the light, glad he had only opened one curtain. My head, like the rest of me, felt heavy. "A little better." If I were completely well I wouldn't have an excuse to stay in bed while my feet healed.

Perhaps it was the strange shaft of bright light, but he looked pale; even his eyes seemed drained of color. "Should I call a doctor for you?" he asked, a crease of worry between his brows.

"No, no, darling. I'll be fine. It's nothing, I'm sure, darling." My words tumbled out and wouldn't stop. "Sometimes it just gets so stuffy at the table with all those people, you know, and I don't think I've been getting enough sleep."

He brushed a stray curl off my neck, the ghost of a smile on his lips. "You seemed to be making up for it this morning."

I tried to smile back, but my mouth wouldn't comply. Then I noticed his clothing for the first time. He was wearing riding boots and had a cloak draped over his arm. "Are you going somewhere?"

He sighed. "My father is sending me to settle a dispute. A couple of noblemen are squabbling over their father's will. I'll only be gone a few days." He paused. "I was thinking you might like to come with me, see the countryside a little."

I imagined it for a moment: getting away from the castle with its gossiping inhabitants. Away from the frowning and disapproval, just the two of us. Then I thought about hours in a carriage, the glass of the slippers against my unhealed feet, people craning their necks for a glance at the famous shoes. "I do want to, darling." The regret tasted bitter in my mouth. "But perhaps I shouldn't go anywhere for a day or so."

"Of course," he said quickly. "I just thought a change might do you good."

"Perhaps I could go next time. Do you have to leave today?"

"Yes." He stood. "Right away. I was only waiting to say goodbye and see if you wanted to come."

"I'm sorry." My illness was a flimsy excuse, but it was all I had. "I'm sure I'll be much better by the time you're back."

He leaned over to pick up his riding gloves from the bed. Then he sat back down, his eyes on the carpet at his feet. "When you were taken ill last night I thought perhaps you might be—"

"No," I cut him off. "I don't think so anyway."

"Oh." His hand squeezed mine, warm and comforting.

We had only been married for a matter of months, but if I didn't show signs of producing an heir soon, barrenness would certainly be added to my list of faults. Mothering an heir was dangerous, though. It would all be down to me if the child didn't please.

Children were expected of us, of course. But this was the closest my husband had ever gotten to mentioning the subject. Was he disappointed? Relieved? I couldn't tell. He was silent, studying his gloves.

At last he stood again. "I really should go." He kissed me on the forehead. It was the way a boy would kiss his much younger sister.

I tried to smile. "I won't keep you. How nice that…" I faltered. I never knew how to refer to my father-in-law. The king had certainly never asked me to call him Father. "How nice that he wanted you to handle this for him. It sounds like an important matter."

He shook his head. "It *sounds* like a childish quarrel," he murmured, half to himself. Then he turned to me, almost angry. "Is anything we do here useful?"

"Of course, darling." I had no idea if that were true; I was certainly useless. But I said it anyway.

He let out a huff of air, his usually straight shoulders falling just a little. "I'd like to think so, but I doubt it."

Then he knelt in front of me, one finger brushing a loose hair from my eyes. "Goodbye, darling." Then, while I was still trying to name the color of his eyes, he stood and strode to the door. When he reached the doorway, he turned back. "Shall I tell them you'll have your meals in your room for a few days? You shouldn't worry about going downstairs if you're not well."

I had to look down so he wouldn't see the tears in my eyes. It was what I was planning to do anyway, but if he told the servants, it would be accepted. They would not frown or look disapproving; the guests at the dinner table would not whisper. "Perhaps that would be best, darling. If you don't mind."

"I'll tell them. See you in a few days."

"Goodbye, darling. Be careful." I looked up.

He was gone.

Ten

For the three days my husband was gone I kept to my rooms, seeing no one but the servants. I hardly even saw them, though. They seemed to know when I moved from one room to another, slipping into the vacant room and dusting, scrubbing, or spiriting away dirty things before I returned.

I prowled from room to room, searching for something useful to do. I read every new book in our apartments. I sketched the view out of every window and arranged and rearranged every object on my dressing table. But nothing eased the restlessness gnawing in the pit of my stomach.

On the afternoon of the third day I sat on the windowsill of my dressing room, my needlework in my lap. Even if I'd wanted to finish the faceless people, the colored threads had become a tangled mess. I would have to unravel it all before I started. And I simply didn't have the heart.

Instead, I drew out the rose I'd stolen from the garden. I had hidden it in my workbasket the day I took it, and it had lain there ever since. The smell had faded a bit, and the petals were ragged, but I preferred it to the hothouse roses the gardener had sent. I hated their perfection.

The room was suddenly too warm. I pushed at the latch to let in some air, but it resisted. I put my body weight hard against the window, and it sprang open all at once, nearly carrying me along with it. I barely stopped myself from falling, clutching the sill with one hand. I froze there, halfway out the window, one hand on the latch, the other grasping the sill. My heart thudded in my throat, and my head spun looking at the ground so far below.

How easy it would be to just let go. I would only have to relax my hands and go limp. Would I float, gently as a leaf, or would I plummet to the ground? Even though my hands had begun to shake at the thought, part of me itched to find out.

Just then a gust of wind blew up, and something small swirled down into the air, gracefully falling to the ground. I couldn't see it land; the object was too small, the ground too far. My own descent would be nowhere near as graceful; I knew that. I made no move to climb back in, though. I simply hung there, half in, half out.

Then I heard a noise below me. There was a lone horseman on the road leading to the castle. He reached a hand up to sweep a lock of hair out of his eyes the way no one else would. It was my husband, returning home. I jumped guiltily and pulled myself back into the windowsill.

The strange compulsion to let go was gone. I looked down at my lap, my heart hammering faster than ever. The rose was gone too. That was what had fallen; perhaps it had obeyed the order to jump while I had not. But my troublesome embroidery remained, its snarl of threads as stubborn as ever. The faceless couple stared up at me, accusing.

I jumped to the floor and pulled off the handkerchief bandages. Stuffing them in a drawer, I reached for a chemise and petticoat. I had wished the last three days away, foolishly pretending my feet would heal best if left to themselves. I'd done nothing more than wipe them clean and replace the handkerchiefs each day, not even looking at the cuts on my skin. Now I was out of time.

I was trying to tighten my stays when I heard him calling my name in the next room. A moment later he came in, looking as though he had taken the stairs at a run. I hadn't had time to put on my shoes, but there was no help for it.

"Hello, darling." I tried not to look worried as I greeted him. "Was it a good journey?"

He put his arms around me. "I'm glad it's over." He drew back and took in my stays. "You're in a state."

"I was just about to ring for the maid."

He shook his head, that slow smile growing on his lips. "I like you better this way."

His smile was contagious. "I can hardly go down to dinner like this."

"Perhaps we'll just eat up here tonight."

He had never suggested this before. "Could we, darling? After all, you've just gotten home. You must be tired."

He sighed, turning me around and tightening my laces. "Father will be expecting me. And we must, of course," he said wryly, giving the laces a final tug, "do what's expected." Once he'd tied the knot, he rested his hands on my waist and dropped a kiss on my neck. "All done."

I sank down on my stool, my spirits dampened. The idea of doing *what's expected* curdled in my stomach.

He knelt in front of me, putting a hand on my knee. "You are better, aren't you, darling?"

"Yes, of course. Much better." I attempted a smile.

"Good." His eyes, some dark color between blue and green, searched mine, as if he needed proof of some kind. "I was worried."

"I am better." I hoped I wasn't lying. "I promise." I leaned a little closer, trying to define the color of his eyes. "I missed you."

He gazed up at me, his fingers trailing down my petticoat. "And I missed you." I tensed as his hand found my foot. He leaned down as if to kiss my instep, then pulled away as the door latch clicked.

"His highness has returned, your highness. Will you be dressing for…" the maid stopped, seeing my husband. "Pardon me, your highness," she said to him. "I didn't realize." She never would have asked my pardon for interrupting. She turned to go.

"That's all right," he told her, motioning for her to stay. He still held my foot in his hand, his thumb rubbing it absently. He frowned, as though trying to remember something. Then he seemed to dismiss his thoughts and stood. "I have to change as well. I'll see you at dinner." And he was gone.

We were alone then, the maid and I.

I had a hope that I hadn't admitted to myself. I hoped if I could fix my feet, if the shoes would fit again, then everything else would fall into place. I would somehow become whoever everyone wanted. I would fit.

I watched the maid, searching for a sign that it had all been worth it. Her face was less grim than usual as she fastened my dress and pinned up my hair, her mouth less hard. And maybe that was why, when she held out my slipper to put it on my foot, I let her do it.

It was a leap of faith. I held my foot out, watching her, just as I'd watched the prince's face all those months ago in my father's house. The shoe slid on with the same ease as it had that day.

And she smiled.

ELEVEN

I was silent as we walked back to our rooms that night. It all seemed too good to be true. I felt lighter, more graceful in my shoes, which didn't pinch in the least. Talking with the guests had been almost easy, and the king and queen had smiled, even at me. Had they felt the difference, just as I had? Did it shine through my skin? Did I now radiate the mysterious *something more* I had lacked? I didn't know how, but something was working.

As we entered our bedroom, though, I had one nagging fear. What if the meat knife had left a trace? A scar, a cut that couldn't be explained away. But if there was a mark, the maid hadn't seen it. She had smiled. Still, I would check when I undressed. I had to be sure.

I was turning toward my dressing room, nearly there, when my husband caught my hand and pulled me back to him. He twined our fingers together and leaned his forehead against mine. "Don't go."

I knew I should pull away, but I couldn't seem to. "I'm just going to change, darling," I breathed. "I'll be right back."

His hands released mine and came lightly around my waist. I could feel the warmth of them though my gown. "Stay." He sat me down on the edge of the bed and knelt at my feet. "Stay with me."

I should go. I had to make sure my feet were completely healed. But for all the deceptions and lies I'd come up with recently, I couldn't think of a single one as he slipped off my shoes. Frozen to the bed, I watched his face, but he wasn't looking at my feet. "Darling," he said softly, "you've got a crack here." He set down one slipper and held the other up to the light. "And on this one too."

I stopped breathing. A crack in both slippers now? For a moment I had no words, but at last I forced something out. "No, darling, it's just the design." My voice was more of a croak than anything else, but I kept going. I had to. "They've always been that way."

His eyes were on me again, a little worried, as if he wanted to argue. But then he set the second slipper on the carpet. He took one finger and traced it along my foot, the top, the arch, the heel, the toes. He kissed the instep and lay his head in my lap.

"You're perfect."

At first, I thought he was right. The next morning, I could almost believe I'd imagined the things the queen always said, the way her ladies looked at me, the feel of the slippers biting in. Curled in my husband's arms, I was safe.

He had only been gone a moment, though, when the doubt came creeping back. He had seen the cracks in the shoes, even by candlelight. Then he'd kissed my foot and called me perfect. But what if there were flaws he couldn't see because of my wish? And if that wish were wearing off, how long did I have before he could see them too?

I sat up with a jolt, suddenly unable to breathe. Hurrying into my dressing room, I pulled aside the heavy curtains and let the morning sun stream in. Then I sat still on the rug with my chin on my knee, my arms around my leg as if I could comfort it. As if it could comfort me. Then I gathered my courage and looked.

I saw nothing. There was no scarring, no scab, nothing. I looked all over one foot, then the other. And I could almost feel it: that overpowering sense of relief, that everything would be all right. It sat just behind my eyelids, ready to rush over me as soon as I knew it was true. But I had to be sure. I went back to the window and climbed onto the sill where there was more light.

Then, bending over my left foot, I saw it. A thin pink line, no thicker than the finest thread, running around my foot where the knife had cut. I studied the other foot; it had an identical line, so light I had missed seeing it before. But now I had seen it, I could never erase it. I would always see it now, even by candlelight. Even with my eyes shut.

Now I could only imagine that feeling of relief, how those hot tears would have felt spilling down my cheeks. Instead, I had swallowed a stone. It lodged at the top of my stomach, just below my heart.

I let myself down from the windowsill and slid onto the floor. I sat there for a long time. Perhaps no one would notice the marks; they were quite light after all. Still, no one must see them, ever. At last, I rose and went to my dresser, numbness spreading from my belly to the tips of my fingers and toes. I put on a chemise and petticoat. Then I went back to the bedroom to get the shoes. They lay on the floor where we'd left them the previous night, like something discarded and forgotten. They winked up at me in the light from my dressing room. They knew I needed them. I leaned down and set them upright, wondering if they knew how much I hated them. Then I slipped them on. I couldn't risk anyone helping me with them now.

Back in my dressing room I rang the bell. I sat on my stool and waited for the maid, who would dress me in a gown that didn't suit me and bring me a breakfast I couldn't eat.

TWELVE

*O*pal, Ruby, and Pearl had not returned to my dressing room. Since the day I offended them by refusing the proposed blue brocade and telling them I had enough gowns, they no longer came to improve me. They sent no more dressmakers or milliners or goldsmiths.

With the aid of my secret knife, the slippers fit again, and dinner seemed to go well for a few nights. But the court's approval was short-lived. I still did not possess the indescribable quality I needed to make me acceptable. So in time, while the ladies did not return, my lessons resumed. Singing with the music master at the piano, dancing lessons by daylight in the deserted dining hall, deportment and elocution in the garden with Madame.

Relax, your highness, deep breath now.

Back straight! Stomach in!

Not like that, my dear. Find your true voice.

The dancing master abruptly stomped his foot to stop the music, then he glared at me. "You are too stiff!" He struck a rigid pose, his arms bent at awkward angles. "You do not *feel* the music in your body. You," he snapped his fingers under my nose with a crack, and I flinched, "are an empty shell. You must be mistress of yourself." He drew himself up elegantly, perhaps showing me what being mistress of myself would look like. "You must be in control." His bushy eyebrows drew together as he took my waist with one hand and my hand with the other. "Whose body *is* this?" he demanded, giving me a little shake.

I didn't know the answer. And besides, my voice, true or otherwise, had gone.

I began to wish I were truly invisible, at least more like my ghostly reflection in the dining hall mirrors and less like a girl whose flesh will not move and speak and act the way it should. I wished I could disappear. But my feet—and my shoes—were all too solid.

I fell into the habit of taking off the slippers when I was alone. I studied the lines in the glass, asking myself if they had lengthened or divided further like cracks on an icy pond. I read them like a book written in a language I didn't understand, trying to find some meaning in their color or their shape.

Other times, I would close my eyes and run a finger over the tiny marks on my skin, feeling for any change in texture. I couldn't forget the thoughtful look on my husband's face the afternoon he returned home. How he'd rubbed his thumb against my foot, right where the little line was. But he'd said nothing, and I could *feel* nothing. The skin was soft and smooth. If I didn't know better, I would have thought my feet were perfect, just like he had said. Then I would open my eyes and look down. I did know better.

As much as I longed for invisibility, I could not have it. About a week after I noticed the marks, I was summoned to one of the castle's many parlors for tea with the queen and some visitors. My husband would be with the gentlemen, doing things gentlemen do, like shooting or riding or hunting. I would have to face the ladies alone.

How I dreaded these teas. I never knew what the visitors would be like; some days were better than others. But the elements were always the same: an ornate room, its inhabitants— brightly colored blossoms in an immaculate hothouse—and me, a weed who had tried to wish herself into a rose.

Perhaps this would be a test, I thought as I chose a gown the color of peaches, covered all over with embroidered birds and flowers. If I could get through the afternoon with no missteps, if I could manage to please on my own, without my husband by my side, it would be a sign of better things to come. Maybe I could even stop the lessons, despite the lines on my feet and the cracks in my shoes.

I put myself in the maid's hands, trusting her to make me as acceptable as possible. While she worked on me, I often stole glances at her in the mirror, hungry for any indication of her feelings, but she never gave anything away. Until today.

When she finished with me, instead of her usual, *Will there be anything else, your highness?* she said nothing. Her eyes met mine in the mirror, and she nodded once. I felt the pressure of her hand on my shoulder, and she was gone.

What did that mean? Was it a scrap of encouragement from a girl who was not so very different from me? Or, like Opal, Ruby, and Pearl, had she been assigned to remind me that even though there was something wrong with me, I must keep pretending there wasn't? I faced my reflection, but the girl in the mirror told me no more than the maid had.

I was halfway to the stairs when I decided to go back for my workbasket. While I wasn't charming or fashionable, I could at least be diligent. But going back only made me late. I arrived, breathless, at the door of an empty sitting room.

There was a polite cough at my back. A footman stood behind me, his arm gracefully pointing down the corridor I had just hurried along. I was in the wrong room. Heat crept up my cheeks as I turned and went in the direction he indicated. Obviously fearing I would pass the door again, the footman caught up to me and stationed himself at the door, a mere two doors down.

Just before the doorway I stopped. The ladies would have seen me pass by; they would have stopped talking and watched the door as one, waiting for the entertainment to begin. I could see it as if I had been there, the ladies breaking off their conversation at the flurry of skirts in the hall, wondering about this odd creature. (Was she a gauche visitor from the country perhaps, or a younger daughter bringing something her mother had forgotten?) The queen, making a sharp gesture to the footman to fetch me before I embarrassed myself further. Opal, Ruby, and Pearl raising their eyebrows, their rouged lips curving up at the corners.

I forced my feet to take the final step into the room. The queen gave me a cold nod, displeased as usual, then made the introductions. I hadn't been to this sitting room before, but they were all the same. Even the ladies themselves seemed the same, though the queen introduced me as if we were strangers. She remembered everyone I had or hadn't met, so she must have been right. I should have known it was our first meeting from the way they looked me up and down. Down and up was more like it, though, because their eyes went directly to my feet, as everyone's always did, hoping for a glimpse of the glass slippers.

Once the baroness and her mother, the duchess and her three elegant daughters, and the dowager countess had looked their fill, I took a seat by the window and brought out my needlework. I had forgotten the mess of threads. Hoping to conceal it in my lap, I began to pick at the tangle with my needle. But the baroness noticed my work. "What a pretty dress she's wearing," she said warmly. "You must make her like you. Your hair is such a pretty color. I've never seen the like. It glows like amber."

"I…" I looked down into my basket, blushing. The queen and her ladies hated it when anyone complimented me. "I don't have a thread to match."

"Oh, well, you can make her eyes green like yours anyway," she said comfortingly. "And you have some gold thread, haven't you? Gold always looks so lovely on a little tapestry like this, don't you agree, your majesty?"

I hoped the queen would give her opinion and let the matter drop. But she didn't. With a snap of her finger, she dispatched a footman to bring my needlework. I surrendered it and felt my face flush as he walked to her chair. It was only a few paces, but it seemed a long way. All the ladies had gone quiet. Opal, Ruby, and Pearl, sitting together on a sofa in the corner, leaned forward.

The queen's judgment was swift. She bent her elaborate curls to the cloth and immediately shook her head, her earrings tinkling as they moved. "But my dear," her eyes fixed mine, round with the seriousness of my crime, "you've started the border before the picture is finished."

My throat was dry. "Well, I, um—" I swallowed a word that wasn't a word. "I hadn't quite decided how to…" I trailed off.

The queen wasn't waiting for my response. She held up the needlework at arm's length, exposing the snarled threads for everyone to see. "My dear, this is quite out of hand. It will not do."

"Yes, your majesty…I mean no, your…" My voice deserted me.

"Never mind." She cast it into the hands of the waiting footman. "I'm sure you'll soon abandon it for another project, won't you?" She smiled around to her guests. "Her highness is always thinking of something new." It was not a kind smile.

Ruby rose and went to the piano. One corner of her mouth tilted up as she shared a private joke with Opal and Pearl. I didn't have to guess the subject. She began to play as the needlework was returned to me, and her music captured the attention and admiration of the entire room. I stuffed the unfinished couple into my workbasket, pretending I hadn't seen the baroness's pitying look. I sat very still, willing myself to become invisible.

But when Ruby's music was over and everyone had finished applauding, the baroness made another attempt to draw me out. "Won't you play for us, your highness?"

"I'm sorry." My voice sounded thin and weak in my ears. "I don't play."

The baroness looked disappointed but seemed determined to know me better. "Surely you must have some hobby?" She gave my hand a warm squeeze.

I wouldn't call bringing growing things to life with my touch a hobby. And anyway, that was unacceptable, in the queen's eyes at least. I loved to tell stories, but when I first came to the palace, the mocking looks of the queen's ladies had been enough to silence me. I only spoke when spoken to these days. I could say I liked to read; it was an answer, at least. I opened my mouth to speak, but Ruby answered for me from her place at the piano.

"Her highness is passionate about gardening." Her blue eyes were wide, brighter than her sky-blue gown; I would have thought she was sincere, had she not been there that day in the gardens.

The queen gave her a sharp look, and Ruby busied herself by looking through the sheet music on the piano. It was all very well to smile about my lack of determination in my needlework, but a princess who put her hands in the dirt was a disgrace that could somehow spread to the queen. It would pool around her petticoats and seep up her skirts. Like a stain.

The baroness seemed to be trying to make the best of Ruby's accusation. "Do you mean you like to arrange flowers, your highness?"

"No, I—I just like growing things." That was too close to the truth. "Things that grow, I mean." I stopped, hoping they would take this to mean I liked to take long walks in the gardens looking at flowers. It wasn't sophisticated or accomplished, but there was no shame in it.

The dowager countess spoke up. "You must choose the flowers you like best and press them into a book, your highness. You can make a collection." She sighed, satisfied at finding a solution for an untalented girl. "That is a very suitable hobby."

"Yes, thank you, ma'am," I murmured into my teacup.

"The gardens here are second to none, madam." Opal's voice floated through the room as I took a sip of tea. "We employ only the finest gardeners."

Pearl made a small sound, something between a cough and a sneeze. I knew it was neither though. It was a laugh.

"Oh, the gardens!" exclaimed the baroness. "Might we see

them, your majesty?"

The queen inclined her head graciously. No doubt she was hoping that we could have a change of subject along with a change of scene. I hoped so too. We all stood, and tea was forgotten as we went through the doors. As she passed me, the queen turned back, fixing me with a warning look, a reminder of what she had said that day in the gardens. *You are a lady, are you not?*

I lagged behind as the ladies strolled around, remarking on the flowers. Opal, Ruby, and Pearl stood together beside a wall of hydrangeas, admiring their showy blossoms and pointing them out to the baroness and the others. The visitors were suitably impressed with the flowers, and even more with the queen's ladies. People always were.

Opal and the others naturally belonged. In the garden, in the drawing room, in the ballroom, anywhere. But it had to be more than their looks that set them apart. Pearl had far more freckles than I did; yet my maid was never satisfied until mine were completely covered with powder. Ruby was rounder than I was; but my stays could never be laced tightly enough. Opal was always more likely to be frowning than smiling, and people could not stay away from her. The queen did not hiss, *smile, my dear,* under her breath. Not to Opal, not to any of them.

They possessed something unseen. I couldn't name it, but there was a kind of magic in it. Women hung on their every word, and men followed them with their eyes, hungry for scraps of their attention. I had studied them since I came to the palace, but I was no closer to discovering their secret. All I knew was that it couldn't be bought, and I feared it could never be learned. Whatever it was, perhaps I should have wished for it when I had the chance.

When they all passed up the steps into the next garden, I tucked myself away from view behind the wall and sat on a step. They turned off the path into one of the mazes, not noticing I wasn't with them.

The flowers beside me were strange things. Instead of leaves, each sky-blue blossom was surrounded by several spidery, branch-like arms, delicate and spiked. At home we always called them *devil in the bush.* Here at the palace, they called them *love in a mist.* It was a more acceptable name, I supposed, but not as fitting somehow.

Most of the flowers had blossomed by this time, but the bud on one was still closed, protected by a cage of tiny spikes. I looked around. I hadn't put a hand on the soil since that day the queen made it clear what she thought of my *fondness for flowers.* It was shameful; *I* was shameful. But the queen was not here. I was alone.

Someone might return at any moment, but I was suddenly reckless. Let them see. I would never belong here, no matter what I did. What difference would it make? I stole one hand into the flower bed, spreading my fingers on the soil. I closed my eyes, anticipating the tingle in my fingers, the warmth creeping up my arm, the lightheadedness. It would only be slight for such a little thing.

But I felt nothing. Nothing at all.

I opened my eyes. Perhaps it was such a small thing, opening this one bud, that I hadn't even felt it. Except the bud hadn't changed at all. The pointed petals were resolutely closed, protected by the delicate, thorn-like branches.

All I could do was stare. This had never happened before. Since that first time at my mother's grave, the magic had always responded to the lightest nudge of my thoughts. I looked around, wondering if anyone had come into the garden without my knowing it. But it was empty, just like before.

I closed my eyes again, willing the familiar feeling to come, the warmth spreading out of my fingers and up my arms. When it came at last, it was weak and short-lived. If I hadn't been expecting it, I might not have noticed it at all. I opened my eyes. The blossom had opened, but not fully. Slowly, I withdrew my hand, as if the mass of flowers would lash out against me if I moved too quickly. As if they would sting me.

When my hand returned to my lap I rubbed it, my thumb

pressing into the palm, my eyes never leaving the half-open bloom. It was just the color of Ruby's gown.

I had opened the bud, I told myself, and it felt the same as always. I couldn't believe myself, though; something was wrong. Before, it was always easy, natural, an extension of my thoughts. But not this time. I was being punished for making a wish I never should have, to secure a love I hadn't earned.

I stood, backing up the steps, away from the flowers with their sharp-edged petals and their angry, spiky leaves. When I reached the top step, I turned away and into the nearest maze, relieved that I could no longer see them, that they could not see me.

I knew I should catch up to the others, but I didn't think of where I was going at first. The maze was cool; the deep green of the yew hedges rising up on either side of me was comforting. I walked on down the shadowed paths, thinking of nothing until I reached the center.

But the ladies weren't there. I couldn't even hear their voices, and I hadn't since I'd stayed behind in the garden. Perhaps they were in the other maze, the one on the other side of the path. I must have turned the wrong way when I came out of the garden. They would be wondering where I was. I could see the frown forming between the queen's eyebrows. *Where is she?* she would hiss to Opal. She would not use my name. Only *she*.

I began to make my way out, but nothing felt familiar now. I had been into the other maze before, and I could navigate its twists and turns. I had assumed the patterns here would be the same, but they weren't. Their curves and spirals made no sense.

I stopped at the entrance to a longer path which curved away gently to either side. I stood for a moment, sweating and dizzy. How could I choose? My sense of direction had deserted me. Right or left?

I chose left and turned onto the path, almost running now. Then I heard someone call my name. Heart banging against my ribs, I turned and froze as a shadowy figure strode toward me. I couldn't make him out at first, but then he stepped into a patch of sunlight.

It was my husband.

"What's wrong?"

"I was just—I couldn't—" It was silly to have gotten lost like that. "Nothing," I managed at last. My stays were too tight. "I was looking for the others."

He looked down at me, his brow furrowed in concern. "Are you hurt?"

I shook my head. What must I look like, I wondered. I was flushed, no doubt. Perhaps I had bits of leaves in my hair. Had I torn my gown? "No." I tried to breathe normally. "I'm fine."

"But you're limping." He led me back the way I had come, to a bench near the entrance to the path. The place where I had chosen to go left.

"Was I?" I murmured in surprise as we sat down. "No, no it's nothing, just a stone in my shoe." That was a lie. But I had to give some explanation.

He gazed at me for a moment, his expression warm. "Is that all?" When I nodded, he knelt and reached out his hand. "Allow me."

"No, no." I jumped up, talking all the while. "It's fallen out now. I'm fine now. Really. We should find the others. They'll be wondering where we are."

But he didn't stand to come with me. He remained kneeling, his eyes on the path. Reaching out finger and thumb he picked up a tiny, glinting something and stood. "Here." He opened his hand, a bit of glass shining in his palm. "It's from your shoe."

"No." I took a step back. "No, darling. My shoes are fine."

His hand hung in the air as he watched me, a worried line between his brows. "Darling, your shoes are breaking. We can get you some new ones."

I shook my head wordlessly.

In the shade of the hedges his eyes seemed a dark, smoky

shade of green. He studied me, as if trying desperately to read my thoughts. I looked away, my cheeks burning. "They aren't why I love you, you know," he said at last.

"Of course not." I forced myself to smile. "But they…they brought you to me." My voice was too high.

"But they'll cut you, darling." The piece of glass winked in his hand. "What happens when they fall to pieces under your feet?"

My smile was so brittle I thought it would break. "I wished for them." I tried to make my voice light, as if it were a small matter. "They could never hurt me."

I could tell he didn't believe me. He didn't say so, though. He only pocketed the piece of my slipper and offered me his arm. He touched me gently, as if I were the thing made of cracking glass, and led me out to rejoin the others. A sick feeling seeped through me as we passed the turning where I'd gone left. When he found me, I was nearly to the entrance. But I had just turned the wrong way—toward the heart of the maze—and I'd been about to lose myself all over again.

I made sure not to limp. There had been no stone in my shoe; it felt nothing like a stone. Now that I was paying attention, I knew exactly what it felt like. How could I not recognize the bite of the slippers against my skin?

How could that be? I had made them fit again, and it had worked. It must be my imagination, I told myself. The thought was reassuring, but I rarely believed myself these days.

When I was finally alone to dress for dinner, I sat down and forced my shaking hands to lift my skirts. The slippers winked up at me as my flesh, red and angry once more, puffed out around the edges of the glass. I pulled the shoes off and held up first one, then the other. The cracks now spider-webbed farther down each shoe. And as I knew there would be, on one slipper's edge, right at the top of a crack was a tiny opening, just the size of the glass fragment in my husband's pocket.

I stared at my feet. The sick feeling crawled over my skin, hot and clammy. It was as if I had never cut them. But that wasn't right, because this time the faint pink lines were there as well. And now with the shoes cutting into them, those lines looked darker, and even thicker than before.

I didn't stop to think. The stolen meat knife hadn't helped for long, but at least I had fit the shoes. And I would fit again. I hurried to the dresser and opened my stocking drawer. My weapon would be waiting there, wrapped in an old pair of homespun stockings. It had lain there, forgotten, since the night I pushed it, wound in its lumpy woolen wrapper, to the back of the drawer. Now my fingers pushed aside the smooth knitted linen and silk, feeling for the wool of the old stockings. But all I touched was the wood at the back of the drawer. Nothing else.

I sank onto my knees, choking down a sob. The other stockings were there, every color, embroidered and plain, neatly rolled. They stared up at me, pristine, never-worn things. I pulled the drawer so hard it nearly came out of the dresser. I yanked out pair after pair of stockings, but it was no use. I couldn't have mistaken the old stockings for any of the others. The old stockings were gone.

The knife was too.

So be it, I thought, pulling out a garter and tying it around my thigh. Wondering what had happened to the knife did me no good. I had gotten a knife before, and I could do it again. The clammy heat was gone from my skin, and my hands were steady. No one had found out last time, I told myself.

It was easily done.

THIRTEEN

*D*eception is easy, I reminded myself as I sat down to dinner that night. So why did I feel so sick? The prospect of adding another deception to my marriage sat like a stone in my gut. My speech to the dinner guests was stilted, my movements awkward. I didn't get the knife tied into my garter well enough, and I could feel it slip as the knot began to untie. I had to drop my spoon a second time as an excuse to bend down and re-tie the knife.

When I sat back up, my husband gestured for a servant to bring me a clean spoon. "A second escape attempt?" He winked, taking the wayward spoon from me. "We'd better set it free." He handed it over and turned back to his creation. He had plucked a raw carrot garnishing one of the platters and was carving it into a flower with his knife.

"My son," the queen remarked to her guests, "amuses himself by thinking he can change something humble into something beautiful."

The only indication my husband made that he'd heard her was a slight tensing of his jaw.

When he did not respond, the queen continued. "It is an optimistic, but misguided way of thinking."

"I see beauty in many things, madam," he replied, not looking up.

The queen sighed. "But things do not change their natures simply because you wish them to. Neither do people." She was smiling, the same way she did when she told the visiting ladies I was always thinking of *something new.*

It was time to get it over with, so I began my performance. I pulled out my handkerchief and patted my face with it. I stared at my uneaten soup. When my husband touched my arm, I blinked dazedly, as if forcing my eyes to focus. In truth, I could see just fine, but the shaking of my hands was real enough. I was suddenly afraid to go on, but the knife was already tied back into my garter and unlikely to stay there during the dancing. It was too late to stop now. I swayed a little in my seat, then collapsed into the arms I knew would catch me.

I lay across him, my head cradled in the crook of his arm, and listened to the hushed voices around me. "What is it this time?" The king sounded annoyed. My husband was dabbing my face with a wet handkerchief and whispering my name.

"Ill again?" came another voice. It was the queen. "I am never ill." I was afraid I had gone too far, but accidental eavesdropping is tricky. Once begun, it's hard to know when to stop. Or how.

The next voice I heard was Opal's. It was low, almost seductive. "Oh dear, how sad." If I hadn't been pretending to faint, I would have thought she was speaking to me. But she wasn't. She was talking to my husband, and it wasn't my supposed illness she thought was sad. It was me.

I wouldn't like anything else I heard; I knew that. I had to work up the courage to pretend to wake up. Before I had, though, my husband had scooped me up and carried me from the great hall. Now I really needed to wake up. Reluctantly, I stirred and opened my eyes. "What happened?" We were in the entrance hall now, and he was still walking, headed toward the stairs.

"Lie still. You fainted." I didn't like the way his brows drew together. He looked angry.

"I'm all right now." I spoke tentatively. "You can let me down. Really. I can walk."

"I've got you." He was walking quickly, as if carrying a child who had thrown a tantrum and must be removed from company.

When we reached the top of the stairs I struggled, trying to get my feet on the floor. "Really, darling, I'm much better now,"

"Nearly there." His arms tightened around me.

When we were in our bedroom at last, he set me down on the bed. "Now," he moved briskly, picking up a taper and lighting it from the fire, "stay there and rest. I'm going for a doc—"

"No, no, darling." I couldn't let him finish that word. *Doctor.* "There's no need for that. I just need to rest. Really, just go back down, and I'll rest. I'm much better now."

When my outburst was finished he stood watching me, his frown deepening. "Are you sure?"

"Yes, really. It was just so warm down there tonight…" I trailed off.

His resolve seemed to waver. He bent to light a candle beside the bed. "I'll just have some food brought up then."

"No," I blurted, too quickly. "I'm not hungry." His frown returned. "I just want to rest. I'll ring for something. Later, if I want anything."

He sighed and turned toward the door.

I needed him to go, but I couldn't help calling after him. "I'm sorry."

He came back in and sat beside me. "What do you have to be sorry for?"

How would I even start? For pretending to deserve him. Not being like the others. Not fitting the slippers.

For forcing him to love me.

I couldn't meet his eyes. "Well," I whispered, looking down at my hands, "for spoiling the evening." I made myself look back at him. His eyes were unreadable in the candlelight. "For making everyone…" I was going to say *worry*. But that wasn't what I had made everyone do at all. I had irritated them, perhaps, or given them an excuse to gossip. But I hadn't made anyone worry. "For causing a fuss."

For just a moment, his mouth drew into a thin line, like he was angry. But then it was gone. He shook his head, then leaned over and kissed me on the forehead. "Get some rest."

When he was gone, I sat on the bed for a long time. I knew I should begin. I should get it over with in case he came back. Still I sat there, unable to stop thinking of how stern he had looked, and how the people had whispered.

They would whisper even more if they knew the truth, I told myself. If they could see my feet, with the glass cutting into them. If they knew the famous slippers held the secret to the prince's love. I didn't believe much I told myself these days, but I knew that was true. So I stood and went to my dressing room, closing the door behind me. Then I untied the knife.

And this time, I cut more.

There was more pain, and more relief to see my feet growing smaller. But I must have taken my time. I had barely cleaned and bandaged my feet when I heard my husband in our bedroom. I ran to the window and tipped out the bowl of wash water. There was a clattering that sounded nothing like water, but there was no time to think about it. I pulled open my stocking drawer and grabbed the first pair of stockings I touched. I was pulling on the second stocking when he came into the room.

He looked puzzled. "I thought you would be in bed."

"I was just getting undressed."

He knelt in front of me, his eyes searching mine. "What have you been doing all this time?" His voice was gentle.

My throat felt so tight I didn't know if I'd be able to speak. Perhaps if I told him something true my voice would work a little better. "Just sitting. Resting."

He caught sight of my feet. "You never wear stockings."

"My feet are cold." The night was quite mild, but what other reason could I possibly have? His hand reached toward one foot, as if to rub it.

I didn't mean to, but I flinched.

His hand closed abruptly, as if I had burned it. He looked at me, eyes unreadable, and stood. Then he walked toward the window as if to close it. Had I left something on the sill? A drop of water or blood? The knife? "That's all right, I don't mind the air, darling, it's only…" I stopped, realizing how odd it all sounded. How much like a lie.

He stood for a moment, just looking at me, one hand rubbing the back of his neck. Then he straightened his shoulders. "I should get back down," he said, a little stiffly. "I just wanted to see if you needed anything."

"I'll just go to bed now. I won't need anything."

He nodded. "Good." And he was gone.

I struggled out of my corset laces and went around the room, making sure I hadn't left anything incriminating behind. The knife wasn't on the windowsill as I had feared. It wasn't anywhere. Then I remembered the clattering sound I heard as I threw out the water. Of course it had been the knife, slipping off the sill. One more knife gone. And if I needed another, I couldn't steal one from dinner. Too much had gone wrong tonight, from the knife slipping to the court's annoyance to my husband's reaction that I couldn't quite name. Disapproval? Anger? I couldn't risk it again.

As I got into bed, I told myself these thoughts were foolish. My feet had never been smaller. I would never need another knife.

That was what I told myself.

FOURTEEN

*M*y husband didn't go away this time.

When I was alone, I peeled off my stockings and glanced under the handkerchief bandages to see if they could come off yet. And, as if my feet knew how much I needed them to heal quickly, they took even longer than before. So I stayed in bed, pretending to be sick.

But I was too convincing. On the fourth day, my husband and his mother came into the bedroom followed by another man. His clothes were simple but elegant, and he was all in black. I had never seen him before, but I knew him anyway. He was a doctor.

When my mother was dying, I watched many doctors at work. I heard their explanations about *low spirits* and *weak constitutions*, as if she had brought her illness upon herself. I smelled the foul purges they tipped down her throat and saw the knives they used to bleed her with. And in the end, I saw that nothing they did helped.

This doctor drew a chair to my bedside. "Your highness." He inclined his head, all politeness. "Her majesty says you are unwell." The queen stood beside my husband in the doorway, still and expressionless. Her disapproval wafted into the room and hovered around me.

"There was no need to trouble you." I tried to imagine some symptoms I could complain of. Something believable, but not too serious. "I'm sure I will be well again soon. I'm only tired."

"Perhaps taking some exercise is all that is required."

Tiredness was not enough, then. "Standing makes me dizzy. I feel better sitting."

He said nothing, but peered at me through his spectacles. His silence was soon too much for me. "I do feel weak."

"Very well, my dear." He reached for his bag. "We will see."

Perhaps my racing heart would be a good symptom, I thought as he examined me. Surely he could hear it pounding through my skin. But what would I say if he wanted to look at my feet?

When it was all over, he had pressed on my neck and abdomen with spidery fingers, looked into my eyes, studied my tongue, my fingernails, even tested the smell and color of my urine.

At last he sat back in his chair, thinking. I knew he'd found nothing wrong, but he must offer some solution. He was here to fix me, just like the seamstress and the others. Like Opal and Pearl and Ruby. So he stood and reached into his bag, bringing out a thin leather strap and a knife. Then he regarded me for a moment, sitting there in the bed with my arms tightly crossed over my stomach. "Nothing to fear, my dear." He looked over his spectacles at me. "It is a simple matter. All we must do is restore the balance of your humors."

We. Was he suggesting this was something I would actively participate in? I had a ludicrous desire to ask if he was going to want my help. Surely at this point I was fairly skillful with a knife myself. But his hand was open, waiting for me to comply. My part was to lie still. I unclenched my fists and surrendered my arm.

He stretched the leather strap to its full length, as if to make sure it was long enough. It obviously was. "You needn't look." He tied the strap around my arm above the elbow, apparently unaware that I was watching his face, not my arm. "There may be a mark here for a short time, but it will soon fade." He turned toward the door. "Young ladies are so concerned with their outward appearance, your majesty, your highness. However, the health of the body is too important to neglect."

My husband gave a slight inclination of his head, not looking at any of us. His arms were crossed over his chest, and his cheeks were flushed. He shifted uncomfortably.

The doctor gestured to the maid, who must have been waiting in the corridor in case she was needed. She came to the bed, a metal basin in her hands. "Now my dear." He held up a warning finger at me. "You mustn't struggle. It will be much easier if you lie still." His hand encircled my forearm as the maid stood at my shoulder, the basin ready. He made a quick cut with his knife. "There, there, now." His voice was stern, as if I had cried out or pulled away. I had not.

"Very good." He straightened up and laid the knife on the little table next to the bed. Then he went to join my husband and the queen, leaving the maid to collect my blood in her basin. As usual, she said nothing, but one arm came around my shoulder, and I felt the pressure of her hand on me. Whether it was meant to comfort or restrain, I could not tell. Until she shifted, moving between me and the doorway with the pretense of wiping a drop of blood from my arm.

"Don't faint," she whispered. "And don't let them see you cry." I nodded. Then she resumed her position at my shoulder.

We stayed like that, both of us looking at nothing. From time to time I caught a stray phrase from the doctor in the doorway, things like *nervous constitution* or *female frailty*. He said the words as if they were something embarrassing for him to even mention. Something shameful.

The queen asked something in a low voice; I couldn't hear what. My husband turned to her, his lips pressed tightly together, but said nothing. "No, no." The doctor shook his head. "There's no indication of that. But not to worry, your majesty, your highness, she is young. There is still plenty of time for that."

I was beginning to feel dizzy, but I would not faint. That would please the doctor, and probably the queen as well. Usually, I wanted to please more than anything, but I had no desire to do it now.

"Pinch me," I whispered, low enough for only the maid to hear. She said nothing, but slowly, she moved her hand underneath my hair and pinched the back of my neck, her nails digging in. Tears sprang to my eyes, but I didn't cry. The pain kept me alert. I nodded once, and the maid's hand returned to my shoulder, clamping down on it tightly. I looked around, my glance falling on the doctor's knife. It was smooth and sharp. Far better than the ones I had stolen from the dinner table.

I started guiltily as his hand closed quickly around the knife and wiped it clean. "You're quite right to look away, my dear." He slipped the knife into his bag. "The sight of blood upsets many of the ladies." He hadn't noticed me coveting his knife then; he had only thought me squeamish. I felt my jaw tighten, just a little. I said nothing.

He looked into the bowl and nodded. "I think that will do very well." He untied the leather strap with an expert flick and tied a cloth around my arm. "There now," he peered down at me, perhaps still hopeful I might faint. "I daresay we'll be feeling much better very soon, won't we, my dear?"

I was worried for a moment that my throat wouldn't allow any sound out, and when it did, it was louder than I intended. "Yes."

"Good girl." He turned back to his patrons. "You see, your majesty, your highness, she is stronger already." He closed his bag with a satisfied snap and walked toward the door. "I advise some exercise tomorrow. It will do her a world of good." And with that, the doctor was gone. The queen went with him, leaving her disapproval hanging in the air behind her.

My husband remained where he was as the maid tidied up and cleared away the basin of my blood. Neither looked at me. When she was gone, he came in and took the doctor's chair beside the bed. I looked down at my hands and dug my nails into my palms. The pain was the only thing keeping me conscious. "She insisted we call for him, darling." He put his hands on mine, and I flinched. "I was worried about you."

"I know," I whispered, still looking away.

"How do you feel? You're very pale."

Pale? Perhaps he had never seen anyone bled before. I swallowed the angry response on my tongue. "I'm fine. Only tired." I tried to concentrate on focusing my eyes. It wouldn't do to faint in front of him either. He would only go back to the doctor, who might decide he needed to bleed me again.

"Perhaps you should sleep now." His hands released mine and settled on his knees, his fingers moving restlessly.

"Yes." I slid down in the bed. "I think I could."

He adjusted the covers. "Shall I sit with you?"

I looked at him finally. My vision was blurring, but I could see that he was pale too. Even his eyes seemed pale. "No. Thank you, darling. I won't need anything. I'll just sleep."

Looking a bit relieved, he nodded, and turned to go. I forced my eyes to stay open until he was gone. Then the room went dark.

When I opened my eyes, I saw that someone had put a cup of wine beside the bed. I reached out and drained the cup, then I rolled over and fell into a deep sleep.

I didn't wake until full light the next day. My body was heavy, as if I was recovering from a long and wasting illness. But, unless I wanted the doctor to return, I had to get out of bed. So I sat up, pulling the stocking and handkerchief bandage off one foot.

"What are you doing?"

I jumped. My husband was sitting in a chair by the window, holding a book and watching me curiously.

"Taking off my stockings." Quickly, I pulled off the other. I made sure the handkerchief came with it and wadded them all up into a ball. "How long have you been there?"

"Since last night." That explained the slightly rumpled look of his clothes. "Are you feeling better?"

"Yes." I said it because I knew I must. "I think I'll get up."

"Good." He rose and walked to the bed.

My heart thudded in my chest as he got closer. As he sat down beside me, I sat up on my knees, hiding my bare feet underneath me. But if I was odd, he didn't seem to notice. He was absorbed with a long strip of leather he had picked up from my bedside table. He studied it as if wondering what it would rather be instead of the strap the doctor had tied around my arm.

I cast about for something to say. "Why didn't you come to bed?"

His fingers tested the flexibility of the leather for a moment before he looked up. "I didn't want to disturb you."

"I don't think anything would have disturbed me."

He looked down again, his cheeks still pale. "I thought perhaps you wouldn't want me to." He made the leather into a series of loops and joined them together between his fingers. They looked like petals. "But we were right to call for the doctor." He tied the loops together with one end of the strap, which dangled below like a stem. "Look how much good it's done you." He held out his open hand, offering me the strangely lifelike flower.

"Of course, darling," I made myself say as I took it. "I'm much better." I hated this conversation. I was fully capable of shedding my own blood. I didn't want to praise the doctor for doing it for me. "So now I'll go get dressed."

He stood and gave me his hand. "I'll help you with your laces."

"No, that's all right, darling." I made my voice bright as I walked toward my dressing room, stockings in hand. "I'll ring for the maid. You've wasted enough time on me already these past few days. I'm sure you have more important things to do." With what I hoped was a reassuring smile, I shut the dressing room door behind me.

I leaned my head against the door. I wanted to call him back, but I knew I couldn't. My feet would look how they would look, but until they were completely healed, I couldn't allow him to see them up close.

I sat down, my back against the door, and held one foot in my hand. The bleeding had stopped, and there were no scabs. They had healed, finally. The only signs of the cuts I had made were the thin pink lines, the same as I had noticed the last time. Hardly daring to believe my luck, I hurried to find my shoes. They slid on with ease, feeling, once again, as if they were made for me.

Because, after all, they were.

FIFTEEN

I almost looked forward to dinner that night. The cuts had healed, and the shoes fit. Now I could begin again.

Before I went to dinner, I sat for a moment, looking down at my arm. Right in the center of my inner elbow was a tiny red puncture wound, where the doctor's knife had cut. I shook the lace of my sleeve over it. If I hadn't been looking, I wouldn't have noticed anything. And even if someone saw it, the idea didn't bother me. This knife-made mark was not my fault. And yet I hated the doctor for a reason I couldn't explain.

I slid one slipper off my heel and ran a finger around the thin pink line, following it like a trail on a map. Then I snapped the shoe back on my heel and looked down at the mark. The glass hid it perfectly. That thin, pink line was such a little thing, but I had made it. It was mine.

That night everyone congratulated me on my recovery and told me how well I looked. I danced every dance, talked easily with the guests, and laughed with my husband. "Don't be long," he breathed in my ear, as I turned toward my dressing room at the end of the evening.

Once the maid had left for the night, I sat down at the mirror to take off my earrings. Studying my reflection, I pulled out my hair pins. I looked the same, didn't I? Funny how a little thing like fitting the shoes could make such a difference. Of course, they were no ordinary shoes.

I rested one foot on my dressing table next to the candle. The cracks on the slipper were no worse. But when I slid out my foot, I noticed something different. The little marks on my skin looked bigger, more like a proper road on a map, instead of just a path.

I tried to swallow, but my throat didn't work. Hand shaking, I held the candle closer. The lines were thicker, and darker as well. I put the shoe back on. The edges still hid the marks, but when I took it off again, there they were, angry and red, accusing.

"Darling, where are you?"

I jumped, nearly crying out in surprise. I sat on my stool, taking deep breaths until I stopped shaking.

Then I opened a drawer and pulled out a pair of stockings. There was no help for it. He couldn't see my feet like this. The stockings were delicate, very finely knit, but they would hide the lines.

What if he didn't mind, part of me whispered. About the shoes, the lines on my feet, or any of it? What if he thought there was more to me than his parents and everyone else could see? What if he would have loved me even without the wish?

I didn't dare to hope that, though, so I covered my feet with the stockings and went in.

And when he kissed me, I could almost forget. The wish, the knives, the trap I'd made for myself. I could almost believe he wouldn't care even if he knew the truth. Until his hand touched the silk around my thigh.

For a moment I stopped breathing. "My feet are cold," I forced myself to say.

He caught the stocking with one finger and began to slide it down. "Let me warm them up." His lips brushed the hollow of my collarbone.

"No." I stopped his hand with mine, my voice too loud. Then I softened my tone, afraid I'd gone too far. "I'd rather just leave them on tonight. You don't mind, do you darling?"

His hand pulled away. "Of course not." His eyes studied mine in the firelight for a moment, as if he were trying to read my thoughts. "You're tired. It doesn't matter."

"I'm not tired." I leaned into him, but he had already turned away and settled himself to sleep. Staring at the shape of him in the dark, I told myself I should be relieved. But that was the problem, wasn't it? I never was how I should be.

I had escaped discovery for another night. So why did I feel this way? As if he had hit me.

"Darling?" I whispered after a few moments. A sigh escaped him, and his breathing slowed, almost as if he had fallen asleep, but not quite.

"Darling?"

He didn't answer.

Sixteen

My head was dull and heavy when I woke.

My husband's side of the bed was cold, and the bed curtains were open. It wasn't late, but the room had an abandoned feel, as if he'd been gone a long time. I lay there trying to clear the fog from my mind and remember what I was supposed to do now. At last I forced myself to get up and ring the bell.

When I asked where the prince had gone, the maid said he'd had to leave the palace and would be back by afternoon. Perhaps it was another assignment from the king, I told myself, trying not to be disappointed. Trying not to believe he was avoiding me.

I spent the morning doing nothing in particular. Reading only increased the heavy feeling in my head, and I couldn't settle to my needlework. I couldn't even imagine how to go about untangling the mess of threads in my workbasket, and just looking at it gave me a sick sense of shame.

By midday my head was throbbing so badly I couldn't finish the meal the maid brought, so I rang the bell to ask for a cup of tea. What I really wanted was not the black tea the kitchen always sent, but mint. It had always helped before, when I could slip out to our garden and put a handful of mint leaves in hot water. Before I came here.

I thought of asking the maid to bring up some mint along with my tea, but I couldn't do that. She would ask why I wanted it. If I told her my head hurt, they might send for the doctor to bleed me again, or worse, examine me further. And when I asked for the tea, the maid's look was odd enough. *Ladies did not ring for tea at this time of day*, her expression said. I was wrong to want the things I wanted.

After she left, I didn't move. I just sat, massaging my temples, trying to make my mind work. I had some idea of where the kitchen was; surely the gardens were nearby. If anyone saw me there, they would think it strange, but surely they wouldn't question me. If I went quickly, I could be back before the maid arrived with my tea.

It was not a good plan; I knew I wasn't thinking clearly. But it was the best I could do with the pain in my head. I took the servant's stairway down to the kitchens and was nearly to the bottom when I almost bumped into an under maid. She jumped and gasped as if I had caught her trying on my jewelry. Then she dropped a curtsy right there on the stair, one arm touching the wall to keep her balance.

"Can I do something for you, your highness?"

If I said I was lost, she would only direct me back to somewhere more acceptable for a princess. There would be no mint. I had been pretending for so long the truth did not come easily, but at last I managed to find a little. "Where is the kitchen garden?"

Frozen in her curtsy, the girl pointed down the last few stairs. "Go left, then out the door at the end of the hallway." Her eyes were fixed on mine, wide with fear. As if I might hit her.

I knew I should tell her not to mention she had seen me here. But all I could do was murmur, "Thank you," as I made my way down the last few stairs. When I looked behind me she was still in place, watching me go.

I hurried down the hallway at the bottom of the stairs, passing kitchens, pantries, and stillrooms. Through the last doorway came a buzz of voices. Several servants were gathered around a huge hearth, big enough to roast an ox in. My maid was there too, sitting on a table and waiting for my tea to be ready. Someone must have said something funny, and she laughed, her head thrown back and her hands clapped together. I had never seen her like that. Her laughter was a joyful, infectious sound. I turned away, a mixture of shame and envy burning into my rib cage.

At the end of the hall I pulled the ring on the wooden door, and I was out. I thought for a moment that I hadn't reached the kitchen garden at all, but one of the ornamental ones. The beds were laid out in geometric patterns with gravel paths between them. Apple and pear trees grew up along the walls, their branches spread tortuously against the stones with perfect symmetry. I had a fleeting thought that I could do wonders with a garden like this.

Passing under an archway covered in grapevines, I made my way past beds of early cabbages and pumpkins, turnips and carrots, until I found the herbs. They were in a circular spot in the center of the garden, each herb in a separate bed like the spaces between the spokes of a wheel.

Inside the circle was a pool with a statue of a mermaid kneeling on a rock in the center. For a moment I forgot my mission and stood gazing at her. She had such a sad expression, but all the same, I wished we could trade places. She had no feet to trouble her.

I made my way around the circle of herbs, past lavender and comfrey, savory and rue. I had never seen a garden like this before. In the garden at my father's house, every vegetable had its plot, but I'd let my herbs grow in a mass. Sage and chamomile wove together under the yarrow—parsley and dill intermingled.

It wasn't like that here. Every herb had its own bed, separated by a neat line of stones. Each plant was neatly clipped, with not a twig or blossom out of place. Even the mint was in a perfectly symmetrical clump.

At home, my mint grew wildly, its creeping tendrils making their way into all of the neighboring space. But here it was tamed, domesticated. Even its smell, when I rubbed a leaf against my fingers, was less pungent than it should have been. It would have to do, though.

But if I took a handful of leaves from this immaculate plant, someone would know, even if no one saw me do it. They would see the missing leaves, the broken stems. *Who's been at the mint?* the cook would demand. Or perhaps the gardener would say that. *I've just pruned it only yesterday.* The cook would shrug. *I haven't used any since then.* And then the under maid would speak up. *Her highness was asking about the gardens, just today.* They would shake their heads. *I've heard there's something wrong about that girl,* the cook would say. *Whyever did he marry her, anyway?*

Whyever indeed? I wondered, trailing my fingers around the base of the mint bed. I wanted to believe it was because I was special, that my wish had only given the prince the same little nudge I gave the roses in the gardens. Or, better yet, that my wish hadn't worked at all and he'd married me because he really, truly loved me.

My fingers struck on something, and I looked down. Below me was a burrowing root that had tunneled under the earth and come back up, ready to spread and make more and more mint. The corner of my mouth turned up in the ghost of a smile. They couldn't tame it after all, and it was just what I needed. There were only two tiny leaves budding from the end of the creeping root, but it would be easy enough to make them spring to life. No one had noticed this little rebel, so taking a few of its leaves would make no difference.

I spread my hand on the earth around the creeper and closed my eyes, willing myself not to think about the last time I had done this. I had tried to put the devil in the bush out of my mind. It was nothing, I told myself. I had been out of sorts that day; there had been too many people in the maze nearby. But the memory came back to me, insistent, its tendrils stealing in around the edges of my mind. *You cannot do this anymore,* it whispered. *You never could.*

I tried to shut it out. I tried not to see the half-bloomed devil in the bush, frozen against me, refusing to open. I told myself I only needed to concentrate, that it was easy and it always had been. I told myself I could do it.

But when I opened my eyes at last, the creeper and its tiny leaves were no bigger. There were no new leaves. I closed my lips together and shut my eyes again. Setting a second hand beside the first, I pushed my fingers into the soil. *Just work,* I begged. *Please please please.* But I felt nothing. And when I opened my eyes, the little root was just the same.

Frozen at the edge of the garden bed, I forced myself to breathe in and out. I had told myself I could do it. But I lied.

I lifted my hands and studied them, palms up. They were not trembling or buzzing with the magic that was mine alone. They were only shaking with some hot, ugly feeling I couldn't name, for, just like my feet, my hands had turned against me.

I grabbed a handful of mint, from the very front of the plant.

I wanted to believe that I had something special. That I *was* something special. But that simply wasn't true. I had needed magic to catch the prince and make him fall in love with me. Magic that was now failing. I could no longer fit the shoes I'd wished for; I couldn't even make things grow anymore. So, what did that make me? A pretender, no better than my stepsisters. A liar, even to my own husband.

A thief.

I clenched my fist around the leaves and hurried from the garden. I ran up the servant's stairway, the sharp scent of stolen mint flying out behind me.

SEVENTEEN

As I approached my dressing room door, the maid was just coming out. All traces of the laughter I had seen downstairs were wiped away, as if they'd never been there. I stopped in the passage as a flutter of women's voices floated up from the grand stairway; it was the queen and her ladies. I was caught. They would see what I had done. The stolen mint dropped from my nerveless fingers as I stood frozen like a hare before a hawk.

But before the ladies appeared, my maid sprang to life. In one swift motion, she snatched up the mint, steered me inside, and pulled the door closed behind us. We stood, straining to hear, but the walls and door were too thick. After a moment, she unlatched the door and opened it a crack, but there was no sound. The ladies had gone on their way. She shut the door again and faced me. I stared into her wide eyes as she pressed the mint into my hands, her fingers gripping so hard I almost cried out. She was telling me something; I just didn't know what. After a few heartbeats, she let go and straightened her back.

"Your tea, your highness."

"I wanted some air."

We'd both spoken at once.

She inclined her head, and I clutched the mint tighter in my fist. Then, without another word, she disappeared out the door.

What had just happened? Had she been protecting me from embarrassment? Or herself from punishment? Had the queen set her to watch me for more sins to add to that book in her head?

Was my failure now the maid's fault somehow? The pounding in my head increased. I couldn't think.

I told myself I didn't care what any of them thought and tossed the mint into the pot, little bits of stem and all. I didn't wait for the tea to cool but drank it down so hot it burned my tongue. It soothed the throbbing in my head, but only a little.

I drank a second cup, hoping it would help, but it didn't. I couldn't help thinking it would have worked if I had been able to grow the mint with my own hands. If I hadn't stolen it.

I decided to really get some air, like I'd told the maid I had. The castle walls were the domain of the palace guard, but they weren't forbidden. And I wouldn't meet the queen or any of her ladies there. I went back to the servant's stairway and climbed up, as high as I could go.

The day had turned cool and windy, but I stayed on the walls, pacing up and down until the pain in my head finally eased. Then I stood still, watching the road that led down from the castle and through the forest. I couldn't stop thinking of the night before, how the prince had said the stockings didn't matter. But how he had turned away from me anyway. I realized I was watching for him, that I wanted to see him as he returned, before he saw me. As if watching him without his knowledge could give me a glimpse into his mind. Or his heart.

I had a fear that sat like a tight band around my chest. I was afraid the one who was once the easiest to please might now have become the hardest. He was slipping away from me, out of my reach. Of course, I should never have been able to hold him in the first place. My wish had robbed him of his free will.

Not that it mattered. I couldn't undo my foolish choice. I could only tell him what I had done. And that was unthinkable; then I would lose him forever. Without him, I had nothing.

I was nothing.

The sun had gone behind the clouds. The wind whipped the trees around so the forest below me moved like a living creature, a fierce and angry one. What would it be like to stand on the forest floor, I wondered, the autumn wind screaming around me and the leaves shutting out the light? Would I be frightened to be lost in it? Or would it be a relief to let myself be swallowed up?

At last a rider emerged from the forest. I could tell it was him by the gentle hand he laid on his horse's neck. As if he knew I was there, he looked up and seemed to see me. He waved as he disappeared through the gates, and a few minutes later he joined me on the wall. He looked bemused as he strode up to me, taking off his gloves. "Were you watching for me?"

I nodded.

"Why? You never do that."

The tight band of fear had moved up my chest and settled like a hand around my throat. What if I opened my mouth and the truth came spilling out? "I was worried," I managed at last.

"About me?"

I nodded again. In a way it was the truth.

He closed the distance between us and put his hands on my arms. "There was no need. I hadn't gone far." He touched my face, and I realized my cheek was wet. "What's happened to you?"

I doubted he was talking about my windswept hair or my cold face. What would he say if he knew? The fear squeezed my throat with thick fingers. "I don't know," were the only words I could force out.

"Never mind." His lips were warm against my forehead. "I'm back now." He put his arms around me, his cloak shutting out the world outside, and I leaned into him, my face wet against the softness of his coat.

Eighteen

*T*he magic that bound my husband to me was cracking.

I tried to pretend it wasn't true, but somewhere inside, I knew. Every night I took off the shoes and the pink lines were the same, and my excuses were the same. But he was not. He would never understand why I had to wear the stockings, and I could never explain.

His puzzled looks soon became distant, even cold. And before many nights had passed, he was sleeping when I came to bed. Or pretending to at least. He didn't know I had betrayed him, but he was beginning to suspect. He knew I'd done something wrong, something to hurt him.

He kept his thoughts to himself, though. In public, he was kind, even attentive. But instead of looking at me like I was the only person in the room, he avoided my eyes. His slow smile that had been for me alone—I only saw flashes of that now.

My maid was different, too, since the doctor came to bleed me. Now, just before she sent me off to tea or dinner or some other engagement, once she had laced and curled and powdered me, she would take me by the shoulders. Her eyes would bore into me, fierce with some unspoken message, then she would let me go.

But when we weren't alone, if someone came into the room, or if she was bringing me something, a shawl or a fan I'd forgotten, she would draw close with the pretense of fixing an earring or a hairpin. *There, there, now,* she would whisper, so softly only I could hear. The same words the doctor had said. *There, there.*

And though I never told her when I had a headache, she had an uncanny way of knowing. For on the days when my head was pounding and I could barely stand the sunlight, on my tea tray, tucked under a napkin I'd find a handful of mint.

I suppose she meant to give me strength. Perhaps once, she'd hoped she could transform me into something I wasn't. But by now, we both knew that whatever was wrong with me was not so easily fixed. It wasn't a stain that could be washed off, or a blemish that would fade. It could only be managed, hidden from view.

But what if a day came when I could hide it no longer? What if I wasn't a girl at all, but an arrow, nocked to the bowstring? What if I was arrow and archer too, drawing the bow tighter and tighter? When I loosed the string, I would fly headlong through the air, unable to change course or slow down. The only end I could imagine was me shattered into a thousand pieces.

Sometimes I believed that strange story was true, and I had no idea how to stop it. I didn't make plans to steal another knife for the next time I needed one. I told myself being ready would only invite the slippers to bite into my skin all the sooner. And I waited.

Waiting is a kind of torture. When my mother was dying, I took no pleasure in the days that remained to us. And now, I couldn't enjoy being the girl who fit the slippers. I was always willing that moment to come, when I would feel that telltale tightness in my shoes. I wanted it over, even though I knew I would feel no better when it was. And the more I wanted it, the longer it took.

When I was alone, I would search for a sign: a thicker mark on my skin, a longer crack in the glass. In company I would lift my heel out of one shoe, to see if it would still come out easily. Then I would repeat the process with the other foot. Which would break first—me, or the slippers?

My smile was hard, like a mask I was looking through. I always had that feeling now, like there was a stone just under my ribs. I could almost feel it if I put my hand there.

How much my husband knew, I couldn't be sure. I couldn't tell him the truth, and we had nothing else to talk about. He knocked on the door of my dressing room one afternoon. "I'm sorry to disturb you."

I looked up from my plate. I'd been pushing my food around to make it seem like I had eaten more than I had. "No, of course not, darling." We were always polite. We did a lot of pretending, even in private. I abandoned my meal and crossed the room, a piece of bread in my hand. "I was finished." I opened the window and began crumbling the bread onto the sill.

"I'm going out hunting." He glanced up from buckling on his belt. "There's a wolf that's been making trouble, going after some of the…" he trailed off, watching me curiously as I picked the bread to pieces.

"It's for the birds. I like watching them." It wasn't a lie; I did like watching them.

The turtle doves from my mother's grave never came anymore. But when I first came to the palace, after the servants took my old clothes, bathed me, and dressed me in something *decent*, after they left me alone at last, I opened the window, and the doves found me. I fed them crumbs and talked to them, just like I had to the hazel tree. After what happened at the wedding, though, the queen's ladies forced the maid to close the window. *Nasty, vicious creatures!* they had shrieked. I hoped the doves might find me again in the palace gardens, but they never did.

These days, a little sparrow came to my window. I didn't know if she was the same one who helped the other birds sort the lentils from the ashes at my stepmother's command. But I liked to think so, and I was always glad to see her.

My husband continued to stare at me. "Are you all right?" For a moment, his voice was different from the formal tone he used with me these days. He almost sounded like he used to. "You're so pale and thin."

Pale. Thin. I bit back an angry retort and kept my eyes on my hands, shredding pieces of bread into crumbs so small they almost disappeared. Wasn't I supposed to be pale and thin? What was the point of all the powder, the gloves, the parasols, if not to be pale? What was the point of the corset, if not to be thin?

When I looked around, he was kneeling in front of me. "And your shoes." He stood and held out his hand. In his palm were not one, but two tiny bits of glass. More pieces of the slippers. "We can mend them." His tone was almost pleading. "Can't we try?"

I opened my hand and let him drop the glass onto my palm. What if we could? What if there were someone who could fix the shoes, someone who could keep the magic intact? Someone who could right the wrongs I'd done. I tried to imagine who it might be: perhaps a shadowy, barefoot figure, cloaked and hooded, dressed in the colors of the earth, stepping out of a green wood. But just like the people in my needlework, I couldn't see a face. Surely such a person didn't exist.

I held the bits of glass out the window, and I let them fall. "I like my shoes the way they are."

It was a lie. Of course it was a lie. Perhaps that was the only thing that would come out of my mouth these days.

He stared at me, defeated. "Why won't you let me help you?"

I shifted my foot in my shoe, my throat closing against any truth that might come out. "I don't need help." Another lie.

His hand reached out to touch my cheek. "But you're—"

"I'm not crying." I wished he would go.

He put his head down and sighed, running a hand through his hair. Then he nodded. "Well." That formality was back to his voice. "Well. We're leading a party into the forest to see if we can find some trace of this wolf."

When the feeling came I almost missed it. "Be careful, darling," I said, flexing my toes in agitation and lifting my heel. Then I felt it.

The shoe did not come off.

An inexplicable surge of triumph coursed through my veins. Then, just as quickly, it evaporated. I should have planned for a knife after all, of course I should have. The first had disappeared; the second had fallen out the window. I had known this, all those anxious days of waiting, and I had thought of nothing. What sort of a knife could I get now?

I only needed a small one, like the one my husband wore at his belt. My breath caught in my throat, remembering the first time I had seen that knife. It was months ago, one of the first warm days of spring. We sat on a woven rug on the edge of the orchard, the trees blossoming all around us. He took an apple from a basket and peeled it with his knife. It was a wizened old storage apple left over from the fall, but the tough skin came off in one curly red ribbon. I leaned back on my hands and laughed, saying how clever he was with a knife.

He laughed too and moved close to kiss me, but then he stopped, looking down at my arms. A little vine had sprung up under my hands and twined its way around my wrists. The buds on the vine opened into delicate purple flowers as he watched. *You are a wonder,* he whispered. Then he kissed me, and the apple was forgotten. We'd been so happy that day.

I turned from the window, opening my mouth to speak, but my dressing room was empty. My husband had gone to hunt the wolf. How long had I been standing there? I hurried out to catch him.

When I stepped into the stables, the warm, animal smell surrounded me. The sense of comfort was so overpowering tears sprang to my eyes. But I was not there for comfort. I rubbed my eyes, smearing the maid's careful handiwork. She would have to fix the damage I'd done.

My husband was talking to the huntsman while a groom saddled his horse. They stopped abruptly when they saw me.

"Darling," I stopped and cleared my throat, trying to summon my voice. "Couldn't this wait? I was thinking how nice it would be to have a picnic this afternoon." His knife was such a little thing, so easily slipped into a pocket. He probably wouldn't even miss it, and I could put it back with his things later. When I was finished with it.

With a glance at the prince, the huntsman moved away and busied himself with his own horse and gear. It seemed he had nothing left to do, but he made a show of re-buckling the saddle and going through the saddlebags. My husband took my arm and led me out of earshot.

He took my hand in a way he never did these days. He studied my face a moment, puzzled, unconsciously rubbing my hand with both of his, as if he instinctively knew I was cold. Then he looked down, a lock of soft, brown hair falling into his face. "I'm afraid it can't wait." His voice was so low I could hardly hear it. "Farmers are losing livestock, and people are frightened."

"Of course." I pulled my hand out of his. "Never mind." Despite everything, he still tried to save me whatever embarrassment he could. I knew I should be glad, but I wasn't. I was only angry.

Behind us the door to the outside banged open, and a cold gust of wind blew in. He shut the door and looked at me curiously as I put my arms around myself for warmth. "Odd day for a picnic, isn't it?"

"I only thought it would be nice if we—" I broke off, feeling the hot prickle of tears behind my eyes again. "Never mind." I pushed through the door, letting it slam shut behind me. The sound of his voice followed me, but the wind swallowed his words. Perhaps he'd called my name. It was the name of someone I should be, but I never knew how. If only I could have some other name. If only I could be some other girl. A girl who didn't lie and cheat and cling to a happiness she didn't deserve. A happiness that wasn't even happy.

I put all my concentration into not limping. The tightness had been long in coming, but now it had reappeared, the pain was intense. I was making my way toward my room when a footman approached me.

"There you are, your highness." He spoke as if I were a naughty child. "The duke is here. He is in the music room."

The duke. My father. I tried to look pleased, but I was sick of pretending. "Thank you." The footman turned in the direction of the music room, one arm extended as if to usher me in. But I couldn't go in just yet. "I'll be in directly."

"Very good, your highness." He stationed himself at the music room door, his face belying his words. It wasn't good at all.

NINETEEN

I sat at my dressing table, my jewel casket in my lap. Not much in it would do. Most of these jewels were presents from my husband or his parents, and they would notice if I didn't wear them from time to time. I would have to commission some new jewelry. At last I settled on a few pieces I didn't think would be missed. I wrapped them in a handkerchief and tied it up with a bit of ribbon. Then I dropped the package in my workbasket and went to meet my father.

The footman was still in place at the music room door. "Are you quite well, your highness?" I must have been limping again.

"Perfectly well, thank you," I had forgotten my feet for a moment, but now I had a sudden thought. "Have you brought tea?"

"Not yet, your highness. We did not know how long you would be." Another reproach.

I nodded. "When you send it, I'd like some apples. Do we have any?"

It was autumn; of course we had apples. His face was expressionless. "Certainly, your highness."

"Good." I didn't need a picnic to get my hands on a paring knife. "Why don't you send us a couple?" He inclined his head again. Apples with tea were not worthy of a response. But I didn't care.

With a short bow, he left. I watched him go, and only when he was out of sight did I walk through the door. I didn't like these visits to be witnessed.

My father never put his arms around me anymore. He stood and began to bow as soon as he saw me. "Father," I reached out a hand, "please don't." But it was too late.

"I wish you wouldn't," I said as he straightened up.

He spread out his hands in apology. "A man must bow to his princess." The corners of his mouth lifted hopefully.

"Not if she doesn't want it."

He nodded. "Of course, my dear."

We said these words every time. He always agreed, then bowed again when he left, even lower than before. That part of our ritual over, I indicated his chair, and we sat. Then came the silence as we searched for something to say while we waited for the tea.

"How well you're looking," he said at last.

I was silent. Even my husband seemed to think I was too pale, too thin. So my father's compliment only confused me. I would have been grateful if I hadn't seen him examining my gown and jewelry, as if taking inventory, remembering every detail, to tell people about later. He didn't see me at all.

"Thank you," I managed at last. "I'm glad you could come." That was my standard greeting for visitors, but saying it to him felt especially stilted. I wasn't even sure if it was true.

His gaze strayed to the piano. "How about some music, my dear?"

"I'm afraid I'm out of practice." He would be pleased no matter how badly I performed, but knowing a knife was coming along with the apples, I was too agitated to play. I could hardly sit still in my chair.

He shook his head, smiling a little. "Come now, you have a lovely voice. Surely you can indulge your poor father."

"I can't sing today, I," I made a coughing sound. "I have a bit of a cold."

That was a lie. I did not have a cold, but my throat was always tight these days. *Let's just leave it for today, my dear,* the music master had said the last time I was in this room, his eyebrows furrowed in concern. *Perhaps you need a rest.* Madame was even more disappointed. With her, as with most of the people of the palace, I often struggled to find any voice at all, much less my *true* one. Whatever that was.

My father's long mustaches seemed to droop. All of him drooped, really. He was wearing his best coat, or it had been his best when my mother was alive. But it was threadbare now, and new trim couldn't make it less shabby.

Finally, the tea arrived. In addition to the teapot and cups and saucers, there was a plate of bread and butter, and one of little cakes. The apples were there too, on a separate plate. It matched the others, but it seemed to have been squeezed onto the tray, haphazardly, at the last minute. I imagined the cook in the kitchen trying to make room for this extra plate and throwing up his hands when it destroyed the symmetry of his beautiful tray. *Don't blame me*, he would have huffed at the footman. *Apples, of all things.*

And there the apples were: peeled and cored, cut into little slices, and artfully arranged on the plate. Of course, there was no knife. Who would need one when the apples were cut up so carefully? My nails dug into my palms.

My father didn't seem to notice my shaking hands as I poured the tea. The footman had gone, so now we could talk without being interrupted or overheard. But he didn't speak immediately. He merely took the tea I offered him, looking around the room and humming to himself between sips. It was always difficult for him to get to the point of his visits, and, as my mind was on the elusive paring knife, I wasn't helping. I worried my wedding ring with my thumb and sat, holding in my disappointment.

Finally, he gathered his courage and spoke. "Your mother and your sisters wished to be remembered to you."

This was my cue. I drew the bundle from my workbasket and put it in my lap, waiting for my opportunity to give it to him. For now he had begun this little stab at me, he must finish. "Your mother would have liked to come with me, but it is so difficult for her to leave your sisters, you understand."

I had not forced my stepsisters to cut themselves, all so they could deceive a prince and steal a life they didn't deserve. That was on my stepmother's head. I hadn't wished for the turtle doves to swoop down and attack them as they left my wedding either. I'd been as shocked as anyone.

And yet.

Hadn't the years of hurt and anger poured out when I told the birds what my sisters had done to fit the slipper? And hidden deep beneath my horror that the doves had blinded them, hadn't there been a fleeting feeling? That they'd gotten what they deserved? Yes, I was culpable. So I would take my punishment.

"Of course I understand." I held out the handkerchief in the space between my father and me. "Please give them this." This was the easiest way to do it. I hated hearing about how he would have come in the carriage, but it desperately needs replacing, or how one of his horses had broken a leg and had to be shot. How some of the glass in the front windows had been broken, and how drafty it makes the house. There were dozens of little details. I had no idea if they were true, but I didn't want to hear them. If I acted first, I heard no more stories, and I preferred it that way. Surely he did too.

"Oh, how very kind, my dear." He tried to seem surprised, and not too pleased, as if I were giving him a bouquet of wildflowers, with no value other than a sentimental one. A present between affectionate family members. One hand fingered the package, subtly, trying to evade my notice. He was feeling its weight, wondering what was in it, and how valuable it was.

His curiosity got the better of him, though; it always did. He untied the ribbon, and the edges of the handkerchief fell away. My present to my stepmother and stepsisters was a matching bracelet, necklace, and pair of earrings, all made of rubies.

I always seemed to give them rubies. I couldn't help it. When I thought of my stepsisters, I thought of blood. I thought of the day the prince and his footmen came to our house, and my stepmother handed the knife to my stepsisters, first one, then the other. *When you are queen*, she hissed, *you'll have no need to walk.* I could still see the red of it, dark and liquid, trickling out of my slipper like a delicate chain of jewels.

I thought of them scornfully then. *They didn't know the prince,* I told the turtle doves when they flew in my window at the palace. *They didn't love him. How could they?* I whispered. *How could they not care about his happiness but only their own?*

Surely I understood my sisters better now. And perhaps I was lucky—that the doves had never returned to give me what *I* deserved.

My hands twisted in my lap as I watched my father run his fingers over the rubies. But I was anxious for nothing; he never seemed to notice the color of the jewels. He held up each piece in turn, as if imagining how they would look on his wife and daughters. Once this little performance was over, he slipped them furtively into a pocket of his coat, murmuring, "You are so good to your family, my dear."

"I hope they will like them."

I didn't know why I played this sick game of pretend with him. Of course, after what the doves had done, my stepsisters would never *see* the rubies. But I doubted they would ever wear them, touch them, or even hear about them. By the time he arrived back home, they would have been exchanged for a horse or a bag of coins; or maybe they would have been used to pay off some gambling debt. I had no idea what he did with his money, only that he could never seem to hold onto any.

I had no money of my own to give him, but I could order all the jewels and fine things I chose. It was the best solution I had.

Once the jewels were safely hidden in his pocket, my father leaned over, crossing the distance between us, and patted my hand. "So good," he repeated.

The worn linen of his cuff had a hole in it, a burn mark, perhaps. I caught his hand and pushed up his coat sleeve. "What happened?"

"What?" He looked down at it and shook his head, bewildered. "I don't—I didn't know…"

"Never mind," I said, sitting on a footstool beside him. "I'll fix it."

In the bottom of my workbasket, underneath the tangle of brightly colored embroidery silks, was a single spool of everyday thread. It was in my pocket the day the prince brought me to the palace, declaring he'd found his true bride at last. I came into my new rooms with nothing but the clothes on my back and the glass slippers on my feet. But when the maid took off my old things and gave me a silken dressing gown to wear while I waited for the bath water to be brought up, I had the strangest feeling. I was sure it was me she'd dropped in a contemptuous pile on the floor, me she would gather up and throw on the fire. So, when she had her back turned, I snatched up the old stockings and ordinary thread and slid them into a drawer, desperate to hold on to something.

The stockings were gone now; they had mysteriously vanished along with the first knife I'd stolen. But the everyday thread remained.

"Oh, no, my dear." My father's fingers twitched feebly as I drew out the thread to mend his cuff. "You shouldn't."

I knew he was right. But my throat ached at the feel of the worn wooden spool in my hand, warm against my skin as if it had been waiting for me all this time. I didn't care what people would think if they saw me. Mending something that needed fixing was nothing shameful.

My needle ready, I reached for his sleeve.

"No, no, my dear," he said again, but weakly. "Your mother can—"

"She's not my mother." I stabbed my needle into the fabric. "Hold still."

Was he ever sorry, I wondered, for preferring my stepmother to me? For the things he had said? I made a row of stitches across the gap in the fabric.

Just a stunted little kitchen wench my late wife left behind her. That's what he called me when the prince's men asked if any other young ladies lived in his house. He said it as if I had nothing to do with him. As if it was careless of my mother not to have taken me along with her, wherever she had gone. My needle moved in and out of the rows of stitches, weaving a new bit of cloth to fill the hole. Was he ever sorry, I wondered. For forgetting her?

My handkerchief was still on his knee. He smoothed it with his free hand, stroking it the way he used to stroke my hair when I was little.

Watching him now, I could almost believe he missed me. And for just a moment, I wanted to lay my head in his lap the way I used to. Back before my mother died. Before he married my stepmother. Before I married a prince.

Instead, I tied the knot and bit through the thread. My darning blended in so well I could hardly see it. The hole was filled, and for the space of a few minutes, I'd been of use. "There." I straightened his cuff and slipped the tarnished silver button into the buttonhole. "No one will ever know."

TWENTY

*T*he hunting party was victorious. But when the wolf's carcass was taken to be skinned and we sat listening to the hunters' stories, my husband sat in silence. He had no love of killing.

That night when I came to bed, he was sleeping, or appearing to, as usual. I lay down beside him and, after a while, pretended to sleep myself. All the while I listened for the change in his breathing that came when he really was asleep. After all these nights, I had learned to tell the difference.

At last, he gave a final sigh, and his breathing slowed. I waited a minute longer, then I eased myself out from under the blankets and pulled the bed curtains closed behind me. My heart hammering, I stole across to the door of his dressing room.

The hinges made a soft squeak, and I stood frozen. But I heard no movement from the bed. Afraid to open the door any farther, I squeezed through the narrow space and slipped into his room. It was too dark to see, so I closed my eyes, reaching out until I touched his belt, hanging on a hook beside the door. My fingers slid along the leather until they met the cold smoothness of his knife handle. I drew it out of its sheath, crept out of his dressing room, and closed the door.

Back in our bedroom, the fire was dying, but the embers still glowed. Silently, I knelt and held a candle into the ashes, using my body to mask the flare of light when the wick caught.

Once I reached my dressing room, I let out the breath I'd been holding. The danger was past now, and I would make no noise; there would be no reason for my husband to wake. The candle on the floor beside me gave little light, but I didn't need much. The scarred, puffy lines on my feet felt magnified now, like leeches on my skin. My fingers knew what to do, and so did the knife.

Behind me, the window slammed open with a gust of cold wind, and the drapes streamed into the room. The maid must not have latched the window properly. My candle flickered, then recovered. The window banged again, but I ignored it as the strips of skin peeled neatly away under my husband's knife. The pain was the sharpest it had ever been. Tears sprang to my eyes, and I gritted my teeth to keep from crying out. But still, I felt lighter with every touch of the knife.

From the floor beside me, something winked in the light of my candle. One of the glass slippers watched me, abandoned, malevolent. I tossed it away from me in revulsion, then I immediately regretted it. *They'll cut you, darling,* my husband had warned. *What happens when they fall to pieces under your feet?* I knew he'd been right. One day, they would shatter when I put my weight on them. And I couldn't afford for it to happen any sooner than it had to. For what would happen then?

But the slipper landed soundlessly on the carpet by the door to the corridor. A shudder ran down my spine.

The second slipper was nowhere to be seen, so I turned back to my work. I wouldn't think of how quickly the scars would come back, how dark or how thick, or how long it would be before the tightness returned or the glass splintered under my feet. I only thought of slipping my feet effortlessly into the shoes.

I heard the blood beating in my ears; I felt the knife and the pain and the lightness and the release. But I didn't hear the door open. I didn't see the light. I didn't feel the wind chilling the tears on my cheeks. Until I heard his voice.

"What are you doing?"

My husband stood in the bedroom doorway.

I stared at him blankly, seeing nothing. I had gone numb. After all my planning and deceiving and hiding, I had nothing left. My body, heart, brain, all of me was empty, except for one imperative: he couldn't see my feet. I threw my nightgown over them, my hand knocking against the candle, which tipped over and rolled under the dresser, the flame guttering. I reached out to extinguish it before the wood above it caught fire. But the night air swirling into the room was there before me, and the flame died in a sudden rush.

Strangely, the last moment of light illuminated something under the dresser. A lumpy, oval-shaped package, something rolled up, with a shiny point sticking out of one end. I stared at the patch of dark where the something was. What could it be?

But it didn't matter. I was exposed at last.

"What are you doing?" he said again. His voice was low, but it struck my ears like a shout.

My throat felt like it was carved out of stone. Each word I forced out was a ragged whisper. "Making them fit," were the only words I could say.

"But why? What difference—" He could not go on.

There was so much I had to say. That I needed the slippers. That I hadn't meant to hurt him. That, despite it all, I loved him.

I wanted to tell him. I wanted to cry. I wanted to scream. But when I opened my mouth, nothing came out. Not a word, not a sob, not a shriek.

He took a step forward.

I scooted away from him, one hand reaching behind me. I had to escape. I should explain. And yet, I thought, with a rush of defiance, if I had it to do over, I would do it all the same. My fingers, scrabbling on the floor, closed on something smooth and cool as a fish. I wanted to laugh. The second slipper waited behind me in the dark. This was where my foolish actions had led. This was the path I stepped on the moment I wished the prince would fall in love with me. I drew back my arm and hurled the glass slipper at the wall behind him with all my strength.

With a sickening crash, my wish shattered and fell in pieces to the floor. It was over.

The prince hardly seemed to see it, though. Despite the open window, the air seemed gone from his lungs. He stood in a small circle of light, one hand protecting the candle he held. With my candle out, he couldn't see my face, or my feet; I was surrounded by the dark. But if the darkness had been complete, I wouldn't have had to see him there, ghostly in the dark, with that look on his face. Like he was bleeding internally.

"How—" he stopped, then started again. "How could you?" He sounded sick.

He knew I had betrayed him, but not how. He thought I had never fit the slippers. That I'd tricked him somehow, just like my stepsisters had tried to do. He thought I was no more his true bride than they were. That I was just like them. I wanted to tell him it wasn't true, that he was wrong.

And if I could have believed it, I would have.

He was coming closer. I scrambled to my feet; I couldn't let him see the damage I'd done, even now. But he wasn't looking down at my feet. It was my face his candle moved ever closer to. The window banged again. The room was filling with cold air, and his circle of light moved closer still.

I stood frozen, staring at his face, but I couldn't read it. There was no color to his eyes; they were only dark. "Tell me," he choked out. "Tell the truth."

The candle was between us now. There was too much light. I wished darkness would swallow me; silently I begged for it. But there he was, waiting for me to say something.

I took a breath and opened my mouth, no idea what would come out. The truth was impossible, but what else was there? He deserved to know, and yet, the words would not come. I couldn't make a sound. My throat was closed against the lies, the truth, and everything in between. The window banged again, sending a gust of cold air into the room, and I breathed out, a long shuddering breath. The candle flame flickered once, then died. We were in darkness.

I couldn't think; I could only run. I turned and flew to the door to the hallway. I was almost there when I heard a splintering, and a sharp pain shot up my foot. I had stepped on something, something jagged. Something broken. I ignored it and groped for the door latch, pulling it open and running out into the blackness of the corridor.

Behind me there was a crash and a pained intake of air. Perhaps he had stumbled in the dark. I heard his voice calling out to me. He is lighting another candle, I thought as I ran, to see where he is going. I had no light, but I didn't seem to need any. In this darkness I had wished for I could think more clearly, see more clearly. I followed the corridor all the way to the stairs and started down them. This was the servant's stairway, the one that led down to the kitchens and the gardens. But I didn't need to go that far. I stopped on the landing and ran out through a little doorway into the dining hall.

The room was empty. There was no music, no conversation; the dancers and wolf hunters and musicians and servants had all gone to bed. The only light was from the dying fire in the cavernous fireplace at one end. By this light I fled the ballroom and the palace, just as I had fled from the ball, all those months ago. The castle door was bolted this time, though. I put all my weight under the bolt and lifted it free, pushing the door open. Then I was out on the steps and into the night air at last.

I was halfway down the stairs when I felt the pain again. The broken thing was still in my foot, pushed further and further in with every step. I sat down to pull it out. It was smooth, its sharp edges slick with my blood. I yanked at it and winced as it cut into my hand, but it came free at last. There were more pieces of whatever it was, but they were so small or in so far I couldn't pull them out. I was out of time.

I turned on the stairs. I had fled the palace before, but nothing was the same this time. The prince hadn't spread pitch on the steps to stick to my shoes and catch me like he had before. The clock wasn't striking midnight, like it had the night my slipper stuck in his trap and I ran on without it. The clock wasn't striking at all, but I knew it was late. I could feel it. I had stayed in this life too long.

Except for the wind, the night was silent. No one was watching. All the better, I thought, passing the locked gates and slipping through an unguarded door in the castle wall. Nothing will stop me from getting away. Of course, before, the prince hunted the girl in the glass slippers. And I was not that girl anymore, so who would want to stop me now?

A trail of bloody footprints followed me into the wood.

PART TWO:

THE WOOD

TWENTY-ONE

I ran.

The wind howled around me, pushing, pulling me deep into the forest, then deeper still, and I ran where it led me. I couldn't see where I was going, but I didn't care. Away, that was all that mattered.

Wispy lines of clouds raced across the moon, dimming the light. The wind blew stronger, and there was a rumble of thunder. From behind me came a muffled shouting and the baying of hounds. Surely this was not the prince and his men, hunting me? Nothing made sense.

The next time the moon appeared, I stopped, turning to look behind me, but I could see no one. All I could see was the forest path, the trees leaning over it and brambles snaking up to its edges, threatening to swallow it entirely. Let them, I thought. Let the forest hide me.

The thickening clouds covered the moon, and I heard the hounds again. I ran faster, my hands out in front of me. I flew deeper and deeper into the wood, whipped by thorns and branches as I ran. But the sounds of the hunt followed me, always a little closer.

If I was their quarry, I had made their job easy. The dogs had only to follow the scent of my bloody footprints. I should have been more careful, but back at the palace, in the dark of my dressing room, the thought that my husband would want to follow me hadn't entered my mind. I never would have believed it.

I ran, my chest bursting, hands and face bleeding where the branches slashed across them. The thunder continued, and the rain began. It came down in sheets, and the wind grew bitterly cold. I ran on, fallen leaves turning slippery and dirt becoming mud under my feet. Let it continue, I thought, let it be a drenching rain that will blot out my scent and make them lose their way.

I ran on and on until at last a gnarled tree root caught my foot, sending me sprawling to the forest floor. I lay there, letting the downpour wash the blood off my feet and thinking of nothing. Even the whispers in my head were silent now. I was tired, so tired of running. I was soaked to the skin, my nightgown ripped and covered in mud. How easy it would be to stay there.

From my place face down in the moss and dead leaves I saw a blinding flash of light, and an earsplitting crash sounded right ahead of me. I cowered at the noise, hands over my head. Then I smelled burning and heard another sound, the slow creaking of something massive falling to the forest floor. In the next flash I could see what had happened. A bolt of lightning had split a giant tree nearly in two. One half remained standing; the other had fallen to the ground in front of me, still connected to the tree at the trunk, high above.

The hounds bayed; they were close now. I didn't think but grabbed one of the branches of the fallen part of the tree and clambered up. Then I crawled along it, up toward the center, and soon I was at the cleft. It was still smoldering, but not burning. The inside of the trunk was rotten and soft where insects had eaten away the wood, making an empty space in the center. Making room enough for me. I folded myself into the little hollow, wrapped my arms around my knees, and waited.

Surely, no one in the palace would want me back. *Good riddance to bad rubbish.* That's what people would say. People like Opal and Ruby and Pearl. People like the queen. But perhaps they wanted to punish me first. Before I got what I deserved.

I held myself tighter, making myself as small as I could. Was this how the wolf had felt that afternoon, before my husband and the other hunters caught it? Did it run like I had, as it heard them come closer with every breath? Did it try to hide, or did it turn and fight? Did it wonder why they were hunting it at all? Perhaps it wasn't really a danger to anyone. Perhaps it had been a toothless, flea-bitten thing, scouring the wood for grubs, too old and ill to hunt. I imagined it, thin and ragged, staggering out into a clearing, facing the hunters and their dogs. It didn't offer to fight them; it only stared. Daring them, begging them, to finish it off.

I could do the same. It was a tempting thought; I had nowhere to go, after all. But I couldn't go back. Besides, the shouts and barking were softer now. In fact, the dogs weren't barking at all; they were whimpering. They had lost the scent. I closed myself into a ball and shut my eyes, almost invisible at last. Running away, it seemed, was the one thing I could do well.

Twenty-two

I must have slept, there in the cleft of the tree, for I started with a gasp, sweating and shaking and sure I was falling from the castle walls. I must have been dreaming. When I could breathe again, I shifted from my cramped position. The rain still fell, though the wind had dropped. The trees around me blocked out most of the light, but there was a little, enough to make me think it was day. Careful not to slip, I crept from the hollow trunk and onto the fallen part of the tree. I slithered down it and dropped to the ground.

My feet hurt, especially the one that had stepped on something sharp, but I ignored them both. I made no attempt to bandage the cuts I had made or pull out any more of whatever the sharp things were. In fact, I didn't even look at my feet. They had failed me, so I didn't care how they felt.

There was no proper path here, only the ghost of a trail, overgrown with brambles and saplings, but it was a start. I began to walk.

When I disappeared after the third ball, the prince had searched for me for weeks. If he truly wanted to find me now, he would come back to the wood. I wondered again what he could possibly want with me. Did he want me to come back so we could pretend we were happy, when he must despise me? Or was I to be shamed? Would I be brought for judgment before the king and queen and all the others, my feet in tatters, before he cast me off?

Or did he only want the truth? That truth I could never bring myself to tell him. I didn't know. I only knew I couldn't stay where I was, so I walked.

The weather had been mild until yesterday. Had it only been the day before that I had begged for a picnic so I could steal a knife? But autumn had begun in earnest now, and sped toward winter as I walked. The wind didn't push me as it had the night before; it only chilled me. The rain was softer now, but cold and constant. I went on doggedly, not knowing what direction I was going, only hoping it was away.

I shouldn't have felt anything as ordinary as hunger. Not when I had left my marriage, my home, anyone who knew me. Anyone who loved me. I pushed aside the emptiness in my gut, just as I did the pain in my feet. But as the light failed I could no longer ignore the gnawing in my stomach. I began to look around for any late blackberries. At last I found a few, but I knew they wouldn't be enough to ease the cramping in my belly.

Before I knew it, I was kneeling, my hands finding the earth under the brambles, waiting for the familiar tingle in my fingers, my mouth watering for the blackberries I would grow. It was easily done. That was what I thought for one delirious moment, but nothing happened.

Before, it would have been nothing to make a handful of blackberries into a basketful. Before the prince, before the palace, before the slippers. But that was all over. I waited and waited, but the feeling did not come. Shivering, I sat back on my heels, lightheaded only from hunger. I should have known, of course. The devil in the bush should have shown me. The mint in the herb garden too. My hands had lost their magic, just as my feet had.

I plucked all the berries off the bush and crammed them into my mouth. They were too soft and tasted rotten on my tongue. But I ignored the churning in my stomach and forced them down my throat. They were all I would get.

I walked on through the deepening shadows. The muddy earth was soothing to my feet, which felt hot all the time now. I refused to think. To think was to give in to the whispers in my head. *A princess cannot disappoint, you know.* But I heard them anyway. *I'm afraid it is a hopeless business.* I shut out the thoughts and watched for the trees to thin, or for a path to appear. But the trees only grew bigger, taller, and closer together. When it was too dark to see, I cleared a space under a thicket of brambles and curled up to sleep.

The ground was hard. It was wet and cold, and again I slept little. When the forest lightened some, I struggled out of my bramble shelter, my joints aching. Tearing free from the thorns catching on my nightgown and hair, I stood. Though the rain had become a drizzle, the air was just as cold.

But I was not cold now; I was hot. Shivering and sweating, I began to walk. My feet burned with every step. Though I had left the slippers behind at the palace, I felt them on my feet again, jagged glass cutting through skin into muscle and bone. I must stop and take them off. I must find a knife. Surely the little pink marks, the lines on the map of my feet, were thicker than ever now. Surely they were bright red. Everyone would see.

But I didn't stop; instead, I stumbled on. The trees rose above me like monstrous dancers in a dark ballroom, their skeletal arms reaching for me, their few remaining leaves waving in the wind like fingers. I couldn't escape them.

I don't know how long I wandered in the wood. Perhaps it was days more, perhaps only hours. I forced myself to keep walking, but my feet betrayed me once again. Sharp pain lanced into me with every step, like flames licking up my legs. I slipped in the mud. It wasn't the first time, but this time I couldn't get back up. The forest was darkening, and night was coming. The trees leaned in around me as wind hissed through the leaves and made them whisper. They were murmuring words, but I couldn't make them out.

Raising my head from the mud, I looked around. I was back at the palace; I had fallen on the ballroom floor. They were all there: Opal, Ruby, and Pearl, all with haughty, handsome dance partners. Madame and the dancing master and the maid. The king and queen. They stared, dancing around me all the while. But they wouldn't help me get up, and I couldn't stand. The glass slippers were growing into my feet; they were in so far I couldn't take them off. The dancers parted, and there was the prince, holding a candle. *How could you?* he breathed. *Tell me the truth.*

I tried to speak, but I couldn't get the words out. I blew out his candle, and he was gone. But I could still see his light. It was up ahead, through the dancers, through the trees. It couldn't be a candle; perhaps it was a house with a lighted window. Illuminated in the light, there was a head, the shaggy straw-colored head of a little boy.

I called to him, but no sound came out. I reached out my hand. Perhaps he would see I needed help and fetch someone. The child's eyes widened as I leaned toward him; then he took a step back, and he, too, was gone. I stretched too far and fell forward onto mud and dead leaves. The trees closed in again, and I understood them at last.

Good riddance, they sighed. *Good riddance to bad rubbish.*

TWENTY-THREE

*T*here was something blissfully cool on my feet, rubbed on by a gentle hand, and I heard voices. They were warm, human voices, no longer the shivery, rustling whispers of the trees. "Bring those dry cloths there," said one, a woman.

Something soft wrapped around my feet. A moment later, firm hands turned me onto my back. I felt a spoon at my lips. "Open up." It was the woman again. "Open up, little bird." The spoon tipped a little broth into my mouth. I tried to swallow, but my throat was parched and swollen, and I ached all over. I coughed. Where was I?

The other voice was a child's. "Who is she?"

The spoon was back at my lips with more broth. "I don't know, my rabbit. A little sparrow very far from her nest, I think."

"Like the other sparrow?" asked the child. "The one whose mama left her, and she couldn't fly?"

"Yes, love, very like that, I think." The woman had a dry voice, like a crackling fire. "And that sparrow got all better, didn't she?" Another spoonful touched my lips.

"She left us."

"Yes, she flew away when she was better. Birds aren't meant to live in houses, Rabbit." I managed to swallow the broth this time. "Good girl."

"But what happened to *this* sparrow?"

What *had* happened? I didn't want to remember; that much I knew. I tried to make myself move, to tell the woman not to answer. To tell her I didn't want to hear.

"I don't know, love," the woman murmured as she continued to spoon the soup into my mouth. "But we'll do what we can, won't we?" I heard a bowl being set down close by. "That will do for now, my sparrow." I felt the light touch of a hand on my forehead. "That will do."

The next time I woke, the hand was on my cheek. It was cool and gentle, my mother's hand; I was sure of it. I tried to speak to her, but my mouth would not work. I reached up to put my hand on hers.

"Rest easy, my sparrow."

My eyes flew open, and I let the hand go with a start. The voice was not my mother's at all. I struggled to breathe as I stared at the woman standing beside the bed. The woman who was not my mother. She was a stranger.

She covered my hand with one of hers. I jumped again, but the pressure of her hand remained steady on mine. "You are safe, little bird. You are safe with us."

At last I nodded, although I wasn't sure what I was agreeing to. She released me, and I unclenched my fingers. There was something strange about my hand; it was naked. My thumb brushed at my ring finger, feeling for a ring that wasn't there.

"The fever has broken." The woman turned away from the bed. "We'll try some more soup." She walked a few steps to a fireplace with a cooking pot hanging in it. "Jack," she called over her shoulder, as she picked up a wooden bowl, "fetch a spoon, my rabbit." There was a rustling sound in the corner of the room.

I must have been a little feverish still, to have thought this woman even a little like my mother. She was nothing like her. My mother had been delicate and fine boned, with a musical voice. The old woman bringing me a bowl of soup had a sturdy frame and thick gray hair, braided and coiled at the back of her head in a knot. Her hands were large and rough, so unlike my mother's. And yet, as one of those cool, dry hands brushed the hair from my eyes and rested on my forehead, the word repeated in my mind: *Mother*. But as I couldn't seem to speak, what I called her in my head didn't matter anyway.

Now the old lady was sitting beside the bed. As she helped me sit up, I looked around. The fire lit a sparsely furnished one-room cottage. There was a rocking chair, a table, and a small sleeping pallet in one corner.

When I was settled, she began to feed me the broth as if I were a small child. I knew I should feed myself, but I let her do it. After a minute I noticed movement behind her. A small, fair-haired head peeked out at me around her shoulder, and a grubby little hand clutched at her waist. It was the boy from the forest. The forest with whispering trees. *Good riddance.* The boy hadn't been a dream; he'd been real. The trees had been real. *Good riddance to bad rubbish,* they had hissed. I had run. From what I wouldn't think of, but I had run and run until my feet gave out. Something was wrong with my feet.

Something was wrong with me.

I flattened myself against the pillow. No air was reaching my lungs, no matter how much I gulped in.

"Little sparrow." The old woman set the bowl on her chair and stepped back, spreading out her hands. "No one will harm you here. It is only me and Jack."

Then, slowly, she put a hand on me, one steady, calming hand. And I could breathe again.

"Jack found you not far from our door," she said. "The little rabbit scampered in to tell me, and we brought you inside." I must have looked disbelieving, for she raised her eyebrows. "You're only a little slip of a thing, and I have a sturdy wheelbarrow." She looked behind her again. "And a good strong helper."

I nodded again, knowing this time I was giving her permission to sit back down beside me. I swallowed another spoonful of soup. The little room was dark except for the light of the fire.

"That was two nights ago he found you. We worried for a while that you might not live. Didn't we, Rabbit?" The boy had stolen up behind her and put his arms around her waist. "But the danger is past now." She squeezed the little hands reassuringly. "She will mend."

My cheeks were wet. Tears were trickling down my face, and I couldn't stop them. I couldn't eat anymore. The old woman set the half-empty bowl on her lap and let me cry.

"You will mend." She laid her cool hand back on my forehead. "In time."

I lay back on the bed, feeling I could sleep. The old woman gathered her bowl and stood, but I grabbed her hand. Mute as I was, my lips formed the word I wanted to say: *Mother.*

TWENTY-FOUR

I did mend. Or I began to, at least. The next morning, I woke to see the old woman tending the fire, and the boy Jack bringing a pail of water through the door. The cottage was brighter by the light of day. Barrels for storing oats and flour were tucked into the corners; sausages and braided onions and garlic hung from the ceiling. Along with the food hung bunches and bunches of dried herbs, and attached to one wall was a shelf filled with bottles and jars.

When she saw I was awake, the old woman brought over one of the jars and a bowl of water. Sitting at the foot of the bed, she pulled up the blanket. "Let's have a look." With deft hands, she unwrapped the bandages from my feet and washed them with warm water.

"Better today." She laid down the left foot and picked up the right one. "I think we've got them all out, don't you, Rabbit?" She glanced at the boy, who had taken up his place behind her. He ducked under her arm to look at my foot and nodded. Then he plucked at her sleeve and whispered something in her ear.

The old woman reached into her apron pocket and pulled out a handkerchief tied in a knot. She carefully untied it and spread it out on the bed beside my feet. "No touching, now," she warned him. "They are beautiful, aren't they? I know you'd like to keep them with your precious things, Rabbit, but they could hurt you. They're no good for feet."

There in the handkerchief were several shards of glass.

No one in the kingdom can work glass like that.

My fever had returned. Even in pieces, I recognized the glass slipper. I remembered throwing it away from me, remembered it landing on the carpet beside the door on the night I fled the palace. I thought it was unharmed, but the cracks must have continued to spread. So that when I stepped on it, it splintered into the sharp, jagged something that forced itself into my skin. The old woman must have painstakingly removed each little sliver from my foot. Catching the light filtering through the window, the glass winked up at me.

Sweating and shivering, I turned my face away. They had been beautiful, once, those fragments of glass. But no longer. Not to me.

Wrapping my arms around myself to contain the shaking, I looked at my feet instead. The bleeding had stopped, but the lines I had made with the knife were swollen and angry. The soles of both feet were covered in cuts and scratches from running barefoot through the woods. The right foot was the worst, though. It had carried the pieces of my slipper all the time I wandered in the forest.

What a mess I had made.

"Not to worry, my sparrow," the old woman said, as if I'd spoken aloud. She opened the jar on her lap. "They look bad now, but they'll heal up just fine." Her fingers dipped into the jar and began spreading on the salve. "There will be scarring; that can't be helped. But they're good feet. They'll serve you well."

I looked down. I had been proud of my feet, once. With their slender toes and delicate arches. *The whole kingdom has heard about your slippers and your lovely, dainty feet.* Now they were puffy and torn, ugly. Good for what?

"Standing, walking," she went on as if she'd heard me thinking, "running, jumping. That's what feet are for." Not for being admired. Not for snaring a husband. Why had I never known that? Why had no one ever told me?

She felt around in her apron pocket and brought out some strips of cloth. Then she laid them out by my feet, preparing to use them as bandages. I fingered them absently. They were fine white linen, and one even had a bit of lace attached.

"I'm afraid I ran out of rags," the old woman said. "And I had to use your gown. But it was so ripped and stained I couldn't mend it anyway." I looked down at the garment I was wearing. It was a simple shift, worn, but clean; it probably belonged to the woman herself. I was glad to be wearing it, and not my elegant nightgown. That fine gown didn't belong here in this little cottage; it didn't suit me anymore. It probably never had.

"I kept the lace from the sleeves. I suppose we could make you a handkerchief or two out of them, with some of the cloth that's left," she offered, her eyes on the bandage she was tying on.

I shook my head.

She glanced up and nodded. "There, you see, Jack," she said. "She didn't mind."

I certainly didn't mind. I only wished I had been able to cut it to pieces myself.

TWENTY-FIVE

I didn't want to get better. I wanted to curl up in that bed and never get out. But my body betrayed me again.

I slept for most of that day, but by evening I felt a little better in spite of myself. While the old woman and the boy ate their porridge at the table, I ate a little sitting up in bed. After the meal was over, the old woman settled herself by the fire with a basket of apples and a knife. Her rough hands deftly cored the apples and sliced them into pieces.

Jack sat at her feet. "Let me do it, Mother," he begged, sitting up on his knees and reaching for the knife. "Please."

"Not yet, Rabbit. You might hurt yourself." Her hand came down to move his away. "You're too little for a sharp knife like this."

Frowning at the injustice, the boy looked over at me, then back at the old lady. "Is she big enough? Would she cut herself?"

She stopped her work and glanced at me. Her knife glinted in the firelight. "Rabbit, anyone could hurt themselves with a knife like this, if they weren't careful."

My face was burning. Something thick was crawling up my throat. How long ago had it been, a week? Ten days ago? How I would have loved to get my hands on a little knife like that. It would have been just what I needed.

But now, away from the palace, I couldn't stop hearing my stepmother. *Make it fit,* she had hissed as she handed my stepsister the knife. *What's a little pain when you can catch a prince?* Her voice in my ear was relentless.

The ugly blackness roiled in my stomach like poison, and my mouth filled with saliva as more and more words echoed in my head.

What are you doing?
Making them fit.

Something was wrong with me. I had pushed it down. I had held it in. I had kept it to myself. But now it filled me up; now it would not be restrained. My body took control and vomited my porridge onto the cottage floor.

In an instant, the old lady was at my side with an empty bowl to catch the rest. "Let it out, love." Her voice was gentle. So was her hand as it smoothed the hair from my face. "Let it all out," she said. "You'll feel better."

When the floor was clean and she'd brought me a wet cloth for my face, the old lady gave Jack a needle and set him to work threading the apple slices on a long strand of thread. I watched him work, my thumb worrying a ring that wasn't there.

But the old lady didn't settle back to her apples; instead, she went to the rafters and brought down a bundle of herbs. She fingered it a moment, testing its dryness. Then she picked up a bowl and brought it over to the bed.

Her eyes were kind, but her penetrating gaze unsettled me. She looked like she knew me, knew all about me, even though I was a stranger. That didn't stop me feeling I should explain myself somehow, tell her why the sight of her knife made me fall to pieces. But she didn't seem to want any explanation. She only said, "Would you like to help?"

I nodded. It was the least I could do.

She handed over the herbs and the bowl. "Just pluck the leaves, and put them in here." Then she laid a hand on my arm. "It's good to have some work to do."

I nodded again, to show I understood. And as she turned back to the hearth, I caught her arm. I should thank her for taking in a stranger; I should explain who I was or why I had ended up at her door with a foot full of glass. I had no words for any of that, but at last I found one: "Mother."

My voice was harsh from lack of use. It was almost a question.

She seemed unsurprised that I had spoken at last. "Most everyone calls me that." She glanced at Jack, as if she knew why I asked, for surely she was too old to be his mother. "I am not his kin, but I am all he has." She brushed her hands on her apron as she returned to her chair. "You and I will have to do, won't we, my sparrow?" I opened my mouth, but I couldn't think what to say. She didn't seem to expect a response, though. "Just the leaves, mind. Not the flowers."

"It's good for wounds of all sorts," she continued as she sat back in her chair with a new apple. "It stops the bleeding, inside and out. It's good for headaches, too, and sore throats. Sickle-wort is good too, but this serves just as well, so I always gather some when I find it." My fingers slowed as her voice washed over me, describing this plant or that, and the good they could do.

"Tell about the sparrow."

I awoke later to the sound of rain on the roof. Inside, the room was dark, except for the light of the dying fire. The bowl and herbs had been removed from my lap and my blanket pulled up around me. I shifted from my half-sitting position and curled up in the bed.

"Well, Rabbit, we found her outside. Back in the spring, wasn't it?" Across from me, I could see the old lady in her rocking chair at the fireside. Jack was in her lap, a fur cloak or blanket spread over him. She spoke with her eyes closed, and the chair rocked gently back and forth. Between the chair and the hearth hung Jack's strings of apple slices, set there to dry.

"After a while, when we didn't see her mother come to feed her, and it was getting late, we brought her inside so the foxes didn't get her. We made her a nest of rags, and you fed her crumbs of bread. In time, she began to fly around inside, and one day, when she was ready, she flew out the door. We were sad. But she left you something, didn't she?"

"A feather," the boy whispered.

"A lovely, brown tail feather. And you put it with your precious things, didn't you?"

Jack jumped from her lap, ran to one corner of the cottage, and knelt there for a moment, his back to the room. In a moment he returned and crawled back under the furs.

"And there it is," the old lady said. "What a lovely feather. I know you wish she could have stayed."

You and I will have to do. That's what she had said. As if she expected me to stay. It seemed like a very long time since I had felt wanted somewhere. And I had done nothing to deserve it. I had eaten her food, slept in her bed, and caused a lot of worry. It wasn't much to recommend me.

I couldn't think of what I had done or what I had left behind; I could not go back. And what was next, I couldn't imagine. I lay there, warm in the bed, watching the woman and the boy, lit by the fire. Outside, the wind howled angrily around the little cottage. I pulled the blanket tighter around me. I couldn't say how, or why, but this little family kept out the storm and the wood, with its malevolent trees and their hissing words.

It was enough.

TWENTY-SIX

I called the old woman Mother from then on. And she called me Sparrow.

Little by little, my voice returned. But she never asked my real name, and I didn't volunteer it. It was better to be a little bird, dust-colored and inconspicuous, than anyone I had been before.

Mother never asked me where I came from either, or what brought me to her door. Whether she thought I would tell her when I was ready, or she somehow knew without being told, I didn't know. But I was grateful.

The morning after the storm, Mother tended my feet as she had the day before. Looking down into her little pot of salve, she frowned. "Be needing more of this," she murmured to herself. When she was finished, she gave me more dried herbs to pluck and sort. As I put leaves in one bowl and flowers in another, she began making more of the ointment. She opened an old leather-bound book on the table and took various jars and bottles down from her shelf, naming each one.

"Comfrey." One by one, she set the jars on the table. "Self-heal. Moneywort." She added a bottle. "True-love. Wintergreen." Her hand stopped as it ran along the shelf. "Rabbit, can you find me some wintergreen? Remember we saw some by the stream?" Jack nodded and disappeared out the door.

I watched as she crushed dried leaves and mixed the powders together, sometimes murmuring directions, other times making comments. "We don't really need it," she said when Jack returned with the wintergreen, "but it makes the salve cooling on the skin." She chopped the leaves and added them to her mixture. "When the fat has turned to liquid, add the rest, then let it cool." Her voice was low, but I heard her plainly. I would have thought she was reading out the recipe from her book, but she never once looked at it.

Jack did, though. He sat on a stool beside the table, one finger running over the page almost reverently. He kept glancing up at Mother as he did it. She was occupied with putting the jars back on the shelf and wiping the rim of the new pot of ointment, but she seemed to know what he was doing.

"Little rabbits must know their letters, did you know that?" He pulled his hand away, afraid he'd done something wrong. "Not furry rabbits," she went on seriously, "but little rabbits who live in houses must. Would you like to know how to read, Rabbit?" He nodded, eyes wide. She studied him a moment. "Perhaps Sparrow could teach you. Can you read, Sparrow?"

I nodded.

Mother looked unsurprised that a girl who had turned up on her doorstep, half-starved and sick and wordless, would know how to read. She only nodded and handed me her book. "There you are, Rabbit." She collected my bowls of herbs. "Sparrow can teach you some letters. It's high time I went to the village." She put the leaves and flowers in separate bottles, finding them a place on the shelf when she finished. "It's not far from here. Only at the edge of the woods."

A village on the edge of the woods. What would have happened if I had ended up there, instead of collapsing at Mother's door? Who would have found me then? A shiver ran up my arms.

On her way to the door, Mother set a stool next to the bed. "Hop up, Rabbit." She patted the seat. "I'll be back tonight." She took a furred cloak from a hook beside the door and tied the strings around her neck. Then she picked up a bag and disappeared out the door.

Jack watched out the window as Mother walked into the trees, and I looked through the book. It was a recipe book of sorts. The recipes were not for cakes or breads or stews, but for syrups and poultices, decoctions and infusions. The pages were made of different kinds of paper, added at different times, with the handwriting changing from page to page. Some pages were made up of drawings of plants with descriptions or instructions scrawled in the margins. This book was the work of many years, and many authors.

When Jack sat up next to me on the stool, he was so quiet and sat so still, I didn't notice. But then there he was, his little hands clutching each other impatiently.

I took an unsteady breath. What if I couldn't speak to him? My voice had worked the night before, but could I trust it to obey me now? I cleared my throat. "A."

That was a beginning. "Let's find a good A." I paged through the book until I found an entry for a burn salve made with adder's tongue. "Here's one," I said, tracing the letter with my finger. "A is for," I glanced around the room for an example, "ashes." Jack followed my gaze to the hearth. Then he quickly slipped down and ran to his strings of fruit drying over the fire, glancing back for my approval. "Apples?" He nodded, and I flinched, remembering how I had asked for apples, that last day at the palace. *Apples, of all things.* And the prince peeling an apple into a long, curly ribbon.

Jack's eyebrows had a worried crease between them as he returned to his seat. I tried to smile, but my lips felt broken. "Very good. Apples too."

I looked back down at the book and searched for a B. "There." At the bottom of one page was a picture of a plant labeled *Bittersweet*. "B is for," I looked around the room again, "broom."

Funny how these words, these ordinary, everyday words, caught in my throat. They had been hateful to me once, when cooking and cleaning made up the days and nights in my father's house. After I was married, I thought I'd never need to say them again. I thought I'd never want to.

People who live in palaces say words like *jewels* and *wine* and *carriage*. They say, *I'll take tea in the rose garden*, and *Fetch me my gown with the gold embroidery*. They never say, *Today is baking day*, or *I'm going to get more kindling*.

I don't know when it happened, when I came to miss those words. But sitting there in Mother's cottage, I realized I had been choking them down for so long. *Wool. Pot. Spinning wheel.* Even thinking them was an act of rebellion.

Jack scratched the mattress at my side with one finger. "Bed?" He nodded. "Yes, B is for bed."

Then he jumped down and returned with a little pot. His lips formed the sound "B?" as he held it out.

I opened it and looked inside. "No, honey starts with H," I said, as he dipped his finger in the jar, then stuck it in his mouth. He frowned at my slowness and tapped at the design of a honeybee on the side of the pot. This time it was weak, but I did manage a smile. "But honey is *made* by bees. You're right."

"Next is C." The remedies in this book were mostly unfamiliar. Meadowsweet for a sour stomach. Infusion of feverfew for an aching head. For a moment I forgot what I was looking for; I even forgot the boy beside me. Hawthorn seeds in wine for pain. A poultice of butcher's broom to knit a broken bone.

When Jack spoke, his voice was so soft I almost thought I had imagined it. "I think you are a princess."

I sat motionless, not wanting to break whatever spell had given him the courage to speak to me. He stayed still as well, kneeling on the stool, his mouth close to my ear. I turned a page in the book. *Boiled rue for colic.* I spoke softly. "You think I'm…"

"A princess," came the whisper again, a little stronger this time.

I turned the next page. *Syrup of nettle for coughs.* "Why do you think that?" The familiar tightness was returning to my throat.

"I know it." He was growing confident now. I turned another page. *Powdered motherwort for the pain of childbirth.* "You had a beautiful dress."

I stopped turning pages. "It was ripped and dirty."

"You had jewels in your feet."

I looked at him out of the corner of my eye. "Do you know any princesses who go wandering through the wood with no shoes in nothing but a nightgown?"

"Well..." He seemed unsure how to answer, as if my question confused him. "You're the only one I know."

I turned toward him, just a little, and held out my left thumb. "Would you like to know how I got this scar?" He nodded. "I was baking bread, and I burned myself on the inside of the oven. Do you think princesses know how to bake?"

He was silent, his brow furrowed.

"I can churn butter too," I continued, and the tightness began to ease. "And milk a cow and spin and knit." I turned my face toward him a little more, looking down so as not to frighten him. "Do you see the freckles on my cheeks?" They had faded in those months at the palace, but they never completely disappeared. Jack nodded. "Princesses keep their skin pale by staying out of the sun." I chanced a look at his face. "Who would want me as a princess?"

"You are," he insisted, his voice still soft. He put a hand to my cheek, wiping away a tear I didn't even know was there. "Maybe you are a sparrow princess. The sparrows will come for you one day. You'll see." He warmed to his story. "They will give you a cloak all made of feathers, and a crown of berries."

"What will my gown be made of?" I asked.

"Leaves," he answered. "Green leaves."

TWENTY-SEVEN

We did a few more letters then: J for Jack, M for Mother, S for Sparrow, and, at Jack's insistence, P for Princess. After that, he brought me a dish of porridge from the pot by the fire, and we ate, me in the bed, he close by on the stool.

I must have slept, for the next thing I remember it was late afternoon. Jack sat by the hearth holding something in each hand. "Don't be sad, Princess," he said softly. "Don't be sad."

What could I say? That I was not sad, that I was not a princess? I didn't want to lie. But what was the truth of me? I couldn't tell.

Jack answered himself though. "But I am sad," he said, in a bit of a different voice. Then, in the first voice, "Don't worry, Princess. We'll take care of you."

I sat up, careful not to interrupt. Now I could see what he held in his hand: two little straw dolls, tied up with bits of rags for clothes. He carried on their conversation intently for a few minutes, with the sad princess lamenting and the other comforting her.

At last, Jack stood and went to the window. The sun was low now. He stood on his toes, hands on the sill, and peered out, repeating, "Don't worry, don't worry," under his breath.

"Do you see her?" I asked after he had looked for a minute or two.

He turned to me and shook his head. "Don't worry."

"I won't," I replied. "She said she would be back tonight. It isn't night yet."

He nodded and went back to the hearth, where the dolls continued their conversation. "Mother, Mother," said one doll, the princess, I thought. "Where is Mother?"

"Don't worry," said the other. "She'll be back tonight. Don't worry."

"But where is she?"

"Don't worry. She's in the village. She will come back to us. Don't worry." I supposed Mother had never left him this long before. His body was tense, and his play was almost fevered.

"Would you like to hear a story?"

When I was Jack's age, I had been enthralled by my mother's stories. After she died, I missed them so much I began to whisper them to myself. There was the story about the man who wanders the world for seven years wearing the skin of a bear, and the girl who wears out three pairs of iron shoes in the search of her husband, and the lovers who meet again after being separated by a water nixie. It wasn't so long ago that I had told my husband those stories. It felt long, though.

Jack turned to me cautiously. "What story?"

"About a little boy." I knew plenty of those as well.

"A lady," he said, putting down his dolls.

My throat tightened as the whispers sounded in my ears. *You are a lady, are you not?* "A lady, then."

"A princess!"

A princess cannot disappoint, you know.

Jack ran to the bed and jumped up and down, clapping his hands. "A sparrow princess!"

I tried to silence the voices in my head. "I don't think I know one like that."

He shrugged. "Make one up."

"A sparrow princess." My mother often made up her own stories, but I only knew how to repeat ones I'd heard before. "I'll try."

He nodded, confident in me. "You can do it."

"Very well then." I made room for Jack beside me on the bed, but he stayed standing, shifting from one foot to another in anticipation.

I licked my lips, and I began. "Once upon a time, there was a sparrow who fell in love with a human prince." My throat was suddenly dry. I didn't know how to do this. "She begged a wise owl to transform her into a girl. The owl warned her that wishes are dangerous, but the sparrow wouldn't change her mind." Somehow words kept coming out of my mouth, whether I wanted them to or not. "She became a human, and married the prince. They were happy together, but the queen, the prince's mother, hated the sparrow princess. She could tell she was only pretending to be a girl."

"I don't know this one." Jack had crawled up on the stool and was staring up at me, eager to hear what happened next. I wasn't sure myself, but this story had a mind of its own.

"One day, the prince went on a journey, and the queen imprisoned the sparrow princess in the highest room of the tallest tower and sentenced her to death at the next sunrise." Beside me, I heard Jack's intake of breath and felt his hand beside mine on the bed, clutching a fistful of the quilt. "The sparrow princess went to the window and called for the owl to help her. The owl could not undo the magic, but she pitied the girl and called all the birds in the kingdom to help. In they all came through the window: Sparrows and robins and wrens. Rooks, ravens, and magpies. Thrushes and mockingbirds and blackbirds."

The story poured out of me as if a dam had broken. "Each bird gave the sparrow princess one of its feathers before it flew away. By sunset, the tower room was filled with feathers from larks, nightingales, and doves, falcons and eagles and hawks. The last bird to leave was the owl, who gave her two more gifts: a needle and a spool of thread. The sparrow princess worked all the night through with her needle and thread, and by sunrise she had sewn herself a pair of wings. As the palace guards threw open the door, she leapt from the window and flew away."

Jack's hands covered his mouth, as if he didn't want to interrupt me in his excitement.

"She flew all day, and by night she was over a dark forest. But before she could find shelter, a great storm blew in. The princess couldn't see. She flew into a tree, and one of her wings broke. She fell to the forest floor and couldn't fly anymore. She was sick and cold and wet and hungry. She would have died if someone didn't help her."

I turned to Jack. "Do you know who helped her?" He shook his head, eyes wide. "A rabbit." His eyes grew wider still. "He was a little rabbit, but very strong and very brave. He carried the princess on his back to his little cottage, where he lived with his—" I stopped, thinking.

"Mother hen!" Jack burst out.

I laughed. It was an unfamiliar feeling. "Where he lived with his mother hen. The rabbit and the hen had never seen such a strange creature. They called her All-Kinds-of-Feathers, but they meant it kindly. They took such good care of her that she was soon better. Her wings didn't work anymore, but they were warm, and the queen's soldiers would never recognize her while she wore them. So she kept them and wore them like a cloak."

"Then the prince came looking for her," Jack went on, taking up the story. "He told the queen he'd love her even if she was a sparrow."

I hadn't bargained on this. I wrapped my arms around myself, suddenly frightened at what might happen next. But I opened my mouth and the story continued on. "He came into the mother hen's cottage, and All-Kinds-of-Feathers made him some bread soup. He said it was delicious and tasted just like the soup his wife made."

I wasn't sure I wanted to go on. But I had begun this story, so I must finish it. "But he didn't recognize her in her feathered cloak, and she was too afraid to show herself. So the prince went away again. And she asked the rabbit and his mother hen if she could stay with them a while." I paused. "What do you think they said?"

"Was she sure?" he asked with a bit of a frown, as if he liked his contribution better.

I nodded, uncertain if my voice would hold.

"They said she could, if she wanted to."

I took a shaky breath. "She did want to, so she stayed. And they lived happily ever after."

He looked at me intently, his head on one side. "Is your name really Sparrow?"

"It is now." I hadn't noticed when he had moved onto the bed to sit beside me.

He nodded. "You can stay with us."

TWENTY-EIGHT

*M*other was back before the sun set. As soon as she was through the door, Jack clung fiercely to her legs and wouldn't let go. "Easy now, love." She settled herself at the table and drew him onto her lap. "Let's see what I've got." From her bag she unpacked a bottle of wine, a loaf of bread, a string of sausages, and a sweet pastry for Jack.

"Now, that one's not for you, Rabbit," she told him as he drew a length of brown cloth from the bag. "It's for Sparrow. We can't have her wearing nothing but a shift when she's up and about, can we?" Her gaze dropped to his breeches, which sat well above his knees. "But maybe we'll have enough for a new pair of breeches. We'll see."

"And," she looked back at me and gestured to the knit shawl I wore around my shoulders, "winter is coming." The shawl had been one of hers, like everything else I had now. "That's good enough for inside. But you'll need a cloak as well." She drew another length of cloth from the bottom of her bag. This was a heavy wool, a darker brown than the first. "I know red cloaks are all the fashion for young ladies, but I'm afraid this will have to do."

She was right about girls and red cloaks. My stepsisters had wheedled and begged until my stepmother sent for enough red wool to make one for each of them. I hadn't even asked if there would be enough left over for me. Of course there was not. At the palace, though, Opal, Ruby, and Pearl would have scoffed at plain red wool. Only silk or satin cloaks were good enough, trimmed in sable or ermine with a muff to match.

"Thank you." I took the thick cloth between my fingers. "It will be just as warm."

Jack was tugging on Mother's sleeve. "Make her one like yours."

"I can't do that, Rabbit." She smiled down at him. "Sparrow is not me. She must make her own cloak. And it will do what she needs it to."

I began with the gown. Mother cut it out, and when I wasn't helping Jack with his letters, I began stitching the seams. The cloth was rough and homespun, but it would be warm. As there was little else I could do from the bed, it was soon finished. When the time came to hem the skirt, my feet were healed enough so I could stand while Mother knelt at my feet and pinned up the cloth.

"I suppose we'll need to find you some shoes."

My stomach lurched at her words. Suddenly lightheaded, I reached out for something to steady myself. I caught at Mother's shoulder, and her hand came up, holding me fast. "What's wrong, girl? Feet hurting you?"

I shook my head. "I'm all right."

She waved me back to the bed. "That was the last one; you can sit down now." She helped me take the skirt off and handed me the needle and thread. As I started stitching, she returned to the subject of shoes. "The baker's youngest girl is about your size, perhaps she's got a pair she's outgrown."

How could I tell her? About the slick sense of fear that crept over my skin at the thought of a shoe touching my foot. Any shoe, even the baker's youngest daughter's. "Never mind," I told her. "I—my feet aren't cold."

It was a silly excuse, but Mother simply nodded and held up the remaining cloth. "Come here, Rabbit. Looks like you'll get your breeches after all."

❧

I was glad of the bandages. When I moved from the bed to a seat by the fire, I preferred to see the strips of cloth tied around my feet, not the ragged mess I knew lay underneath.

I was stitching Jack's new breeches one afternoon when we heard a knock. I must have jumped, for Mother stopped beside my chair and laid a hand on my arm. She gave it a squeeze, then she walked to the door.

I don't know who I expected. The man standing at the door in the failing light was no one I knew, of course. He was a traveler, he said, who had lost his way in the forest. "Couldn't point me to the next village, could you, good mother?"

Mother peered outside, then looked the man over. "You'd better stay with us tonight. It's nearly dark and looks like snow. I'll set you on the path in the morning."

"Much obliged to you, ma'am." He removed his hat with a flourish as he stepped inside. "I'm not completely empty handed, though." He pulled two birds out of a sack on his back and handed them to Mother. "At least I've something to offer. Caught them earlier. No good being lost and hungry both, is it?"

He leaned his walking stick in a corner and set down his packs and bags. From all he was carrying, I guessed he was a tinker or a merchant dealing in small goods. Or perhaps he was a little of both.

"Your servant, young lady." He nodded to me as he made his way to the hearth. Warming his hands, he looked around the room, taking it all in. When his gaze fell on Jack, who watched him from behind my chair, he leaned down, hands on his knees. "And are you the master of the house?" When Jack said nothing, the stranger turned to me with a wink. "Well, sir, I thank you for your hospitality."

As Mother settled down beside me with the birds and a cloth sack, the stranger began to tell us how he'd lost himself in the forest. I laid down my sewing, and Mother handed me a bird, setting the bag between us. I stroked the feathers the wrong way, so they stood up a bit, and began to pluck them. Funny how these things came back, as if I'd never been away. I fell into the rhythm of the work, listening to the conversation around me.

The stranger was just what I had thought him: an odd job man, a peddler, even a storyteller, and he entertained us with stories as we cleaned the birds and waited for them to cook. He told tales he'd picked up on his travels: about the man who cheated death, the girl without hands, the boy who couldn't feel fear.

As I put away the supper dishes, the stranger moved his chair back to the fire, got a pipe out of his coat pocket, and filled it. Then he sighed and stretched his booted feet toward the flames. "Many thanks, good mother," he said. "I've not eaten a better meal, even at the palace."

I sat back on my stool, my legs suddenly weak.

"You've been to the palace, have you?" Mother asked him. Her voice was hollow in my ears.

He took a pull at his pipe. "I always save the best stories for last," he said, waiting for his audience to gather around him. Mother took her usual seat in the rocking chair with Jack at her feet. Jack arranged his straw dolls carefully in his lap, his eyes wide. His princess doll was newly dressed in a lace gown I had made with a scrap of my old nightgown.

"I suppose you'll have heard all about the prince's new bride," he said, lazily blowing a smoke ring into the room. They were waiting for me. I walked to the hearth to retrieve my sewing, moving as quickly as my healing skin would allow. The sound of my bandages scraping across the floor grated in my ears. When I had my sewing, I sank to the floor beside Jack and tucked my feet under my skirts. It was not my usual place, but it couldn't be helped. My feet would carry me no further.

I didn't want to hear this story. I didn't want to hear about the poor, motherless girl who planted a hazel twig on her mother's grave and watered it with her tears. I didn't want to hear about the glittering gowns she wore, the prince's tireless search for her, or the brutal blinding of the deceitful stepsisters. I didn't want to hear about the sparkling glass slippers.

But he told it all. All except for that last wish, of course.

I bent my head over my work and tried not to hear. Stitch, stitch, stitch, went my needle. I heard him anyway. It didn't sound like my story, I thought. This kind, lucky girl, beautiful in all the right ways and everything everyone wanted, was not me. She didn't have to wish for the prince to fall in love with her. He saw her for who she was, and she saw him. They loved each other instantly.

This stranger was a skilled storyteller, but he didn't know the truth.

I drew my shawl around my shoulders, feeling cold, even so close to the fire. I had an uneasy dread that the stranger would continue his story past its end, to reveal how the girl was not the true bride after all. How she was found out, dragged back to the palace, and punished for her presumption. I forced myself to sew some more. Stitch, stitch, stitch. But how can he continue, I wondered. It was my story, after all, and even I didn't know how it ended.

At last, with the traditional, "And if they have not died, then they are there still," the stranger was silent. He took a long pull on his pipe, and it was over.

Happy ever after.

Jack tugged at my sleeve. "Has he seen her?" His whisper was so low I could hardly hear it. My throat tightened as I drew breath to speak. Jack tugged at me again, insistent.

I told myself I didn't know this man, so I had nothing to fear from him. "Did you ever see this princess, sir?"

Knowing the question came from Jack, the stranger addressed him as I went back to my sewing. "See her? Oh, yes, sir."

My needle froze, mid-stitch.

"Told you I'd been to the palace, didn't I? I pass through there a few times a year. If I've something to sell, or they have some pots need mending. If nothing else, I can tell a story or two to entertain the great folks. They don't let me mix with them of course, but I can go into the grand ballroom and spin a yarn for their amusement." He spread his hands with a smile. "It's a novelty, you see, for them to lay eyes on a simple fellow like myself."

I remembered him now.

"I've seen this princess, and a beautiful thing she is, too. Lovely gown she had on, a pale blue it was, with jewels around her neck, even in her hair." I remembered that gown; it was the blue taffeta. "But her clothes and jewels were nothing compared to her. A picture she was, sir, a picture. Eyes green as leaves and hair the color of honey. Unusual color, I grant you. About the same color as your young lady's there, though. Fancy that!" I was too exposed sitting there at Mother's hearth. If only I had a hooded cloak covered in feathers to pull around me. But wishing did no good. I bent my head back over my sewing so the telltale hair fell around my face and hid it from view before he could think of any more similarities.

I remembered all of it now. That night at the palace, his stories were different ones, tales more suitable for his elegant audience. He told a story of a prince seeking his lost wife, and one about the frog king's faithful servant, who had three iron bands bound around his grieving heart to keep it from bursting. Then he told another about a princess who must watch the geese while her maid usurps her place. That tale he dedicated to me with a courtly bow. When the princess married her prince at the end of the tale, the storyteller bowed to me again with a wish that *our princess* would have all of the happiness and none of the woes of the goose girl.

Everyone in the great hall looked at me. By this time, I had been at the palace long enough to know that anything I was naturally inclined to do was wrong. In my father's house, I would have asked him into the kitchen to share my meal. I would have told him a story in return. I couldn't do those things here, of course. What could I say that wouldn't sound awkward? Surely nothing, so I gave him a small smile and stayed silent.

Easy and graceful as always, my husband came to my aid. He beckoned the storyteller forward, tossed him a ring from his finger, and drank his health.

I was the one who should have done those things.

Now, in Mother's cottage, the stranger seemed to be thinking of that same moment. "Funny, lost-looking little thing, she was," he mused, his voice no longer the mysterious storyteller.

Then he roused himself. "But you'll have heard all about how she came to marry the prince." He spoke slyly, his storyteller voice returning. Jack nodded, and the stranger blew another smoke ring. "That is only the beginning of the tale. I was just at the palace, not a week ago." There was silence as he waited, drawing out his audience's curiosity.

Jack tugged at my sleeve again. I looked down to see him pointing at my hand. "I've just pricked it with my needle," I whispered, looking at the drop of blood on my thumb. "It's nothing." I took a handkerchief from my pocket and held it to my thumb as the stranger went on.

"The palace is in an uproar." He paused for effect. "For our princess has vanished." Beside me, I heard Jack's intake of breath. The stranger heard it too. "Where has she gone, sir?" He leaned toward Jack, his eyes wide. "No one knows. She disappeared on the night of a terrible storm, and hasn't been heard of since."

"Was she abducted? Has she run away? No one knows. But the king and queen have sent out their hunters and trackers in all directions, searching for any sign of her. They have sent soldiers and diplomats far and wide to enquire after her. But they have heard nothing. The whole palace is transported with worry. Their majesties fear for her safety. All are desperate for news of her, and yet they learn nothing."

Jack, who had heard tales of giants and witches without flinching, climbed into Mother's lap and whispered in her ear.

She shook her head. "People can't fly, love."

The stranger cocked an eyebrow. "Did she fly away, sir? Likely as anything else, I say. Some say perhaps she has been captured by enemy soldiers and held for ransom. But no demand has been sent. The king and queen would pay any price, it is said, to have her returned."

Surely this was the end of his story, for what else was there to tell? "However," his voice came again, softer than ever, "there are those who tell a different story. Some of the palace servants whisper that their majesties only make a show of wanting her returned, that they wish she would stay lost."

Through my curtain of hair I could see Jack, intently whispering in Mother's ear. "Don't worry, Rabbit." She rubbed his back with one calloused hand. "She'll turn up when she's good and ready."

"But perhaps she does not want to be found, good lady," the storyteller continued. "They say the fine folk of the palace tried everything they could think of to make her into a proper princess—according to *their* standards, of course. Some say even the poor girl's maid was charged with bringing her up to snuff, and they sacked her when she couldn't do it." His voice was barely a whisper now. "But others say the maid wasn't sacked at all, that she'd had enough of their majesties' unkindness to her mistress, and that she refused to work for them anymore."

Don't faint, my maid had said. My vision blurred with sudden tears. *And don't let them see you cry.* And still I hadn't believed she was on my side. Who else did I not trust that should I have?

"And what about the prince?" The words hung in the air for a moment before I realized I was the one who had said them.

The stranger chuckled. "Ah, the young ladies always want to know about the prince. Well, young lady," he inclined his head to me, "I'd like to be able to tell you how the prince is pining away, how the poor lovesick fellow is pale and grief-stricken. I'd like to tell you how he haunts the castle walls, day and night, waiting for news of his beloved, vowing that he will not eat or sleep until he gets her back." He paused, and the smell of his pipe smoke floated around me. "But I can't tell you any of those things."

"I suppose he agrees with his parents," I replied, "and thinks he is better off without her. Maybe he thought he loved her at first, but he sees it wasn't true love after all. And now he regrets marrying her."

Why could I not be silent? "She's awkward." My words kept coming out and out and would not stop. "And too much trouble. She isn't any more fit to be a princess than her stepsisters. Perhaps it will be embarrassing for him, but he doesn't miss her."

I had said too much, but my words had a will of their own. "He must make a show of looking for her, but he'll be just as happy if he never finds her."

When at last I stopped speaking, I heard nothing but the scraping sound of the stranger tamping down the tobacco in his pipe. Then he spoke again. "There are those who whisper that, young lady. But what the prince himself thinks, no one really knows. Because the prince is gone." He took another puff on his pipe as the rest of us sat in silence.

"Folks say the night the princess disappeared he went right out to search for her and didn't return for three days. When he finally did return, it was only to speak to his parents and pack some things. No one's seen him since. Some say he's wandering the country searching for her. They say he wears her wedding ring on a chain around his neck so it's always close to his heart."

I closed my right hand over my left, over the ring that wasn't there. Why would he do that? Hadn't the spell broken with the slippers?

"Some folk say he's off to find himself a new wife." The stranger shrugged one shoulder. "Throwing a ball—what kind of a way is that to find a wife, they say."

What kind of a way indeed? But surely it was no worse than being put under the power of a foolish wish made by a selfish girl. And what would the prince decide now that the magic was all over? I could not tell.

The stranger puffed on his pipe again. "And that, good folk," he spread his hands, "is my story from the palace. It's not the sort

I usually tell. Most people don't like a story without an ending. Just not satisfying, they say. But I like them, myself. Unfinished stories are the most exciting, don't you think, sir?" Jack must have shaken his head. "No? Well, like I said, most folks prefer an ending, and a happy one too, but it can't be helped. If I'm ever in these parts again I'll try to do better for you."

"Well, we're obliged to you for your stories sir, and your news." Mother's rocking chair scraped the floor as she nudged Jack off her lap and stood. "But now it's high time little rabbits were in bed. Why don't you sleep with us tonight, and our guest will have your bed."

I stood and led Jack to the bed I shared with Mother. "Tell me about All-Kinds-of-Feathers," he whispered as I pulled up the quilt.

My throat felt raw, as if I was the one who had been talking all night. Or as if I had been screaming. "I think we've had stories enough tonight." I couldn't face going back to the fire, so I climbed into the bed as well while Mother fixed Jack's pallet for the stranger to sleep on. Our guest didn't seem ready to sleep, though. He took out a little whistle and began to play.

I turned my face to the wall. I tried to shut the stranger out, but his music flowed around me, lonely and sweet. Jack shifted restlessly; perhaps the stories left him too excited to sleep. I lay beside him listening, sure I had heard the stranger play that tune before, and wishing he had never come to remind me of how little I was wanted.

When I woke up later, the cottage was dark. I felt the warmth of Mother's body at my back. Jack's hands were tangled in my hair, as if he had fallen asleep stroking it, and his face was pressed up next to mine. His cheek was wet. Or maybe mine was.

The cottage was quiet now, except for the sound of the stranger, snoring faintly beside the fire. I wiped my cheek dry and freed my hair from Jack's hands, careful not to wake him. I stared into the dark, thinking about the stranger and his story.

I had said too much. I never should have opened my mouth. But what was the point in wishing my words unsaid? I had said them, and he may have recognized me already. How well had he seen me, that night at the palace? It was dim here, even by the fire, but it would be bright enough in the morning.

And if he recognized me, what then? Would he make his way back to the palace and tell them where I was? Or would he go on his way and let me be? Beside me, Jack whimpered in his sleep. I turned back toward him and his hand fell on my cheek. He quieted down then, his fingers lightly patting me. "It's all right," he murmured as his hand moved back into my hair, "all right." I didn't know who he was comforting, but my eyes began to feel heavy.

The stranger must do what he would. I could not stop him.

Twenty-nine

*I*n the morning, the stranger said nothing to me, other than to thank me when I set a bowl of porridge in front of him. I was silent too. I left my hair unbound and kept my eyes on the floor. It was all I could do.

As he prepared to go, the stranger gave us each a gift. For our hospitality, he said. He had mended a pot handle for Mother; she would accept nothing else. And from one of his bags, he found a little wooden whistle and presented it solemnly to Jack. "Make a noise with that, sir, if you'll make no other." Jack took it, saying nothing. Then he ran through the door and galloped around outside, blowing it all the while. We followed him out into the weak sunlight. A little snow had fallen during the night, just enough to dust the ground.

The stranger reached into a pocket. "And for you, young lady." He spread several ribbons across his hand and invited me to take one. "Perhaps to trim a dress with, or for your hair." He pointed to one with intricate flowers woven through it. "The ladies of the palace were quite taken with this one."

Of course they were. I could see Opal scrutinizing the ribbons. He would have had to lay them out on a table, so she didn't have to risk touching his hand. She would have laid a slender finger on this ribbon or that, a slight frown on her face, before settling on the one she liked. She would have pointed at it, not even deigning to speak. Ruby and Pearl would have nodded that they would have that one too.

The stranger held the ribbons a bit closer. "I've only the one flowered ribbon left. It's yours if you'd like it." I hesitated. "Pretty face like yours," he went on, "you'd be just like one of those fine ladies."

"What do I know of being a fine lady?" It was true, after all.

His thumb inched the ribbon toward me, just a bit. "Well, you know what you like, don't you?"

It was a simple enough question. Still I was silent, looking at the ribbons spread over his hand. When I was back at the palace, I would have chosen that ribbon with the flowers, just because the others liked it. I wouldn't even have considered what I thought about it myself. I would have worn it, hoping it would have given me that *little something more* the ladies said I lacked. Until Opal smiled at me pityingly and said, *Really your highness, it came from a common tinker.*

"Yes," I heard myself say at last, as I pulled out a plain black ribbon from underneath the ornate ones. "I like this one." I straightened my shoulders, drew the ribbon under my hair, and tied it back from my face so I could meet his eyes. "Thank you for your present, and your stories."

The stranger inclined his head as he tucked his ribbons back away. "Not such a lost little thing after all, are you, young lady?" He watched me as if he had discovered some never-before-seen creature and didn't know what to make of it.

I kept my eyes on his. "My name is Sparrow." For the first time in such a long time, my voice was clear in my ears.

He leaned down and shouldered his packs. "A good name. May it bring you good fortune. Perhaps one day you will tell me a story, one with a proper end." And with that, he walked away, toward the path Mother had pointed out. Then he disappeared into the trees, leaving me wondering what a proper end could possibly be. I could not imagine one. I was hiding in the woods from a world that didn't want me back. And my husband—could I even call him that? The prince, then, was rubbing the fog of my wish from his eyes and setting off to search for a new wife.

I don't know how long I stood there in the doorway, staring into the wood. After a while, Mother draped a shawl around my shoulders and called Jack inside. Still I stood there in the snow, watching the trail of the stranger's footprints.

At last, I heard the creak of the door and the low tooting of a whistle, like the mournful coo of a dove. Jack took the new whistle out of his mouth. "Mother says you'll catch your death out here in your bare feet." His brows lifted anxiously.

"I'm not cold."

He tugged at my skirt, pulling me toward the door, "But you can't get better from your death," he insisted, his face suddenly blotchy as if he might cry. "You're just dead, and you won't come back."

What had happened to this boy, I wondered. I knelt down. "Did you know that birds have special feet?" He shook his head. "They can perch on frozen branches and not mind it at all. If they feel a little cold, they can hold one foot up and get it warm in their feathers. Then they switch feet and warm the other one."

He held up one foot. "Like this?" I nodded and held up one foot too. "Even sparrows?"

"Even sparrows." I held out my hand, and he took it. "Let's go in."

I closed the door and drew down the bolt, shutting out everyone and everything. Now the world was only Mother and Jack and me. I settled into the rocking chair, pulling the shawl a little tighter around my shoulders, for I did feel the cold now. A little.

I wondered what Mother would say to me, now that our visitor had gone. What would she say about his strange story, and the even stranger things I had said in reply? But she said nothing; she only continued taking bottles from the shelf and arranging them on the table.

When she spoke at last, it was only to say, "I'm glad you've come, Sparrow. I need you to read out this recipe for me. My eyes are not as strong as they were." She handed me her book, open to a page with directions for a cough remedy. "Let's make sure I've got all the ingredients."

Dog rose hips, cinquefoil root, juice of colt's foot, honey. Her fingers touched the bottles and jars as I said their names.

"And?" she'd say if I paused too long.

Wine, syrup of alehoof, dried horehound.

I liked the feel of these words on my tongue, even though I was fairly certain Mother didn't need me to say them aloud. She never seemed to read the book, although she always spread it out on the table when she was making something.

"Are you getting a cough?" I asked as she crushed the horehound leaves between her fingers and dropped them into the wine.

She shook her head. "This time of year, people from the village will be wanting it soon enough." She gestured to the book. "Go on." She reached for the honey jar.

I looked down and found my place. "Add honey."

After the remedy was finished and bottled, and all the ingredients put away, I put aside Mother's book and returned to my sewing. The breeches were almost finished. Jack sat at my feet as I worked, stacking the spools of thread from the sewing basket into towers, or making patterns with them on the floor. But when I tied the last knot, I looked up to find him gone. I heard his voice, though, as I gathered up the spools.

"Princess, Princess. Where are you?" He was in a corner, his back to the room, with his little straw dolls. One of them, at least. I couldn't see the princess doll. "Please come back, Princess. Where are you?" The voice of his imaginary prince sounded as if he were the one lost, and not the one who had lost someone. It was an empty sound; it curdled in my stomach.

"Look, Jack," I said, "your breeches are ready. Come put them on."

He came slowly, and when he reached me, he held out his doll. "He can't find her."

"The king's men are looking for her." I didn't want to say that, but whenever that worried expression came onto Jack's face, I found I said whatever I could to make it go away.

His face brightened a little. "Will we see them?"

I hadn't thought of that. It was bad enough to have one traveler coming through, one man who had seen me once before. But what of the castle guards, hunters, or servants, who would be more likely to recognize me? What if they came here? My skin felt hot and cold all at once.

"Oh, I doubt it, Rabbit." I felt Mother's hand on my shoulder. "We're not that easy to find here, all tucked away in the woods."

She knew about me; I was sure of it. Not everything, but she knew I was the runaway girl from the palace. And still she said nothing, she merely gave my shoulder a squeeze before taking the breeches out of my hand and holding them up. "Oh, what a fine little rabbit you'll be now," she told Jack. "Let's see them on you."

The night the stranger left, I sat up gasping into the dark. I was falling. I could not breathe. I was dying. "Sparrow," said a voice at my ear. "Sparrow, wake up." Someone was holding me. Someone was rocking me as if I were a little child. "You were dreaming."

The fire was dying in the hearth. Mother's arms were around me, and I could breathe again.

She stroked my hair. "Do you know where you are, love?"

I nodded as I sank back into sleep.

"I'm home."

THIRTY

There, there now.
You mustn't struggle.
Smile, my dear.

I knew I had been ill for a few days when Mother took me in. But once my feet were bandaged and I was out of bed, I couldn't stop feeling I was waking after a much longer illness, a fevered delirium that had lasted weeks, months, perhaps even years. I was no longer the girl who mindlessly ducked her stepmother's blows and slept in the cinders. I wasn't the girl who wished herself a love she hadn't earned. Or the girl who cut herself to fit a life she didn't deserve. Who I was now, though, I didn't know. Hopefully someone better.

Autumn was passing into winter. And Mother was right; the villagers soon came for her cough remedy, and other potions as well. First it was the weaver's wife, whose husband had a fever. Then the miller's daughter, wanting something for her mother's cold. Then the smith, whose baby was poorly.

"Another foundling, Mother?" asked the seamstress, whose middle daughter had a sore throat. *Probably nothing, but you can't be too careful,* she'd said. She had been watching me, sizing me up, though not unkindly.

Mother was at the table, mixing the syrup of hedge mustard and honey. She merely glanced over at me. "How about some tea, Sparrow?"

I hung the iron kettle over the fire and searched for something to brew. There was nothing here to make the sort of tea they would have served at the palace, of course, but plenty of the plants hanging from the rafters would do just as well. I reached above my head, crushing the dried herbs between my fingers and breathing in their scents. Mint, chamomile, lemon balm. I decided I liked the sharp, earthy smell of the sage. I picked off some leaves and crumbled them into our cups.

As the tea was brewing the seamstress tried to coax Jack onto her lap. "Oh, come now, ducky, my little ones are all too big to fit in my lap anymore." Jack shook his head, but he grinned and blew his whistle at her from across the table. She winked at him and sat back in her chair. "Well, maybe one day. I remember when you wouldn't even come out when I came to visit." She turned back to Mother. "You've done wonders with him. I don't know how you do it."

Mother gave a little shrug, a half-smile on her face. "I do what I can."

The seamstress turned to me, where I was stirring honey into her mug. "What she *can* is a good deal better than most."

I knew full well the wonders Mother could do, but I said nothing. I just nodded and handed her the tea. She glanced at the light coming in the window. "Thank you dear, but I really should be getting back." But she took a sip anyway. Then she wrapped her hands around the mug, breathing in the scent of the tea. "That's good." She looked up at Mother. "I think you ought to keep this one."

More villagers came, and I made more tea. In between times, I cut out the dark brown wool and made it into a long cloak with a deep hood. After that, I worked at teaching Jack his letters and helping Mother. At first, it was only plucking leaves or sorting seeds and petals. I avoided things like peeling and chopping. Just looking at Mother's knife made a sick, shameful heat creep over my skin.

I had to be busy, though; it kept me from thinking. I had my thick wool cloak for protection now; it hung on a peg beside Mother's patchwork fur one. But I still didn't want to think of the king's men, out there looking for me, or of how I might see them if I stepped outside. I didn't want to think at all.

They had looked for me before, of course, seeking the girl who fit the slipper. But it was different then. Every day my stepmother and stepsisters repeated the latest gossip about the prince, out hunting for his true bride. And I waited, on hands and knees, scrubbing the floors. I waited, face smudged with ash and skirts sodden with wash water. I waited as the king's men came closer, ever closer to my father's house.

My life was rushing toward me, about to begin. I couldn't stop it, and for the most part, I didn't want to. But still I waited, frozen. I didn't come forward to claim my life, this life I had set in motion with a thoughtless wish. I did nothing as it closed in around me, trapping me into what I wanted all along. What I thought I wanted. Only at the last minute, when my sisters' feet were in bloody ribbons, did I step out to meet this life and claim my place in the sparkling slippers.

Now, though the slippers were broken, I waited again. But for what, I didn't know. Not a beginning. The beginning of that life was over; so was the end. So why did I feel unfinished? And why was it so hard to hear Jack with his dolls, calling, as he did so often these days, "Princess, Princess, where are you?"

I knew the man I'd married was not really wandering the forest calling me in that plaintive, abandoned voice. *Please come home, Princess.* Some days I heard Jack's voice in my head long after he was silent. If I didn't shut it out, the prince's voice would mingle with it, repeating and repeating and repeating.

Why won't you let me help you?

How could you?

Tell me the truth.

Any distraction would do.

It was one of these times, when there were no seeds to pound or leaves to crush, that I reached across the table to where Mother was chopping roots. "Give me something to do," I said.

If she saw the way my hand shook as it closed around the handle of her knife, she didn't mention it. She simply pushed the uncut roots across the table. "Nice and fine now," was all she said.

Not right away, but in time, I cut and chopped and sliced with ease. I hardly thought at all about the harm I could do with a knife like that. The harm I had done.

I learned to make infusions and syrups, and Mother asked me to read out recipes almost all the time now. And even though her eyes were keen enough to thread the smallest needle, and she seemed to know all the recipes by heart, I did not mind. There was something calming about her book, its words, even the ink on the pages. When we were finished and had cleared away the bottles and jars, I would hold it in my lap, running my fingers over the words.

Make the flowers and leaves of lady's bedstraw into an oil by leaving them in the sun. Then mix with wax to form an ointment for burns. I sat there by the fire more and more, silently repeating the words to myself. *To ease labored breathing, take an infusion of rampion flowers.* They were a talisman almost. A defense against the whispers that returned and returned.

Seed of the peony, powdered and mixed with wine, eases bad dreams.

Juice of the meadow pimpernel, taken in red wine, will protect the heart.

THIRTY-ONE

It was after midwinter when they came. I was sitting by the fire with Jack, and we were practicing letters. Mother had no ink or paper to spare, so we wrote in some ashes I had scooped onto the hearth and let cool. "Very good," I said, after he had done each of our names. I wiped the letters away with one hand. "Now what would you like to write? Any word you want."

Jack was decided. "Princess."

I should have guessed. "Very well, then. What do you think is first?"

"P."

I nodded, and he grasped the twig he was using as a pen and began to scrape it through the ashes. "Good. Now R, then I."

When he got to the N, he stopped and looked up at me. "How does it go?"

I traced an N in the soot with my finger above the letters he had done. He studied it, then went on. We were working on the first S when the knock came at the door. Jack's S was on its side, more like a picture of a mountain than a letter. I smoothed the ash with my hand and made him an S to look at so he could try again.

I hardly noticed the knock. We had fairly regular visitors these days.

It was only when Jack stiffened beside me that I realized they must be strangers. There were two men at the door. I looked long enough to see that one was dressed in the uniform of the castle guard before I turned away. The king's men had come. There was coughing and stamping of feet in the doorway as they knocked the mud off their boots. Their voices came closer. Mother had invited them in.

I could not move. I had never asked her to hide me if the king's men came. I had been so sure she knew who I was, that she had guessed it all, and that she knew I didn't want to go back. But I had never told her that. And even if she knew, what could she do? Here they were. They were talking to her, and she was talking back. But I couldn't understand their words; my heartbeat was too loud in my ears.

"Sparrow." I did not answer Mother's call. The men stood between me and my new cloak; there was no way it could protect me now. I pulled my braid over my shoulder, my fingers starting to untie the ribbon. "Sparrow, is the soup ready? We have guests."

I stopped unraveling my braid and put the ribbon in my apron pocket. I could not hide behind my hair. It was too late, and Mother's cabin was too small. They had found me.

My body obeyed without my permission. I checked the pot over the fire, then went to the shelf for the bowls and spoons. Dishing out the soup, I willed my hand to stay steady. Only a few drops sizzled into the fire.

I must simply tell them, I thought as I walked across the floor. I must tell them I don't want to go back. Surely they wouldn't take me by force. But if they insisted, I must go willingly. I couldn't cause Mother and Jack any more trouble. They had done far too much for me already. The small space between the hearth and the table, only a few steps, seemed so long. I gripped the bowls tightly and watched the soup inside. Slosh, slosh.

"We're on our way back to the castle now." The man in the guard's uniform was speaking. "And we wouldn't trouble you, only the folk in the last village were saying you're good with potions and such, and he's got a nasty cough." He jerked his head toward the other man.

"My girl can fix you something for that, can't you, Sparrow?" Mother was saying as I reached the table with the bowls. I nodded as I stood next to the man in the guard's uniform. Any of the castle guards had surely seen me around the palace at some point. This man would know me. I slid the bowl of soup in front of him and waited.

"Thanks, love." He wrapped his hands around the bowl and turned to me. I straightened my spine, not daring to breathe out. His smile was apologetic, as if he knew I didn't want to be found. "Haven't got a spoon, have you?"

I froze for a moment, unable to make sense of his words, but part of me understood. My hand fumbled in my apron pocket for the spoons and held one out. He turned away without another word and started in on his soup.

The other man had his elbows on the table, his face in one hand. I put the second bowl in front of him. He looked down at my sooty hand and glanced up to thank me. But before he could, he turned away, coughing. I had seen his face, though, and I knew who he was—my husband's huntsman. He'd been with my husband on the day of the wolf hunt, the day I had so stupidly asked for a picnic. The day I had run away. If the guard didn't recognize me, the huntsman surely would. But he said nothing. He just coughed, a hoarse, hacking sound. It must have hurt.

His forehead was warm, but not hot. "No fever?" My voice wasn't falsely bright anymore as it had been that day in the stables. *Darling, couldn't this wait?* But I had the same feeling I had back then, of a hand around my throat.

He continued to cough, but shook his head. *A syrup of colt's foot leaves, mixed with powdered wild sunflower root, brings relief for a dry cough.* I turned back to the hearth to hang the kettle in the fire. The huntsman had his task to do, and I had mine, even if it was for the last time.

I brewed him a tea of licorice root, stirred in the mixture of colt's foot and wild sunflower, and sweetened it with honey. All the while, the guard talked. He was talking of their mission: the search for the princess. How they had been far and wide, from village to village, house to house, looking for some sign of her. Jack, once he learned that these were the king's men he had hoped to see, stood behind Mother's chair, clutching the back of it and hanging on the man's every word.

"She did this before, you know," the guard was saying as I brought the huntsman his tea. "Little minx leads the prince on a wild goose chase just to make him want her more." I sucked in a breath at a sudden burning on my hand. I had spilled the tea.

I set the mug down in front of the huntsman, wiping it with my apron. "Drink it down while it's hot." It was something a princess would never say. And though I had to force the words out, they were strong and clear.

"And he wanted her all right," the guard went on. "Had us searching every house, just like now, only with this little shoe. Ridiculous." He leaned back in his chair with a snort of a laugh. He watched me gather up the empty bowls and the spoons. "Thank you, love. Delicious. Did you make it?" I inclined my head toward Mother. He looked disappointed. "Well, very good soup."

He returned to his story, including the rest of us. "I was there when he found her, you know." He snorted again. "Sooty little scullery maid, is what she looked like to me. But she fit the shoe, so there you are. Cleaned up nice enough, I suppose," he finished with a knowing smirk.

I looked at the guard properly for the first time. He hadn't had a beard then, but I recognized him now. I could see him, standing clean-shaven in my father's kitchen. It was the day the prince and his men had come, and he came in to ask for a rag and a little water to wash my stepsister's blood out of the glass slipper. Both sisters had already tried it on and both had been caught in their deception. He spoke to me as one servant to another, in confidence. *What some people will do, just to get ahead—would you believe it?* He mimed slicing his foot with a knife.

Well, my girl, his highness says every girl must try it on. How about it? Wouldn't you like to meet the prince? Maybe it's your lucky day. It was all a bit of a joke to him. *No knives though, right?* He patted me down with his beefy hands, grinning as he checked my apron pockets. *If you don't fit, you don't fit.* I never told anyone the way his hands lingered on me before he gave me a mocking bow and gestured for me to walk before him into the next room.

Washing the soup bowls in Mother's cottage, I felt the guard's eyes on me again. He clearly didn't know me, but why should I be surprised? He had hardly believed it the first time; only the glass slipper had provided any proof. Now there was no slipper, there was no wish; it was all only shards of glass. I still had my feet, but they were as different from their former selves as those shards were from the shoe they had been.

The guard sighed. "And now she's at it again, and we're on another fool's errand. The prince can't wait to get his hands on her. He's got half the men in the palace out looking for her. But you mark my words, he'll give her a good hiding when he finds her this time."

The huntsman was shaking his head. He must have heard all this before. "He won't." His voice was raspy from coughing.

"He should." The guard leaned across the table, pointing one finger at the huntsman. "It's no way for a princess to act. No way for a wife to act. Do you know they found a knife in her dressing room? All wrapped up and hidden away under her dressing table."

What did he mean? I had used my husband's knife that night. I had abandoned it, along with everything else. I had not wrapped it up; I had not hidden it.

Then I remembered: the swirling night air, the sound of the banging window. The candle rolling under the dressing table. And underneath the table was the *something* I couldn't understand: a lumpy package with something sharp and shiny poking out from one end.

But I understood it now. It was the first meat knife I had stolen from dinner, wrapped in a pair of old stockings. The knife that had disappeared. The one I couldn't find when the slippers became too tight for the second time. I thought someone had found it and taken it back. But it had only fallen out of the back of the drawer like ordinary objects do.

"And what was she going to do with that?" the guard was saying. "Call her a princess if you like, but I wouldn't share my bed with a common little slut who would murder you in your sleep as soon as look at you. He's better off without her."

The huntsman shook his head again. "No. I was with him on the night she disappeared." He took a gulp of his tea. "I've never seen him like that. Not himself, you know?"

"And?"

The huntsman rubbed the stubble on his jaw. "He just said, 'She left. She's gone. We've got to find her.'"

"See, she did run off. I told you how it was." The guard crossed his arms over his burly chest. "You mean to tell me he wasn't angry?"

"Not until later. We were in this forest three days and didn't see a sign of her. We came back to the palace, and he saw the king and queen. Afterward he came out and told me to organize the search parties. He said we must find her, no matter what." He coughed, but only a little. "He was angry that time. He mounted his horse and left right then. Haven't seen him since."

I tried to imagine my husband's anger. Was he like a man waking up out of a magic fog? Like someone who sees he's been duped?

"Well, king and queen talked some sense into him, didn't they? Told him she wasn't acting like a proper wife, and he agreed. He'll take his belt to her now." The guard stretched his feet out in front of him, the matter settled in his mind.

The huntsman shrugged and drained his tea. Then he cleared his throat as I took the mug from him. "That's better already."

"So how about you, my man," I heard the guard saying as I washed the mug, "have you seen a lost princess anywhere around here?"

Jack was still behind Mother's chair, but he nodded, an eager expression on his face.

I stood still, the mug and dishrag hanging in my hands, and watched. Would they believe him? Would they believe it if a little boy told them what they were searching for was right in front of them? I doubted Jack would speak, but he could point his finger easily enough.

The guard's eyes opened wide in mock disbelief. "You have? Where is she then? Hiding in this forest somewhere?" He was enjoying his game, while I was on fire from the inside. "Or is she in the village?" I could not breathe. "Maybe she's in your little shed outside?"

Jack shook his head.

"Well, where then?"

Jack's eyes darted to mine, then Mother's, his confidence faltering. He looked back to the guard, and his hand moved. But he wasn't pointing at me; he was holding out his princess doll.

A little air came back into my lungs. The guard looked at it for a moment then roared with laughter. He put out a hand to ruffle Jack's hair. Jack was too fast though, and ducked back behind Mother's chair before the guard could touch him. "Well, little man," said the guard, when he had finished laughing, "You must tell her that the prince says to wait for him where she is, and he will find her. Will you do that?" Jack nodded.

I was safe.

THIRTY-TWO

*L*ater I sat by the hearth, Mother's book in my lap. I wasn't reading; I was hardly even thinking. I just stared at the fire. The king's men had come all the way to Mother's cottage to summon me back to the palace, and I had not gone.

Jack sat at my feet, whispering intently to his doll. "He will find you," he told her again and again. "Stay here." He looked up at me for the briefest of moments, then back down at his doll. "He will find you."

He will find me; that's what the guard had said. Why stay, though? Had the magic continued somehow, and the prince's love remained? But if he wanted me back, why wouldn't he have ordered whoever found me to bring me back to the castle? Was he clear-headed at last, now that the spell had broken? And if that was true, why bother looking for me at all?

My fingers shook as I ran them over the book's worn pages. What did it matter, anyway? These two men, who had known me at the palace, had come here. They saw me with no glass slippers to mark me but no cloak to hide me either. I spoke to them and served them food, and they left empty handed because they saw no princess. She must never have existed in the first place.

So I must forget.

If only I could stop remembering what it was like to be her, this princess who was so wrong. *Her highness is passionate about gardening.* If only I could silence the hissing in my head. *You're so pale and thin.*

And now these men had come, grudgingly searching for a prize no one wanted to win. *Sooty little scullery maid.*

I must forget her, and I would. I would banish her from my thoughts. I looked down at the book in my lap, my fingers tracing the drawings and words. *Goat's rue, wood sorrel, clary.* I tried to memorize each page, blotting out this hated girl with each new remedy. *To ease the pain of toothache, steep rest-harrow leaves in vinegar and wash out mouth. Lavender, to calm the passions of the heart.*

I jumped and nearly cried out when I felt a hand on my shoulder. But it was not the men, recognizing me at last. It was only Mother. "Easy, love." She pressed my shoulder firmly, waiting until my breathing slowed. She turned my hand over and laid three copper coins on my palm. "A good day's work, Sparrow." I looked up, puzzled. "For the medicine."

I had sent the huntsman off with a little bottle of the coltsfoot and wild sunflower mixed with honey; these coins were his payment.

I touched them with a finger. It wasn't unusual to be paid for our remedies; we often were. But the payments were different here: a few eggs or a sack of grain, a chicken or some sausages. Once, when Mother had nursed a child through a bad fever, his parents gave us a nanny goat. People gave what they could, and we always found a use for it.

But the cool metal coins felt unfamiliar on my skin. At the palace I had never needed money, though I could only imagine how much was spent on me. When I arrived there, a new wardrobe appeared almost magically: linens, gowns, jewels, and more. I never knew who decided what I would need, or how much it would cost to make me into the girl I was supposed to be. And before, in my father's house, I would sometimes pay the tradesmen who came by, bringing us something from the village. But it had never been my money; I hadn't earned it.

I had earned this money though, these three little coins.

"You keep them," I told Mother. "I have no use for them."

She let me put them back into her hand and took them to a jar on her shelf. "Perhaps we'll need them one day." She dropped them in and went back to the seeds she'd been pounding into powder before the men came.

But Jack couldn't be tempted to return to his writing lesson, and I couldn't settle to anything. I stayed in the chair, curled around Mother's book, whispering the words to myself, over and over, like a prayer. *Pluck dove's-foot early in the autumn. Crush the plant between fingers and lay upon the wound.*

The next morning as I was getting out of bed, Mother stopped me. "Let's have a look at those feet." She sat down beside me and unwound the bandages first on one foot, then the other. She hadn't put ointment on them in a few weeks, but still she checked them every so often. She turned my feet this way and that, her cool fingers running over the cuts. At last she gave my feet a little squeeze. "How do they feel?"

Her question surprised me. "They—" I had been trying not to think about them for so long. "They don't hurt."

Mother nodded approvingly. "I don't think you need the bandages anymore, unless you want them." She went to stir up the fire, leaving the unraveled bandages on the bed.

I hadn't looked at my feet since I'd first arrived at the cottage, but now I bent my knee and gathered one foot into my lap.

The cuts had healed, and the foot was no longer swollen and angry. But my skin was crossed with scars: some made with the knives I stole, others by the shards of the glass slipper.

Mother had said it that first day—she said there would be scars. How could there not be, with cuts like those? I sat staring, wondering how Mother could bear to touch them. Didn't they disgust her? Of course healing was what she did; she was used to imperfection and didn't mind it. They weren't her feet.

But they were mine. This was me now.

"They're good feet, Sparrow." Mother was putting a log on the fire. She wasn't looking at me, but she knew. She always knew.

I picked up one of the bandages, placing it under the arch of one foot, then wrapped it around my ankle. I wasn't ready to go without them, not just yet. Jack had come to sit beside me on the bed and watched me anxiously. "Good feet," he whispered, not quite a question.

"Yes." I tied the bandage so tightly it almost hurt. "Of course they are."

I said that, and maybe I even meant it. But the next day, the next week, as I took off the bandages and put on clean ones, I wasn't so sure I could keep meaning it. I began searching in Mother's book for a remedy for scars.

At first I skimmed, looking for any mention of scarring. Her book was in no particular order, not by affliction, cure, or plant. The book had been written little by little, each new author adding her own knowledge. When I didn't see anything about scars, I began to look at entries about wounds and cuts. Still I saw nothing.

I could ask Mother. She had the contents of her book committed to memory, plus more knowledge besides. Sometimes she sat with the book and a pen and ink bottle, making notes and additions. If there was a cure for me, Mother would know it. But whenever I thought of asking her, I found I couldn't say the words.

So I continued searching on my own, thumbing through the pages. I had faith in this book by now. Mother worked a kind of magic with her syrups and tonics. It was an ordinary, everyday magic, but magic nonetheless. Somewhere in her book, surely there was some magic for me.

THIRTY-THREE

It was a strange winter. Instead of staying frozen, the little stream outside Mother's cottage would freeze and thaw, then freeze again. The warmer spells didn't tempt me to go outside though. I stayed in, studying Mother's book by the fireside when I had nothing else to do. But Jack was happy to venture out when he could, and Mother sent him to fetch water every day.

"Don't get yourself wet today, Rabbit," she said one morning as she wound a knitted scarf around Jack's neck. "It's very cold out." He wriggled out of her grasp and was out the door, one end of the scarf trailing behind him. A gust of wind blew the door open for a moment before Mother pulled it shut.

I was building up the fire when I heard a splintering crash outside. There was a cry, too, but it was cut short. I found myself outside and running toward the stream without knowing how I had opened the door or even gotten to my feet.

I fell to my knees at the stream's edge, where Jack's legs and arms thrashed in the water. I couldn't see his head. He must have been trying to break the ice and lost his balance when he succeeded. He didn't weigh much, and soon he was out and in my arms, coughing up the water he had swallowed.

"Give him here." I turned and found Mother behind me holding a blanket. She took him and strode back to the cottage, wrapping the blanket around him as she went.

As I knelt to retrieve the bucket, I looked down. My clothes were red with blood, and it wasn't mine. The cold soaked into me as if I were the one who had fallen into the stream. I ran inside, the bucket dropping to the ground behind me.

Mother had settled Jack on her lap beside the fire. He must have cleared all the water from his lungs, for now he was howling loudly. He was usually so quiet it seemed impossible he could make so much noise. Mother was unflappable, though, holding the reddening blanket around one of Jack's hands and rocking him a little.

"It's not long, but it's deep," she told me as I closed the door. He must have cut himself on a jagged piece of ice. I went straight to the shelf of herbs and potions, gathering things I thought Mother would need. *Wash a deep cut with juice of the meadow pimpernel. A mixture of cobweb and honey stops the bleeding and draws together the lips of a wound.* I set the bottles on a stool beside her along with some rags (more remnants of my nightgown) and a large spider web I'd harvested from a corner of the ceiling with a broom handle.

She looked at my offerings, nodding as she took in each one. "Very good," she said. "We just need one more thing." I glanced toward the shelf, wondering what I had forgotten. Would she prefer hound's tongue? Would she want to stitch the cut, rather than use cobweb? I looked back at her. "Strawberry jam."

I pictured the page in Mother's book with the detailed drawing of the strawberry plant. The leaves are useful, *boiled in water will aid digestion*, the roots, *cooling to the liver*, and even the juice of the fruit itself, *to ease sunburnt skin*, but I couldn't remember anything about jam. Perhaps it was on a different page.

Mother's voice drifted over Jack's sobs as I reached the shelf. "Don't forget the spoon." I returned, pulling the stopper out of the jam pot. She drew out a large spoonful of jam and put the spoon in Jack's uninjured hand. He took a breath, ready to howl some more, but stopped. He took another deep shuddering breath, then stuck the spoon into his mouth.

Mother smiled at me in the sudden silence. "Now we can get to work."

By the time Jack had finished his third spoonful of jam, Mother was nearly finished bandaging his hand. He paid little attention as she held the rag dipped in meadow pimpernel to the cut, then drizzled in some honey and packed the cobweb over the top. After she tied the last knot on the bandage, she left me to help Jack out of his wet clothes and returned the bottles to the shelf.

He hardly seemed to notice me as I pulled off his shirt. Absently, he stepped out of his breeches and drawers and held up his arms for me to put a dry shirt over his head. All his attention was on his bandage; he wouldn't take his eyes off it.

"Will I die now?" He watched his hand as he turned it back and forth.

"Of course not," I told him as I undressed and put on a dry shift. "It's only a cut."

"Will I be very ill?"

"No." I gathered him up and sat in the rocking chair, drawing my shawl around us both. "Mother has fixed you, and you'll heal up nicely now."

He looked up at me at last. "You had a cut, and you were very ill, and we thought you would die."

"Sparrow had many cuts." Mother returned to the fireside with a cup of sweet cherry wine mixed with a little red poppy juice. "They were dirty and untended." She handed Jack the cup.

"And I was hungry and tired and cold," I whispered.

"And sad," Jack added.

I nodded.

For a moment I didn't say anything; I just rubbed my bare ring finger with my thumb. Remembering made my head ache, so I tried to stop. I tapped Jack's cup to encourage him to drink. "I was all alone," I murmured when he at last took a sip. "I had no Mother to put cobwebs on my cuts, and no Jack to come and help me."

He looked up at me again, the corners of his lips smeared with wine. "Until I found you."

I nodded again, but said no more. I was thinking. What if I had known Mother before, when I lived at the palace? Would I have known to put cobwebs on my cuts—those wounds I had given myself? Of course, I couldn't have told her what I was doing any more than I could have told someone else. Someone like my father. Or my husband. She wouldn't have approved—of the wishes, the knives, the pretending—any more than they would have. I wondered, though, if I'd known her then, would I have cut myself at all? Maybe I wouldn't have needed her cobwebs and honey, if I'd known Mother.

Jack stirred in my arms. "I want to pet the fur."

Mother reached over and took his empty cup. "Very well." She set it on the table and returned with her cloak, which she laid on his lap.

For a moment, he was silent, holding it up to his cheek, his eyes closed. It was a curious garment, made out of different kinds of fur, all patched together. I had noticed that much before, but seeing it up close, I realized there were other fabrics peeking out underneath the furs. Not everywhere, just here and there: rich brocades and silks, woven linen, coarse, knitted wool. It shouldn't have been beautiful, but it was somehow.

"Fox and ermine and mink." Jack sleepily touched each bit of fur as he named the animal it came from. "And badger and wolf and cat and…" He looked up at me. "Tell the story."

I looked over at Mother, now busy at the table chopping roots. "She doesn't know it, Rabbit," she said. "You tell it."

His eyes widened at being given such an important task. He straightened the cloak with his unbandaged hand and began. "Once there was a queen with long golden hair." He turned the corner of the cloak over, searching until he found a braid of red-gold hair, stitched into the fine wool lining. He traced the braid with his finger, then went on with his story. "She got sick and she told the king not to marry…" The poppy was doing its work too well, and Jack yawned. "No one but the princess had such golden…"

He touched the braid again, his eyelids drooping. "She said no," he whispered, as if this part confused and distressed him. "She said only if her father gave her the impossible things she asked for, for surely he couldn't…But he said it would be done. And it was…She put the beautiful gowns in a walnut…" He rubbed his eyes and pulled up a patch of soft, brown fur. "Gold as the sun," he murmured, exposing an exquisite piece of golden silk. "Silver as the moon."

Jack must have heard this story many, many times. But I felt sure he was leaving out important parts, half asleep as he was. Still, his fingers knew where every part of the story was on the cloak. "Bright as the…" He yawned again. "She ran from her father, and the forest hid her. No one would recognize her in her cloak with all its kinds of fur…Donkey…" He touched each fur in turn. "And dog and mouse. Bear and hare and hart and…"

He was asleep.

I drew the patched cloak around us, my fingers running through the furs. What an odd story. Jack's disjointed telling gave it a nightmarish quality I recognized. I had not been born a princess. But the story of the golden-haired girl's flight from her palace was familiar enough to raise the hairs on my arms. It made me remember the girl I longed to forget.

That girl I used to be, with all the things I did to fit—to please—was beginning to seem like someone I didn't know. I had a feeling this girl I was in the wood, this Sparrow, was who I was from the start. Or who I should have been, at least. She would have known right away that pleasing was impossible, as impossible as pretending to be someone she wasn't. In fact, I could not imagine her at the palace at all, not as a princess, a lady in waiting, even an under maid. And the longer I spent as Sparrow, the less I could imagine ever being anyone else.

But I could not forget everything about the palace; I couldn't forget the prince. Where was he, and what was he doing? Had he seen the truth of the slippers at last? Or did some trace of love remain? Was he searching for the princess, or someone else entirely?

Someone new.

"Tea is ready, Sparrow," called Mother. "Let's let him sleep."

I put Jack to bed on his pallet by the fire, covering him with his blanket. I hung the mottled cloak back up beside the door and smoothed the fur with my fingers. Mother had been right when she said I didn't know the strange story of her cloak. But by this time she had heard me tell Jack plenty of stories. How could she have been so sure I wouldn't know this one?

Unless it was her own.

THIRTY-FOUR

Mother and I sat at the table with cups of lemon balm tea, and I watched Jack sleeping. There was always a little crease of worry between his brows, even when he slept. "What happened to him?" I asked.

Mother glanced over her shoulder at Jack before she spoke. "Last year there was a fever. Not a house in the village was spared."

"I remember." People where I was called it a plague. My stepmother and stepsisters refused to let anyone into the house, sending me out to buy anything we might need. I doubted they would have let me back in if they hadn't needed me to cook and clean and keep the house running.

Mother nodded. "But Jack's family…" She took a sip of her tea, then shrugged. "It was the worst for them. Father, mother, grandmother, sisters, brothers. He was the only one left. I was going from house to house doing what I could. Many of his family died before I even arrived, and the rest followed soon enough. Except the little rabbit," she said with a ghost of a smile in his direction.

"Could you have helped them," I asked, "if you'd come earlier?"

She shook her head. "Some people recovered, some didn't. There's no cure for a fever like that."

A rush of heat flooded my skin. I couldn't believe there was nothing in that book of hers that could have saved Jack's family.

Recently, I had been telling myself a story. It had never happened, and now it never could. But sometimes it came to me anyway: Mother comes in to see my own mother when she is ill. She puts a hand on her head, asks her where it hurts. She asks what the doctors have said, and what they have done. She shakes her head when she hears about the leeches and the purging. She reaches into a pocket, bringing out one of her bottles and telling me how much to give her and how often. She says she will come back, and when she does, my mother is feeling a little better.

I knew it was foolish to think of these things. We couldn't change the past. But it was comforting somehow, to imagine Mother could have made her well again.

I tried to keep the anger out of my voice. "Was there nothing you could do?"

"Sparrow," she said gently, "there is always something we can do. But it doesn't always cure them. Sometimes all we can do is lessen the pain a bit, or sit with them and ease their passing."

My mother's doctors had done none of those things, and my father hadn't either. The doctors had packed up their potions and sharp instruments and left, telling my father to prepare himself. My father had disappeared into his room and paced the floor, praying for her recovery. He did not sit holding her hand, or tell her stories, or sing to her.

I did. But only for a while.

As she looked less and less like the mother I knew, as she grew gaunt and quiet, I began to wish her away. I didn't want this ghostly mother, this death-like thing. Ashamed and sure she could sense my betrayal, I deserted her. It was an old servant who witnessed her last breath. Not my father. Not me. And it was the same old servant who came to find me, hiding in the branches of a pear tree, to tell me it was all over. She did what Mother would have done. I could have done those things, and I should have.

But I didn't.

I didn't want winter to end. I wanted to stay curled by Mother's fire, hidden from the cold and the world outside. People braved the weather to visit us sometimes, though. They came for what I now knew were the usual reasons: toothaches, coughs, sore throats, broken bones. Now and then Mother went to the village for supplies, or to visit someone in need of help. She looked at me sometimes as she put on her cloak, as if wondering if I would like to put on mine and join her. But she never asked, and I never went.

I couldn't forget the trees that circled the cottage, threatening and disapproving. I couldn't forget their whispers on the night Jack found me. *Good riddance. Good riddance to bad rubbish.* I'd been delirious then, but even now I couldn't help feeling the trees didn't wish me well. They looked different these days, stripped of their autumn leaves. They were skeletal and sharp, sometimes tipped with ice. As long as I went no farther than to the stream for water, or to the little shed to milk the goat, I was safe enough. But I had no desire to venture beyond the clearing where they grew thick. So I stayed—in Mother and Jack's circle of protection.

I was eager to earn my keep, and I did all I could around the cottage. I swept and cooked and kept up the fire. I washed and scrubbed and polished. I knitted and spun and mended. These were the same things I had done in my father's house, but it was different here. I did them willingly; there was a pleasure in helping Mother and Jack. I felt welcome, even wanted. Everything was different here.

I also did tasks I had never done in my father's house. I boiled leaves into thick syrup. *A decoction of pennyroyal brings about clear sight.* I used Mother's knife to chop roots, then I steeped them in vinegar. *An infusion of butcher's broom relieves an aching head.* I plucked delicate leaves from dried plants and crushed them into a fine dust. *Powdered motherwort, taken in wine, soothes the troubled heart.*

I knew I couldn't make things grow the way I had before. That part of me had withered at the palace. It had died there; I was sure of it. But it pleased me to recognize a plant by its scent or the shape of its leaves or the feel of its root. Even the things that might have seemed dull absorbed me: scraping bark, grinding seeds, plucking endless petals and sorting them from the leaves. If I was working hard, I could drive away the whispers. *My son has told me of your fondness for flowers.* If I was busy, I could forget.

At first I hung back when visitors came. I feared their curiosity. But soon I realized most villagers looked at me with only a mild interest, as if noticing a farmer has acquired a new cat. They didn't ask who I was, where I had come from, or why. It made me wonder how many Jacks had occupied Mother's house over the years, how many Sparrows.

Mother seemed happy to let me stay in the background, fetching syrups and tonics and making the tea, while she chatted with visitors at the table, listening to the latest news.

I had never been there, but bit by bit, the village came to me. The butcher came for something for his wife who had a new baby. The blacksmith's wife needed a salve for burns. The cobbler's apprentice had a sour stomach.

The miller's daughter lingered in the doorway, not at all eager to come in like most people. "Rose," Mother said gently, "shut the door, love, or we'll all catch our deaths." The girl complied, but then stood near the door, as if trying to decide whether to stay or go right out again.

I left the roots I was chopping and fetched a loaf of brown bread from the shelf. I cut it into thick slices and spread butter on each one. Just as I was about to hand out the plates, Mother set a jar of jam beside me. "I hope you'll try some of our blackberry jam." She sat down at the table, patting the stool beside her.

The miller's daughter murmured her thanks and took the offered seat, still looking as though she might run at any moment. Mother made no indication that she had noticed, but smiled and asked after the miller and his wife and their other children. When the girl had replied that they were all well, Mother nodded approval, then cocked her head to one side. "And yourself?"

The girl fixed her eyes on the plate of bread and jam I had set in front of her, her hands worrying each other in her lap. "I am—" She halted, her eyes still downcast. Her hands looked so like my own had at the palace, fidgeting with my wedding ring, that I felt an unspoken kinship with this girl. At last she gathered her courage. She looked straight at Mother, a hard look in her eyes. "I want a love potion."

"Oh." Mother looked thoughtful. "Has your father picked you a husband you don't like?"

She flushed. "No, no." She managed a weak smile. "He wouldn't do that. It's not for me. It's for…" She trailed off, looking at me for help.

"Him," I finished. Rose didn't know me, but she sensed that kinship too. She was right, of course. Who would know better than me, the lengths you would go to? When you wanted something that badly?

She nodded, her eyes filling, and it all came out in a rush. How the innkeeper's son had come courting her. At least she thought it was courting. How extra errands brought him to the mill, and he always wanted her to wait on him. How he would walk her home, whenever he saw her in the village. How he asked her to meet him in the square for the festival, in the meadow for a picnic, by the millpond after dark. She told us of gifts of ribbons and wildflowers, of promises and stolen kisses.

She was the only one for him, he told her. He was hers forever, he said, and she believed him. Until she gave him too much. Until his visits became less frequent and his kisses distracted. Until she saw him with the merchant's golden-haired daughter. But he would never be allowed to marry that girl. The merchant's daughter could make a far better marriage than an innkeeper's son, and the merchant knew it. And besides, that girl could never make him happy, Rose told us, but she could. If only he could see. If only he could be made to see.

She trailed off at last, collecting a tear with one fingertip and studying it, as if even the pain this boy caused her was precious.

Mother had gotten up and busied herself with the kettle during her story, leaving the two of us alone at the table. I glanced at her now, wondering what she was making. In all the time studying her book, I had never seen a recipe for a love potion, or anything like it. So what was she making? A tea of vervain, to calm the nerves? Or juniper berry, in case there was an unwanted baby on the way? I leaned forward to catch the scent from the steaming mug Mother set down, but it smelled the same as the tea she served me a moment later.

Mother returned to the table and sipped her tea, eyeing the girl over the edge of her mug. "Now then, Rose." She set down her mug. "A love potion is a serious matter. Is this lad worth it?"

Rose laid a coin on the table, her eyes defiant. It was likely all the money she had in the world.

Mother waved the money away. "Is he worth the trouble, I mean."

"I love him," Rose said simply, her eyes shiny. "More than anything."

"Does he get a choice in the matter?"

The girl stared at her clenched fists, unable to meet Mother's eye. My shaking hands were balled into fists too, as if in sympathy. I stuffed them into my lap to hide them. "I'd be good for him," she said.

"If you care for him that much," Mother asked, "would you really want him changed?"

"Changed?" Rose looked up, puzzled. "No. I want him the way he is."

Mother placed her calloused hand on the girl's slender one. "It seems to me that the way he is," she said gently, "*who* he is, is a fellow who is in love with someone one day, and someone else the next."

"I just want it to be like it was before."

Mother shook her head with a bit of a smile. "We can't go back to before, love," she said. "And if we could, how could we find out what comes after?"

Rose exhaled in what was almost a laugh. "And what's after? Seeing him with her? Being his cast-off?"

Mother fixed her with the same penetrating look she often used with me. "I imagine there's something else in store for you. Finding someone worth waiting for perhaps? Someone who chooses to love you and you alone, without a potion. Don't you deserve that? Doesn't he?"

There were more tears after this, but in time Rose quieted, and Mother was able to persuade her to drink her tea and eat her bread. "The blackberries were sweet this year, weren't they?" She gathered the dishes as the girl wiped a trace of jam from her lips. "Now, I never like to let anyone leave empty-handed. How about I send you home with some more tea, for later?" She rose from the table and began putting some herbs in a bit of cheesecloth. Knotting the ends of the little bundle, she put the tea in the girl's hand. "Just you drink that up tonight before bed. It'll do you a world of good."

Murmuring her thanks, Rose stood. "It's a lonely walk back to the village," Mother said as the girl put on her shawl, "why don't I send Sparrow with you for some company?" Rose smiled shyly, and Mother ignored the look that must have been on my face. "You can try out your handiwork," she told me, draping my new cloak around my shoulders. Then she inclined her head toward her clogs which sat by the door.

I approached them, wondering what would happen if I put them on. Would they close around my feet, biting in as the glass slippers had done? They were nothing like them, of course. They were not delicate; they had no intricate designs swirled into them. They were working shoes, sensible and ordinary, made of wood. I had worn a pair of shoes like this, after my mother died. I wore them for cleaning out the pigsty and walking through the apple orchard and going to market. There was no shame in shoes like these.

So why did my stomach clench at the thought of putting my feet in them? Why did I feel as if something thick were crawling up my throat?

I turned to Mother. "I won't be cold."

She made the barest nod of her head, and turned to her bag of rags in the corner. She drew out some strips that must have once been a thick old blanket and handed them to me. I tied these around my feet, and Rose and I left for the village.

Keeping my eyes on the path, I tried not to think of the trees above and around me as we walked. Rose seemed glad of the company and didn't seem to mind my silence. She imagined Mother was right about the innkeeper's son, she said, and perhaps she should wait for someone who would treat her better.

I nodded, but said nothing. My idea of love had only caused harm, so who was I to give advice? I knew nothing of love.

"Maybe," she said after a moment of silence, "maybe I should go to the Looking Glass to see my true love."

I must have stared at her blankly.

"You know, on the mountain. Don't you know the story?"

I shook my head.

"On the other side of the wood there's a mountain," she said. "And at the top of the mountain there's a well. The water in it is clear as glass. And if a girl looks into it at sunrise, she will see her true love. Or maybe it's in the light of a full moon, I forget." She sighed. "It might make the waiting a little easier. And then I'd at least recognize him when I saw him."

We walked in silence a little longer. I thought I'd met my true love, but I hadn't trusted that love to grow of its own accord.

"There's another story too," Rose said after a moment. "That on top of Looking Glass Mountain there's a handsome prince, encased in a coffin of ice so clear you can see right through it."

A shiver ran through me. "What happened to him?"

"I can't remember," she said, frowning. "He's under an enchantment perhaps. Or his heart was pierced with a piece of ice that grew and grew all around him to form his prison."

Suddenly she laughed and nudged my shoulder with hers. "You and I should go up there together. Surely he'd do for one of us."

"He must be so cold," I whispered.

Rose nodded. "He must be." Then she brightened. "What about you? Do you have a young man?"

"I—"

Why did I hesitate? "No."

She had turned to look at me, a little smile on her round face. "But you did have."

I nodded.

"What happened?"

How could I explain it? I hardly knew myself. "I ruined it."

She wanted to hear all about me and everything I had lost. Perhaps it comforted her to think about someone else's heartbreak, instead of her own. I didn't want to talk about it, but the words came out anyway. Not everything, of course. But I told the truth: how we met at a ball, how the first time he came to my house he thought my stepsister was me, how I thought his family liked me, then I learned I was wrong. How I'd done something I shouldn't have to make him love me. How I didn't fit in his life. How I ran away.

Rose gave a little sigh. "Where is he now?"

I shook my head, my hair getting in my eyes. "I don't know." I was thinking of the storyteller and what he said about the prince and the ring he kept close to his heart. Wondering if that part was true. "He's happier without me, I'm sure."

She sighed again. "What if he's not?" She was the kind of girl who was always on the lookout for a happy ending, even if it wasn't hers.

I pulled my cloak around me. "Then I am wrong."

THIRTY-FIVE

The village was a small one, smaller than the market town I once lived near. There was a cluster of shops around a square, the church, the inn, and the mill in the distance. I only saw it from the edge of the woods, though, refusing Rose's offer to warm up by her fireside. I told her I was not cold and that I had better get back. A whole village full of people, even a small one, was too bustling, too crowded, too much like the world I was hiding from in Mother's quiet cottage.

Rose seemed to be thinking the same thing. Her cheeks were wet again, but she pressed her fingers under her eyes, pushing outward as if she could erase her tears and the hurt that caused them. Then she gave me the ghost of a smile and squeezed my hand.

As she turned to go, something fell out of her apron pocket. It was the bundle of tea. I caught it up and called out, running out of the trees to hand it to her. As she walked away again, I realized I was standing in the middle of the lane; I was almost to the square. I put up my hood and hurried back into the trees, my heart pounding in my chest.

What was I so afraid of? Even the king's men hadn't recognized me. Did I expect the king and queen to ride through this out-of-the way place? Or even the prince himself, in a carriage with his new bride?

All I knew was that I was relieved to be back in the shelter of the trees. I leaned against an oak, feeling its trunk solid and strong under my fingers, and my heartbeat slowed. Those trees, so menacing in the autumn, were welcoming now. It was a relief to see their bare branches closing over me as I went deeper into the wood and back toward the cottage.

I had told the miller's daughter more than I had told anyone. But I couldn't stop thinking of the things I had not said about that day the prince had come to my father's house. I told Rose he had mistaken my younger stepsister for me. And that was true enough; for with a little help from my stepmother, she had fit the slipper. *Don't be a fool,* my stepmother had hissed, holding out the kitchen knife. *When you are queen, you'll have no need to walk.* I was watching from the passageway when she paraded the poor girl out, calling, *It fits! It fits!* I only got a glimpse of her face as they passed me, but I saw the tears running down her cheeks.

That only explained part of the prince's bewilderment, though. The other part, of course, was that he didn't recognize her. He masked it well, offering her his handkerchief and taking her arm as she limped over to him. But I could see it as he studied her face, perhaps thinking all those candles and mirrors in the great hall hadn't made it light enough to see the girl properly, this girl he had been seeking. Perhaps he thought if she smiled, the expression would be familiar.

Or maybe he was thinking that trial by shoe wasn't the most sensible way to find a wife.

He said something to her, cocking his head and leaning closer to listen for her response, hoping perhaps to recognize my voice between her stifled sobs. He recognized nothing, of course, and after a few minutes of speaking with her he seemed to realize he wouldn't. But he remained courteous and kind, gesturing to the door where his carriage and horses waited.

He knew by now she wasn't me, but he would marry the girl who fit the slipper. He had said so, and he wouldn't break his word. That made me love him all the more. But as they reached the door, my stepsister fell against him, catching her breath. He tightened his hold on her arm to steady her, and, looking back, he saw the trail of blood. It stretched from the kitchen all across the floor, only ending at his bride's skirts. His face grew pale and he scooped her up into his arms, carrying her toward the fire.

A wall then blocked my protected view, and I was about to risk moving farther into the passage when my stepmother swept by me, my older stepsister's arm grasped tightly in one hand, the bloody slipper in the other, her mouth set in a hard line. I flattened myself against the wall to let them pass. When they had gone by, I peeked again into the entrance hall. The prince was calling for one of his footmen to send for a doctor. My younger stepsister was curled into a ball on a settle near the fire while my father stood behind her, patting her shoulder with an awkward hand.

My stepmother was quick about her work. *Make it fit!* She and my older stepsister were soon back with another victorious, *It fits!* This stepsister was made of stronger stuff, though, and she did not cry. She was also considerably taller than me, with much darker hair. The prince would have known at once she wasn't me.

The flash of disappointment that crossed his face almost made me burst out into the hall, but something held me back. What it was, I still couldn't say. I only knew that once my older sister was discovered in her turn and I stepped around the corner at last, his expression, that slow smile, had been worth waiting for.

But what good was remembering? He would never look at me that way again. I had done the same thing as my stepsisters. They had tried to win him with a knife, and I had tried to keep him with one. We had all deceived him.

So was there no true bride for the prince after all? I saw him now through the eyes of the miller's daughter, not happier without me, and now through the eyes of Jack and the storyteller, searching the kingdom with my ring around his neck. *Princess, Princess, where are you?* I felt the sudden stinging of a headache between my eyes.

Funny, how I never really put myself in his place. I always assumed I knew what he felt, but I was only imagining. And what if I had imagined things all wrong? I rubbed the bridge of my nose, trying to pinch the headache away.

I was knocked off balance by the whirlwind that was Jack, throwing his arms around my legs and nearly sending us both to the ground. "You're back!" he breathed into my skirt. "Mother says you'll catch your death." I had entered our clearing without even noticing. He took my hand, pulling me toward the cottage. I let him lead me, but as I went, I looked back at the trees behind me. Those trees that stood between me and the rest of the world.

I shuddered, wishing there were a hundred times more of them, twice as tall and twice as thick. They were friendly now, but somehow, they weren't protection enough. After all, what could protect me from the memories of the girl I had been? The girl I didn't want to be anymore.

I squeezed Jack's hand as we walked toward the door. "Don't worry," I said as he dragged me in, his face intent, "I'm not frozen."

He frowned. "Your hand is cold." But then his face lit up, remembering something. "Did you put one foot into your feathers?" he cried, stopping and lifting up one foot.

"Oh." I smiled as I remembered telling him how birds keep warm by putting a foot into their feathers. "I suppose I forgot to."

He looked up at me seriously as I hung my cloak beside Mother's. "You need feathers."

I sat by the hearth, stretching my feet to the warmth of the fire and blowing on my hands. There was a pungent scent to my fingers, and I breathed it in, wondering what it was. Then it came to me, the tea for the miller's daughter. I had picked it up to give it to her, and the scent lingered on my skin.

Mother was swirling honey into two mugs of tea. She raised her eyebrows in question when she saw my eyes on her. "What was in that tea?" I asked. "Is there a potion for heartbreak?"

She shook her head. "I can't bottle time, Sparrow. That's the only cure I know for heartbreak. And I don't make love potions, either."

"Is there such a thing?" I blurted out. "Can someone be made to fall in love?"

She handed me a steaming mug and sat down at the table with one of her own. "Perhaps." She looked thoughtful. "But it wouldn't last. Falling in love is only the beginning of a real, lasting love. Sometimes being in love leads to true love, and sometimes it doesn't." She gave me one of her appraising looks. "There may be temporary sorts of magic, to make one feel in love. But no magic in the world can make true love. That takes bravery and honesty and hard work. You must see your love as they truly are. And let them see you in return. No pretending."

My body ached all over. That sounds impossible, I thought, wrapping my cold fingers around my mug.

Mother was still watching me. "Love works a magic all its own, Sparrow. But it cannot be forced."

I stared into the surface of my tea. What of my wish, then? Had it worked for a time and then failed? Had my husband and I ever felt real love? I wanted to believe we had. But I had pretended far too much for that. "So what did you give Rose?" My voice was toneless.

"It was only tea, same as this."

I inhaled the steam that curled around my face. It was the same as the scent on my hands.

"Just mint," she said, "and a little thyme." She returned to the shelves and began putting her jars in order. "I thought it might soothe her head. All those tears can bring on a headache sometimes. Even the ones unshed."

Jack was kneeling in one corner of the cottage, taking something small from a chink in the wall. A moment later he stood beside my chair opening a little wooden box. Inside was a collection of a small boy's treasures. There was a perfect acorn, a smooth, sparkling gray stone, a few dried violets, and a small brown feather. This box must have contained what Mother had called his *precious things*, the night she told him the story of the first sparrow they'd taken in.

He picked up the feather and held it out.

"For me?"

He nodded. "So you won't be cold."

THIRTY-SIX

That night, I sat beside the fire with my cloak in my lap. I took out Mother's sharpest needle, a thimble, and a spool of ordinary thread. Threading the needle, I wondered about the cloak made of all kinds of fur. Had it provided more than warmth for the princess in Jack's story? Not just a disguise but transformation? Had the girl disappeared inside it and not come out again until she was someone new?

Was it possible to remake myself?

I didn't know, but I set to work anyway. I stitched the sparrow's feather Jack gave me onto the hood of my cloak.

That was the beginning.

The next morning, after bringing in wood and milking the goat, I took a walk around the clearing. When I came inside I had a small handful of feathers: black and brown and gray, from tails and wings and breasts, small and large and in between. That night when my work was done, I sewed them on beside the sparrow's feather.

When they saw what I was doing, Mother and Jack collected feathers too, and every night I sewed on more. My cloak was warmer than it had been before, and the rain beaded and ran off

201

the feathers. It became a strange, mottled thing like Mother's, but with a shine all its own.

And as my cloak transformed, time went on, whether I wished it to or not.

Mother, Jack, and I continued our quiet life. The seasons changed, and I took on new tasks. I helped Mother in the little garden she kept in a sunny spot, and soon enough she left it all to me. "You have a way with growing things," she said, watching me thin the turnip seedlings. "I've never seen them come up so quickly before."

"It's only the weather."

Mother's voice trailed after her as she walked away. "You know it isn't."

I didn't know that. What I knew was that my hands were barren now. I didn't feel anything I used to feel—the warmth, the tingling when I set my hands on the earth was gone. I refused to hope that feeling would ever come back. I was content working the ordinary magic of digging and weeding and watering.

That was what I told myself.

When it was warmer, we began to take walks in the wood to gather one thing or another. Mother showed Jack and me the best places to gather wild strawberries in spring or how to recognize creeping lady's-tresses in summer. And always, we looked for feathers.

We stopped to rest one day, and Jack lined up our baskets to compare them. After a time, he looked over at me. "You have the most strawberries."

"You have the most feathers." I pointed to his coat pocket with a grin.

But Jack was undeterred. He turned to Mother. "They just pop up wherever Sparrow puts her hand." He turned back to me with narrowed eyes. "How do you do that?"

There was a time when I would have been proud, to have someone notice a thing like that. *Are you doing that?* my husband had asked. A time when it was true. *You are a wonder.* But that time was over, and I didn't want to think about it. "I just have my eyes open for them, that's all." I cast around for a reason to change the subject. "Look." I pointed at a small purple and yellow flower beside Jack's hand. "It's a little stepmother."

"What?"

I plucked the flower and showed it to him. "Haven't you heard this story?"

He shook his head. "Tell it."

"Once there was a king and a queen," I said, "and they had two beautiful daughters. But the queen died, and in time the king took a new wife, who had two daughters of her own. The new queen wanted no one to be more beautiful than she was, so she made her stepdaughters dress in dark, solemn colors. So here are the two stepdaughters." I pointed to the two deep purple petals.

"But she and her own daughters dressed in gold." I pointed to the three yellow petals. "Now, there were five green thrones in the throne room for the queen and the princesses, but the jealous queen made her stepdaughters share one throne." I plucked off both purple petals, leaving the one tiny green leaf underneath. "And there it is. Now, the queen's own daughters got one throne each." I picked off two yellow petals, revealing a single tiny leaf under each one. "So how many thrones are left?" I asked Jack.

He counted on his fingers. "Two."

"So why did the stepdaughters have to share, if there were five ladies and five thrones?" I asked. Jack shrugged. "Well, the queen's dress was grander than her daughters', and her skirt was so full," I pulled off the final, largest petal, revealing the two leaves that supported it, "that she had to have two chairs to sit upon."

Jack grinned and reached for the bare stem. "I want to do it." He looked around for another flower, but didn't see one.

Mother and I looked too. Usually where there was one little stepmother, there would be more, so I reached back to the place where I'd found the first. But it must have been the only one to bloom so far. There was another blossom budding, but the petals hadn't opened yet. I leaned on my hand, looking further into the underbrush.

The soil was warm beneath my palm, and a tingle shivered up my fingers.

I sat up, pulling my hand away as if the soil had burned me. Beside me, Jack was watching the closed blossom intently. But it wasn't closed anymore; it was fully open. "See!" He pointed at me. "That's what you do."

I plucked the blossom and looked over at Mother, waiting for her to comment on Jack's vivid imagination. She didn't laugh, though; she only leaned forward and squeezed my arm. "You're as white as a ghost, love," she told me. Then she turned to Jack. "She just coaxes things to life, doesn't she?"

I shook my head. My throat closed at the mere idea of believing that was true. Jack and Mother watched me, an identical expression of satisfaction on their faces. Silent, I handed Jack the flower so he could tell the story. Then I put my hands in my lap so they could bring me no more hope.

Many times it was the three of us, walking through the woods together. Other times Jack and I went without Mother, or I went alone. I didn't mind the trees now. I knew they kept me safe. From what exactly, I didn't know, but it was enough to be in their shelter. And even when it grew too warm to wear my cloak, I always had it to come home to, with a few new feathers to add.

And while I preferred the wood, after my first visit to the village with the miller's daughter I began to venture out a little more. As winter turned to spring and the bilberries ripened, I sometimes went with Mother on her visits, carrying her basket and watching as she tended her patients. In summer when the villagers were busy with haymaking, she watched as I dressed wounds and soothed fevers.

I learned to set bones and stitch cuts and, as always, I mixed potions and teas and poultices, each one a little bit of magic under my hands. We witnessed births and deaths. There wasn't much to do in those cases, except to sit beside the bed and ease the pain if we could. But we went, and as Mother said, there was always something we could do.

By autumn, when the acorns fell from the forest oaks, if Mother was busy, I would sometimes go alone. The villagers eyed me cautiously at first, but in time, word must have spread that I hadn't harmed anyone, and even those I hadn't met didn't complain if I came without Mother.

Perhaps I was not a pretender here.

My son has told me of your fondness for flowers.
Your touch works wonders.
A tea brewed with mint and wild thyme,
to soothe an aching head.

I refused to think about the time passing, but it did, whether I thought of it or not.

One day in the autumn I returned from walking in the wood, my basket full of blackberries and their leaves. They were probably the last berries we would find, for it was growing cold and the leaves were falling. When I neared our clearing, I climbed over a dead tree that had fallen in the path a few weeks before. I should take our ax to it soon, I thought; the woodpile was getting low. I stopped to pick up a large black feather from the ground and went inside.

Jack met me at the door, tossing away his dolls and hopping up beside me at the table. He and I sat a while separating the berries from the leaves. Every so often he took a berry for himself, saying, "That one's no good. I'll have to eat it," and grinning up at me with an increasingly purple mouth.

I had just taken a berry for myself when Mother said, "You know, Sparrow, it's been a year now since you came to us. I remember it was hunter's moon when Jack found you. And hunter's moon was last night."

She looked up from her knitting and corrected herself. "A year and a day then."

I looked at the blackberry I had been holding to my mouth, thinking of the rotting berries I had eaten when I was lost in the wood, those few days before the hunter's moon. I set the fruit back in the basket, uneaten.

Mother spoke again. "When the spring comes, we need more second sight."

"Second sight?" I didn't remember hearing that name before, or seeing such a plant in her book.

Mother nodded, her eyes still on her knitting. "Pearly white petals, blue-green leaves—all shaped like teardrops. It's a rare plant, we'll likely have to go up Glass Mountain for it. Good for drawing splinters and other things embedded in the skin." She looked up and around the room until she saw her book, lying on the table, but she made no move to get it. "Good for old wounds."

We were busy with the blackberries for the rest of the day, setting the leaves to dry for tea, making jam with some of the berries and a pot of ink with the rest. As I cleaned our supper dishes, I was still thinking about what Mother had said. A year and a day. In the stories my mother and that traveling storyteller told, it was a magical period of time. In the space of a year and a day quests were completed, changelings returned from other worlds, and true loves lost were found.

And what of my year and a day? I had no answer. All that time ago I had appeared on Mother's doorstep, friendless, sick, hungry. She and Jack had given me shelter and companionship and a place in their household, far more than I had a claim to. Sometimes I wondered if I should leave the shelter of the wood and Mother's cottage. If I should go back into the world. But where would I go? And why?

I glanced over at Mother, wondering what she would say if I asked her. She had always treated my presence with a calm acceptance. She seemed happy enough to have me, but I wasn't hers, any more than Jack was. Did she hope I would fly away, leave her and go back into the world like the first sparrow she took in? As usual, her appearance told me nothing. She sat by the fire, absorbed with writing in her book, so I didn't ask. I didn't want to disturb her.

And I feared her answer.

THIRTY-SEVEN

I never asked Mother's opinion, or her advice. I told myself I could ask her some other day. There would always be time.

We went to bed that night, as always. But the next morning the cottage was much lighter than usual when I opened my eyes. Mother always woke early, just as it was getting light, and Jack and I followed quickly after. We tended the fire and made breakfast; we drew water and fed the goat. We began our day.

But not this morning.

I lay in bed for a moment, wondering why I had slept so long. Jack was awake but still on his pallet by the fire whispering to his dolls.

I could feel Mother beside me in the bed, so I sat up slowly, not wanting to disturb her. She was always a light sleeper, but this morning she didn't wake. She didn't move at all.

A prickle crept up my spine. Her stillness was wrong. Something told me not to look at her, not to see why the bed felt different. But I did. Her mouth was a little open; her eyes were closed. Her body was stiff and cold.

She looked peaceful, I told myself. She was only sleeping. But I knew that wasn't true; working with the old and sick of the village had made this sight familiar. Mother was dead.

My thoughts crowded in on me all at once, telling me it could not be, not like this, not with no warning at all. She hadn't been sick or in pain. Not that I knew of, at least.

My heart pounding in my ears, I whispered her name. I shook her gently; I laid my head on her chest to listen for a heartbeat or feel for a breath. But there was nothing. I knew it, but part of me kept insisting that it wasn't true. That she wouldn't just leave us this way, that the next time we spoke she would have to explain. But another part of me whispered there would be no next time. We would never speak again.

But I couldn't listen to that whisper. Not now. Jack was stirring on his pallet by the fire; he was getting up. I sat in the bed, one shaking hand on Mother's motionless form, and tried to gather the courage to turn around. How could I tell him he had lost yet another person he trusted, another person who loved him?

Another person who loved me.

I stared at the wall, forcing my lungs to breathe in and out, but no words came. My head went back and forth, saying over and over the words I could not say aloud. *No. No. No.*

"Did she catch her death?"

A chill seeped through me. The whisper had come from my shoulder. Jack had crossed the room without my knowing it, and now he stood beside the bed.

"Yes." I didn't turn around. I covered my mouth with my hand, holding in the sound that threatened to come out next.

"How?" He sounded so very small. "She wasn't sick."

I forced myself to face him. His face was pale, his hair still tousled from sleep. His eyes, wide and dark, were fixed on me. A bit of sleep was caught in his eyelashes. I pressed my lips together, hoping my voice would be steady when it came out. "Sometimes it just happens that way." Mother's voice sounded in my ears as I spoke. They were her words; she had said them over the summer when an old man in the village died suddenly. He had been healthy as far as we knew, but Mother had told his daughter that sometimes people's hearts just stop beating. They stop breathing, and we don't know why.

Jack was not looking at me now or at Mother, but down at the floor, both hands clutched around his princess doll. "It just happens," I said again. "Sometimes." A lock of his hair was sticking up. I reached my hand out to smooth it down, but he took a step backward, still not looking at me.

Something in my stomach was crawling up into my throat. I tried again. "Jack," I said, swinging my legs off the bed and kneeling on the floor, "come here." I held out both arms to him. "It will be all right." But now he took several more steps back until he was out of my reach. "It will be all right." I sounded like I was choking.

He was now against the wall beside the hearth, as far away from me as he could get. His eyes still on the floor, he stroked his doll and shook his head back and forth. "I know." His voice was so faint I could barely hear him. "I know."

The whisper in my head told me I must get on with things. I must show Jack the world had not ended, even though it felt that way.

I must get off the floor.

So I did. I pushed to my feet and stood for a moment, wondering if I could stay upright. Then I ran to the door, my mouth filling with saliva, and fell to my knees outside, retching. My stomach was empty, but that didn't seem to matter.

When the heaving stopped, I wiped my mouth and got up. I was shaking still, but perhaps now I could begin. I told myself there was much to do, and there was nothing for it but to make a start. I went back inside, my body moving as if someone else controlled it, not me. Jack had hidden himself away under the table. I could hear him whispering to his dolls, *I know*, and *It will be all right*, and *She caught her death*.

I built up the fire and sent Jack out for water as Mother always had. He came obediently when I asked, but as soon as he finished he disappeared under the table with his dolls. He spoke to them in whispers, his back to the room.

That day I told myself not to think, to pretend it was someone from the village. Someone I hadn't known well. But I wasn't as good at pretending as I had been before I left the palace.

Our table wasn't big enough for laying a body on, so I left Mother on the bed. These were tasks I had done before in recent months: undressing a body, washing and redressing it to prepare it for burial. I told myself it was nothing new, but before I dressed Mother, I did something I had never done with any of the village dead. I smoothed out her everyday gray wool gown on the table, and scissors in hand, I lifted the hem and cut out a piece of the turned-under cloth. Then I slipped it into my pocket and folded the hem back down. The missing piece didn't show, and there was plenty of room left on my cloak to stitch it on somewhere. I had to have something.

Standing beside the bed, the gown in my hands, I stopped myself. If Mother had a finer gown than this one, I had never seen it. But I told myself she would approve. This was the life she had chosen; this was the gown she had worn. I began to dress her, hoping the work would keep me from thinking. It didn't, though. The same whispers ran through my head over and over, just like Jack's words to his dolls.

She caught her death.
I know.

Around midday, I was fetching a shovel from the shed when a man appeared at the opposite edge of our clearing. He was a stranger, with the look of a man who often sleeps out of doors. He wore simple clothes, leather boots, and had a bow and arrow strapped to his back.

"Is this the house of the healer woman?"

"Who needs her?" My words came out automatically. There was no point in asking; it was just my usual response.

The man's words tumbled out. "It's my master. He has a wound just here." He indicated the palm, at the base of his thumb. "And nothing seems to help. He bears it patiently, but I know it pains him." He rubbed his hands restlessly on his trousers. "He didn't send me, but he is in the village, could—"

I cut him off. "The old lady cannot help him. She is dead."

"Old lady?" He looked confused.

"Just this morning. And I must bury her." He didn't seem to understand me, so I said it again. "She cannot come to your master. I'm sorry."

The man was shaking his head. "Not an old woman. In the village, they said a young woman named," he paused, trying to remember, "well, it's a bird's name. They say she wears a cloak of feathers but no shoes, even in winter."

It was a cold day, but I wasn't wearing my cloak. It would only get in the way during the task I had in mind. But he wasn't looking for my cloak; his eyes were on the ground beneath my skirts. At my feet. My toes and heels were bare, but the rest of my feet were wrapped, as usual, in bandages. There was no need for them anymore; still, I couldn't bring myself to wear shoes. The strips of cloth protected my scars from the curious glances the villagers would have given them. Apparently they noticed the bandages instead.

The man was still talking, about how his master was a kind man, how he hated to see him in pain and wished something could be done for him. How he was sure I could do him good if I would only come, that he was only in the village.

At last I raised a hand to stop him and went inside to Mother's shelf of medicines. I found a small pot of ointment and took it out with me. It was the same recipe that Mother had used on my own wounds, made with comfrey, self-heal, and true love. I had made up this pot for myself months before when the last one had run out, but I had only used it once. If the man's master didn't mind my finger mark on the surface, it would serve him well enough.

I pressed the pot into the man's hand. "Clean the wound first." His hand closed around the pot, but he made no move to pocket it. "Dry it well, then rub this in, morning and evening." He opened his mouth as if to try again to convince me to come with him to the village. "I must bury Mother," I said. "I cannot come to your master. I'm sorry."

Finally, the man seemed to hear me. "Your mother." His eyes darted to the shovel I had leaned against the cottage door. "I'm sorry."

I nodded. I wanted to thank him, but my mouth would not make the words.

The man looked around our little clearing then, taking stock of the dwindling woodpile, the shed, the cottage. His eyes went from the shovel and back to me, looking me over. His eyebrows furrowed. "Is there anything you need?"

I crossed my arms over my chest. It was a cold day, but that wasn't why. "No thank you." Somehow I squeezed the words out.

The line between his brows deepened, and he looked around the clearing, as if wondering if anyone else was around. "I'll fetch some help from the village. If there's something—"

My arms tightened, winding themselves around my ribcage, like I was keeping something within my chest from bursting out. "No." My voice pushed through my closing throat at last, loud and fierce. "I will manage. I don't want anything." The man took one step backward, toward the edge of the trees, looking torn. "That potion should help him," I said, more softly now.

He took a few more steps, then seemed to remember something. He came back to me, pulling a small pouch out of his pocket and fumbling for a coin to pay for the ointment. I shook my head. "You keep it," I said. "I don't need it."

He seemed to give up trying to help me at last. He made a small smile and bowed his head to me. "Thank you." Then his face brightened a bit. "Sparrow. That was the name."

I watched him go. Then I picked up the shovel.

THIRTY-EIGHT

I could have had help from the village if I had asked. I knew that. Some of the women would have come to prepare the body, and some of the men would have dug a grave in the churchyard. Mother could have had a service at the church and prayers said and flowers strewn over her grave. But I didn't want anyone's help. Mother was mine; she was mine and Jack's, and I wanted to do everything for her. I had earned the right.

So after the stranger left, I began to dig. Jack and I found a place for Mother's grave behind the cottage at the edge of the clearing. It was peaceful there. I couldn't make a tree grow to watch over her, but there were trees enough; we were in the wood after all. And when the spring came, there would be a carpet of bluebells growing all around.

It was not an easy task, but it was simple enough. One foot on the shovel, pushing down with all my strength, cutting into the earth. One shovelful after another, tossed to the side over and over and over again. I was lucky there had been no hard freeze yet. The soil was loose enough at the top, like good garden soil, but the deeper I dug, the denser it became. I fought against roots and stones and chunks of clay.

Jack helped clear away the dirt with a bucket, until the hole became too deep for him. Then he stayed at the top, peering anxiously down at me from time to time, and I dug until the failing light forced me to stop. The grave was probably not as deep as it should have been, but it took all my strength to climb out of it. My feet and gown were caked in mud and my hands covered in blisters.

It was full dark by the time Jack and I finished our usual chores and returned to the cottage. Mother's burial would have to wait until the morning. Back inside at last, it was all I could do to cut us each a slice of bread and bank the fire for the night. My limbs were heavy, like all the blood had drained out of me. I wanted nothing more than to curl up in bed and think of nothing, know nothing until the morning, or longer if possible. But the bed was occupied, and as soon as Jack had eaten his meager supper he dragged his pallet away from the hearth and under the table. There he hunched into a ball, as far away from me as he could get.

I let him go; Jack was a puzzle I must solve another day. I went to the bed. Earlier that day, when I had finished preparing Mother's body I had covered her with the quilt. I didn't want to take it from her now, so I took my cloak from its hook by the door and settled myself by the fire. Next to the still-glowing cinders, I wrapped myself up, curling into myself as tightly as I could, just as I had done in my father's house.

The floor was hard, and the ashes were quickly cooling. But even after all this time, a spot beside the hearth felt all too familiar, and I was soon asleep.

It was still dark when I woke the next morning, a fistful of fur in one hand. I must have covered myself in Mother's cloak instead of my own the night before. I lay there, wishing I could return to the oblivion of sleep, but I hurt too much. My muscles burned from the hours of digging the day before, and there was a heavy pain behind my eyes.

Sometimes, Jack crept into bed with Mother and me after we had gone to sleep. I half-expected to find him curled on the floor beside me, his hands in my hair. But as I turned over, trying to find a comfortable position, I knew I was alone. In the dark I could make out his eyes, glowing like a cat's from under the table. I sat a moment, my fingers idly stroking the fur cloak. Then I got stiffly to my feet and stirred the fire into life. There was much to do; I might as well begin.

I went through my morning routine like a sleepwalker, fetching water, milking the goat, fixing porridge neither of us had the stomach for. I told myself I was tired, and no doubt I was. But there was more; I dreaded what was to come. Once breakfast was over, though, I couldn't think of a single reason to put it off any longer.

"I have to wrap her body up now," I told Jack. "Do you want to kiss her?"

Jack shrank back a little and shook his head. "She's not her."

I nodded. "I know."

I kissed her anyway, on the forehead, because I never had when she was living. But Jack was right; this cold shell wasn't Mother anymore.

My body was numb, and my hands worked automatically, as if they weren't attached to the rest of me. I wrapped her body, tightly as I could, in the sheet. As I finished, Jack tugged on my skirt.

"Does she want her all kinds of fur?"

I knelt beside him. "What do you think?"

He nodded.

I got Mother's cloak and stood beside the bed, not quite sure what to do with it. At last, I spread it over her body.

"Fox and ermine and mink." Jack stood beside me, murmuring. "Donkey and dog and mouse."

I looked down at him, thinking of the gray wool I'd snipped from the hem of her gown. "Would you like a piece of the fur? To keep? I'm sure she wouldn't mind."

"Bear and hare and…" He stopped, his fingers twisting hopefully. "Rabbit?"

With Jack on my lap and the cloak over us both, I snipped a thread and began picking out the stitches around the bit of rabbit fur. As I worked, Jack continued whispering the story of the princess and her fur cloak. "The forest welcomed her." He stroked the fur on his lap. "She made herself useful." Then he lifted the fur hiding the golden silk and ran one finger over it. "Happy ever after."

I handed him the rabbit fur, now free of threads. "What did she do with her fine gowns?" I snipped another thread.

Jack must have asked Mother the same thing, for he knew the answer by heart. "She cut them up and made them useful," he said as I picked out the stitches holding on the piece of golden silk. "They became bandages and patches and pockets and handkerchiefs. They were only fabric, after all."

I smiled and handed over the piece of gold silk. I liked Mother's answer. Holding up a corner of the cloak, I studied it. I didn't know it the way Jack did, and I wanted to remember every bit of it: the piece of sheepskin, the wolf's fur, the parchment-colored linen. I was about to lay it down, when something winked at me from the underside of the cloak. I pulled it close, hearing Jack's surprised intake of breath. In the bottom corner, their sharp edges bound with red thread, were three shards of glass, sewn onto a piece of fine, white linen.

I had never thought to wonder what Mother had done with the pieces of the slipper she took from my feet. I only knew I had never wanted to see them again. My eyes closed, I forced myself to breathe in and out. In and out.

"Can we keep them?"

I opened my eyes. How could I explain the damage the glass shards had done? But then again, I had only found my way here because of them. I picked up the scissors and snipped a red stitch. "Perhaps I can find a place for them."

At last the glass shards and the white linen scrap from my nightgown were free. I wrapped the glass in the fabric and put it in my pocket, then I laid a hand on Jack's shoulder. "Are you ready?"

Abruptly, he grabbed a piece of the cloak in each fist and plunged his face into the furs, his body rigid. I wrapped the cloak around him, but I sensed he didn't want me to hold him. I drew my arms back, cautiously, as if he were a wild thing. When he sat up, his face was red, but his eyes were dry.

I was suddenly afraid I was doing something wrong. Perhaps we could keep Mother's cloak. Why rob Jack of something, anything that gave him comfort?

"We don't have to bury it with her."

His eyebrows knit together in worry. "It will help her sleep."

"You know she won't wake up?" I brushed his hair from his face, and he nodded.

"I know."

I brought the wheelbarrow in from the shed and set it next to the bed, and with Jack holding it steady, I maneuvered Mother's body in, little by little. The stiffness had left her now, so her body slumped to the bottom of the wheelbarrow as I eased it out the door. Jack and I had to stop several times on our way to the grave to adjust our load. Mother must have brought me in the door the same way when Jack found me, just over a year before. She had made light of getting me inside this way, but it must have been hard work.

At last we reached the grave and shifted Mother out onto the ground beside it. Jack and I knelt beside her body, her cloak folded between us. "Have you ever been to a burial?" I asked. He shook his head. "Well, usually someone says a prayer over the body before they put it in the ground. Once it's buried, they put some flowers on the top." Jack nodded, not looking at me. "Do you know any prayers?"

He shook his head, so it was up to me. I had known some prayers, once, but I couldn't think of anything that fit. Nothing I could say would ever be enough. Mother had taken me in and brought me back to life: a life which must now continue without her. Even if I could have found the right words, they wouldn't have come out; my throat was too tightly closed. I bowed my head and sunk my fingers into the fur of her cloak. I had to hope that somehow she could know my thoughts.

Beside me, Jack had put one hand on the cloak too. He was whispering something. "The forest welcomed her. She made herself useful." He spoke so softly, if I hadn't heard those words earlier that day, I wouldn't have understood them.

Together, we repeated them. *The forest welcomed her. She made herself useful.* It was enough.

Jack tugged at my sleeve, the way he used to when we first met, and I leaned down so he could whisper in my ear. "Will she be cold?"

"No," I said. "She'll have her cloak."

He looked down at the shrouded body, then leaned into me again. "Will she be scared?"

"No," I said again.

He studied his hands, which were curled into fists in his lap. He spoke so low I could barely hear him. "Will she miss us?"

My shoulders made the ghost of a shrug. "I don't know." I should have said no, but I couldn't somehow. "But if there's any way she can keep on loving us, she will."

He jumped up suddenly and ran into the cottage, coming back right away with his dolls. He held them out to me. "So she won't be lonely."

I tried to assure Jack that Mother didn't need his dolls, that she wouldn't be lonely, but he insisted. So at last, I tucked them inside the winding sheet. Then I stood at the end of the grave holding out the cloak, and I let it go. Its fall was surprisingly slow for the weight of it, almost like the rose falling from my window at the palace all that time ago. It settled gracefully onto the earth, ready for its owner.

I had no way to ease the body into the grave, so I rolled her in, as gently as I could. The body landed with a muffled thud.

Jack turned away, hiding his face with his hands. I didn't want to see either, but I made myself look down. Mother's body lay crumpled on her cloak.

I had done it all wrong. I couldn't leave her like this.

"Wait a moment," I told Jack, and lowered myself down into the grave. I ignored his faint noise of protest. There was little room to move, there in the earth. I placed one foot on either side of Mother's body and reached down. Perhaps I should have asked the villagers and had her buried in the churchyard. I straightened the body, drew the cloak around her, and fastened the ties around her neck. Doing it all myself was the only way I could say all those things I had never said. In life, she always knew what I was thinking; perhaps she would do the same in death. I wanted to believe that.

When I climbed out of the grave, Jack was gone. Perhaps he'd gone looking for some flowers to put on the top. I began to push at the pile of earth beside the hole. It tumbled in, clods and roots and bits of clay. Soon Mother's body was covered, and I continued filling the hole, first pushing from the pile, then using the shovel as the mound of dirt dwindled.

I thought Jack would be back shortly, but he wasn't.

When I finished covering the grave, he still hadn't come out, so I went inside to look for him. But he wasn't there. I walked around the edges of the clearing calling his name, first softly, then shouting.

He did not come.

I ran back inside, my heart hammering in my chest. I looked under the bed, in the bedclothes, under the table, even under his little pallet. There weren't many places to hide in our little cottage, so my search was over quickly. I even tried places I knew he could not be: inside barrels and sacks of grain, behind my feathered cloak hanging on its peg by the door, but he was nowhere.

He never ventured outside the clearing on his own, a cold voice whispered in my ear. But he must have gone into the wood;

there was nowhere else he could be. So I closed the door behind me and started toward the trees, fighting the rising panic in my chest. He must have gone searching for some flowers for the grave. I tried not to think of the way he shrank from me the day before. Or the frightened sound he had made when I disappeared into the grave to fix Mother's body.

Whatever his reason, he was gone.

I stood for a moment on the edge of the path. One way led to the village, the other out of the forest toward the mountain. Jack would surely avoid the village, whatever his thinking. He would willingly go there with one of us, but he never spoke to anyone, preferring to observe from behind our skirts.

So I chose the mountain path. I shouted Jack's name as I walked, looking up trees and down hollows as I went. Birds took flight, and hares and foxes bounded away at the sound of my voice, but I didn't care. If Jack could hear me, that was all that mattered.

I walked on, calling until my voice gave out. A promising noise led me off the path, but he wasn't there. I hadn't been paying any attention to where I was, and now I was just walking. I had no intention of going home without Jack, but I was no longer sure where home was anyway.

I walked more slowly, without the heart or the voice to shout anymore, but I could listen. It was a still day, with little wind to disturb the leaves. My ears became accustomed to the sounds of the wood: a vole scurrying through the litter on the forest floor, a woodpecker knocking on a tree, the call of a thrush. At last I heard something that didn't fit. A snuffling sound, close to the ground. I stopped, waiting for it to repeat itself, but there was only silence.

I turned slowly in place, studying the bushes and underbrush and fallen branches. I still saw nothing, but I knew what I'd heard. It was the sound I heard before Jack crawled into our bed after a nightmare, or if he'd hurt himself but didn't want us to know. I sank down right where I was. He was hiding; otherwise he would have come out or at least called to me. He could move much faster than I could, and I didn't want to frighten him.

I sat there, my eyes closed, just listening. In time, I heard the noise again, off to one side in a tangle of brambles. But I didn't turn; I didn't even move for a few more breaths. At last, though, I spoke, my face still turned away from him. "I'm hungry, Jack," I said, slowly and softly, like I was talking to a wounded animal. "Are you hungry too?"

There was a shifting in the brambles, then more silence. I spoke again. "Shall we go home now?"

I heard a shaky inhalation, then a whisper. "We can't."

I slumped in relief. "Why not?"

"We'll catch our deaths."

I allowed myself to turn toward his voice, just a little. "Jack." I tried to keep my voice calm and steady. "Mother didn't die of anything catching."

He repeated my words of the day before. "It just happens."

"Yes. It just happens like that sometimes. Maybe something was wrong, but we didn't know it."

I heard the snuffling noise again. "It will happen to you. Then I'll be alone."

My fingers itched to reach through the brambles to him, but if I made one mistake he would be gone again. I tightened my hands on my knees to keep them in place. "It sometimes happens like that to people who are old. It wouldn't happen like that to you." I paused. "Or me."

"Something could."

"It could." Jack's experience had taught him this was true, and I wouldn't deny it. "We can't know what will happen. We just have to go on and do the best we can."

There was a shuffling in the brambles, as if he were drawing farther away from me. "She left me alone." I could hardly hear him now.

"I know, Rabbit," I whispered. "She left me alone too." There was more shifting in the brambles. "But wouldn't you rather be alone together?" He didn't answer. "I can't promise nothing will ever happen to me, or to you. But that may be a very long time off. Can't we try?"

Can't we try? Whose words had I repeated just then? Whose voice whispered through my head?

Jack was silent. I didn't know how else to convince him. After all, when someone had wanted to help me, that year and a few days ago, I had run away too. So I knew just how he felt. I was numb all over; there were no words left in me. I curled into myself, there in the leaves, and closed my eyes.

I must have fallen asleep, just for a little while, but then I woke with Jack kneeling next to me, his face close to mine and his hand on my cheek.

"Sparrow." I opened my eyes. "I'm cold."

I stayed where I was, not wanting to make any sudden moves. "Me too," I said. "Do you want to go home?"

He nodded, backing up a bit. His face was streaked with dirt and tears, and his hands were covered in scratches from his time in the brambles. I got stiffly to my feet and looked around me. There were some hours of light yet, but I still had no idea where we were. Jack stood next to me, his arms wrapped around his thin chest.

"Do you know which way to go?" he asked.

I shook my head. "Do you?"

He shook his head too, his eyes wide and solemn.

"Well." I turned and looked around us, choosing a space before me where the trees weren't quite so dense. "Let's make a start."

After an hour or so we found a path, but it wasn't a familiar one. Again I chose a direction and continued walking. Jack did not hold my hand, but followed silently behind me. The light was failing, and I was beginning to think we should try to find a tree to take shelter in for the night when we heard a voice. It was a man, calling out somewhere ahead of us.

And I knew his voice.

All the breath rushed out of me as if I had fallen. In the silence after the voice died away, I could feel my blood beating, pounding in my ears; my body screamed at me to run, but toward the voice or away from it, I couldn't tell. Direction didn't matter, though; I was frozen to the forest floor, unable to move.

Then the first man's call was answered by another man, and I could breathe again. It was someone from the village, I told myself. It was only the surprise of hearing another voice breaking the quiet of the wood that made my legs suddenly weaken.

What other reason could there be? It couldn't be anyone I'd known from before, in one of my other lives.

I couldn't tell what the men were saying; they were too far away, but they sounded relaxed and friendly enough. I took another breath, nodding encouragement to Jack, and we went toward the voices.

Sometime later our little path met a bigger one. We stood, wondering which direction to take. The new path had an odd look about it. The brush and leaves were trampled down, and small chips of wood were scattered everywhere. On either side were some large branches, laid there as if on purpose.

Beside me, I heard Jack's intake of breath, and I realized where we were. We were nearly to the entrance to our clearing, where the dead tree had fallen. The one I had planned to chop for firewood the night before Mother died. But the dead tree was gone, except for its branches, which had been pulled neatly out of the way. Someone had cut up the tree and carted it off. What they didn't take, they had stacked on the side of the path.

I was so relieved to be home I didn't wonder who had taken the tree. Until I saw what they had done with it. As we entered the clearing, Jack headed straight for the cottage, but I turned toward the woodpile. We needed more wood inside, and I had lost the opportunity to get what I could from the dead tree. But our woodpile had been replenished. In fact, it was better stocked than

I had ever seen it, with neat stacks of split logs, most of a very large tree. The very tree that had just disappeared from the path.

I looked around the clearing for a sign of who had been here, but it was empty. I walked around the cottage and saw nothing, except a bunch of ivy and dog violets on the mound of Mother's grave. In the chaos of Jack's disappearance, I hadn't put any flowers there myself.

Someone else had done it for me.

Too tired and cold to stay out any longer, I returned to the woodpile. I reached for a log, then stopped. On the very top of the pile was a scrap of cloth, tied up in a knot at the top. It was much like the handkerchief full of rubies I had given my father, only simpler. The cloth was coarse and homespun, and it wasn't tied up with a ribbon. All the same, it was a gift. I was sure of it.

I picked it up and untied the knot. Inside was a tiny figure carved out of wood. It was a bird, no bigger than a walnut, its delicate beak and feathers skillfully carved. It was not painted, but its tiny eyes seemed bright and alive somehow. I curled my chilled fingers around the little thing. Everywhere my skin touched it, I felt warmer.

Inside, Jack took the bird from my hands with a look of wonder on his face. He held it up to the fire to examine it, as if it were something precious, made of gold or jewels, not wood. After turning it around and looking at it from every angle, he looked up at me.

"It's a sparrow," he said, with all the certainty in the world. He stroked the feathers with one reverent finger. "Who made it?"

I shook my head. "I don't know." I couldn't stop thinking of the voices we'd heard that day. "It seems we have a friend. It must be someone from the village."

For who else was there?

THIRTY-NINE

That night, winter arrived. The next morning frost covered the ground and the trees, and the little stream was frozen solid. I was lucky I had no more graves to dig; the earth would have been too hard. I wanted nothing more than to wrap the covers over my head and never come out again. But there was a goat to milk, water to boil, and more firewood to bring in. I got up.

My body was heavy as I went through my morning routine, like I was walking through mud. I tried to think of what Mother might be doing so I wouldn't leave out anything important, but my mind was as sluggish as my body. Once I had done the chores that seemed essential and choked down some food, I sat in Mother's rocking chair by the hearth, her book in my lap. Despite the fire, it was cold. But I had a vague feeling it was me that was cold, and not the cottage. I took my cloak from its peg and wrapped myself in it.

Jack had refused to eat. He was under the table again, holding a silent conversation with the wooden bird. I should make him some more dolls, I thought, to replace the ones we had buried with Mother. But for the moment, he was happy with his little carving. And besides, I couldn't seem to get out of the chair. Part of me wanted to open the book in my lap, to feel the reassurance of its pages under my hands, to trace the delicate writing and drawings with my fingers. But I couldn't. I just sat there, eyes closed, my arms wrapped around it, and rocked.

We weren't allowed to be quiet for long though. By mid-day, we began to have visitors. The miller's daughter, Rose, and her youngest sister were first, bringing a loaf of bread. The blacksmith's wife was next with a pot of jam, and her friend from one of the nearby farms brought a few eggs. Apparently word of Mother's death had gotten out.

As my body went through the motions of making the tea and slicing the bread, I wondered how they'd heard. I hadn't set foot in the village since Mother died, so it wasn't me. But everyone seemed to have heard from someone else.

"Well, it was that fellow Ash and his man told my John," said one woman, "and he told me straightaway." I must have looked at her blankly; I didn't know anyone named Ash. "You'll know them," she said with a nod, as if her saying it would make it true. I shook my head.

"Oh, yes," she said, nodding again, "you know, those fellows, strangers, came through town a week or so ago. The one fellow has his hand all bandaged up. They put them up over at Blackhorse Farm. The man said his master needed to rest himself as he wasn't well." It was the man who had come for the ointment then, and the master with the wounded hand.

The lady was going on with her story. "Didn't seem to do much resting though. There was a fence needed mending, and those fellows said they'd seen a likely copse of saplings nearby on their way into town. So they went there, gathered the wood and rebuilt most of the fence. I'll bet they were sorry to see them go at the farm." She nodded to herself once more and took a sip of tea.

"They're gone now?" Rose looked a bit disappointed.

"Oh, yes, bless you, love," replied the lady, pleased to have useful information. "Off they went yesterday afternoon. Odd time of day to be starting off if you ask me," she continued, "but I suppose they know their business." Her tone implied they didn't really. Then she turned her attention to me. "Now, love, why don't you and the lad come to us? We've got a little room in the attic where you can stay, and you won't be any trouble."

Jack and Rose's little sister had been playing beside my chair, and with the lady's words I felt his body stiffen. I felt the same way. The lady and her husband kept a few dairy cows outside the village. They were kind enough people, but the thought of leaving Mother's cottage made me feel like I had a stone in my belly. I thanked her and told her Jack and I could manage where we were.

"But you're so young, love." she said, her brows furrowing.

The lady's friend, who kept a few pigs and had brought us some sausages, disagreed. "She's no younger than our Katie was when she married. She's old enough to look after herself, and the lad too." She peered around the table to smile at Jack, who disappeared into the folds of my skirt.

The dairy farmer's wife now shook her head as vehemently as she had nodded before. "She's not old enough to marry."

The friend replied with an exasperated expression. "Of course she is, Martha, don't be daft." My cheeks felt hot as I busied myself collecting the empty mugs. Something wasn't right about me, I knew that. Had I been too young? Maybe that was why I'd made such a mess of it all.

And what would Mother have said? Perhaps she would have said it wasn't age exactly. I tried to shut out the women and hear her voice in my head instead. *You must see your love as they truly are. And let them see you in return. No pretending.* I hadn't seen the man I loved as someone worthy of making his own choice. I hadn't trusted him to see me and love me back. How was that love at all?

Perhaps Mother would have said that. Perhaps not. It was useless to wonder, though; I would never again know what she would say, not ever.

The dairy farmer's wife seemed to admit defeat about my ability to take care of myself, but grudgingly. "Well, I don't like the thought of you all alone out here in the woods, love. You be sure and tell us if there's anything you need. Or if you change your mind." The ladies rose to go, wrapping their shawls around themselves. At the door, she turned back. "I'll just send my Jamie to chop you some firewood."

"Thank you." I pointed outside. "But someone's already been."

"Hmm." She raised her eyebrows, a little put out that someone else had thought of it first. "And a good job of it too. Who was it?"

I shook my head. "I don't know. We weren't here."

"Hmm," she said again, her eyebrows raising higher. "A mystery." She patted me on the shoulder and turned. Then she turned back, pointing her finger at me. "Don't forget," she said. "If there's anything you need."

I thanked the ladies and closed the door behind them. Rose stayed a while longer, but eventually she left too, putting her arms around me and promising help if I needed anything.

If you need anything. That's what everyone says when someone dies, and it was good of them to say it. I knew they meant it, but no one would be able to give me what I needed. Even if I knew what that was.

I turned from closing the door the last time to see Jack, under the table where he had been all afternoon. But now he had two little wooden figures in his hands. I knelt beside him to get a better look. Hearing me, he stopped his whispering and turned, holding out the second figure.

I took it in my hand. It was a wolf, sitting with its tail curled around its legs. There was a graceful wildness to it, very like the bird's. In fact, I was certain they were both made by the same hand.

"Where did you get it?"

Jack shrugged, unconcerned. "She brought it."

"She who?" As the cottage had been filled with nothing but *shes* all day, that wasn't a helpful answer.

Jack held his hand out for the wolf. "To play with."

I set the little carving on his outstretched palm. "Do you mean Kitty?" The miller's youngest daughter. He nodded. "Did she say you could keep it?" Jack's fingers tightened around the wolf and he turned away. "Did you take it from her?"

Jack was a generous soul, and my question clearly stung him. He turned further from me and crossed his arms tightly around himself, one little animal in each fist. "She left it here," he said, louder than normally.

I sat back on my heels. "Well, maybe she wanted you to have it, but maybe she just forgot it by accident. Next time we go into town we'll have to ask her." I reached out a hand to stroke his hair, but he pulled away. "And I'll make you some new dolls. How will that be?"

I could barely hear his response. "I don't want any."

FORTY

I made the dolls anyway, but Jack barely looked at them.

They were small things, no bigger than my palm, but a good size to be playmates for the wooden bird. I used stitches for the eyes and mouths, and bits of spun wool for hair. Then I made breeches and a shirt for one and a dress for the other. I had no more lace from my old nightgown, so I used the finest bit of rag I could find, a bit of green linen. I decorated the little gown by embroidering it with leaves, and I made a tiny feather cloak to go around her neck.

I'd wanted to surprise him, so I worked on them by firelight after he'd gone to sleep. I hoped to please him, but when I put them in his hands, Jack was silent. He avoided my eyes and returned to his place under the table. When he settled himself there, he laid the dolls purposefully to one side and began whispering furiously to the bird and the wolf. I watched for a while as he made a little house out of sticks and folded his piece of rabbit fur from Mother's cloak, laying it inside for a bed. The tiny house was only big enough for the two wooden figures, and the rag dolls lay by his feet, unwanted.

I didn't want to make Jack return the wolf, so I put off going to the village as long as I could. And to tell the truth, I had reasons of my own for staying away. I dreaded seeing the villagers, even though they had always been kind to me. Surely they would see me differently now, as if my grief was a smudge on my face. Or a scar. Something that marked me as other and alone. Their visits of sympathy had been kindly meant, and I appreciated them. But I didn't want to go among their noisy, chatting market stalls and inns and houses. The thought of it was as heavy as a stone around my neck.

But not long after I finished the dolls, I found we were out of flour, and I needed more thread and a new needle. So we went at last to the village. I insisted Jack take the wolf, and was surprised to see him putting the rag dolls in his pocket as well, even though he'd hardly looked at them since receiving them. I hoped it was a good sign.

Once we finished our other errands, we turned toward the mill. Rose was pleased to see us and hurried us into her kitchen to fix us some tea. Kitty was by the fire, stringing some wooden beads on a length of woolen thread and singing to herself. She looked up as we approached. I glanced at Jack to see if he would ask if she had meant to leave the wolf, but his lips were tightly shut.

"Kitty," I said to her, "when you came to play with Jack, did you leave something behind?" Kitty said nothing but watched me with wide eyes, and I stepped aside, revealing Jack behind me. He held out one fist with the wolf inside it. Kitty's mouth opened in a smile, and she reached out her hand. But Jack quickly pulled the wolf back and held out his other hand, which was clutched around the two rag dolls. Now I understood. He wanted to trade.

He opened his hand to let Kitty see the little dolls, and she sat up on her knees to examine them. After a moment she shook her head. "My dog." She held out one chubby hand.

I knelt beside Jack. "She just left it accidentally, Rabbit," I said. "Please give it back." I thought for a moment he was going to throw it at her. He didn't, but he didn't hand it over, either. Instead, he brought the bird out of his pocket and held a brief but silent conversation between the two figures.

He saw me watching and glared at me. "She said goodbye," he said, indicating the bird. "So did he." He held up the wolf.

I nodded. "Good."

At last, Jack opened his hand for Kitty to take the wolf. She snatched it back, and Jack turned away, arms folded.

Rose knelt beside her sister and cajoled her into giving up the wolf for a minute. "So this is what you were on about." She turned to me. "She wouldn't stop talking about how she lost her dog, but we didn't know what she meant." She turned back to her sister. "Where did you get it anyway?"

Kitty snatched the wolf back. "Man," she said, as if that explained everything.

Rose frowned. "What man?"

"Outside."

Rose turned Kitty's face toward her. "Did you know him?" Kitty shook her head. "A stranger?" Kitty nodded.

"You know you mustn't speak to strangers."

The little girl shrugged. "Good man."

"Did you see Jack's?" I asked Rose. "It's very like it, but we don't know—" I turned to Jack to ask him to show the little bird. But the door to the outside was standing open. Jack was gone again.

He hadn't gone far this time. He was sitting by the millpond, throwing in stones with fierce intensity, so I sat down a little way away, hoping he wouldn't run. His face was red and blotchy, but he wasn't crying. "They had to say goodbye," he said, loud enough for me to hear. "They had to say goodbye." He repeated it again and again.

"It's good to say goodbye," I said at last. "When you can." I reached out a hand to touch him, but he flinched away from me. "Are you ready to go home?"

He didn't answer, but rose and started down the path, walking very fast.

Jack's body was stiff and hunched as he stalked through the wood ahead of me. He refused his soup that night, and instead, he stole under the table with his bread where he pretended to feed it to his bird.

After my soup was eaten and the dishes cleaned, I sat by the fire in the rocking chair, my cloak wrapped around me and Mother's book on my lap. I did this most nights, but never had the courage to open it. I don't know what I thought would happen when I did. Would I find it wiped clean of any trace of her? Or would the smell of her come flooding back as my fingers touched the pages? That smell of dried lavender and mint and freshly turned earth? I didn't know which would be more unbearable.

The book wouldn't help me now; I knew that. There was nothing in it to tell me what to do for a grieving child. But I had to have something. Even the touch of those pages might help me feel less alone. My hand hovered above the cover, about to choose a page, when I felt Jack's arms come around my legs, hard. Perhaps he wanted to hit me, but he chose this savage embrace instead, burying his face in my skirt.

My fingers uncurled from Mother's book and reached down, slowly, as if he really were a wild rabbit from the wood. My hand rested on his head, barely touching him, and he didn't pull away.

After a few moments, he climbed into my lap. I laid Mother's book on the floor and wrapped my cloak around him. We rocked in silence for a long time. At last he spoke, so softly I hardly heard him. "Is she the same princess?"

"The same?" I looked down. Jack was holding the little rag girl in one hand. He stroked the feathers on her cloak gently, and turned her in his hand as if he had never looked at her properly before. Perhaps he hadn't.

"As the last one, the one who went with Mother."

"No." My voice was toneless in my ears. I wasn't sure what story he wanted me to tell, but I knew the girl in the lace gown was not the same as the girl with feathers on her cloak.

"She's not All-Kinds-of-Feathers?"

I took a breath, then I let the story begin. "She is, but she's not the same as she was. The one before, that was before she left the palace. This," I touched the new doll's gown, "is her after."

"She looks different now?" Jack was watching me closely.

I shrugged, not sure how to explain. "She has different clothes. She feels different too. She loves living in the woods, and she'd never leave the little rabbit. But since the mother hen went away, she's…she's…"

"Sad again?"

I nodded. "All-Kinds-of-Feathers and the little rabbit both missed the mother hen very much. And sometimes she didn't know if she was doing everything right and she also missed…" I couldn't go on.

"She missed her prince?"

I sighed. "Yes. But she was afraid she wouldn't see him again."

Jack touched the doll's hair. "But she's going to stay with her rabbit?"

"Yes." I leaned my face into his hair.

"Maybe tomorrow…" He sighed and yawned. "Maybe tomorrow I'll make them a bigger house." He held up the wooden bird. "I still like the sparrow best." He looked up at me, his eyes wide in the firelight. "I'm sorry."

I tightened my arms around him. "It doesn't matter."

"I can't help it," he murmured, running one finger along a black feather on my cloak, then a pale gray one. "Raven," he whispered. "Dove."

I kept rocking as he touched a red feather. "I know."

He yawned, nestling his face into the hollow of my shoulder. "Robin."

FORTY-ONE

*J*ack was true to his word. He made a stick house big enough for the wooden bird and the two rag dolls. The bird was still his favorite, though, and sometimes he played only with her. I thought about making him a wolf out of rags, but I feared he would reject it. Instead, I sewed the scrap from my nightgown and the shards of the glass slipper into my feathered cloak. I used red thread, just as Mother had done.

Instead of hanging my cloak on its peg beside the door, I usually draped it over the back of Mother's rocking chair by the fire. When Jack and I sat there, I would wrap it around us, and he would name the feathers. *Rooks, ravens, and magpies. Falcons and eagles and hawks.*

Alone together, Jack and I continued on. I held him when he woke in the night crying. And when I startled awake in the mornings, sure it was me I had buried behind the cottage, Jack put his hands on my face and said my name, over and over until I could breathe again.

And when I got up, I did what was needed. I fetched water and firewood. I milked the goat. I fixed meals we didn't always feel like eating. I swept the floor and cleaned the dishes.

I had been through this before, and it was familiar. This emptiness. And yet, this time I had no hateful replacement ordering me around, wearing my mother's clothes and jewels. No one filled up her rooms with the scents of harsh perfumes until I could no longer remember her delicate scent, that irreplaceable *something* I would never know again.

This time no one trampled or threatened me. No one looked down their nose at me or disapproved, and that was one comfort. But in a way it didn't matter. It was no easier to get up every day, to do those things I used to do when Mother was here. Things like chopping roots and crushing leaves and mixing potions. Things like sweeping and spinning and tending the fire.

Things like breathing.

When my own mother died, there was no end to my tears. The storyteller at Mother's hearth told us how the motherless girl watered the hazel tree with her tears. That was not true. So much bitter salt water would have drowned that little tree. But now, without Mother, I was dry. I hadn't shed a single tear since finding her cold in our bed.

I didn't want Jack to see me cry, but surely it was wrong not to. I told myself I must be heartless.

I didn't really believe myself, though; surely heartless did not feel like this.

Still I didn't open Mother's book. Perhaps I was saving it for a time when I really needed it, a time when nothing but seeing her handwriting on those familiar pages would comfort me. It was something to look forward to, a treat I promised myself. Although what I had to do to earn this treat, I didn't know.

In the end, I didn't choose when to open it. It was not a reward or a consolation but to check a recipe I couldn't remember. The shoemaker had accidentally driven a nail into his finger, and the wound had festered. I was missing an ingredient in the infusion I was making to cleanse it, but I couldn't remember what it was.

Mother would have known it. She wouldn't have had to check the book; it was all inside her head. But I was not Mother; the shoemaker would have to make do with me, so I had to open the book. I left the ingredient shelf and went to the fireside to pick it up. As I sat down in the rocking chair, I felt the shoemaker's eyes on me. I glanced over at him, but he wasn't looking at me, exactly. He was looking at my feet.

I tucked them under the chair and opened the book. It was as it always had been, mismatched pages, written by generations of different hands. But I didn't feel Mother's presence or hear her voice; I wasn't even thinking of her. As my fingers turned the pages, my thoughts were on the shoemaker. I suppose he, more than most, would wonder why I wasn't wearing shoes in the dead of winter. Doubtless he was looking at Mother's wooden clogs, sitting by the door. I wouldn't wear them, but I didn't have the heart to move them. Not yet.

I glanced up. The shoemaker wasn't looking at Mother's shoes but at my face. His white brows were slightly drawn in, almost worried, as if I was written in a language he couldn't read. I looked back down at the book, turning quickly to the page I needed. As I did, something caught my eye, something different. It was a color of ink I had never seen before.

Could there be a page in Mother's book I had never memorized, never even seen? I had flipped past the page so quickly the flash of color was gone before I was sure I had seen it, and now I had found the page I needed. I would have to look again later.

I closed the book and added the forgotten ingredient, *juice of knotgrass,* to my infusion. I avoided the shoemaker's eyes as I tended his finger and bandaged it up. But I could feel him watching me with that slightly worried expression. He said nothing, though, until I gave him a jar of the mixture and a pot of salve to take back home with him.

"Thank you, my dear." He stood with a smile. "It feels better already." He patted his pockets, feeling for something. "Now we must discuss payment." He seemed to find what he wanted and drew it out. A tape measure. "How about I take your measure for a new pair of shoes?"

All the strength drained from my muscles as I imagined unwinding my bandages and the old man taking my scarred feet in his gnarled hands. I couldn't breathe. Did he know the kind of damage a pair of shoes could do? The kind of damage someone might inflict to fit them? Or would he be shocked by my scars? I took a step back, my hands shaking.

I had worn nothing but bandages on my feet for more than a year, maybe I would never wear shoes again. I couldn't let him go to all that trouble.

Finally, I squeezed some words out. "Oh no, no thank you." My hand fluttered, warding off the tape measure. "Not for me. Perhaps when Jack needs a new pair." Truthfully, it probably wouldn't be long until he did. The shoemaker's watery blue eyes had that slightly baffled expression they had worn earlier, and he drew the tape measure in toward his chest, holding it in both hands as if to shield it from me. Doubtless he wondered why such a little thing, such a simple object, could trouble anyone so much. But I couldn't explain myself to him.

I couldn't explain myself to anyone. I could only run away and hide.

The shoemaker looked around for Jack, perhaps thinking to examine his shoes. Jack retreated further under the table, his hands closing protectively around his wooden bird.

The shoemaker must have thought that whatever ailed me was catching, but said only, "Very well, then, my dear, when you are ready," and gave me a bit of a bow. "You know where I live."

After Jack was asleep that night, I sat back down in the rocking chair and opened Mother's book. For a moment I feared the mysterious page would have disappeared and I would never find it again. But then there it was; it wasn't a completely new page after all. On the top of the page was an entry I recognized, a quick note with an extra use for rest-harrow: *mix an infusion with vinegar and wash the mouth to ease the toothache.*

The rest of the page had been empty. It wasn't now.

Mother had filled the space that remained. But unlike the faded grayish entry for rest-harrow, this was written in a purple ink. Near the top of the page, just under the rest-harrow entry, she had drawn a flower with delicate tear-shaped petals and leaves. The flower's head drooped gracefully on a willowy stem. Underneath, in Mother's confident hand, was its name: *second sight.*

Then I remembered Mother sitting by the fire the night before she died, writing in her book, that night we'd made the blackberry ink. This was the plant she said we needed.

Her entry was uncharacteristically brief. There was no recipe for how to use it, only a drawing of the flower, the name, and its use: *It draws what is deep inside.* Under this, taking up most of the rest of the page was another drawing, this one of a structure. It looked like a ruin of some kind, an abbey perhaps, or a castle. There was a crumbling tower at the back, but the rest of it was only walls; the roof had fallen away. Under this, Mother had written two words: *Glass Mountain.* In the margin on one side, she had written: *Well.*

And that was all.

I studied the page for a long time, memorizing every stroke from Mother's pen. It was only another entry in a recipe book, a picture of a plant and a note about where to find it. It should have been enough, just seeing something new from her. But I wanted to believe it was more: a last letter from Mother, for my eyes alone.

My fingers ran over the blackberry ink, tracing each line. Why had she drawn this ruin? There were no other drawings like it in the book. She had said the plant was rare; maybe this ruin was the only place to find it. She said second sight was good for drawing things embedded in the skin, but she said something else too. If only I could remember, perhaps I would know what she'd been trying to tell me.

It was late when I went to bed. And as I lay there, on the edge of sleep where thoughts become jumbled and confused, I heard Mother's voice. *Good for old wounds.*

Good for old wounds. That's what she had said. I carried those words into sleep with me. And all night, sleeping and waking, I turned them over in my mind, repeating them over and over to myself. What sort of wounds, I wondered. A broken bone, not properly set, that aches when the weather turns? The sores of the bedridden invalid, which fester if not tended properly?

Or had she meant scars like mine? A naked reminder of past hurts.

My sleep was restless, almost feverish. Every lump in the mattress felt like a stone. Late in the night I threw off the quilt despite the cold and fell deeply asleep at last, but I woke again before it was light, hunched against the cold. Giving up on more sleep, I got up and sat in Mother's chair, wrapping my cloak around me.

Could there really be a cure for me? I was beginning to think not, but if there were, Mother would have known it. Maybe if I had gathered up the courage to ask her, she would have told me long ago. She would have told me properly, instead of with a few mysterious lines in her book.

Maybe she only wanted to jot down a few notes, a reminder to go to Glass Mountain in the spring to get some supplies. But why the elaborate sketch of the ruin, then? If she had been there and planned to go again, she would know the place. She had obviously remembered it well enough to make a detailed drawing.

In fact, she had the contents of the entire book memorized. I had long known that. By the time I had arrived at Mother's cottage, the book was not for her anymore. It must have been once, when she was young and got it from some other woman. Who that woman was, I never thought to ask. Perhaps it was the woman with the crabbed, spidery script, or the one with the neat and flowing hand, who ended her letters with a curling flourish, or the one who began all her entries with an elaborate capital letter, like she was a monk in a monastery writing an illuminated manuscript. Each of these women had filled the book with her own knowledge and experience. She had used it to remind herself of what she had learned. Then she left it behind for the one who came to take her place.

Now Mother herself had left it behind. We had not been kin, but Jack and I were all she had; we were her heirs, and this was her legacy. Jack could follow this calling too, if he chose. But for now, this book was my inheritance. Why else would she have had me read her recipes when she knew them all by heart? She hadn't needed me to. But she had known that in time, someone would come after her, and if I showed the interest and aptitude, it might as well be me. So the book was mine then. I was the someone who came after, and what she wrote in it was for me alone—one final message. Her last words.

The room was growing lighter now with the first rays of the sun. When Jack sat up in bed, I asked him if Mother had ever taken him to Glass Mountain. He shook his head. "She wanted to go there." I hung up my cloak and began to build up the fire. "So you and I will go, in the spring when the weather warms up."

I turned to see Jack watching me, his hair still tousled from sleep. "Why?"

"I don't know," I told him, "but I want to find out."

PART THREE:

THE MOUNTAIN

FORTY-TWO

Good grazing land, folks used to say.
There's a little village not far off; Needle, it's called.
Water as clear as glass.

Glass Mountain filled my thoughts. It was a place I'd never been, home of a plant I'd never seen, except drawn in blackberry ink. I had no idea how to use the second sight when I found it. Still, Mother had written about it in her book.

She'd wanted us to go up the mountain for it, so we would go. It was something to hope for.

But we couldn't go until spring, and I was restless all through the winter.

In the meantime, I asked the villagers what they knew. While Rose was sure Glass Mountain was the same as her Looking Glass Mountain, none of the other villagers mentioned magic wells or enchanted princes. They told me how to get there and a bit about the nearby village, but they knew little else. Part of me wanted to write down all they said in Mother's book. I couldn't bring myself to do it, though; it was still hers. I could read it, but nothing more. Instead, I kept every word in my memory and repeated them to myself, over and over and over again.

The villagers all knew about Mother's death by now. Still, I dreaded seeing a stranger in our clearing, someone from farther away. Someone who knew Mother but hadn't heard. I dreaded not being who they wanted, and having to explain myself.

When the old woodcutter's son came to our door, he didn't ask me any questions, and I was grateful. He only said his father had a bad cough and could someone come to see him. He apologized that they were so far away, a couple of hours walk through the woods.

"I wasn't sure I could get away to come today. It's just the two of us, you see," he said as he strode along the path, quickly getting ahead of Jack and me. "I had a load of wood to take to the village, and some repairs on our roof to make besides."

Realizing I had stopped to wait for Jack, he turned back. "Oh, losing you, am I?"

"Our legs are not as long as yours," I replied.

The annoyed glance he shot at Jack was gone in an instant. He returned and stood beside me, cocking an amused eyebrow as he studied my feather cloak. "That's a funny thing."

"It does what I need it to."

"It hides your prettiness." He stretched out a finger as if to run it down one of the feathers, then drew it back as Jack ran the last few steps to us.

I looked away, my cheeks suddenly hot. "It's warm. It keeps the rain off. That's what a cloak is for."

"Suit yourself." He laughed down at me, offering his arm.

I shook my head. "We can manage." Jack had reached us now.

He shrugged and went on with his story. "Anyway, last night these fellows came by looking for work and offered to help me with the wood. So I had time to fetch you."

It was a good thing the strangers had come along, for the old man had a fever as well as the cough. He had refused to take to his bed, though. He sat in a chair by the fire, a blanket wrapped around his thin shoulders. *I don't worry much until they take to their beds,* Mother had said to me once. *Though sometimes they surprise me.*

I decided not to worry much either, though the cough sounded bad. I cleared a place to work at the table as the patient's deerhound watched me from its spot beside the hearth, its tail thumping in approval.

The old man was in good spirits, telling his son he planned to feel poorly much more often if it got him a visit from a pretty girl. "Or perhaps," he winked at the younger man, "I'm not that ill at all, and you just wanted the pleasure of the young lady's company on the walk here."

"It was certainly a pleasure, Da." The son laughed and glanced at me. "I'll fetch her for you as often as you like."

I looked down into my basket and suppressed a shudder. The younger woodcutter was, in truth, old enough to have children my age at least. But, *It's just the two of us,* he had said. There wasn't a woman around the house, or any sign of one. Or any children, either.

Even with my back turned, I could feel his eyes on me. I didn't want to be gazed at like that—as if I had something he wanted and he was wondering how he could get it from me.

I smoothed the hairs on the back of my neck and set to work chopping onions for a poultice. Jack, who had been hanging back by the door, became a little braver and stepped nearer to the fire, patting his knees and calling for the dog. The dog wagged his tail and moved to stand, but sank back with a whine as soon as he put weight onto his front paw.

I stopped my work and knelt beside the dog, stroking its coarse, gray fur. "What's wrong with him?" The dog's tongue lolled out, his mouth forming a good-natured expression that was almost a smile.

The old man shrugged. "He was like that when he came here."

I continued to pet the dog, hoping to gain his confidence enough to touch the sore leg. "How long have you had him?"

"Oh, he's not ours," he said with a wave of his hand. "Belongs to that lad with the funny…" He paused, trying to remember a name. "That Henry's master."

"Those men helping us," the son explained. He spoke louder for his father's benefit. "Henry's the master, Da."

The old man scowled. "Why does he call the other fellow 'Master' then? And he's always fetching things for him?"

The younger man shrugged dismissively. "I don't know, but if you'd them seen out working, you'd see it's Henry knows what he's about, and tells his *master* what to do."

By this time I had managed to stroke my way down the dog's body to his foreleg. When I reached the sore spot, he whined and pulled away. As gently as I could, I ran my fingers over flesh and bone until I found the problem. "The leg's broken."

The old man nodded. "Thought it was so," he said. "Told the young fella. He was hoping some rest would set him right, but I said not."

The son gave his father a skeptical look, then glanced at me, one corner of his mouth tilting upward. "Can you fix it?"

"I can splint it," I said, "but he'll need to stay quiet for a while." At my direction, the son trimmed two thin strips of wood, and I began. The break was clean, so I bound the wood tightly to the leg with some strips of rag as the dog looked on, his tail still thumping.

As I finished, Jack crept up beside me and knelt by the dog's head, stroking his ears and patting his back. "Sparrow fixed you," he whispered. "You'll feel better now." The dog submitted to Jack's attention patiently, giving him an occasional lick on his hand or nose.

Once he had finished helping me with the splint, the son disappeared outside to fix the roof, and I breathed a little easier. While the onions cooked, I fixed a remedy for the fever. As I did with everyone these days, I asked the old man if he knew anything about Glass Mountain.

"Of course," he said as I poured some water from the kettle into a clay mug. "No one goes there much anymore." This was what everyone said. I nodded and reached into my basket for the ingredients I needed. *Syrup of coltsfoot.* "Folk used to though, when I was a lad."

"Did they?" No one had said that before. "Shepherds grazing their sheep, you mean?" I took out another bottle. *Root of swallow-wort, dried and coarsely chopped.*

The old woodcutter shook his head. "No no, lass, for the well."

"What do you mean?"

The old man was pleased to have an interested listener. "Oh, Looking Glass Mountain is a magical place."

No one besides Rose had called it Looking Glass Mountain. My hand stopped, hovering over the basket. I forced my hand to move again. *Dried horehound leaf.*

"There's an old ruin up at the top," he went on. "Some say it was a palace, some say a monastery, but no one knows for sure. But people from miles around used to go to visit the well up there. The water in it was so clear, folk called it the Looking Glass. Glass is a magical stuff, you know."

I nodded, my throat tightening. How could I deny it? An involuntary shudder ran up my spine.

"Folk went to see their future," he continued. "Maids would look in to see who they would marry, young lads would look in to see how they would make their fortunes. Most of all they'd go for the healing. Folk'd say water in that well there, clear as glass, would cure whatever ails you."

I stood still, the bundle of horehound clutched in my hand. "Did you ever go?"

He waved a hand. "No, no. I've been healthy all my life. Never sick. Perhaps I ought to go, when the weather warms up. Just for my joints, you know." He held out a gnarled hand, fingers distorted with rheumatism.

I smiled. "I'll bring something for your joints next time."

"No, no." He waved away my offer. "Don't bother." Then he grinned. "Unless you find you're missing me. It'll give you an excuse to visit." He broke into a hearty laugh that ended in a painful fit of coughing.

I hadn't brought Mother's book, but this recipe was one I knew by heart. I could see the words on the page without any effort. *Steep swallow-wort and horehound leaf in boiling water.* People used to travel to Glass Mountain from miles around, that's what he had said. *Stir in syrup of coltsfoot and honey.* To drink from the well with water as clear as glass. Was that what Mother had meant by writing *Well* in her book? *Drink as hot as can be tolerated.*

"Drink this down," I told my patient, "as quickly as you can. It will taste bitter, so the faster, the better."

He took the mug and sniffed it; then he wrinkled his nose. "Smells awful." I nodded. He bent back his head and downed the whole mug. "Tastes worse," he gasped with satisfaction. "I always say, the best medicine tastes the worst. That's what I'd tell my lad," he gestured upward, to the roof where his son was working, "when that lady came to tend him, you know, the wise woman from the woods. Back when he was a boy and took ill."

My throat was suddenly dry. "Mother."

The old man nodded, coughing a little. "Yes, her. I thought he'd bring her today, but he came back with you. Busy with someone else I suppose."

It was the conversation I dreaded having, but there was nothing for it. "Mother is dead, I'm afraid," I told him.

His eyes grew bright, with fever or with emotion, I couldn't tell.

"In her sleep." For some reason I felt I owed him more of an explanation than that. But I had none to give.

He sat, not saying anything for a few moments, just nodding his head and looking into the fire. "Not many of us left anymore. From those days."

At last, he held out the empty mug. When I took it, he grasped my hand and patted it. "Well, you'll do very nicely, lass. Your potion tastes every bit as nasty as hers used to. You'll do very well indeed." He began to laugh at his joke and was overwhelmed by another bout of coughing.

"I thought that awful stuff was supposed to help," he gasped when he could breathe again.

"It will." I took the mug back to the table. "Give it some time. And this will help too." I shifted the collar of his shirt so I could lay the poultice on his chest.

He took a whiff of the onions and nodded approvingly. "That smells awful too." He leaned back and closed his eyes. "It ought to work wonders."

I thought so too. I set aside ingredients for another cup of the tea for him to drink that night and in the morning before we returned. I was impatient to ask more about Glass Mountain, but he needed rest, not more talk. The next day would be soon enough.

As I packed up my things to leave, I saw the old woodcutter beckoning to Jack. He sensed Jack's wariness and waited patiently for him to approach. I couldn't hear if he said anything, but after a moment Jack nodded and went closer.

When we said our good-byes, the man's son thanked me again and again. Jack threw his arms around the dog's neck and gave the old man a shy wave. I raised my eyebrows. "He's taken quite a liking to you," I said. "That's more than most people get out of him."

My patient winked. "I have my ways." He grinned as I touched his forehead to feel for fever. He was still quite hot, but I told myself with rest and another cup of the tea at bedtime he should be much improved by morning.

Sometimes they surprise me, Mother's voice whispered in my ear before we had gone many paces from the cottage. I stopped and turned, wondering if we should stay. But we had the goat to milk at home, and if we waited much longer, we would be making our way through the wood in the dark.

As I hesitated in the woodcutter's clearing, I heard the jingle of a harness.

"That'll be those fellows, back from the village," the younger man called from the doorway, where he had stayed to see us off. "They'll be glad about the dog."

I nodded, thinking I should stop and say hello. But my feet made no movement toward the door. Suddenly, I didn't feel like meeting anyone new. It was time to go.

"Sure you don't want me to walk with you?"

I shook my head and waved. "We'll be fine." I had needed him to bring us today. After all, we hadn't known the way, but the idea of another walk with him made me uneasy. "We'll come again tomorrow."

That night, I curled in Mother's rocking chair while the soup simmered over the fire. I wrapped my shawl around me and closed my eyes, thinking of nothing. The cottage was quiet, except for the fire crackling and Jack's voice from his place under the table. "I've found you," he whispered over and over. "I've found you."

I opened my eyes. Jack had one little figure in each hand. That was nothing new; sometimes he played with both the wooden bird and the girl in the feathered cloak. But the little doll lay on his lap. Cautiously, I stood and took a few steps to the table. Jack was so engrossed he didn't notice me until I was crouched beside him. "What's that?"

Jack jumped and pulled the toys into his chest, protecting them. "He gave it to me," he said, his eyes wide. "It's mine. For me. He said to take it." The words came out in a rush. Then he stopped, breathing heavily and clutching the toys, afraid I would snatch them away.

I sat back on my heels and held up my hands to prove I meant no harm. "May I see?" Slowly, Jack opened his hand. On his palm was another carved wooden figure. This one was a hare, ears forward and one tiny paw lifted, as if it were ready to run.

When I didn't reach to take it, Jack opened his other hand to reveal the bird. "She knew she had a friend," he said, "but she didn't know who. But now she found him." He touched the hare's nose to the bird's beak. "I found you," he whispered. "My friend."

"Who gave it to you?"

"The man."

Just what the miller's little daughter, Kitty, had said about her wolf. "What man?"

He was surprised I didn't know. "The man today. The coughing man."

The old woodcutter. When he called Jack over before we left, he must have given it to him then.

Jack drew the hare a little away from me. "I can keep him." His solemn eyes were fixed on mine.

I didn't reach for the little creature, though my fingers itched to touch it. It was so like the other two. I had a feeling that if I held it, I could feel its tiny heart beating.

"Of course you can," I said. "He gave it to you, so it's yours." The little frown that had been between his brows relaxed. "Did you say thank you?"

His gaze dropped to the floor. "I forgot."

"Well, you can thank him tomorrow when we go back."

I stood up to check on the soup, and Jack went back to his toys. "Thank you, my friend," he whispered. "Thank you."

FORTY-THREE

*J*ack could not thank his new friend the next day. Overnight it began to snow, and the wind whipped around and around our cottage, wailing and crying and blowing the snow in gusts. In the morning we woke to a world of white, with the snow still falling fiercely. We would not be going out any time soon.

I stood at the table, fixing ingredients for another tonic for the woodcutter. My fingers knew what to do. They chopped and crumbled and poured without my thinking, so my mind was free to wander. The old woodcutter would be well enough without us. I hoped so, at least. Despite my unease about the way the younger man had looked at me, I was anxious to be back. What else did the old man know about Glass Mountain and the well called the Looking Glass? Mother had never mentioned any water that healed or foretold the future. It seemed like something she would have shaken her head at. And yet, she had written the word *Well*. But Mother couldn't tell me anything anymore.

Maybe the woodcutter could.

And again and again, my thoughts returned to another question. Was the old woodcutter the carver of the little wooden animals? Surely he wouldn't have traveled all the way to our cottage to leave us a pile of wood and a carved bird. I couldn't imagine his son doing it, either. And neither one had known that Mother was dead. How could they have known how welcome those gifts would be?

Snow fell off and on for two days, transforming the wood outside our window into an unfamiliar landscape. The third day was cloudy and gray, with wind whirling the snow into phantom shapes. But the fourth morning was calm and sunny. As I was washing the breakfast dishes, there was a knock at the door.

The old woodcutter's son stood outside, his frame filling most of the doorway. I took a step back. Why had he come to collect me? I'd said I would return on my own. Was the old man worse?

He said nothing. It must have been a cold, wet walk through the snow. His cheeks were red and his trousers soaked to the knee.

I opened the door wider and let him in. "Would you like some tea?" I gestured to a chair beside the table.

"Thank you." He came in only far enough to close the door behind him. "There's no hurry."

I fetched a cup and added some mint and chamomile. "I wanted to come before," I said. "But I wasn't sure I could find the way with the snow and—" I broke off. The woodcutter was still standing, his hat in his hand, looking at his boots, which dripped melted snow onto the floor. I pulled out the chair. "Please, sit down."

He did, but continued looking at the trail of water on the floor. At last he looked up when I handed him his tea. He thanked me with a faint smile. It was not unfriendly, but it wasn't the same smile of a few days before. "We'll be ready soon," I told him. "Dress up warm, Jack. We're going out."

The woodcutter held out a hand. "There's no need."

"He's better?" I took my cloak from the peg by the door. "Perhaps I should come anyway, just to—" I turned back and stopped. He was watching me, a bit of a flush on his cheeks.

I came back to his chair, a shiver of cold running down my spine. "What is it?"

"You don't need to come." He paused, as if not knowing how to go on. "He's…" His expression was almost embarrassed. "He's past helping now."

My face went hot as I realized what he was trying to say. His father was dead.

I took a step back, feeling something hard behind me. It was the table. I held on to it with both hands. I had dropped my cloak. "Oh." My voice echoed in my ears. "When did—"

"It was the day after you came, the first day it snowed so hard." His story came rushing out. "He seemed no worse that morning, but that afternoon, the cough got worse. I thought maybe we should give him some more of the tea, so I poured some more water on those herbs you left, and I put the poultice on again. By that night he wasn't coughing so much, but his breathing wasn't easy. But he slept at last. He went in the night." He drank his tea thirstily, as if that speech had left him dry. "He was peaceful enough."

He looked up at me, then, concerned. "You should sit down. You've gone pale." He stood to bring me a chair.

"I'm well," I said, waving for him to sit back down. He brought the chair anyway and guided me into it. Why does it often happen that way? Why do the loved ones of the dead do so much comforting of others, the people who are supposed to comfort them?

He took his chair again, across from me.

"I'm sorry," I said at last. "I didn't think…I thought he would recover."

He nodded. "Me too. He was a stubborn old dog." His smile didn't reach his eyes, and he looked away, cracking his knuckles. "I reckon I thought he'd go on forever. But we can't." His eyes met mine. "Can we?"

I shook my head, but I knew he wanted more from me than that useless gesture. I should say something wise, something comforting. I couldn't rid myself of the feeling I was obliged to give him something. I didn't want to consider what, though. I tried to think of what Mother would have said, but my imagination failed me.

"We can at least come and help," I said at last. "Prepare for the burial, I mean." The idea of walking through the wood to the now empty woodcutter's cottage unsettled me even more than it had before. But I would have done it for anyone else; so would Mother. I reached down to pick up my cloak.

He caught me by the wrist with a hand that encompassed much of my forearm. I froze, but he didn't seem to notice. "There's no need. We've already done it. The fellows staying with us…" He dropped my wrist, his eyes on the floor. "With me. They were a great help. They helped me get him ready, and helped with the grave and all of it."

I sat back in my chair, unconsciously rubbing my arm where his hand had come around it. I had failed to help the old man, and now there was nothing I could do. But surely there was something I should have done. I should have left more of the swallow-wort and coltsfoot. I should have told the son how to make another poultice. I should have tried a different mixture.

I should have stayed.

The woodcutter was watching me. "I'd rather it had been you to help me."

My throat was suddenly dry, but I found my voice at last. "I'm grateful they were there. For you." My eyes were on the bed where I had washed and dressed Mother's body, but I wasn't seeing it. "It's lonely work."

"Lonely," he repeated, nodding. "It's lonelier now they've gone."

I said nothing. It was my fault, but did that mean I owed him something? Something I couldn't give? The hairs on the backs of my arms stood on end.

"I should be off." He stood abruptly and walked to the door. Then he turned back; I thought it was to look for his hat. It was on the table, but he didn't see it. He was staring at me again. "I'm sorry to be the bearer, you know, of bad news. But I—I wanted to see you. We're both alone now and—"

I rose and picked up the hat. "I'm not alone."

"You know what I mean." He dismissed my argument with an impatient wave of his hand and took a few steps toward me.

"We—I mean I. I don't have much money, but I've always got enough to get by. You'd never starve." He glanced toward Jack, who was huddled by the hearth, watching. "You could bring the boy. I'd take care of you."

He was looking at me like I was the only one in the room. But he didn't see me like my husband had. This man saw only something he wanted to consume. He didn't care what might be left afterward.

His voice was low but rough somehow. "We could take care of each other."

Suddenly, he moved to close the gap between us, his hands shooting toward me. Before I realized what I was doing, I had pushed his hat into his hand, holding him at arm's length.

He stopped and stared down at his hat, as if he couldn't quite understand what it was and why he wasn't holding something else. He looked back at me, his face draining of blood and his jaw tightening.

I straightened my spine. "I can take care of myself."

His mouth opened, and his fists clenched on the hat as if he wanted to rip it to pieces. Then he jammed it on his head and strode out the door, letting in a rush of cold air.

My cloak lay puddled on the floor where I had dropped it. Forcing myself to move, I returned it to its place, pulled the door closed, and drew down the bolt with trembling hands. Seeing nothing, I turned and sank to the floor. A moment later I felt Jack's hands on my cheeks. "It's all right," he whispered, the way he did when I woke in the night gasping for air. "All right."

He shifted into my lap, and we sat, saying nothing. Then he held up his two wooden animals. "Did that man make them?"

I hadn't asked the woodcutter who made the little wooden hare, or if his father had ever told him anything about Glass Mountain and the plant that grew there. How could I, when he came to tell me the old man was dead? When it was my fault? When I'd said no.

I laid my chin on Jack's head. "I don't know." Whatever the old man had known, I would never know it now.

"Why does everyone want to take us away?" he whispered.

I shook my head. "We're staying. This is where we belong."

FORTY-FOUR

I went page by page through Mother's book, searching through the remedies. Should I have used hyssop for the old man's cough? Would butter-bur or wood sorrel have broken his fever? I went over and over what I had done for the old woodcutter and what I could have done. What I should have done.

In bed at night, the entries in the book crowded into my thoughts and dreams as I mixed and remixed different potions and poultices, wrapped the old man in blankets to sweat the fever out of him, or put on snow-covered rags to cool him. But it didn't matter. I hadn't helped him, and now I never could.

I had begun to think I had a gift, that Mother had chosen me on purpose to take her place. And maybe she had.

But she was wrong to trust me.

The snow was beginning to thaw a little when Rose came to bring me to her mother. "She says it's nothing, she's just a little down," she said, standing in the door as Jack and I wrapped up for the walk. "But something's wrong. I know it."

As we trudged through the snow, Jack running before us and climbing onto the drifts, Rose told me she'd been seeing a lot of the baker's son. How they'd known each other all their lives, but something was *different* now. It was as if they were seeing each other for the first time. "I'm taking things slowly, though," she said, then she blushed. "He says I'm worth waiting for."

Rose had been right about her mother. Something was wrong; I knew it as soon as I walked into the bedroom. The room had a familiar scent to it, sweet and a little rotten. Just like my mother's room had smelled at the end, when the surgeons had gone and there was no one left but me and her. I set my basket on the floor, Mother's voice sounding in my ears. *I don't worry much until they take to their beds.*

When Rose went to make the tea, the miller's wife placed my hand on her belly, guiding it to the hard knot on one side. She watched me, but I think she knew what I would say. She had known it for some time as she felt it growing inside her. I sat still on the bed, feeling like I was the one with something hard and alien inside. Something spreading through my veins and turning them to stone. At last I made my head nod, telling her what she knew was true. She patted my hand and nodded too.

She glanced toward the next room where her daughter bustled about. "My Rose will need a friend."

I squeezed her hand. "She has one."

"Couldn't you bleed her?" asked the miller, when I told him his wife was dying. She had gone to sleep, and we were talking in hushed voices at the kitchen table.

I shook my head. "It wouldn't help."

"What about a potion? Can't you make her something?"

"I know of nothing that would cure this." My heartbeat filled my throat and ears, and my stomach was sick. Everything I had learned from Mother wasn't enough. I wasn't enough. This

Sparrow, whoever she was, was an imposter, just as much as the girl with the glass slippers had been. I had failed the old woodcutter, and I was about to fail again.

The miller curled his hands into fists, his eyes reddening. "Mother would have known."

Perhaps she had. But she never told me how to cure this creeping, spreading death, and there was nothing about it in her book. We would have to get by with me and what I knew.

Rose followed Jack and me out the door. She caught at my hand. "I don't think I can bear it," she said.

I hugged her tightly. "You can."

She would have to.

"Is there nothing you can do?" The words seemed to catch in her throat, as if she could barely force them out.

I had asked Mother nearly the same question once, when she told me about Jack's family. Her answer came out of my mouth now before I knew I was speaking. "There is always something we can do."

We went to the mill nearly every day. I made the miller's wife willow bark tea to ease the pain and gave her syrup of wild poppies to help her sleep. And I did other things. I made meals and watched the younger children. I sat by the bed and read aloud. I helped Rose with the washing and the mending and the baking. Little ordinary things.

And I went to other villagers who called me for the usual reasons, the hurts I could heal. Coughs and fevers, scrapes and cuts. Stomachaches and earaches and toothaches.

Winter passed away, and the miller's wife faded, her skin becoming paper-thin and her voice a whisper. Her sleep was restless, so I made the poppy syrup stronger as the snowdrops peeked above the snow and opened up. I made it stronger still as the trees showed their first buds.

But as I mixed and tended and bandaged, my thoughts had gone ahead of me. They were up on Glass Mountain with the plant called second sight. They were working out the route we would take to get there, what we would bring with us, how long it would take. I took Jack to the shoemaker's for a pair of sturdy boots; I mended our clothes. I baked hard biscuits that would keep a long time. I sifted through my herbs and potions, deciding which to take along and which to leave behind. I don't know when it started, this feeling that I was incomplete without them.

When the blackthorn blossoms opened, the miller's wife fell into a deep sleep without the aid of poppy syrup. Her heartbeat was weak and her breathing shallow. I took turns with the miller and his children sitting by her bedside reading or telling her stories. Or sometimes doing nothing at all, just being near her.

On the third morning after her mother dropped into this deep sleep, I arrived to find Rose sitting outside on the low wall around the mill yard, her hands uncharacteristically still. She had the shadowy, wasted look of someone who has nursed a loved one through a long illness, someone who has worried too much and slept too little. When she looked up at me, her eyes were red-rimmed but dry. I sat down next to her and put my arms around her. It was over.

We sat that way, saying nothing, as Jack followed one of the mill cats around the yard, trying to pat it. It was peaceful there in the sun, but there were things to do, so at last we went inside. Rose insisted on making me tea and a slice of bread and butter. She was already slipping into her role as comforter of the people who didn't love her mother as well as she had.

Over and over again the miller thanked me for all I'd done for his wife, but I couldn't stop thinking of what he'd said at first.

Can't you make her something?

Mother would have known.

"I wanted to do more," I said into my cup of tea.

He put a calloused hand over mine. "If you could have done, you would have."

I nodded, suddenly feeling stifled in this little village. I had done what I could, those *somethings* Mother always talked about. But it hadn't been enough.

The morning after the burial, we left for Glass Mountain. I'd asked Rose if she'd like to go with us. We'd been standing beside the grave in the churchyard, and the villagers were filing out. She shook her head. "No, my father couldn't spare me right now." She looked toward the side of the church where the baker's son waited, then she glanced back at me, blushing. "Perhaps I don't need to see into the Looking Glass after all." Then she tilted her head, and one corner of her mouth lifted. "But maybe you do."

FORTY-FIVE

It felt odd, letting the fire go cold in the hearth.

I fastened my cloak and stood gazing at Mother's wooden clogs, the bag open in my hands. We would be walking a long time. Perhaps I would want them at some point, and there was a little room left. The bag wouldn't close properly with the shoes inside, but it would have to do.

I looked around to see if there was anything else I needed. Only one thing caught my eye: Mother's book. But now there wasn't room.

I took out the clogs and slid in the book.

Mother had told me long ago that mine were good feet, that they would serve me well for standing or walking or whatever I needed. So I sat in her chair and wrapped them in thick, clean strips of rag that had once been a woolen blanket. I sent Jack out ahead and shut the door behind me.

We started into the woods. And as the trees closed in behind us, I had the strangest worry that Mother would wonder where we had gone. But Mother always knew, I told myself, even the things I didn't tell her. Especially those things. I found the forest path leading north, and we began to walk.

The trees were mostly leafless still, but ferns uncurled on the forest floor at our feet, and a haze of green buds emerged around us as we made our way. The first night we slept in a charcoal burner's hut. It would likely be occupied once summer arrived. But it was empty now, with no one to mind us passing through.

We spent the second night with a couple of elderly ladies in their cottage. There were no other houses nearby, and they were happy for the company. "It's lovely to see young people," said one lady, who was small and thin, as she bustled about her hearth dishing us bowls of porridge. "We always invite them to stay, don't we, dear?" The other lady, who was taller and round, had settled down for a nap in her chair by the fire, a cat on her lap. She roused herself and nodded.

"That's what I was telling those last two lads." The thin lady settled herself to sit at the table beside Jack and me. "Usually it's the lads who come through, though, isn't it?" She rubbed at the chilblains on her fingers. "Such a help they were, with tapping the birch trees. They came along at just the right time." She leaned toward me and lowered her voice. "She doesn't get around so well these days. It's her joints; they pain her."

"My ears are well enough, though," the round lady called.

"Just telling the young people how we welcomed the help with the birch wine, that's all."

"They were both sweet on her, that's why they were so helpful."

The thin lady giggled. "Get on with you. I'm old enough to be their granny."

The round lady grinned and leaned back in her chair, closing her eyes. "The boys always fancy her."

The thin lady waved away this thought in mock exasperation. "They were looking for a girl, don't you remember, love?" she said pointedly. "Not an old lady like me." She turned back to me. "Someone they'd lost, you understand. Or one of them had." She put her chin in one hand, staring dreamily at nothing. "It was a sad story; I just know it." Then she looked back at me, folding her hands in front of her. "They didn't tell much of it, though. Just said she was missing and had we seen her."

My skin felt hot, as if I had a sudden fever.

It had been over a year since we had seen the king's men, and in all that time we'd heard little about the search for the lost princess. But the lady had not said it was a princess they were looking for anyway. And I could hardly imagine palace guards and huntsmen stopping to help these ladies with their wine. Surely no one was looking for me after all this time.

What would I do if there were? I wrapped my arms around myself, suddenly cold.

The thin lady's eyes were still on me. "They didn't say anything about a little boy, though. I suppose they weren't looking for you." There was a hint of a question in her tone.

I gave her a small smile. "I suppose not."

I knew nothing about making wine from birch sap, but there was something I could do for our hosts. Before we left the next day, I fixed a salve of wallflower and hemlock for the round lady's joints and one of pennywort for the thin lady's chilblains. We said our goodbyes and returned to the path.

It was still light when we came to the edge of the forest, though the sky was cloudy and the air smelled of rain. As the trees cleared, the land sloped down to the valley below. Needle, the village I had heard about, was ahead—the valley beyond it dotted with farms. Behind those farms was Glass Mountain, rising up toward the clouds.

Jack ran ahead, but I stopped at the edge of the forest, my chest suddenly tight. My feet stayed rooted to the forest floor, unwilling to leave the protection of the trees.

Realizing I wasn't with him, Jack turned, his expression worried. I raised my hand and waved. "Go ahead," I called. "I'm coming."

I stepped out of the woods.

FORTY-SIX

*I*t was raining and nearly dark by the time we reached the village inn, an old wooden building with a needle's eye painted on its sign. The next morning the rain had stopped, but there were still puddles in the village streets when we went out. As we bought bread, cheese, and apples at the market, I asked if there was a healer in the village. It was my last chance to find out anything more about the second sight or the well beside the ruins.

"My neighbor's a midwife, and she does potions as well," the baker told me as I paid her for a loaf of bread. "But I'm afraid she's gone to visit her daughter. Lives quite a ways off. She won't be back for weeks."

I told myself it was just as well. Now that the mountain was within my sight, I was more anxious to be there than ever.

"Is someone ill?" she asked, knitting her eyebrows in concern.

"No, I only—"

"Oh, very good." Her worried expression relaxed, but only a little. "I was sorry to tell them at Valley Farm that she wasn't here."

My mind was instantly on the contents of my bag. "Did someone there need her?"

"Don't know if it was serious." She shrugged. "Mary was up here yesterday. She's got a new hired hand who's hurt himself somehow."

Jack tugged on my skirt. "Are we going to the mountain now?"

Glass Mountain rose up on the other side of the valley, its peak shrouded in fog. My feet itched to move on and meet it, but the mountain and I would have to wait.

I laid a hand on Jack's shoulder. "Not yet."

I had work to do.

Though the water at the top of Glass Mountain was said to be clear as glass, the mountain itself was green. It grew greener and greener as we walked across the valley. We couldn't begin our climb yet, but Valley Farm sat right at the base of the mountain. We were nearly there, at least.

When we arrived in the yard, the farmhouse door slammed open and a woman ran out. She rushed past me, holding out her arms to Jack.

"Tom!" she cried, breathless with some emotion. "Tom! Where have—" Jack clutched my skirts and ducked behind me. The woman stopped short, her hands falling to her sides, and looked behind us. We weren't who she wanted.

"I'm sorry to bother you," I began. "I was passing through. They told me in the village you wanted a healer. I came to see if I could help."

"Why?" She continued to look past us, her hands covering her mouth as if trying to hold something in. "Is he injured? Have they found him?"

"I—" I faltered. "The baker in Needle told me Valley Farm needed someone. To help a man who was hurt. Are you Mary?"

She let out a breath and ran a hand over her head. Her kerchief came off in her hand. She looked at it as if wondering what it was, then she stuffed it in her apron pocket. "Oh, I see," she said at last. "The man you want isn't here. He's gone with the others."

More waiting. I had come right to the base of the mountain, but now it was farther away than ever. "I came to see if there was anything I could do for him. Is he better today?"

For the first time she met my eyes. "I am Mary," she murmured. "I've forgotten my manners. Please come in."

Mary led us into the house and offered us chairs. There was a lump of dough on the table, but she didn't return to kneading it. She wandered around the kitchen, not able to settle to anything. She picked up a folded cloth and refolded it, then took a pan off a hook and put it back.

After a moment, she seemed to remember she was not alone. "The men have all gone looking for my Tom. He wandered off this morning while I was mending the sheep's pen." She approached the dough on the table, but seemed unsure what to do with it. "I thought your boy was him at first, but now I see he's bigger. I've been all over, but he's nowhere. So everyone's gone out looking. But someone has to stay in case he comes back." She held out her hands, dismayed at their emptiness. "So here I am."

It was mid-afternoon now. "Surely he can't have gone too far," I said, "if he's only little." I tried not to remember how far Jack had gotten into the woods the day we buried Mother.

"Yes." Mary smiled, though her eyes looked red-rimmed. "Likely he just fell asleep somewhere and they'll be back with him any minute." She dusted her hands on her apron. Then she dropped them at her sides, leaving the dough untouched.

I took my cloak off and stood. "Let me help."

"I'm not making much progress, am I?" she said with a shaky laugh. "You're very kind." I took her place, and she walked away from the table, her eyes on Jack. "I thought he was my Tom," she murmured, to no one in particular. Then she turned away, her gaze going to the window.

"This hired man of yours," I began, thinking to keep her mind off her son for a little while, "I heard he was injured."

At last she stopped her restless moving and sat down. "His hand was bandaged up when he arrived, a week or so ago. He kept saying it was nothing, just an old hurt, but the other fellow says it bothers him still." She looked thoughtful a moment. "You can tell it does. When he picks anything up, he sort of winces. Doesn't like to complain, I suppose."

I put the dough aside to rise and made a pot of tea with some chamomile from my pack. Mary was up again, pacing from the window to the hearth then back again. "They're both good workers; we were lucky to find them," she said, peering out the window. "So I went for the healer to see if she could help. Henry, that's the other fellow, he said they always ask, but they've only once found someone whose potion helped at all. But that was months ago, and the stuff's all gone now."

"That's a long time for a wound to go without healing." I spoke more to myself than to her, wondering what sort of wound it was, and what sort of potion had helped it.

"Maybe you know them," she said. "Henry and Ash."

I glanced up, but Mary was not looking at me; her eyes were on my feet.

"Henry and Ash?" I rolled those names around on my tongue, trying them out. *Henry and Ash.* My hands moved slowly, as if through water, while I set a pair of teacups on the table.

"Oh, it's just that they said the healer who gave them the potion wore no shoes, and had a cloak of..." Her eyes found my feathered cloak, draped over a chair. "So I thought perhaps..." she trailed off as I poured the tea. I said nothing as the names repeated in my head. *Henry and Ash.*

"I didn't mean anything by it." Mary looked contrite, as if she thought she'd offended me. "You know nowadays, times are hard. Sometimes people must go without, mustn't they? It's no sin." Her eyes were on my face now. "So you don't know them?"

Did I? I remembered the man who had come on behalf of his master, the morning Mother died. His master with the wounded hand. And later the women saying Ash and his man had been staying at Blackhorse Farm.

Henry was a common enough name.

Ash wasn't, though, unless you were talking of trees.

"I might know them," I said at last. "I made a potion for a man with a wounded hand, some months ago. But I never met him."

"Sparrow," she said suddenly.

I put a second hand on the teacup I was holding to keep it from spilling. Whether or not I knew them, Henry and Ash knew me.

"They said her name was Sparrow. Ash said the only thing that's been any good was her potion, and he hopes one day to thank her for it."

"I don't have anything made up," I said, more to myself as I handed her the cup.

It would have been best to wait and see the wound, but now I was the one who couldn't be still. I picked up my cup, then set it down. I had already wiped the table with a cloth, but I did it again.

At last I made a decision. "I'll do what I can." I opened my bag and let the familiar scents surround me. *Comfrey.* I laid the ingredients out on the table. *Self-heal, moneywort.* I measured and chopped, feeling my breathing go slow and even. *Wintergreen. True-love.*

The kitchen was quiet. Jack sat cross-legged on his chair, whispering to his wooden animals, and Mary watched me blankly, as if she saw nothing at all. *When the fat has turned to liquid, add the rest, then let it cool.* I poured my mixture into one of Mary's empty jam pots, and it was finished.

There was a sound outside, and we all jumped. Mary sprang up to open the door, and I busied myself putting away my things. Any minute now the farmhands would come in with the little boy. Henry and Ash would come in. I remembered Henry a little, a simply dressed man with red-brown hair and beard. But I had never met Ash. So why did I picture him with a warm, slow smile and eyes of a color I couldn't name?

I knew that was foolish. The magic in the slippers had surely broken with the glass. Unless the wish had never worked in the first place. But I would never know that now.

My bag was packed, but no one came in. Mary stayed at the door. My tea was cold now, but I sat and swallowed it down anyway. It was something to do.

At last Mary ushered someone in, a young man. He wore simple clothes and breathed heavily, like he'd run here. His hair was wet; yesterday's rain must have returned. I glanced at his hands, seeing they were weathered and a bit dirty, but neither had a bandage. Whoever he was, he was not Ash.

"This is Roland from Steepside," Mary told me. "His baby's ill. Can you go?"

When I arrived at Valley Farm, I couldn't wait to leave it and be on our way up the mountain. Nothing had changed, but now my body moved reluctantly as I stood and set down my teacup. As if I was unwilling to leave. "Of course." My hand closed around the strap of my pack. I walked around the table, checking that I had everything. I had a feeling I was leaving something behind, but it was nothing I could see.

"It's not far," Roland said, "only I've been to the village first and I heard you were here."

"Of course." My voice was dull in my ears as I fastened my cloak. "I don't mind walking." Then I turned back and picked up the little pot of salve. I put it on a windowsill near the door where it would cool more quickly. I turned to Mary, who was holding out a couple of coins. "I hope Ash—" I stopped, not knowing what I hoped. "He can use it morning and evening." My fingers closed around the coins she pressed into my palm. "I hope it helps."

There was nothing more to be done, so Jack and I followed Roland from Steepside out the door into the rain. I looked behind me at the farmhouse as we walked away, choking down a disappointment I couldn't explain.

FORTY-SEVEN

*T*hey were right to call for me.

It was the sort of thing most adults recovered from: spots, high fever, no appetite. But it was dangerous in a child this young, and I was afraid. I mixed the potion for the fever and pain into some honey. *Cinquefoil for ague. Licorice root for a painful throat. Mulberry syrup soothes inflammation.* Then I made a wash of spoonwort and lupin seed to calm the red spots on the baby's skin.

I wouldn't leave until I knew she was out of danger, so Jack and I stayed. And we waited. The spring rains continued, Roland went out to work, and news trickled in from the outside world. "They found little Tom," he announced on the second night when he came in, shaking the rain off his coat. "Yesterday it was." He kissed his wife Janet, then the baby in her arms. He frowned at the heat of the child's skin. "No better?"

She shrugged. "No worse," she said with a sigh. "At least she's sleeping." Roland nodded, hanging his coat on a peg by the door and settling into a chair. Then he was silent, just watching his daughter.

"So where was Tom?" Janet asked after a moment. "Is he all right?"

"Hmm?" he said, as if he'd forgotten. Then he blinked, remembering there was more to tell. "Oh, he's fine. He'd wandered off up the mountain a little way. Those new boys at the farm found him." He turned to include me. "Tom's the little lad from Valley Farm. They were looking for him the day I came to find you."

I nodded. "Mary was telling me."

He told us the story, then, of how the little boy was nearly to the edge of a ravine, how the earth was weakened by the recent rains. How the new farmhand named Ash arrived just in time to scoop him up before a piece of the edge broke off and slid right out from under him. How the farmhand grabbed at a tree root on the way down and hung there, getting the boy to hold on around his neck so he could climb to safety.

"And no one was hurt?" I heard myself ask.

"Tom's got hardly a scratch on him." Then Roland looked thoughtful. "Though Ash did have an old hurt on one hand that opened back up with all that climbing."

An old wound, reopened, might need stitching, I thought. "I suppose they would have sent for me, if they'd needed anything."

Roland turned back to me, nodding. "I reckon so. It must not have been that bad. The little lad rode home on Ash's shoulders and thought the whole thing was a grand adventure."

Just then the baby woke, crying fretfully, so we heard no more of Roland's story, if there was more to tell.

But I couldn't stop wondering about the man with the wounded hand. What would Mother have done for him? What would I do? But no one had sent for me, so wondering did me no good. Ash was not my problem to solve.

During the third night, the baby fell into a sound sleep at last. By the morning, she was much cooler, and finally wanted to nurse. "Go on and have a rest." Janet's hand fluttered toward the bed in the corner of the room. "You've hardly slept at all."

I wrapped myself in a quilt and lay down, thinking only to rest for a few minutes. But I had spent the last few nights dozing in a chair, and the bed was so soft.

Later on I half-woke, hearing rain on the roof and feeling Jack curled up beside me. Other sounds blended with the rain— sheep, men's voices, a dog barking—the voices were almost familiar. But surely they only reminded me of ones I knew from long ago. Before stepmothers, princes, and castles, before wishes and slippers and glass. Back when I was safe from all those things. I put my arm over Jack and sank back into sleep.

It was midday when I startled awake. I had slept too long and didn't know where I was. Then I remembered. I was at the foot of Glass Mountain, and I had long wanted to be at the top of it.

By afternoon I was walking along the base of the mountain. The baby was sleeping peacefully; even Jack didn't seem to need me. I was on my own.

I went where my feet led me, going nowhere in particular. Just walking. I didn't realize I was going to Valley Farm until I was nearly there. My thoughts had gone on before me, though. Again, I was wondering about the farmhand and his strange wound. Wondering how it had happened in the first place, and why it wouldn't heal after so long a time.

But it wasn't only curiosity, I thought when I looked up and saw the farmhouse ahead of me. If he had reopened the wound, perhaps there was something more I could do for him, I told myself, my heart thumping wildly for some odd reason.

I opened the gate, feeling like an intruder.

Mary was in the yard hanging laundry on the line. She looked at me blankly for a moment before she recognized me. "Oh," she said finally, "how's the baby?"

"She's improving at last," I said. "I understand they found your son. I would have come sooner but the baby was quite ill, and I didn't want to leave her." I couldn't seem to stop talking. "But I wanted to see if there was anything I could do now."

Mary waved her hand, dismissing my offer. "Oh, no, he wasn't hurt a bit, thank heavens." She looked over her shoulder, a half-smile on her face, at a boy a year or two younger than Jack who was chasing a puppy around the yard.

"I'm so glad." I waited to see if she would mention Tom's rescuer. But she didn't. "I understand your man hurt his hand again?"

Mary nodded as she fixed a shirt on the line with a couple of wooden pegs. "I gave him some clean rags to wrap it with, but he wouldn't let anyone see to it. He said it wasn't much worse than before and he would trust in your potion to do him good." She picked up a petticoat and frowned at it. "White as this, he was, though." She pegged the petticoat onto the line.

I looked around the yard and saw no one but Mary and her son. "Since I'm here, should I ask if he'd like me to look at it?"

"It's kind of you, but they've already gone up with the sheep. I don't expect them back till the summer." She shrugged. "Tom was quite down in the mouth about it." She fixed the last shirt on the line. "He'd gotten so fond of them, Ash especially, what with him spoiling the boy and making him little toys. We were all so grateful, of course. But I told Tom, that's what we hired them for." She picked up her basket and balanced it on her hip. "Would you like to come inside?"

I shook my head. "I'd better get back. They might need me."

That was what I said.

But I was as useless and out of place at Steepside as I was at Valley Farm. We had been at the foot of Glass Mountain for days now, and I couldn't shake off the feeling I was missing something, that if we did not leave soon, I would be too late. For what, I didn't know, but I had stayed too long.

FORTY-EIGHT

*G*lass Mountain was a lonely place. As Jack and I made our way along the sheep walk, the only living things we saw were a mountain hare in the grass and a red kite soaring above us. The villagers had said we wouldn't meet anyone, and we didn't.

But we were not alone.

There were fresh hoofprints and tracks on the sheep walk, and one night we found the remains of a recent campfire. It was in a sheltered spot, a curve of rock almost like a cave, but open to the sky. Whoever built the fire had left nothing behind them but ashes, and I felt sure enough they weren't coming back, so we decided to stay for the night.

I laid a new fire on the bones of the old one and got out my flint to light it. As I bent over the branches and twigs I had gathered, a gust of wind blew the hair off my neck, prickling my skin. I looked over my shoulder, suddenly uneasy. Who had slept here and how long ago? Where were they tonight?

Who were they?

The old woodcutter had told me people used to climb the mountain to learn their future or drink the healing water at the well. And the villagers said shepherds grazed their sheep here sometimes. The only people we would meet, then, would be ordinary people doing ordinary work, or troubled people hoping for something extraordinary. No king's men, no princes. No one to fear.

When the tinder caught, I sat back on my heels and reached behind me for my bag. But instead of the worn leather, my fingers brushed against something hard and smooth. Turning behind me, I saw a flat stone, perfect for cooking on. Had the fire builder used it then left it behind, traveling light?

On top of the stone was a strangely shaped scrap of wood. I picked it up to toss it into the fire but stopped as soon as my fingers curled around it. I'd thought it was a thin bit of branch with a few twigs still attached, but when I held it up in the firelight I saw it was the carved figure of a stag.

"Our friend made it," breathed Jack, who had come up beside me.

"Our friend?"

"You said we had a friend." He held out his hand for the little carving. "Our friend who chopped our wood and gave us the sparrow." He was right, of course. This little creature could have come from no other hands. I could almost feel the warmth of the carver's clever fingers where the wood touched my skin.

Beside me Jack huffed impatiently. I looked down and realized I was holding the stag against my chest with both hands. Like I expected to feel its heart beating against my own.

I smiled at my foolishness and gave the little creature to Jack. He grinned and held it up. "The stag prince." He settled down beside me. "Tell a story."

"The stag prince." Thinking, I walked to the stream nearby to fill my little cooking pot. I'd never heard a story of a stag prince, but I was well accustomed to telling stories of my own these days.

"Once, a rich man was traveling through a forest, and he lost his way." I moved the flat stone next to the fire and set the pot on top of it. "It was growing dark, and the man was afraid. He was even more afraid when a stag appeared and spoke to him. He said he would lead the man home if he would give him a gift." Reaching into my pack, I brought out a sack of lentils and put a few handfuls into the pot. "The stag said the man must give him the first thing to greet him on his return home. Knowing that was sure to be his faithful dog, the man agreed. But when he arrived, it was not his dog, but his daughter—"

"All-Kinds-of-Feathers!" Jack burst out, holding up his wooden sparrow.

My hands stilled for a moment on the wild greens I'd collected on that path that day. "All-Kinds-of-Feathers." Jack frequently insisted I add All-Kinds-of-Feathers into my stories. Why did it unsettle me so tonight? "All-Kinds-of-Feathers loved her father," I went on after a moment's pause, "and she was glad to pay his debt." My hands went back into motion, ripping the greens and dropping them into the pot. "She agreed to marry the stag prince and went with him to his castle in the heart of the wood."

Jack settled down cross-legged, the wooden sparrow, hare, and stag in his lap.

"At first, All-Kinds-of-Feathers was afraid of the stag prince, but he was gentle and kind, and she soon lost her fear of him. Every night he removed his antlers and his skin, leaving them on the hearth rug. In the morning, he was always out of bed before it was light, once again a stag." I took out an apple for us to share as we waited for the lentils to cook. "She was curious, but he told her she mustn't ask him any questions until they had been married a year and a day."

I sliced off a piece of apple and handed it to Jack. I had never gotten the knack of peeling an apple the way my husband had. We would have to eat the peel. "All-Kinds-of-Feathers agreed, and she kept her promise a day, a week, a month, a year. But then she could wait no longer. Surely there would be no harm in stealing a look at him. Just a peek." I smiled as Jack took in a horrified breath. "So, that night, after he had shed his skin and antlers and fallen asleep, she crept out of bed and lit a candle. Leaning over the bed, she saw her husband was a handsome man, with warm brown hair just the color of his deer skin."

The next piece of apple was for me, but I found I couldn't eat it. I handed it to Jack and went on. "As she moved closer, a drip of wax from her candle dropped onto his bare skin. At once, he woke and jumped from the bed. *If only you had waited,* he cried, *one more day. I would have been released from the spell that binds me. Now I am cursed forever, unless you can find me. You will not see me again until you have worn out three pairs of iron shoes.* With that, her husband turned into a swan and flew out the window."

Jack was staring at me, crestfallen. I gave him another piece of apple. He took it but didn't eat it.

"He was out of sight before she got out the castle door. All-Kinds-of-Feathers left the castle immediately and apprenticed herself to a blacksmith, where she worked until she had made herself three pairs of iron shoes." Glancing down at the remains of the apple in my hand, I sliced Jack another piece. "Then she set off. She walked the world over, day and night, with no food or drink until she found him at last at the top of a mountain."

"Was he a swan?"

I thought a moment, remembering the story Rose once told me. "No, he was a man again. But he lay dead, encased in a coffin made of ice so clear it looked like glass. All-Kinds-of-Feathers laid her hands on the coffin, thinking to melt through the ice with the heat of her skin. But though the ice melted a little, her hands soon cooled; she felt herself freezing too. She had failed."

Jack stared up at me, his brows drawn together in worry. "Hot tears spilled down her cheeks onto the coffin," I continued, then I gave his clenched fists a squeeze. "And in an instant, the ice melted away. Her husband opened eyes of a blue-green color she couldn't name. And the curse was broken at last."

Jack's hands relaxed a little. "Happy ever after?"

For a moment, I couldn't speak. "Yes," I said at last. "But first, she said she was sorry for not trusting him, and he forgave her. She became a blacksmith, and he became a woodsman, and they never went back to the palace. And sometimes they fought, and sometimes they were sad, but they always loved each other. And they were happy ever after."

My chest was tight, like there was a great stone sitting on it. I thought I'd reached happy ever after before. But perhaps it was never as simple as that.

I handed Jack the last piece of apple. He was watching me, that worried wrinkle still between his brows. "Sometimes sad but happy ever after?"

I nodded. "Everyone's sad sometimes. I'm sad sometimes."

"Me too." He stood, putting his toys in his pocket. "We can still be happy ever after?"

"Yes." I hoped it was true.

Jack moved away from the fire to finish his apple and play with his new animal. I could hear him speaking for the sparrow and the hare, welcoming the stag as if they'd known each other forever. Like they had been separated for a lifetime and reunited at last. *I missed you. Me too. I'm sorry. I know.*

That night, after Jack had curled into his blanket, I sat up beside the fire, staring up into the dark. The mountain loomed above us in the blackness. High up, I saw a light. Was it a house? Or had the fire builder made another camp? I rubbed my eyes; they were burning from the wood smoke. It was probably nothing.

Beside me, Jack rolled over and touched my hand. "I was supposed to thank him, but I couldn't," he whispered. "He's dead now."

"Who?"

"The coughing man in the woods." He plucked at my sleeve. "Are there dead people on this mountain? Is Mother here?"

"We don't know if he carved those things." I stroked his hair. "Maybe it was someone else."

A shiver crept up my spine, and I pulled my feather cloak tighter around my shoulders. "Mother isn't here, Rabbit," I said into the dark. "There's no one dead here."

Just before I closed my eyes, I looked back up the mountain. The light was still burning.

FORTY-NINE

It took us three more days to reach the ruin. As we neared the top my pace slowed. My feet grew heavy, like they were weighed down by iron shoes.

I wanted to think I was only tired from the journey, but I knew there was more to it. I was used to hiding myself, running away. It was what I did. I ran from my father's house, from a prince with a glass slipper, from an unfriendly palace, from my own deception. But I had no experience making my way toward something. It made me uneasy.

On that last afternoon, the sheep walk turned off to one side. But by that time we could just see a crumbling tower above us, so we left the path and continued upward. Someone else had come that way, too, and not long ago. The grass was trodden down, and a few bits of wool had snagged on the brush here and there—somewhere above us, a dog barked. My skin prickled.

The ruin was tucked into a hollow with the top of the mountain rising up behind it. Many walls still stood, though the roof had long since fallen in. Most of the front wall remained, its arched windows empty. I recognized the back wall with the crumbling tower, and my breath caught in my throat; it was just how Mother had drawn it.

Jack's hand stole into mine. "Is this it?"

Before I could answer, a long-legged gray deerhound came bounding out at us from one side of the ruin, barking excitedly. Jack ducked behind me, peeking out at the dog. Then he stepped out and allowed it to lick his face. The dog danced around me joyfully, then went back to Jack, tail wagging enthusiastically.

Watching Jack with his arms around the furry neck, I realized we knew this dog. I had set his broken leg at the woodcutter's house. The old man had said he belonged to *that Henry's master.*

I straightened my back, my heart hammering in my chest. I should know what this dog's presence here must mean, I told myself. I should know. Men named Henry and masters with wounded hands and carvers of wooden animals swirled and shifted in my head. I couldn't quite sort them out. But I knew I was about to.

I knelt beside the dog, burying my fingers in his coarse fur. He sat obediently, mouth open in what was almost a smile, and didn't flinch when I felt the mended leg. It had healed well.

The dog jumped up and bounded off toward the ruin. Then he returned for us, whining, and ran off again. He wanted us to follow him. I wrapped my arms around myself to stop a shiver.

We walked toward the skeleton of the main building and in through the front entrance. The space inside had once been a huge rectangular room, likely the nave of the church. But there was no ceiling, and the floors had given way to grass long ago. One doorway was blocked by a small evergreen tree, cut down and laid across it like a makeshift gate. In the room beyond it was a small flock of sheep. The dog gave them a sniff as we went by, but he did not stop. Instead, he crossed the room and led us through a pillared archway into a walled courtyard. He loped on through another doorway, but I stopped where I was, unable to take another step.

The rest of the mountain was alive with wild garlic and strawberries and spring grass. But this courtyard, once a garden perhaps, was overgrown with dry, brown vegetation. There was nothing living here at all. However, in one corner of the courtyard there was something: dead vines climbing up its stones and surrounded by a low wall was a wide, round well.

I forgot the heaviness in my feet; I forgot the dog. I even forgot his master. This was why I was here. This was one of the last words Mother had ever written, one of her last words to me: *Well.* I could see no water from where I was, but if there were a Looking Glass, if there were a well with healing water as clear as glass, it would be here. I walked toward it, rubbing my hands on my skirts. My fingers itched, and my skin buzzed in anticipation. The sun was setting; it would be dark soon. But there was just time enough. I would see it now.

I realized I was wrong about the garden being dead. One small shoot of green grew up right at the base of the well. I knelt, forgetting even the well for a moment. For there it was: a slender shaft with pearly white petals drooping from the top and blue-green leaves at the base. It was the second sight, just as Mother had drawn it. And as far as I could tell, there was only one.

I sat back on my heels, shaking away the restless feeling in my fingers. Perhaps there were others up against the walls of the courtyard, or hidden under the tangled brown vines. Or perhaps I was too early, and this was only the first one to bloom this spring.

"Thank God," said a voice behind me.

I jumped, feeling like I had been caught trespassing. The dog had returned. Henry's master's dog. And this time he brought a man.

I stood, brushing my hands on my skirts, and I realized I knew the man as well as the dog. He was the one who came the day Mother died, the man who served the master with the wounded hand, the man who took wood to the village with the dog's master. The man named Henry.

His clothes were homespun and plain, like when we had met before. But now he looked unkempt somehow. After many days climbing the mountain and many nights sleeping outside, I imagined Jack and I looked much the same. But something about him reminded me of Rose after her mother died. His hair was ragged, and he was pale and worn, as if he hadn't been sleeping. As if worry had been eating him from inside out.

"Sparrow." He held his hands out, pleading with me. "Please help him."

"What's wrong?" I didn't need to ask. Something in his face told me what he would say.

"I think Ash," said Henry, one hand still outstretched. "I think he's dying."

I closed my eyes. My breath came out partly a sob, partly a word. *No.* All this time I had been wondering, thinking surely we would meet some day, this man named Ash and I. But not like this; there had been enough people I couldn't help. I didn't want to add this man to my list.

Since Henry's arrival, Jack had taken his habitual place behind me, one hand clutching my skirts. But now he ran forward. "I know your dog," he said. "Sparrow fixed his leg when the coughing man gave me the rabbit. I was supposed to say thank you but then he died and I couldn't."

Henry looked down at Jack, a puzzled expression on his face. Silent now after such a long speech to a stranger, Jack held out the little wooden hare.

Henry knelt for a closer look. "Ash, he makes these little creatures." He glanced up with the ghost of a smile. "He's very handy with a knife." Jack now drew the other wooden animals out of his pocket and held them up.

Henry touched the sparrow with one calloused finger. "He wanted to thank you for the medicine. I told him about your mother, and he wanted to do something for you. But you weren't there."

"You brought us the firewood," I whispered.

It was their voices we heard the day Jack ran away. They had stocked our woodpile and left flowers on Mother's grave. They left us the little sparrow, wrapped up in a handkerchief. Ash had made Kitty's wolf, the hare at the woodcutter's, the stag beside the campfire. *He's very handy with a knife.* He was little Tom's rescuer and our mysterious friend. His was the voice that set my heart racing, that day in the wood.

And now he was dying.

I looked toward the doorway, my throat closing.

Henry was still kneeling next to Jack. "Will you come?"

My feet felt like they had sunk into a layer of mud. "I don't know if I can help him." I had failed enough to know success was far from certain. If I did everything right, it still might not be enough. Mother had known it, and by now I knew it too.

Henry stood. "Please." He took a step backward, like I was a wild animal he did not want to frighten. "Just come and see him. He's been asking for you."

I picked up my pack. It was not many steps, but my legs were heavy and slow. Walking was like wading through a flooded field. But I forced my feet to the doorway, and I went through.

There is always something we can do.

FIFTY

There was little light inside. The room was open to the sky, but the sun had sunk behind the back wall. All I could see was the shape of a man stretched on the ground. I knelt beside him.

"It's the old wound." Henry had followed me in. "It opened up again not long ago, and it's been getting worse. He's been fevered the past few days. We knew you were at Steepside, because you left the medicine, you see, and he's been asking for you, that I go down and find you." He knelt at the man's other side. "But I was afraid to leave him on his own. He's too weak."

The man called Ash was breathing, but not conscious. His skin was so hot I pulled my hand away from his forehead. He didn't move when I reached for his hands. I found the bandaged one and began to unwind the strip of cloth. As I unwrapped the last of it, the wounded hand closed around my wrist. "Sparrow," he said, in a voice raspy from disuse.

I laid my other hand on his chest to stop him sitting up. "I'm here." He fell back easily, as if he had been talking in his sleep, and his hand dropped from my wrist.

"Do you have any water?" I asked Henry.

He stood. "There's a stream nearby."

"What about the well?"

He let out a huff of air. "That was why we came up this far. For the healing waters clear as…" He shook his head, shoulders drooping. "But it's gone dry."

Dry. That was why I hadn't seen any water as I walked up to the well. The water, clear as glass, wasn't low. It wasn't there at all.

Henry headed out, the dog at his heels.

Jack hovered in the doorway, not wanting to leave me, but not wanting to stay in the dark with the sick man. I nodded my approval, and he ran off after Henry and the dog.

I laid Ash's forearm in my lap and lit a candle so I could see. In the circle of candlelight, the open wound at the base of his thumb shone red and angry. I could stitch it closed, but I didn't like to until I had released the poison. The skin around it was swollen and hotter than the rest of his fevered body. And when I touched it, I felt something hard under the skin. Something alien and strange.

I gazed at his hand in the candlelight. It was calloused, with dirt under the nails, the hand of a man who worked outside. I had tended hands like this before, and yet there was something different about this hand and its clever fingers. It was the hand of a man who chopped wood and built fences. A man who herded sheep and rescued lost children and carved little animals out of wood. A man who was handy with a knife. I traced his fingers with one of mine.

As my finger moved down his palm to his wrist, I could see the redness from the wound spreading up his arm in thin lines, feeding into thicker lines like streams feeding a river. I followed the lines with the light of my candle as they moved up toward his heart. Toward his pulse, beating too quickly in his throat, toward the several day's growth of stubble on his chin.

The glow of my candle spread over his body. In a heartbeat I would see his face.

I stopped, the candle shaking in my grasp, and a drip of wax fell toward his bare skin. My hand shot out to catch it. The wax burned into my palm, I let out a hiss of pain, and the flame died in the rush of my breath. We were in darkness.

Rubbing the hot wax away on my skirt, I took my pack outside where there was still a little light. I hadn't seen his face after all, but what did that matter? I must get on with it. He had a high fever and a festering wound spreading poison through his body. There was also a hard knot under his skin that I didn't understand, but I knew enough to begin.

I needed a tonic for the fever and a dressing to draw the poison. The fever remedy was easy enough; in my pack I had elderberry syrup, blue-bottle, and butter-bur. That was a start. But the wound was more difficult. Clary would be best, laying the leaves on the skin and letting them draw the poison. Mother grew some in a sunny spot near the cottage, but it was unlikely I would find any here. So, I worked with what I had: honey, a little flour, and chopped wild garlic, mixed into a paste.

When Henry and Jack returned with the water, Henry began to lay a fire in the courtyard. "Could we have that inside?" I asked. "So I can see?"

Henry looked apologetic. "The light hurts his eyes."

He wanted to spare his friend any discomfort. He had decided Ash would live, then, that I would save him. His certainty weighed on me. I nodded and rose, taking my remedies with me into the shadows. My body dragged, like I was made of stone.

I lifted Ash's head and put the little bottle of tonic to his lips. He was still when I tipped a little of the liquid down his throat. But at least he was breathing. I brushed his hair away from his burning forehead and washed the wound with water and vinegar. I couldn't see what I was doing, but I didn't need to. I closed my eyes and felt my way, like walking a familiar path on a moonless night. I smeared the honey and garlic paste onto the wound and wrapped a clean cloth around his hand.

All this time Ash did not move. I must have hurt him, cleaning and tending to the wound, but he didn't stir. It was best for him to rest and let my remedies do their work, but I wanted him to wake. I wanted to hear him speak again, to hear my name on his lips. I needed to know he wasn't past speech.

I took a spare bit of rag and dipped it in the water. My fingers shook as I ran the cloth over the fevered skin of his arms, his chest, his shoulders. There was something about the feel of his body under my hands, something I couldn't quite name. Something that made it hard to breathe. The cloth reached his face, and again I brushed his hair back. Then I kissed his forehead. I don't know why I did it; it should have felt wrong.

But it didn't.

Ash stirred then, and I froze, my hair still trailing over his face, his chest. He clutched my hand with his wounded one. Then he sighed. "Your fingers are cool," he whispered, laying my hand over his eyes. *Your fingers are cool.* After those words and that gesture, my heart beat wildly against my ribs for a reason that I couldn't explain.

His hand was burning through the bandage; after a while, though, he relaxed. I sat back and began to draw my hand away, but he reached for it again, holding it against his chest. "Don't let go." So I didn't. I covered our hands with my other hand until his breathing slowed and sounded like sleep.

FIFTY-ONE

I stayed beside Ash all that night, with his hand burning into mine. Despite the heat of it, I did not let go. Our hands fit together, as if they knew each other well.

When I slept, I dreamed I was in the courtyard, following a hooded figure in a mottled cloak. It was still the decayed, abandoned place I had seen in the twilight, but wherever the woman's bare feet stepped, the dead, brown plants came alive. It was soon a lush, green garden, filled with creeping vines and flowers and herbs of every kind. The woman in the cloak was Mother; I was sure of it. She was walking toward the well. I called her name, but she did not stop. I laid my hand on her furred shoulder, and she began to turn her head. But it was not fur I touched—it was feathers. The woman I followed was not Mother but—

The dream already fading, I woke, gasping into the dark.

I was cold and couldn't remember how I had ended up in this place. Jack was curled on the ground beside me, nestled under my feathered cloak. I must have thrown it off me in the night, though I still grasped it in one hand, the feathers slick and cool under my skin.

Ash's hand had fallen out of mine, and his body was still. Still like Mother's. I gasped with the sudden memory of waking next to her rigid form, touching her cold skin. I shook him, but he didn't wake. My heart thundered in my ears, and I couldn't seem to calm my ragged breathing. I couldn't feel his chest moving. I could feel nothing but my own blood beating against the skin of my hands. I put my ear to his heart and my fingers to his throat, straining to hear something, to feel something.

His pulse was weak, but I felt it at last. I let out a sob of relief and stayed where I was, my body warming with his heat, listening to his heartbeat and his breath. And asking myself why they felt so familiar.

I sat up with a shiver. I was foolish to have thought him dead; his body was far too hot. If anything, the fever was worse now, and his skin was dry, like he was baking in an oven. My potion wasn't working. I hadn't done enough.

Mother told me we couldn't cure every ill, and I knew she was right. I knew it all too well. Perhaps this hurt was past helping. Was now the time to find those other *somethings* I could do? To resign myself to sitting beside Ash and holding his hand while he died? Those things I had done for my mother until I abandoned her. Those things I had done for the miller's wife because I could do nothing else.

I felt a sudden burning under my skin, as if I were the one with the deadly fever, not Ash. No, I told myself as I fumbled for my pack and stole out into the courtyard. Not this time. I knew I had more failures ahead of me, enough to last a lifetime, but they could wait. I would not add this man to my list of regrets.

I told myself it had nothing to do with the feel of his hand in mine, or the sound of his breath in my ear.

The sun was rising now, and the sky was growing light. I knelt and reached in the bag for Mother's book. There must be something else. There must be. What else might draw the poison? Dill oil? Barley water? Decoction of ragwort? I must be missing something.

I let the book fall open and looked down. I could just make out the page in the dim light. It was the drawing of the crumbling tower behind me: the entry for second sight, written in blackberry ink.

It draws what is deep inside.

I could hear Mother's voice, the night she wrote those words. *Good for old wounds.*

All this time I had hoped the second sight would heal my scars, but I had a better use for it now. I dropped the book and ran to the well.

The garden was gray in the half-light, and beside the well was the one little plant I had seen the previous night. There was no other trace of green. But perhaps I hadn't really looked before; there must be more, I told myself. There must be. I crept along the stones of the well in the dimness, trusting my fingers could lead me to something living. But all I touched was cold stone and dead vegetation.

I completed the circle at the single stem of second sight. There were no others. Not one. I turned back to the doorway I had come from, remembering Ash's faint heartbeat. I was out of time. This one plant would have to be enough.

I knelt beside the second sight, my fingers trembling above the soil. But I didn't pull it from the ground; I didn't even know how to use it. Should I pound the root into powder? I had no time to dry it. Should I distill the seeds in wine or vinegar and tip it down his throat? I had no time for that either. Fresh leaves were good for drawing poison, but the leaves were so tiny. They would barely cover the wound. How could they possibly be enough?

I ignored the tears spilling down my cheeks and into the earth. I curled my fingers into fists to steady my shaking hands. Then I shook them, trying to banish the itchy feeling that had stolen over them.

Only they were not shaking. They were not itching. Something inside me, held in check for so long, had broken loose. My hands were tingling.

And I understood at last. I closed my eyes, letting out a breath that was half sob and half laugh. At the palace, I had buried my own nature. I strangled it and let it wither. But it was far from dead; Mother and Jack had seen it.

She just coaxes things to life.

That's what you do.

It was what I did. I could feel it coursing through me from the soles of my feet to the tips of my fingers. I laid my hands around the second sight and touched the soil. This one tiny plant would be enough. I would make it be.

The magic poured from my hands and into the earth like water, stronger than it had ever been before. The familiar heat grew under my palms. The tingle spread, up my hands and into my arms and across my chest as the green shoots pushed up through the earth.

I don't know how long I stayed that way, perhaps a few heartbeats, perhaps much longer. Something was touching my shoulder, tugging at my sleeve. Someone was saying my name, again and again.

"Sparrow. Sparrow." The voice was pleading. "Wake up."

My strength was draining out, like blood seeping into the earth, little by little. My cheeks were wet and my eyelids were heavy; I could barely drag them open. But the voice was urgent, almost tearful. When I opened my eyes at last, I saw Jack kneeling in front of me, his eyes wide, a line of worry between his brows.

"I have to—" I gasped.

Jack put his hands on my cheeks. "You made enough."

I shook my head. "He's worse," I panted. "I need more—"

"More of these?" Henry was beside me too. I blinked at him, trying to clear my vision. In his hand was a stem of second sight. Something in me remembered there had only been one. I snatched at it, lurching forward onto a thick carpet of blue green and pearly white. In the dimness, I couldn't tell how far the second sight had spread, but around the well it was everywhere— under my hands, under Jack's knees, under Henry's feet— everywhere.

Jack laid his cheek against mine. "Sparrow," he whispered. "You can stop now."

Behind the wall, Ash lay in shadow, but I could manage well enough by touch. The wound was still dangerously hot, but when I unwrapped the bandage, I found the salve had done some good. The strange lump under the skin had come to the surface and came away in my fingers, a hard, sharp sliver of something. Something I knew the feel of.

I made my way back outside the doorway and held it to the light. It was glass. A shard of glass so finely wrought a little boy might even think it was a precious jewel.

I leaned against the doorway, my legs trembling. I had tried so hard to forget that night. The shatter of the glass slipper under my foot in the dark. The crashing noise behind me as I ran down the hall. The pained intake of breath as a body fell to the floor, onto the jagged pieces I had left behind. A wound that would not heal.

I knew what damage that glass could do.

The space where Ash lay had not brightened that much when I returned to him, but I could see him well enough now: his face, pale with illness, the muscles of his arms and shoulders, grown sinewy with constant working outside. He had changed since the last time I saw him, in the glow of his candle. But he was still the man I married, the man who fell on the shards of my slipper that night at the palace. The man whose hands could twist a piece of cloth into a swan or carve a bit of wood into a sparrow.

Ash was my husband.

FIFTY-TWO

I sank to my knees beside Ash and took a handful of second sight leaves from my pocket. I ripped a few of them to release their juice and laid them on his wound. Something warm and wet dropped onto the leaves in his palm. I did not brush it away. A little salt water wouldn't hurt him now. I wiped my face and closed my hand around Ash's, pressing the leaves into his palm, my vision blurring and my head spinning. The weakness that had begun in the garden as I brought the second sight to life was closing in. Everything grew dark around me as I laid my cheek against his chest. But I held tight to his hand. *Don't let go,* he had said. And I would not.

My cheek was wet, and there was a hand on my head, stroking my hair. Perhaps it was Henry or Jack, trying to rouse me. I squeezed Ash's hand tighter. I would not leave him; I would not let go.

His hand twitched in mine, and there was a groan under my ear. I sat up, and his other hand slid off my head. His eyes were open, though I doubted he really saw me.

"I've been…" Ash's voice was still fevered and weak. "I've been looking for you." His eyes closed, and he sighed. "But you found me." His wounded hand squeezed mine, and he relaxed into sleep again.

Something cut painfully into my palm. I winced and drew my hand from his. When I uncurled his fingers, I could see it:

underneath the leaves was a second piece of glass. I laid a finger on the edge; it was still sharp.

This piece was bigger than the first and still lodged in his flesh. I dug my nails around it and pulled, but it was slippery in my grasp and wouldn't come out with my fingers alone. My bag was still outside, so I looked around for a tool of some kind.

What I needed was a knife.

Beside one wall was a small stack of Ash and Henry's possessions. There were a couple of bags, a neatly folded coat, a belt—and hanging from the belt was a knife. As I drew it from its sheath, I saw it was Ash's: a knife that carved flowers out of carrots or animals out of wood or peeled apples into long, curly strings. The same one I took from his room that night at the palace.

I hesitated; using it seemed almost wrong. I had done such damage with that knife.

Then I gripped it tighter. The knife might be the same, but I was not. Perhaps I could never make things right, but I had to try, even if I hurt him more. I made a swift cut and levered out the shard of glass. Ash cried out, but the sliver had come out in my hand at last, as long as my little finger and sharp on every side.

I pressed more second sight leaves onto the wound I had made and tied a strip of cloth around his hand. His pale face had gone whiter still with the pain, and he watched me with wide eyes. "I'm sorry," I whispered, holding up the piece of glass. "It's out now."

He continued staring at me. His eyes were clear, and there was plenty of light now. I realized he knew me at last. He opened his lips to say my name, but I didn't want to hear it. That old name had never suited me, and I didn't want to be that girl anymore. I put my hand on his lips to stop him saying her name.

He closed his eyes and breathed into my fingers, "Sparrow."

❧

I sat back on my heels. Ash had fallen into a peaceful sleep. His skin was still quite warm, but he was no longer delirious, and the red lines branching up his arm were fading to pink.

"When can I say thank you?" Jack had stolen in behind me. He stood at my shoulder, the wooden sparrow and hare clutched in his fingers.

"Maybe when he wakes up."

He looked down at Ash, a crease of worry between his brows. "Is he very sick?"

"He has been." I held out the slivers of glass. "He'll feel much better without these."

Jack stretched out one finger, then drew it back. "You had those in your foot, and you got better."

I nodded, staring down at the glass in my hand. I had no idea what to do with it. Mother had sewn my shards into her cloak, and now they were in mine. But Ash had carried his for so long; it wasn't my place to decide what to do with them.

I took a spare bit of rag from my pocket and tied the glass pieces into it; they would keep. Ash must make his own choice.

Jack stood still, watching me. "Mother said not to ask you and you'd tell us when you were ready."

I bowed my head, my throat tightening. The words were so like her I could almost hear her voice.

"I'll tell you the story some time," I said, my voice catching. "I promise."

Jack looked at his boots for a moment, then leaned in to my ear. "Do you want to see the sheep?"

I nodded, smiling in spite of myself. I slipped the rag bundle with the glass shards into my pocket and got to my feet.

"We let them out," he said, running toward the courtyard. "I helped. You can—" He stopped and turned back, noticing I wasn't with him.

I had stopped in the doorway, steadying myself with one hand. Earlier, by the well in the dawning light, I had grabbed a few handfuls of second sight. I had stuffed them into a pocket and run. I hadn't stopped to see how far they had spread. But now, in the full light of day, I could see nothing but new life, just like in my dream of the cloaked, barefoot figure. Second sight radiated from the well in every direction like ripples on water. I could even see their pearly blossoms growing up beside the courtyard walls.

But that wasn't all. The rest of the garden, dead and brown just the night before, was green and growing everywhere. Mountain thyme and cottongrass and heather mingled with the second sight, creeping vines trailed up the walls, brambles and fruit trees were covered in blossoms. The scent of it made me lightheaded.

The garden was alive. All of it.

When I looked back at Jack, he gave me the slightest of shrugs.

"We told you. It's what you do."

Henry was sitting by the fire, baking oatcakes on a flat stone. When I sat beside him he was quiet, as if afraid to speak, afraid to hope. "Will your flowers," he said after a moment. "Will they help?"

"I think so."

His shoulders slumped in relief, and he let out a long breath. "He knew you could do him good."

I shook my head. How could Ash have known that? How could he have even thought it, after all the harm I'd done?

We sat in silence for a bit. Henry flipped the oatcakes while I watched the sheep through a gap in the courtyard wall. Jack went cautiously among them, patting each one in turn. "Did you tell no one who he is?" I asked Henry at last.

He looked up sharply, then he shrugged. "He doesn't want to be found. He won't go back to the palace without his wife."

He began sliding the cakes out onto a tin plate, shaking his head a little.

My cheeks felt hot. "And no one else wants her back, I suppose?" As soon as the words were out of my mouth, I wished I hadn't said them. I didn't care what anyone at the palace wanted.

"The king and queen wanted to give up the search. They said maybe she's dead, and it's for the best. Then he could mourn her properly and marry again someday."

I smiled a bit. *Good riddance to bad rubbish.* "Someone more suitable this time."

Henry shook his head. "Oh, no, he won't hear—" he broke off, staring at me, then he sat silent a moment, his face reddening. "It's you, isn't it? You're the princess."

I shook my head. "No," I said. "Not anymore."

FIFTY-THREE

That afternoon I sat in the heather, sorting through a bunch of second sight we had picked. Jack lay on his belly, picking the petals off each flower and making a neat pile. When he had plucked them all, he began to lay the petals on my feet, pressing each one onto my skin with a deliberate finger.

On the other side of the wall the dog barked, and Jack sat up with a start, pulling off his boots. I smiled at him. "Won't your feet be cold?"

He shook his head as he started on his knit stockings. "I won't be cold. I have good feet." He stood. "Like you."

I must have looked puzzled, for he sighed and explained. "Sparrow feet." And he was off, running with his arms outstretched like wings.

It seemed such a long time ago, that day I had told him birds' feet didn't get cold.

I leaned down to gather the second sight petals from my feet. And that was when I noticed it. My bandages were gone; all that was left was some of the cloth tied around my ankles. On our climb up the mountain, they had worn completely away, and I hadn't even noticed they were gone.

I untied the scraps of cloth around my ankles. Then I packed up the piles of leaves, roots, and petals we had made and went to check on Ash. I left the bits of my bandages in the heather for the sparrows to use in their nests. I didn't need them anymore.

Ash's skin was cool now, and the pink lines up his arm continued to fade. I laid my palm on his chest, feeling his heartbeat and repeating to myself that he was improving.

He stirred and opened his eyes; in the shade of the wall they looked drained of color, gray as the stones around us. He covered my hand with his bandaged one, wincing a little.

My throat went dry. Over all the time we'd spent apart, I had imagined us meeting over and over. I had told myself not to, and I had done it anyway. But when it came to what he would say, what I would say, my imagination failed me. And now the moment was here, I felt more at a loss than ever.

There was one thing I knew, though. Ash, this new name, felt right. Better than *darling,* better than his princely name, that name I was always too shy to say out loud. So I began there.

"Ash." It felt like magic on my lips. It gave me the strength to go on. "Ash," I whispered again. "I told you how I wished for the gowns."

He nodded once.

"And the slippers."

His eyes were sad. "I loved your stories."

"I…" My mouth was so dry I could hardly say the words. "I made another wish."

And starting with that last wish, I told Ash the truth. About the foolish wish, the tightening slippers, the cracks and broken pieces of glass, the stolen knives. The pretending, the hiding, the lying. The secret that grew and grew until it shattered.

Blood drained from his already pale face as I spoke. "Was it all a lie?" he asked when I had finished.

I shook my head. "I was no good at love; I know that. When we met, you were an escape. Someone I could run away to, but I—"

He cut me off, pressing my hand with his. "We were both running."

I didn't know what to say. Back at the palace, he had always seemed so sure. But here, on top of a mountain in the shelter of a ruin, even sick and weak as he was, I had never seen him so at home. How strange that I had never seen that I wasn't the only one who didn't fit.

"Yes. We were both running." Something was coming loose in my chest. "I know I made a mess of it all. But I've loved you the whole time." I stroked a lock of his hair off his brow. "But I was afraid you wouldn't love me back. So I wished…"

"I was in love with you already, you know," he said softly. "Even before you made that wish, you were perfect in my eyes. I'm not sure that's real love. But that's what I felt. You could do no wrong."

I huffed out something between a sob and a laugh. "I've done plenty wrong."

He closed his eyes and rubbed my hand with one thumb. "Me too."

"I was selfish. I chose *for* you."

He looked up at me again. "I was selfish too, marrying you." I didn't know what he meant, so I said nothing. "I knew what it was like at the palace," he went on. "What they're all like. I should have known you wouldn't be happy there."

I looked down at our joined hands. "How could you know? I didn't know myself."

When I looked back, Ash was looking away from me. "I should have known." He squeezed my hand tightly. It must have hurt. "But I thought it was true love. I thought that would be enough."

I heard Mother's voice in my ear. *There may be temporary sorts of magic, to make one feel in love.* "But the wish was only temporary?"

"Perhaps. You stopped talking. You wouldn't let me help you. You shrank from me."

Yes. I had done all those things as the glass was tightening on my feet and the cracks were spreading across the slippers. Had the magic been unraveling all that time? Or had the wish never worked in the first place?

"I could see I wasn't enough for you," he went on. "And I began to wonder if I'd ever loved you at all. Then one day I looked at you." His eyes were bright with tears. "And you were different. I saw you as I see you now. You didn't tell me stories anymore. You were awkward, quiet, miserable. You weren't perfect anymore. But you never were, of course. I just didn't realize it."

"And you realized you didn't love me anymore?"

"Sparrow." His gentle laugh was almost a sigh. "I wouldn't have looked for you all this time if I didn't love you. Your leaving wouldn't have hurt so much if I didn't love you. I wasn't in love, but I loved you like I never had before."

No magic in the world can make true love, Mother had said. *That takes bravery and honesty and hard work.*

"But you," he said softly. "You couldn't see me."

You must see your love as they truly are. And let them see you in return. No pretending.

"No. I didn't see you." Just remembering made my throat close up. "And I was too afraid to let you see me. If you saw, if you knew who I really was, what I'd done, you'd despise me."

Love works a magic all its own, Sparrow. But it cannot be forced.

"I didn't know," he paused, "what you'd done. What you were doing. But I knew you were hurting me. I thought I knew you." He looked back up at me, his eyes intent on mine. "But I didn't. Not then."

A curious smile turned up the corner of his mouth, becoming that slow smile that warmed me from inside out. "I don't think I know you now. This Sparrow I heard so much about. The healer with bare feet and a cloak of a thousand feathers. She mixes potions to ease pain and sets broken bones. Everywhere I went I had just missed her. I hardly believed she was real, but there she was, leaving me ointments and mending my dog's leg."

"And sometimes, I'd find traces that I wanted so badly to believe she'd left behind." He reached into a pocket and put a small brown feather into my hand. Tied around it was a bit of black thread, the same thread I used to sew the feathers into my cloak. "I began collecting these, thinking one day we might meet and I could return them."

He lowered his voice, confessing, "It wasn't long before I wanted to find Sparrow as much as I wanted to find you."

He drew my hand to his lips and kissed my palm. "I should have known she was you, with all that magic in your touch." He brought my fingers to his cheek, leaning into them.

"Can I now, Sparrow?" It was Jack's voice, from the doorway.

We both jumped, Ash letting go of my hand. Jack came over slowly, looking between Ash and me. "Ash," I said, "this is Jack."

Jack said nothing and stood still beside me, eyes on his feet. "Go on, Rabbit," I whispered.

"Did you make these?" He thrust out his hands, cupped together in a bowl. The sparrow, hare, and stag were cradled inside. "I have to say thank you if it was you."

Ash turned over on his side to see the little carvings more closely. "It was me."

Jack edged behind me a little. "Thank you."

"Do you like them?" Ash's voice was gentle.

Jack nodded. "I had a wolf, too. But he had to say goodbye." He stepped forward, drawn out by Ash's warmth. "They were all friends before," he went on, setting each one down in the space between the three of us, "and then they weren't, because they couldn't find each other. But then I found the sparrow."

FIFTY-FOUR

Is anything we do here useful?
Good for old wounds.
It's what you do.

*T*hat night I lay awake, watching the moon move across the
sky. The air was cool, but I was warm under my cloak with
Jack on one side of me and Ash on the other.

I should have been sleeping, but my racing thoughts
wouldn't stop. What would happen now? Ash and I had found
each other, and I wanted to stay there forever, among the ruins
on top of a mountain. But we couldn't do that, whispered a voice
I couldn't seem to silence. He was a prince with a palace and a
kingdom to go back to; I was a healer who lived in the wood. I
had never belonged in his world, and I certainly did not belong
there now.

When the sky began to lighten I got up, too restless to be
still anymore. I spread my cloak over Jack and Ash and stole
outside. Wrapping my shawl around me, I paced the courtyard,
stopping at last at the well. I knelt beside its stones, looking into
its shadows and wondering when it had gone dry. Had Mother
ever drunk the water, or had she only written *Well* so I would
know where to look for the second sight? But the well gave me
no answers; I could see nothing in its depths except darkness.

"It's so green." Ash's voice was soft with wonder. He stood
behind me, putting on his coat with care, as if he ached all over.

I turned back to look into the well, my breath catching in my throat. If there had still been water there, clear as glass, I would have seen him reflected there beside me.

"Everything was dead when we came," he said, sitting down on the wall. "Did you do this?"

My empty fingers twitched, impatient for something to do. I reached out and plucked several of the tear-shaped leaves from the carpet around the well. "I needed more of these, for your hand, and there was only one. I was afraid it wouldn't be enough." I straightened up and sat beside him on the wall. Shivering in the morning air, I tied my shawl tighter around me. When I looked back at Ash, his eyes were intent on me, reflecting the shadowed green of the courtyard. He said nothing, though, and my words kept spilling out. "I've failed enough. I couldn't fail you again. I wouldn't."

"So you grew a whole garden of them?" The warmth of his voice surrounded me. "For me?"

I nodded.

"Do you love me that much?"

"I do," I whispered.

"Yes," he breathed. "I think perhaps you do." He looked again at the green all around us. "You really are a wonder."

When he turned back, I looked down, suddenly unable to meet his eyes. "I don't think we'll need them all, though." I held out my hand. "Let me see."

Ash gave me his hand, and I unwrapped the bandage. Then I cleared away the old leaves, running my finger over the wound. There were no more slivers of glass, and the redness was lightening to pink; perhaps all the shards were out at last. I ripped the new leaves, breathing in their clean scent.

As I re-wrapped the bandage, Ash leaned his forehead against mine. When I finished we stayed that way, not moving, and I kept hold of his hand. "Sparrow?" he whispered. I didn't speak. If I was silent, perhaps we could stay that way forever, and nothing would have to change. He slid his hand free and put it over his heart, feeling for something. Then he reached inside his coat. "I've been keeping something for you."

He brought out his closed hand and held the other over it, like he was protecting something precious. "You left it behind. I didn't know if you meant to, or if you might ever want it back."

He opened his hand, and I jumped to my feet. In his bandaged palm was a ring with the gems set in the shape of a rose.

They say he wears her wedding ring on a chain around his neck so it's always close to his heart.

That was what the storyteller had said. He'd been almost right, after all. My thumb moved inward to touch my bare ring finger, but the old habit felt unfamiliar now. At some point in the woods, I had stopped feeling for that ill-fitting circle of gold. It didn't haunt me anymore.

I didn't mean to, but I took a step back. My cheeks were wet. I wiped them and shook my head. "I don't want—" I couldn't look at Ash, and my hands dropped to my sides, gathering a handful of my skirt in each fist. I suddenly felt just like that girl again, the one who had run from the palace with a foot full of glass. "I can't go back there. I—" My voice failed me.

But I was not that girl anymore. I straightened my spine and looked up. I expected Ash to look at me with the wounded look he'd had that night, but perhaps he was not the same either. He sat, simply watching me, as if he knew I had more to say and was waiting to hear it.

"I have a place now. Where I'm welcome. I'm—" the words from Mother's story felt right on my tongue, "useful." I looked down at my hands, searching for something else to say, another way to explain. "I can't go back."

Ash stood, and his voice closed the distance between us, as if his lips were right at my ear. "I would never ask you to."

His fingers moved to close around my ring, but I put my hand over his. "I can't wear it anymore." His eyes closed, and a tear slid down his cheek. I took the ring. "But perhaps I have a use for it."

"Then take this one, too," he said, sliding his own ring from his finger and offering it to me. "They belong together." His eyes were so sad I could almost name their color.

I couldn't speak. So I held out my hand, and he laid it in my palm. I reached into my pocket, feeling for something I could use to keep the two rings together. My shaking fingers brushed something at the bottom. I brought out a piece of black ribbon and something else. It was a tied-up bit of rag, a little package with a strange sharpness to it. A familiar sharpness.

Realizing what it was, I untied the knot. Then I smoothed out the cloth on my palm, revealing the two slivers of glass I had taken out of Ash's hand. He looked at them, puzzled.

"You've been keeping these too," I said. "All this time."

He stared at them, sickened. Then he shook his head. "I didn't realize…"

"No wonder your wound wouldn't heal." I felt sick, too. I wanted to crush the glass to powder. But that was not for me to decide.

Ash's eyes were rimmed with red, but their expression was peaceful. In one swift movement, he lifted the bit of cloth from my hand and emptied it into the well. The shards of glass caught the light and clinked against the stone as they fell. Then I couldn't see them. They were gone.

I breathed in like I was unaccustomed to air. Like I'd been holding my breath for a lifetime. My cheeks were wet again; Ash's were too. I knew I couldn't expect him to stay with me. Not when I'd caused him so much pain. Not when I couldn't go back to the palace with him.

I wiped my face, threaded the black ribbon through the rings, and tied it in a knot. "They'll be together," I promised. I held up the rings to show him and stopped, my eyes wide. The ribbon I'd tied them with was the one the storyteller had given me.

Ash studied me with those eyes a color I still couldn't name. "What's that smile for?"

"This ribbon," I said, dropping the ribbon into my pocket. "I'll tell you the story some time. Will you come and see me, one day when you are king?"

The mountain air was sharp and clear in my lungs. The man standing there was a stranger to me, just as I was to him. And we were both free now.

Ash was shaking his head, as if he didn't understand me. "I don't want to be king. I want to hear all your stories. I want to be where you are, always." He opened his hands, as if inviting me. "Wherever you are."

I leaned in to him, raising my chin so our cheeks were touching. "I want that too." I breathed him in. "Ash." He smelled of the mountain, of woodsmoke and pine, and his skin was warm against mine. "Can we start again?"

His breath caught, but his arms stayed frozen in place, as if I were some wild thing he didn't want to frighten. "Sparrow." His voice was low in my ear, almost a sigh. "I have no money and no prospects." I opened my mouth to speak, but he went on, words tumbling out. "But I don't care about those things. I'll do any work that's honest. I can chop wood and build fences. I'm good with animals, and I—"

"And you're very clever with a knife." Taking his hands in both of mine, I leaned back, thinking of the picnic and the curly strip of apple peel that seemed so long ago. Perhaps I should have known the hands that chopped our wood and carved Jack's animals were these hands. There was so much about him I didn't know; I knew that now. But I wanted to find out.

I was smiling now, but Ash's face was serious. "Is it really what you want?"

I nodded, my hands sliding up to his shoulders. "It's what I want."

At last, his arms came around me, his hands warm at the small of my back, drawing me close. Before, I had always waited for him to kiss me. But that was before, and I did not want before.

FIFTY-FIVE

*A*s Ash recovered, he and I began to tell each other the stories of our lives apart. He told me how he and Henry had traveled. How he had learned every skill Henry could teach him as they found work as farmhands, woodsmen, shepherds, any work that was offered along the way. And how everywhere they went, to villages or farms or forests, they had searched for me.

I told him how Mother and Jack took me in. How I had stayed in the wood, hiding from the world and learning everything I could from Mother and her book. How Mother had died, and the things that happened after.

We were in the courtyard when I told him what had led me to the mountain. I sat on a low wall, Mother's book on my lap. Ash sat in the grass below me, carving a new wooden animal as I told him about the second sight.

"She didn't say it would help me, but I had to come and see." My gaze strayed to Ash's hands, carving the graceful curve of a neck. He was making a swan.

"Doesn't it hurt you?" I asked.

He lifted his head from his work and looked out at the garden. "It does," he said after a moment. "It always hurt before, with the glass in it." He set the knife in his lap and stretched his bandaged hand. "I suppose I thought if I could be useful, work hard enough, please someone," he held up the swan, "do enough good, perhaps one day I could earn the chance to make things right. And if it caused me pain, so much the better."

"It sounds like a punishment. You don't deserve that."

He shook his head. "Not a punishment," he said. "A penance."

I nodded, thinking of all the sweeping and chopping and mixing and healing. I knew about penance, too.

He leaned down to pluck one of the second sight stems, turning it between finger and thumb. "I'm used to the pain now." He turned to me, his eyes searching mine. "Did they help you too?"

I shrugged. "I haven't tried."

"There's plenty here." He gestured with his knife.

I shook my head. "It doesn't matter." There must have been a moment when I stopped minding my scars, but I hadn't noticed it. It had stolen in so quietly.

I looked down at the book in my lap. It was open to the second sight entry. I picked up the pen beside me and opened the pot of blackberry ink. As I held the pen over the page, a whisper in my head asked if I dared to put my writing next to hers, to add my own words.

I answered it by dipping the pen into the ink. Just underneath Mother's last words, *It draws what is deep inside*, I added my own: *Bruise leaves and place on wound to bring out the poison*. I set the book down to let the ink dry. The wet ink was darker, brighter on the page, but the sight of my handwriting beside Mother's pleased me. It was right.

As I wrote, Ash had taken my foot in his hand. He traced the lines of each scar, his finger traveling the path that led me from palace to wood to mountain. The scars had faded, but they would never disappear.

"How could you do it?" Ash's voice was gentle, curious.

My foot stilled in his hand. I couldn't help thinking of the last time he had said those words, and the accusation in his voice. "You said that before." He glanced up at me. "That night. You were so angry."

"I was," he said. "Angry at my parents and the rest of them, for the way they treated you." He looked down at my foot, covering it with both his hands. "At myself, for letting them do it."

"And me." *How could you?* he had said.

"Yes." He bowed his head, and for a moment he was silent. "For not telling me," he said at last. "For not trusting me."

"I was afraid you'd think—" His eyes met mine; I was so close to naming their color now, I was sure of it. "You would think I had deceived you, that I was just like my sisters."

"No." He was shaking his head. "I thought you didn't want me anymore. That you didn't love me. But that wasn't all I meant." He swallowed, looked up at me, and started again. "How could you hurt yourself like that?"

I found I had no answer, at least not one that made sense to me now. At last I said, "They don't hurt me anymore."

His mouth curved with the ghost of his slow smile. "They're perfect, you know."

I laughed then. I couldn't help it. Whatever they were now, whatever I was, it was hardly perfect. "How can you say that?"

His hand slid gently off the top of my foot, and he pressed his lips against my scarred skin. "Because they're yours."

When he looked back up at me, I finally knew. His eyes were exactly the color of second sight.

We left Glass Mountain at mid-summer, driving the sheep home to Valley Farm. Henry stayed on to help with the shearing and eventually the harvest. He promised to visit us when the weather turned cold.

Jack and I returned to Mother's cottage. Our cottage. Ash found work and lodging at Blackhorse Farm, and we saw him nearly every day. We told each other more of our stories, and we took our time.

As the days cooled into autumn, the storyteller knocked on our door, bringing another offering of birds. "I can't say I've come by accident this time." He looked down, knocking the mud off his boots. "But I hope I'll be welcome all the same."

I opened the door wider. "Of course."

He took off his cap as he stepped over the threshold, his eyes roving around the cottage, taking in the little changes like the feathered cloak hanging by the door, the ax and bow leaning against one wall, and the long-legged gray dog who raised his head and thumped his tail in welcome. But he stopped still when he saw the man at my hearth mending a hole in his coat. He nodded at Ash, who nodded back.

He turned back to me, his head cocked a little to one side. "I wonder if you have a story for me this time."

He began the storytelling as we ate. Some tales we knew, like the one about the devil's grandmother and the one about the girl who married a hedgehog, and one we did not, about the missing princess and the prince who disappeared in search of her. For he had been to the palace recently and had the latest news.

"Not only the princess," he said, "but now the prince himself is thought to be dead."

Ash looked up from the knife he was sharpening, and his fingers stopped in their work. He stared into the fire as the story went on, his eyes reflecting its golden glow.

"The king and queen are beyond broken-hearted," the storyteller went on, "but they have settled on a nephew to succeed the king, should their son never return."

The cottage was still except for the pop of a log settling in the fireplace. "Most folks say that's not much of an ending. They wish I'd tell a different one." He took a puff on his pipe and blew a smoke ring into the air.

"I do." Jack turned in my lap to face me. "I wish that too."

"Wishing is a funny thing, young sir." The storyteller winked at me. "More often than not, it takes us down roads we never expected to travel."

I tightened my arms around Jack as he blew out a discontented huff of air. "I have a story too," I told him. "Would you like to hear it?"

Ash glanced up, and I held his gaze, looking at him like he was the only one in the room.

There are not a thousand feathers in my cloak. At least I don't think there are; I have never counted. It isn't finished, though, and I don't think it ever will be. I wear it when it's rainy or cold, and when it's warm, it hangs on a peg by the door. Next time I need it, it will be ready. And in the meantime, I add in things that belong. More feathers, scraps of fabric, even my gold wedding ring, sewn into the lining. Ash's ring is there too. My plain, black ribbon joins them, weaving in and out and around the rings in a curling design I stitched onto the fabric. They are together, as Ash said they should be.

We wear rings of birchwood now. Ash made them from the same branch, smoothed them, and rubbed ashes into the wood to bring out the delicate design he'd carved onto the outside: a circle of tiny feathers. When it had been a year and a day since we met again on the top of Glass Mountain, Ash said goodbye to Blackhorse Farm and came to live with Jack and me.

We live quietly, here in the wood. We don't have jewels or fine horses. We never have much money. But the forest welcomes us; we have what we need. Folks pay us in whatever way they can: eggs, flour, cloth, and we accept it willingly.

Mother's little garden is alive with turnips and cabbages, carrots and onions. I also grow pennyroyal and mint and second sight and whatever else I need for my work. Our visitors say they have never seen a garden thrive like this in the middle of the wood. I tell them it is only the weather. But it isn't.

I have made several more entries in Mother's book. I still call it her book, but it is my book now. I have written in my discoveries, or other things worth remembering. At first, I wrote with the blackberry ink, and when that ran out, I made some out of walnut. The ink itself doesn't matter, of course. The book accepts my writing. I am one of its many authors, and my writing is at home on its pages.

I have found more uses for second sight. They fill the page around Mother's drawings and spill onto the next, my writing mingling with hers. *Juice of the leaves relieves inflammation of the eyes. The seeds, taken in wine, will ease congestion in the head. A tea of the powdered root, mixed with honey, soothes the troubled heart.*

No more slivers of glass came from Ash's hand, and the wound closed at last, leaving a small scar at the base of his thumb. It still pains him at times, when the weather turns, or a stranger comes with news of the palace or the life we left behind. Perhaps it will always hurt; the glass left its marks on both of us after all, and not all of them are visible. Sometimes we fight, sometimes we are sad, but together, we work a magic all our own.

I have no use for shoes these days, or even bandages. Everywhere I go now, I go barefoot, my scarred skin a map of where I have been and what led me here. But it is nothing more. Mine are good feet, just as Mother said. And whether I stand or climb, walk or run, they will carry me. They are useful.

I am useful.

ACKNOWLEDGEMENTS

The path of *Glass and Feathers* has been a long one. From its beginnings as a poem called "Sliver," I have been writing this story nearly half my life. It was one I desperately needed to hear, but it wasn't the tale I thought. And it didn't ring true until I understood what I was trying to tell myself. I am so grateful to the people who have supported me along the way.

My girl with the glass slippers doesn't have a fairy godmother, but I do; she is my editor, Kate Wolford. From the time I discovered *The Fairy Tale Magazine (Enchanted Conversation*, back then), it was home. Thank you, Kate, for loving my characters and their story, for giving me the room and the guidance to help them grow. I could not imagine a happier ever after for *Glass and Feathers* than FTM and The Enchanted Press. This collaboration has spoiled me for any other publishing experience that might come after.

Speaking of collaboration, thank you to the rest of the FTM team. Art Director Amanda Bergloff is unflappable and unstoppable, creating a stunning cover, gorgeous layouts, and always making *The Fairy Tale Magazine* a thing of beauty. And Special Projects Writer Kelly Jarvis is such a talented writer, a comforting presence, and a smart, supportive woman I am glad to know. And thank you to FTM's tech goddess Kim Malinowski, poet and pen pal extraordinaire who had my back every two weeks with a *Glass and Feathers* Saturday Slowdown on social media, and intern Madeline Mertz for her beautiful TikTok videos.

To everyone who has helped spread the word about the book, by posting or doing interviews or inviting me to guest blog, thank you. I am especially grateful to my promotional team:

Kristen Baum DeBeasi, Liz Coleman, Liz Husebye Hartmann, Kelly Jarvis, Madeline Mertz, Kim Malinowski, Marcia Sherman, Gypsy Thornton, and Lisa Vlsek. #TeamSparrow, you are a wonder! Thank you for braving the wilds of social media promotion with me.

I also want to thank the members of the online community of fairy tale and folklore lovers. *The Fairy Tale Magazine*, The Carterhaugh School of Folklore and the Fantastic, and Fairy Tale Forum are at the warm, magical heart of this family and have welcomed me with open arms. And to Carterhaugh's Dr. Sara Cleto and Dr. Brittany Warman, thank you for teaching a lesson about untellable tales right when I needed to hear it.

To the early readers of *Glass and Feathers*, back when it was still called *After*: Natalie Cammaratta, Terri Cline, Angela Holmes, Peter Judd, and Priscilla Van Der Weele, thank you for encouraging me to keep going.

Thank you to FTM's beta readers: Amanda Bergloff, Kelly Jarvis, Sally Schreck, Marcia Sherman, Gypsy Thornton, and Kristin Whitehair, for your kind and thoughtful feedback.

Dad, Shelley, Kris, and Shelly: thank you for your love and support going back to before I'd even thought of this book. And to my mom, who once said, "Yes, but when is she going to start writing?" I took some detours, Mom, but, in time I started.

To Meghan Russell and my fairy godsister, Gypsy Thornton: thank you for being tireless cheerleaders and warm, loving shoulders to cry on.

Finally, thank you to my family. For everything, really, but to name a few things: for analyzing and talking over story points, telling me when something just wasn't right, teaching me how to use Instagram, and loyally liking every post. To Ayden, who is brave, for teaching me about birds and letting me make him tea. I'm so glad you're with us. To Molly, who is bold, for her compassion, for being my grocery partner, Dunkin co-conspirator, and so much more. I'm humbled and proud to be your mom. To

Charles, who is my best friend and true love, whose tears cured my blindness and showed me a way through the thorns. I love you more than I ever imagined.

321